"A page-turner that perfectly captures the lore of Appalachia with superstition, suspense, and sweet love. Mountain beauty hides the secrets of a murderous family's past—until Tessa and Zeke unearth the truth. *The Sound of Falling Leaves* completes my must-have list for a Southern story filled with intrigue, romance, and unforgettable characters."

DIANN MILLS, best-selling author of *Airborne*

"As an Appalachian native, I'm a bit particular about books set in my beloved mountains. In *The Sound of Falling Leaves*, Lisa Carter has composed a story that honors the beauty and heritage of the region and its people while taking readers on a trek as serpentine as a mountain road. Get ready to white-knuckle your way through each new twist and gasp at the beauty of redemption and love."

LYNN H. BLACKBURN, author of the Dive Team Investigations series

"Lisa Carter deftly weaves small-town corruption, generational blood feuds, and the haunting ballads of the Appalachian Mountains into a suspenseful, moving story of second chances. You will remember Zeke and Tessa long after you turn the last page."

CONNIE MANN, author of the Safe Harbor and Florida Wildlife Warriors series

"Romantic suspense at its heart-pounding best. You'll root for the restoration these two broken people deserve."

LYNNE GENTRY, award-nominated coauthor of *Ghost Heart* and *Port of Origin*

"Lisa Carter's Southern mysteries always thrill, and this one is no exception. She once again carries us into the heart of the mountains with a dark and intricate tale of danger, family intrigue, and romance. With its tightly woven suspense and engaging characters, the story keeps the pages turning and the reader on the edge of her seat."

RAMONA RICHARDS, author of *Burying Daisy Doe* and *Murder in the Family*

"Compelling characters. A twisted plot. Finding justice for terrible wrongs. A beautiful love story. It's all in *The Sound of Falling Leaves*. The story will grab you on the first page and not let go until the end."

PATRICIA BRADLEY, author of the Natchez Trace
Park Rangers series

THE SOUND *of* FALLING LEAVES

LISA CARTER

 GILEAD PUBLISHING

The Sound of Falling Leaves
Copyright © 2020 by Lisa Carter

 **GILEAD PUBLISHING**

Published by Gilead Publishing, LLC
Wheaton, Illinois, USA.

This is a work of fiction. Names, characters, places, and incidents are products of the author's imagination or are used fictitiously. Any similarity to actual people, organizations, and/or events is purely coincidental.

Scripture quotations are from the King James Version.

Library of Congress Cataloging-in-Publication Data
Names: Carter, Lisa (Lisa Cox), 1964– author.
Title: The sound of falling leaves / Lisa Carter.
Description: Wheaton, Illinois : Gilead Publishing, [2020]
Identifiers: LCCN 2020025878 (print) | LCCN 2020025879 (ebook)
Subjects: GSAFD: Romantic suspense fiction. | Christian fiction. | Love stories.
Classification: LCC PS3603.A77757 S67 2020 (print) | LCC PS3603.A77757 (ebook) | DDC 813/.6—dc23
LC record available at https://lccn.loc.gov/2020025878
LC ebook record available at https://lccn.loc.gov/2020025879

ISBN: 978-1-68370-096-8 (printed softcover)
ISBN: 978-1-68370-097-5 (ebook)

Printed in the United States of America
20 21 22 23 24 25 26 / 5 4 3 2 1

For the radiant Bride of Christ—
wherever you are,
you know who you are.

Set me as a seal upon thine heart, as a seal upon thine arm;
for love is strong as death; jealousy is cruel as the grave.
(Song of Solomon 8:6)

For such is His love for you—He has set a seal upon His beloved.
A love stronger than death. A love that has overcome the jealous
cruelty of the grave.

The Spirit and the Bride say, "Come," to the faith-becomes-sight
happily-ever-after for which we were made.
"He who has said all these things declares: Yes, I am coming soon!"
Amen! Come, Lord Jesus!
The grace of our Lord Jesus Christ be with you all. Amen!
(from Revelation 22:17, 20–21)

And to the late Bobbi Lewis—you were that godly older woman in my
life. Thank you for the tea. The tissues. The hilarity. And the letters.
For seeing me through the early years of marriage and motherhood.
For being there when I lost a child. It was you who told me, "Never
forget that God is good. And that He loves you devotedly."
I so look forward to our sweet reunion in that sweet by-and-by.
—Lisa Carter
2020

Chapter One

Zeke Sloane stood in the autumn-bronzed shade of the pecan trees that bookended the farmhouse, waiting.

Old Dicy Goforth had called from the rehab center early this morning. She'd told him to be on the lookout for the arrival of her niece. And he'd been none too pleased at this further complication of his plans.

When the BMW turned off the main road and steered through the crossbars of the Goforth orchard, his lungs contracted. In a flume of dust, the coupe topped the rise on the long, graveled driveway, framed by apple trees laden with fruit ready to be harvested. The car came to a stop in front of the house. He pushed off from the rough bark of the tree.

A young woman emerged from the vehicle, and he straightened. His gaze swept over her. In dress slacks and a creamy silk blouse, she remained motionless beside the car. A smoky quartz color, the car was as classy as its well-heeled owner.

They stared at each other a long moment. The silence stretched. The knot in his gut pulled taut.

Finally, she extended her hand. "I'm Tessa Goforth."

Stomach tanking, he ignored her outstretched hand. "I know who you are."

Dicy's niece dropped her hand. "You must be the new orchard manager, Ezekiel Sloane."

He folded his arms across his chest. "It's Zeke."

Tessa's eyes narrowed. "You were here when Aunt Dicy fell."

He didn't care for her tone. "And you weren't."

She bristled. "That's not fair."

"Dicy was in the hospital for a week. She's been in rehab another week." He curled his lip. "Nice of you to finally check on her."

She went rigid. "Why didn't she call me as soon as it happened?"

He scowled. "Because she didn't want to be a burden to you."

Tessa scowled back at him. "Aunt Dicy isn't a burden to me."

Somehow the distance between them had shortened. He found himself looming over her. Had she moved toward him, or had he taken a step toward her? "You're the only family Dicy has left."

On her toes, she was all up in his face, glaring at him. "Aunt Dicy knows I'd do anything for her."

Bitterness rose at the back of his throat. "Except be here when she needs you."

Her gaze grew stormy. "I'm here now."

Zeke shook his head. "She's needed you long before she broke her leg. Where were you when Dicy was worried about the orchard?"

She came down onto her heels. "What's wrong with the orchard?"

"It's been too much for her for quite some time."

Tessa swallowed. "She never said anything."

"She wouldn't, though, would she? But that's why she hired me to take over the management of the orchard. Since you're so disinterested in your family legacy."

"Hold on a minute." Tessa cocked her head. "Are you from Roebuck County?"

Zeke opened his mouth and then clamped his lips together. "No."

She raised her eyebrows. "Do you have any experience managing apple orchards?"

Zeke pinched the bridge of his nose. "No, I don't."

Her mouth twisted. "Kind of convenient, your showing up right before my elderly aunt falls and breaks her leg."

Zeke knew better than to let her get to him, but she did anyway. "For your information, since it's obviously been too inconvenient for you to bother to ask Dicy, I've been working the orchard since last winter."

"Well, like I said before, Ezekiel . . ." Her chin came up. "I'm here now. Dicy is no longer your concern."

"Your aunt has made the orchard my responsibility." He widened his stance. "And harvest is our busiest time of year."

She gave him a look. And if looks could've killed, he reckoned he would've been dead where he stood.

"As you pointed out, the orchard is *my* family legacy." She jabbed her finger in the air between them. "Not only do I intend to help Aunt Dicy get back on her feet, but I'm also planning on helping with the harvest."

"Just don't get in my way."

Her mouth went mulish. "Don't get in mine."

Zeke clenched his teeth. "Gladly."

"*I'm* glad we've come to an agreement of how things stand."

He snorted. "Hardly."

She headed into the house. He went back to work. But fifteen minutes later, she found him outside the barn. "I'm leaving to visit Aunt Dicy at the rehab center."

Bent over the tractor engine, he didn't bother looking up. Dicy should've replaced the antiquated John Deere decades ago, but for sentimental reasons she hadn't. Therefore, he spent hours each day keeping it up and running.

"Did you hear what I said, Ezekiel?"

Irritation burned at his stomach.

She shuffled her expensive and ridiculously high-heeled shoes. "But I'll be back."

"Whatever," he mumbled.

Over the next few days, she spent some time with her aunt, but most of her waking hours she hung around the house or the orchard. She was like an exotic, hothouse orchid mysteriously planted in the middle of an Appalachian mountain meadow. She didn't belong here. Nor did he. He just pulled it off better.

Jittery as a june bug in July, she made him uncharacteristically nervous. So ever alert to her whereabouts, he always kept her within his line of sight. The wisest course of action when confronted with an unknown species.

Leaning his weight against the top of the ladder, he peered through the leafed-out canopy at the open door of the apple shed. She wore a pair of torn-at-the-knees jeans—the hundred-dollar kind ripped by some fashion designer—and a simple long-sleeved tee.

He would've bet last week's paycheck that without makeup Tessa

Goforth would be pale and washed out like other redheads he'd known. But like so many things when it came to her, he would've been wrong.

There was a lot about her that confused him. She was not how he thought she'd be.

Compared to the photos Dicy proudly displayed on the mantel in the house, at some point in the recent past, Tessa's natural slenderness had become a painful thinness. There were shadows under her eyes. Coming and going like he did, he'd seen the farmhouse lights blazing at all hours of the night.

Her face often forlorn, she was too quiet—except for when arguing with him. Or questioning everything he did. Or looking over his shoulder. She reminded him of one of those obnoxious, needling burs in the meadow. The kind that stuck to clothing and were the very devil to pluck off.

For his own sanity, that afternoon he set her to grading the picked apples and out of his way. So, hair swept out of her face and fastened in a high ponytail behind her head, she sorted the Staymans.

As for that hair of hers? He almost fell out of the tree thinking about her hair. Red didn't begin to describe it. A fiery golden copper, not unlike the heirloom apple he held in his hand.

Her knee-buckling tresses. Waves of curls. The mouth-gone-dry strands of silk. The stomach-clench—

Zeke didn't like redheads. Yet his heart thumped inside his chest.

He grimaced. The thumping certainly wasn't because of her. More likely, it was the result of the crisp mountain air. Tucking the Rome Beauty into the canvas pick sack slung across his body, he climbed down the ladder.

Zeke had taken his eyes off her just long enough to get his feet on solid ground but suddenly, she emerged from behind the gnarled trunk.

Hand to her throat, she jolted and stepped back a pace. "I-I didn't see you there."

Whereas unfortunately, he saw her everywhere. He grunted.

"Always so eloquent, Ezekiel." She smirked.

He'd always hated his full, given name. And somehow sensing that, she used it against him at every turn. "Says the ginger."

Those green foxfire eyes of hers flashed with annoyance. From which he took not a small amount of satisfaction. The dislike was mutual.

He didn't know what it was about her that riled him so much. Probably a gut reflex to the hair. Her hair . . . Perspiration had curled stray tendrils of her hair around her neck. He rubbed his tingling fingers down the side of his jeans.

Tapping her running shoe on the grass, she shot him a searing glance. Not hard to imagine her opinion of him—a crude, not-so-bright mountain hick.

Worthless. Shiftless. A good ole boy. Exactly how he wanted her to think of him. And safer for them both.

She closed her eyes for a second before frowning at him. "I'm headed to town to see Aunt Dicy."

He scanned the horizon above the ridgeline. "Once the sun gets behind the trees, the light goes quick. No streetlights outside of town. You're not used to driving the mountain roads."

"I can't tell you how much I appreciate your concern."

She was good at sarcasm. A defense mechanism, Dicy had warned. But he didn't enjoy being on the sharp end of her tongue.

"However, you're not my father, Ezekiel."

Thank God.

"And I'm a grown woman."

He was well aware of that. Too aware. She had this husky, spoken voice . . .

Tessa wrinkled her nose. "Orchard manager, that's your job title, right?"

Such a flatlander snob.

"The title does not mean you get to manage me."

"Somebody needs to," he growled.

The look she gave him scorched the earth between them. "When I want your advice, I'll ask for it." Ponytail swinging, she stalked down the orchard row toward the white frame, two-story farmhouse.

Good riddance. He shucked off the strap of the pick sack. Time for him to call it a day too.

She wasn't his problem. With her gone, he could focus on what was of real interest to him in this backwater end of nowhere in the Blue Ridge mountains of North Carolina.

Fitting in with the local boys. Ingratiating himself with the Cozart political machine that ran this county in the heart of Appalachia.

And making himself indispensable to a gang of murderers.

❖ ❖ ❖

She couldn't seem to stop herself. Once again, she'd been rude to Aunt Dicy's orchard manager. Tessa stomped up the back porch steps and into the farmhouse.

That first day when she'd gotten out of the car, they stared at each other for what seemed an inordinate amount of time. Pinpricks of awareness had danced along her spine.

She'd waited for him to say something. He'd seemed to wait for her to speak first. Neither said anything.

There was just something so irritating about him.

With eyes like blue lasers, he'd glowered at her after she introduced herself. As if she was the biggest disappointment since green ketchup. Or New Coke.

Go figure.

She changed out of her work clothes. In the living room she grabbed her purse off the chair where she'd left it last night. Scattered across the coffee table, Aunt Dicy's vintage album collection mocked her. She'd clean up when she returned from town.

Fun as the little exchange with Sloane had been, she was running late. Dicy would wonder what was keeping her. She flew down the back steps, threw her purse into the Beamer, and slid behind the wheel.

As she pulled away from the house, her gaze cut to the rearview mirror. Sloane had his dark head bent over the John Deere again. What was it with men and machines?

Better question—what was it with men?

She'd never met one she could trust. Or depend upon not to abandon her when the going got tough. And now, her trust having been proven so tragically misplaced in New Orleans, she feared she could no longer rely on her instincts, either.

Turning out of Goforth Gap Orchards, she hit paved road and headed toward the county seat of Buckthorn.

Over in Asheville—as the crow flew, not too far from Roebuck County—Thomas Wolfe once said a person could never go home again. He might or might not have been right. She had no idea.

You had to first have a home before you could go back to it.

The closest she'd ever come to home was Aunt Dicy and the orchard. So when her great-aunt called to say she'd had a bad fall in the midst of the busy apple harvest season, Tessa got a neighbor to look after her condo and then drove north without hesitation. Dicy hadn't asked her to come. She hadn't needed to ask.

Despite what that lanky, backwoods Neanderthal thought of her, she wasn't the one taking advantage of Aunt Dicy's broken leg. With his cocky, womanizing swagger, Sloane had somehow managed to con her seventyish aunt into giving him the job as orchard manager. And also occupancy of the little cabin across the creek on the other side of the meadow.

Tessa strangled the steering wheel. Fields flashed by on either side of the road. Small, isolated farms tilled for generations. Rolling hills. She'd forgotten how glorious autumn could be in the Blue Ridge.

She didn't know why she and Ezekiel Sloane couldn't speak without sparring, but there was something about him that raised her hackles. Something secretive in his blue-sky eyes. Something seething below the laid-back, country-boy demeanor.

It was clear he resented her presence at the orchard. But she wasn't the one who didn't belong. She couldn't believe sharp-as-a-tack Dicy had been taken in by the likes of him.

Although honesty compelled Tessa to acknowledge that, with the sensuous mouth of his framed-by-dark-beard stubble, he did resemble one of the good-looking outlaw country music singers. The type that appealed to a certain sort of woman. But not to her, or as she would've supposed, her elderly aunt.

Perhaps there was another explanation for Sloane getting the job. Maybe Aunt Dicy's mental faculties were in decline. Tessa hoped not.

But no matter, she'd protect her aunt from a grifter like him. One look at him and Tessa could tell he was up to no good. She wouldn't allow

Aunt Dicy to be taken advantage of—not on her watch. She'd come just in the nick of time.

Tessa wrenched her attention to the ear-popping, backcountry road that corkscrewed around the mountain range between the orchard and the nearest town. Roebuck was one of the most sparsely populated counties in North Carolina. She hadn't visited since Uncle Calvin's funeral, but not much in the landscape had changed. There was only one town—Buckthorn—and a profusion of crossroad communities.

Apple orchards dotted the valleys. Hardscrabble farms clung precariously to the sides of the mountains. The population was working poor. By necessity, most Roebuck citizens made the daily one-hour commute to nearby Asheville, where there were more job opportunities.

She entered the Pisgah National Forest.

The national park comprised a significant portion of the county. Much of the rest of the county had long ago been designated as a wilderness area. Roebuck was a land of deep gorges, broad valleys, and hidden coves. Hollers is what they called the coves here.

And the people in the mountains spoke an English that Tessa, who'd been trained to also sing in Italian, French, and German, sometimes needed a dictionary to translate. Quaint, old-fashioned words.

When the gas light flicked on, her gaze darted to the gauge. Still enough to get to town. She'd meant to fill up yesterday, but after leaving her aunt, she'd needed to buy groceries. And, desperate for a decent cup of coffee, she'd detoured over the mountain pass to Asheville. She should've filled the tank then. After her visit to Dicy this evening, she absolutely must remember to get gas.

Rounding the last vista, she wound around the slope, careful to take the curves slowly. Not much shoulder on the road. Nothing but a flimsy metal barricade to keep her from hurtling into a chasmic abyss.

Gaze fixed on the winding yellow ribbon of asphalt, she didn't risk glancing over the side. Even just thinking about the plunge made her insides do a nosedive.

Heights didn't used to bother her. But since the fire . . . She inhaled sharply.

Don't think about that now. Her knuckles whitened on the wheel. *Can't ever . . . Mustn't ever think about that night.*

Because thinking about that night meant thinking about Anton. Though every time she closed her eyes, she saw him . . . one of the reasons she no longer slept well. She bit back the rising tide of nausea.

Stop it. Stop it. Stop it.

Tessa beat the wheel with her palm. Thinking did no good. Remembering didn't change a thing, didn't bring anyone back from the grave.

When the road straightened out, she accelerated. As if speed could help her escape the demons of that night. She'd been so stupid. So naive.

She shook her head and a cloud of hair came loose from the bun at the nape of her neck. With a swipe of her hand, she brushed it out of her face. *No more thinking.*

Her life—the life she'd known—was over. Earlier this week, Aunt Dicy's phone call had come as a godsend.

Though where God figured into that night of hell, Tessa hadn't a clue. And from her vantage point, when desperately clinging to the highest pinnacle of the opera house, He'd been conspicuous in His absence.

Shying away from old memories, she left the Pisgah behind. The deeply canopied forest gave way to the sunny valley below.

Hemmed in on one side by the mountains, on the other by the French Broad, the little hamlet of Buckthorn boasted two stoplights. Portions of Main Street were part of the Appalachian Trail itself.

At the edge of town, she crossed over the bridge spanning the river. Below the bridge, buses from the local rafting company were parked at a put-in spot. In the summer, the French Broad became crowded with a flotilla of inner tubes and kayaks floating along its course. But this time of year, rafting, like the apple harvest, was nearing the end of season.

She drove past a few Victorian homes converted to bed and breakfasts. Clusters of through-hikers congregated on the wooden picnic tables outside The Burger Depot. Retired from the railroad tracks that also followed the river, a caboose had been remodeled and now served meals out of its tiny kitchen on wheels, food truck style.

Tessa pulled into the small parking lot beside the bright-red caboose. She'd promised to bring Dicy a milkshake, burger, and fries. She got out of the car.

After placing her order at the window, she sank onto a sun-warmed bench to get her emotions under control. Orange rubber rafts bobbed farther down the river as enthusiasts enjoyed the October white water.

The deep breathing exercises the therapist had given her to avert the anxiety attacks had done nothing to ease the day terrors, so she'd reverted to an old childhood habit of finding the music in the sounds around her. A game she'd played for so long, she didn't remember when or where she learned it.

Yet nothing held the nightmares at bay. She'd resisted the lure of pills or booze thus far. But if fresh air and hard work didn't do the trick? A lump settled in the base of her throat.

She wasn't sure how many more nights she could take, too terrified to fall asleep. Every time she closed her eyes, the continuous loop of horror replayed in her head.

Even here in the open, she felt exposed and vulnerable. Would she ever feel safe again? She did a quick scan of her surroundings, something she did constantly since the fire.

At a nearby table, the hikers in their expensive outdoor gear and boots were probably one of the final groups attempting to make the Maine-to-Georgia trek of the Trail before the snow arrived.

The hikers were a mixture of men and women. Gap-year students. Those battling midlife crises. The geriatric couple most likely aiming for one last adventure in their sunset years, a swan song of sorts.

She knew about swan songs. She shuddered. *Stop it. Think about the hikers—*

Never very outdoorsy or athletic, she preferred Prada to Patagonia. And she'd had enough adventure—if that's what one called what had happened to her—for a lifetime.

Roughing it in the wilderness wasn't her idea of fun. Never physically brave, she'd nevertheless been a risk-taker when it came to her career. This scared-of-her-own-shadow person wasn't who Tessa was. Or at least, who she'd been. But that Tessa, a rising operatic star, was gone forever. Burned to death in the ashes of the Théâtre de l'Opéra. As good as dead.

If only she'd listened—really listened. Perhaps if she hadn't been so focused on her career, she could have stopped Anton . . . *Don't go there.*

Therein, lay madness. Like the madness that had terrorized her. Nearly ended her life. Destroyed her voice. Forever robbed her of song.

Dicy's phone call had been the impetus Tessa needed to move forward. Without hesitating, she'd fled civilization to care for her aunt. For the foreseeable future, she'd decided to hunker in this isolated backwater to lick her wounds and regather her shattered nerves. An added bonus would be proximity to the folklore center to research her dissertation.

She'd wanted to die that night in New Orleans. But death had forsaken her, as had the music. Her punishment for failing to stop him, for failing to save the others.

The fear and the regret were eating her alive.

Physically shaking herself, she refocused her mind and tuned her inner ear to the sounds around her.

Listen, listen. What do you hear?

The *clackety-clack* bump of cars passing across the bridge. The chatter of the hikers, as cheerful as a bunch of squirrels. Gradually, the intrusive noises faded, like onion skin peeling away to the pearl at its core.

Her breathing slowed. Her heart rate subsided. The tight coil within her loosened.

Listen, listen. What do you hear?

She heard the steady roar of the river, rushing past to the rapids downstream like musical notes suspended in the air. Lilting, floating over the sandbar. The streaming water playing in time with the flowing current.

If she opened her mouth, she was sure, almost sure, this time she could resurrect the exact pitch from the sepulchre of her throat. That life-giving, effervescent tone would pour out of—

"Order up!"

Tessa jumped, cutting her eyes at the now-empty tables around her. She'd gotten lost again. For how long this time?

After staggering to her feet, she retrieved Aunt Dicy's order. She wasn't getting any better. Perhaps this was as good as she would ever get.

Clutching the grease-stained, white paper bag, she hurried to her car. She paused, gazing at the dark water lapping against the bank below. If this was as good as she'd ever get, why not just—

The chargrill aroma of the burger rose in her nostrils. Dicy was counting on her. And she'd promised to give the mountains and the orchard a chance.

For what? Healing? She pulled out of the parking lot no longer sure healing was an option.

And what was worse, no longer sure that's what she even wanted. Not anymore.

Chapter Two

In the late afternoon sun, the gold-leafed dome of the neoclassical courthouse gleamed. Driving down Main Street, Tessa glanced out the window.

Typical, small-town America.

A hardware store. The Cozart Auto Repair Shop, and lots of buildings with the Cozart name. Law office. The Cozart-Roebuck library. Cozart Real Estate Development.

The bakery was new, though. And on the other end of town, the medical campus was also new. Change had managed to make its way over the steep mountain ranges. At least, to some extent.

Progress, but still no coffee shop. She could use a cup about now. Too much caffeine kept her unable to sit still, but mainly, it kept her from having to close her eyes.

After parking, she bypassed the emergency entrance and headed toward the rehabilitation center for post-op patients.

White gravel crunched beneath her open-toed, brown suede ankle boots. The double glass doors slid open. She skirted past the not-so-small bronze plaque affixed just inside the Cozart Medical Complex. The doors whooshed shut behind her.

Inside the thoroughly modern facility, an antiseptic smell assaulted her nostrils. Hurrying down the hallway, she almost lost her balance on the slippery, clean, tile floor.

Overhead, someone paged a doctor, and from a distant corridor, the rattling wheels of a cart squeaked. No one manned the duty station.

Mountain life was casual. And as a consequence, no check-in was required. Everybody knew everybody plus their fourth cousins.

Down the hall to the left, turn right at the elevator, around the corner, second door on the—she ran smack into a man.

He dropped his cell, and the phone skittered across the linoleum.

Bouncing against the wall, she lost her hold on the paper bag. "The milkshake! Don't let it—"

His hand shot out, catching the bag in midair, saving Aunt Dicy's dinner from disaster and a close encounter with the floor.

"I'm so sorry." Tessa bit her lip. "I wasn't looking where I was . . ."

The startling blue of his eyes momentarily robbed her of breath. Intense eyes. Intelligent. Amused.

She had the odd sensation she'd met this stranger before, once upon a time. Yet not him exactly.

With a start, she realized he was waiting for her to take the bag from him. Flushing, she reached for it. But he didn't let go. Not right away.

"I should be the one apologizing." His lips twitched. "I need to get my head out of my phone"—he cocked his very attractive head—"before life passes me by."

She made a wry grimace. "Or knocks you off your feet."

He laughed, exposing strong, white teeth. "As you say."

For the love of Verdi, he was handsome. Like movie star handsome. In Buckthorn. Who would have ever guessed?

She put her hand to her throat. At least she'd changed out of her work clothes before she left the farm. And put on makeup. A redhead had no eyes without makeup.

The statuesque roles had invariably gone to her, being tall for a woman. Yet he was a few inches taller, just shy of six feet, and slightly older than her, around thirty.

He vaguely reminded her of Dublin. With the thick black hair, he was darkly handsome like some of the men there. Black Irish, they called them across the pond.

"I don't believe I've had the pleasure." He stuck out his hand. "I'm Colin."

No brogue, however. American English, with just a hint of a drawl. An educated, cultured Southern drawl. Unlike Sloane and Roebuck natives who favored jeans, boots, and flannel, Colin wore a well-tailored suit.

Sans tie, however. The open collar of his shirt exposed a strongly corded neck. The hue of the shirt set off the blue in his eyes.

Her hand, possessing a mind of its own, slid into his. "Tessa Goforth," she breathed.

This time it wasn't amusement that flickered across his face. She was almost sure they'd never met. Was it her name that prompted the flare of recognition?

She'd been so afraid of men since the fire. Repulsed after what Anton did to Sandy. Afraid she'd never feel attraction for any man again. It was such a dizzying relief to feel normal.

Or almost normal.

"Not quite Lauren Bacall." His fabulous eyes narrowed like a sommelier, trying to identify just the right note in a wine. Pear or apricot? Oak or— "Ava Gardner perhaps?"

She'd always spoken in a lower range than most women. Her musical trademark. Her speaking voice had quickly rebounded from the effects of smoke inhalation. Her singing voice hadn't been so fortunate.

He hadn't let go of her hand.

"You like old movies." So did she.

Dearest Debussy, those eyes of his.

"You don't look like a smoker."

She dropped her hand. "I'm not."

"I didn't mean to offend."

On a woman, his full mouth might be called "pouty." On a man, his chin might be considered a trifle weak. These days, trust didn't come easy.

"I only meant your voice is lovely."

What was with her? A man, handsome and admiring, yet she probed for flaws. Her not-so-brave new reality. "You didn't offend me."

"Buckthorn is so small." He leaned closer. "How is it, beautiful Tessa, our paths have not crossed before?"

The trapped feeling hit her like a wave. She reared. Her shoulder blades scraped the wall. Panic leaped in her chest. She swallowed. "I-I . . ." What was wrong with her?

The paper bag with Dicy's poor, mistreated supper crinkled between them.

"We've just met." He gave her a boyishly sweet smile. "But I would love to take you to dinner."

The Tessa who'd sung to packed houses would have wanted him to take her to dinner. Tessa, the cowering wreck unable to force the music from her throat, wanted nothing so much than to lock herself away from the rest of the world for good.

He swept back the dark lock of hair that had fallen onto his smooth forehead. "Mayhap there are other things besides a familiarity with old movies we might discover we have in common."

Fear, not attraction, sparked in her gut. Her heart raced. Her breaths became shallow. Why couldn't she—*You're being ridiculous.*

Mayhap . . . Who said words like that these days? But that was Roebuck County, a place out of time.

It had been almost a year since the fire. The therapist had pushed Tessa to take back her life. Encouraged her to pursue new interests. Finish the graduate work begun years ago, before success took her by surprise and life became a whirling kaleidoscope of sound, color, and music.

"Keep moving forward," the counselor had said. "One step at a time." Was dinner with a handsome stranger another in a long line of baby steps? It didn't feel like a baby step. It felt monumental.

She was so sick of being a coward.

Tessa moistened her bottom lip. "I-I would like that, Colin."

From the corner, his phone buzzed insistently. He snatched his cell off the floor. Glancing at the screen, he frowned. "My family . . . Cozart business." He let out a sigh. "Rain check, lovely Tessa?"

A not so tiny part of her felt immediate relief. The rest of her experienced a sting of disappointment. It wasn't so much about Colin, but that the longing for something more, that for which she'd been searching, had to be postponed once again.

Rain check. Snow check. Sun check. Whenever check. She'd be better prepared and ready next time. She would.

"That would be great, Colin."

"If you wouldn't mind me calling you . . ."

Mind having a handsome man talk to her? What was to mind? "I wouldn't mind."

Turning that languid gaze of his full force upon her, he handed her his phone. "Would you put in your number for me?"

She set the bag beside her feet. And somehow, despite her real befuddlement in the face of his devastating, Greek-god virility, she managed to remember her cell number.

"Perfect . . ." He checked what she'd typed before tucking the phone inside his blazer. "Duty calls." He made a move as if to go. Reluctantly, or so she told herself.

She lifted the bag. "Me too. My aunt."

Touching a hand to his forehead, he gave Tessa a one-finger salute. "Until we meet again." He disappeared down the corridor.

She took a long overdue breath. Had she actually forgotten to breathe?

If he bottled even a tiny part of that charisma of his, he'd make a fortune. He had a way of making a woman feel as if she were the only person in the room, the only creature he had eyes for. No one had looked at her like that in a long time.

She was so tired of being the crazy, opera lady victim.

Tessa shook herself free of his spell. Because that's what it was. She was a connoisseur of sounds, and his voice was like a velvet purr. He played with words the way she played with notes.

A vast improvement over monosyllabic Sloane. She practically had to draw blood to pry speech from him.

From the cut of his suit, if whatever family business Colin did so successfully ever failed, he could have a future on the screen. The camera would love him. If there was one thing she knew, it was stage presence, which he possessed in spades. Today was turning out to be not so bad after all.

After meeting Colin, Nowheresville, USA, didn't seem nearly so unappealing. But suddenly ripe with all kinds of tantalizingly, distracting possibilities. And considering what she'd gone through, if anybody on earth needed a pleasant interlude, she did.

Here in Buckthorn, it came as no surprise he was a Cozart.

Outside Dicy's room, Tessa faltered at the sound of raised voices.

"It would be in your best interest, not to mention hers, if she gets out while she still can," a man's deep voice growled.

"You've sunk so low that you've taken to threatening old ladies, have you, Judson?" Her aunt's voice was shrill.

Tessa rushed through the open doorway. "What's going on here?" Hastening to her aunt, she glared at the fifty-something man looming over the hospital bed.

Beneath the tidy, gray beard, his features tightened. "It's not a threat, but a warning you would do well to heed, Dicy Goforth."

Tessa reached for the switch to summon a nurse. "I'm calling security."

He gave a short bark of a laugh.

"There's no need." Dicy's lips thinned. "Mr. Cozart was leaving."

Judson Cozart's blue gaze assessed Tessa, leaving her feeling once again oddly vulnerable and exposed. "Ah, the niece."

Dicy's mouth twisted as if she'd tasted something sour. "Your network never lets you down."

That seemed to amuse him.

"You've said what you came to say, Judson."

"And you best tell her what I said." The humor vanished from his face. "Nineteen days and then my dozers roll. Whether she's gone or not."

"Get out," Tessa hissed.

With a meaningful scowl at her aunt, he strode from the room. Her aunt collapsed against the pillows.

"Aunt Dicy, should I—?"

"I'm okay." Her aunt fussed with the lace collar on her gown, but her arthritic-shaped hand shook.

"What did he want you to tell me?"

"Not you." Folding her shaking hands one over the other, Dicy lay them atop her lap. "Someone else."

"Judson Cozart . . . Any relation to Colin?"

Dicy's eyes, blue like faded denim, sharpened. "You've met Colin?"

She gestured toward the door. "A few minutes ago."

"Ain't that ever the way." Her aunt's countenance had taken on that sour lemon look again. "Where there's one viper, there's bound to be two."

"Colin didn't seem like that."

Dicy snorted. "Scratch the surface and none too deeply, they're all like that. Colin is Judson's nephew. His brother Ransom's son."

"I could see the family resemblance. The eyes. Something in the smile."

Her aunt reached for the Styrofoam cup on the bedside table. "And the ruthlessness."

She handed the cup over the bed rail to her aunt. "Colin seemed perfectly—"

"He's the charm behind the muscle. Next-generation Cozart, God help us. Slick as a moss-covered log in the rain." Dicy took a sip from the straw. "The velvet glove encasing the iron fist."

"From the looks of things in Buckthorn, the Cozarts—"

"Cozarts run this town, missy." Her aunt handed Tessa the cup. "You'd do best to steer clear of 'em while you're here."

She pursed her lips. "The uncle—Judson—is a jerk, but the rest of them can't be as bad as you're making out."

Dicy's shrewd old eyes narrowed. "Colin's already managed to turn your head, has he? Cozarts don't do anything without an agenda."

Tessa stiffened. "Do you find it impossible that a man—an extremely handsome, intelligent man—could actually find me interesting?"

Her aunt waved her hand. "Don't go getting your pantaloons in a wad. That's not what I'm saying."

Pantaloons... She shook her head. "Colin wants to take me to dinner one night. I see no reason not to go out with him."

"All them Cozarts are easy on the eyes, I'll give you that. Colin tends to be their front man." Dicy grimaced. "And Judson's the enforcer."

She rolled her eyes. "You make them sound like some sort of Appalachian Mafia."

"Not far off the mark. The Cozarts stick together." Dicy's mouth hardened. "But then so do we."

"Who is *we*?"

The old woman heaved a sigh. "You've got a lot to learn about folks hereabouts, Tessie. Other than God, family is the most important thing."

She set the cup on the nightstand with more force than necessary. Her aunt was right about one thing—she didn't have much experience with family. Thanks to her dysfunctional childhood.

Dicy smoothed the coverlet over her legs. "But no matter what I say, you're going to do like you want. Always do. Like your dad. Stubborn. Hardheaded."

"I am not like my . . ." She pressed her lips together.

A relationship with her emotionally unavailable father had been a wish-true dream that remained a never-shall-be reality.

Dicy took her hand, her grip surprisingly tenacious. "Your father was never interested in the source of the strength your uncle Calvin and I taught you."

But Tessa wasn't strong. Not at all. Not anymore.

"Hobnob with the Cozarts, and you'll be playing with fire." Her aunt patted her hand. "And after what you've been through, honey, I'd hate to see you get burned."

The unspoken "again" hung between them.

"So would I, Aunt Dicy," she whispered. "So would I."

Chapter Three

Not long after the taillights of Uptown Girl's BMW disappeared over the rise, Zeke's cell phone pinged.

He glanced at the text. He'd been summoned—a command performance from the almighty Cozarts. He sighed.

Zeke didn't know why he so enjoyed pushing Tessa's buttons. Although she gave as good as she got. If nothing else, the bickering snapped her out of the fog of gloom that had perpetually dogged her since she arrived. That and he reckoned he had to take his fun where he could find it.

He knew better than to head to the Cozart estate as is. He jogged through the apple trees. The tangy sweet aroma wafting from the row of Virginia Beauties reminded him of Tessa.

But not so much anymore. Because clearly anything sweet about her, she'd long since relegated to childhood.

Which Cozart needed him tonight? And for what this time?

He'd been here almost a year with nothing to show for his efforts. But slowly, with frustratingly small steps, he was coming closer to finding concrete evidence that would put them away from decent society for the rest of their collectively disreputable lives.

Zeke had to be patient. His progress felt minuscule, but he couldn't afford to rush things. Yet a lurking fear gnawed at his belly. The fear that one day they'd demand he do something to prove his loyalty that crossed the final line of decency.

He'd been operating on the thin, razor-sharp line so long, he wasn't sure he'd recognize the edge if he saw it.

Dicy had been good to him—taking him in and welcoming his

undercover investigation. She was part of a growing number of Roebuck citizens eager to throw off the shackles of the Cozarts' fifty-year autocracy.

On the other side of the meadow, he crossed the narrow wooden bridge, just wide enough to drive his truck across. The orchard was surrounded on two sides by the national park. The southwest was bordered by a designated wilderness area. To the east, town.

And the cabin was a sweet deal too. Fulfilling a long-suppressed Daniel Boone, coonskin-cap boyhood fantasy.

Two hundred years ago, the cabin had been the original homestead for the first Scots-Irish Goforths. They came down the Appalachian Trail and settled the rugged, isolated terrain of Roebuck County.

From the cabin porch, he could hear the burbling of the stream—the branch, as locals called it. A small tributary of the French Broad, the third oldest river in the world. Geologically, a river even older than the mountains.

He'd arrived in the starkness of winter, the mighty oaks and maples under which the cabin sheltered then barren of leaves. As he'd gradually worked his way into the good graces of the Cozarts, he'd watched the trees leaf out in spring with the apple-green shade of new growth.

Later came the blossoms. To Zeke, the never-to-be-forgotten perfume of the pinkish-white petals meant summer, Roebuck County, and his grandfather. Happy times.

He stepped inside the cabin and toed out of his work boots. On a clear day, he caught glimpses of the Appalachian Trail high atop one of the ranges. A glint of metal from a canteen or sunglasses. Maybe a hiking pole belonging to one of the through-hikers.

And always he agonized about Kaci. Where she was. What had become of her?

He tore off his shirt, slipped out of the dirty jeans, and cranked the shower. No time for the water to heat in the pipes—he stepped under the cascading rivulets and flinched at the chill.

Imagination could be a curse. At night he'd awaken thrashing, tangled in the sheets, drenched in sweat after imagining the worst of scenarios. Hoping to God she hadn't suffered during whatever it was they'd done to her.

Closing his eyes, he lifted his face to the showerhead and let the water flow over him. Toughening up for whatever they'd demand of him this time.

He'd have to hold his tongue—temper too—and do their bidding. Whatever it took to get closer to the Bureau's ultimate objective. And there was still nothing on Kaci. No closure there.

In his gut, he believed the Cozarts were responsible for her disappearance. For a local girl's tragedy too. He just didn't know which one of the family had done the deed. Not yet.

But he would. God help him—no, God help *them* when he found out what they'd done to her.

He took a shuddering breath. After soaping quickly, he rinsed, shaking the droplets off himself like a wet dog. He climbed out of the shower and grabbed a clean shirt and jeans from the closet.

Five more minutes and he was on his way toward evil incarnate—the Cozarts. Passing under the crossbars near the road, he glanced in the rearview mirror at the orchard.

He lost his parents while overseas with the Army and Kaci more than a year and a half ago, but he'd lost himself long before that.

Assistant Special Agent in Charge Reilly had no idea of Zeke's connection, tenuous as it was, to Roebuck County. If he had, Zeke would've never stood a chance of landing this assignment. He'd gambled no one in Roebuck County would recognize him and took the risk.

But Dicy had remembered, opening her home and heart to Zeke. She'd become very dear.

If GrandPop could see him now . . . If GrandPop knew what might be required to exact justice . . .

Zeke set his jaw.

GrandPop had taught him the ways of the wood. Instilled within him a respect for God and for people everywhere. Insisted the strong must always protect the innocent.

"I'm trying, GrandPop," he whispered to the windshield.

But what if the innocent were already lost? Where was justice to be had then?

One-handing the wheel, he ran his hand through his still-damp hair. GrandPop wouldn't have liked the direction his thoughts had taken of late. Nor approved of the darkness brewing within him. A darkness he feared might someday, if given the right motivation, overtake him completely.

He cut across national parkland, taking a seldom-used service road, bypassing town and gaining an extra ten minutes. The Cozart ranch, where the majority of the clan unhappily resided together, backed up to the park. They probably considered the Pisgah within their purview as well, just as they did the rest of Roebuck.

They ran the county like their own personal fiefdom.

Coming out of the tree cover, he sighted Ransom's two-story wood-beam-and-glass mansion on the ridge. Leaving the dirt road behind, he followed the winding pavement to the summit. As he parked beside the other cars, he ticked off the identity of each owner.

Judge Ransom's white Caddy. His wife's sturdy green Range Rover. Still living with his parents, Pretty Boy Colin's sleek red Corvette. Judson's Yukon Denali. Only two missing—

A black-and-tan Roebuck County Sheriff's cruiser pulled beside Zeke.

Great. Not quite a coven, but close enough. Zeke slung open his door and got out.

High Sheriff Merritt Cozart slammed the door of his patrol car and joined Zeke on the blue slate walkway. "Son . . ." He tipped the brim of his regulation hat to Zeke.

But not your son, thank God. He kept his thoughts to himself. Of the Cozarts, he actually found Merritt the most likable, the most approachable. Yet he wouldn't have trusted the burly man as far as he could throw him.

The high sheriff was as crooked as they come. With the aid of an insidious network of informers, Merritt and his handpicked deputies ran Roebuck County.

Depending on one's family standing with the Cozarts, a person could get away with murder. Someone already had.

Zeke was a realist. In his line of work, he had to be. Kaci had disappeared over eighteen months ago and probably died soon after she went missing.

But nothing happened in Roebuck the sheriff didn't know about.

Whoever killed her—even if it wasn't a Cozart—Merritt would know who had.

Masking his true feelings, Zeke arranged his face into a more amiable facade. "Sheriff."

An imposing bulk of a man around fifty, Merritt broad-shouldered his way past his sister-in-law's flower beds. Like the well-trained guard dog he wanted the Cozarts to believe him, Zeke followed, pausing beside the sheriff on the large stone steps.

Barking broke out on the other side of the massive oak door.

Merritt rolled his eyes, the same startling blue as the rest of his clan. "Anjanette and them dogs."

Suddenly, the door flew open. Anjanette Cozart glowered at them. "'Bout time."

The sheriff rested his meaty fists on his gun belt. "Been busy today."

Zeke hung back, letting Merritt take the grief. Of a similar age as her brother-in-law, Anjanette ran the family like Merritt ran the county.

Her gaze ping-ponged between the men. And Zeke, seasoned professional that he was, felt ready to confess to anything—stuff he hadn't even done—just to get those creepy, pale-blue eyes off him.

Even Merritt shifted from foot to foot.

"Well, get in here." Making a sweeping motion, she stepped aside. "We're waiting on you."

They no sooner stepped over the threshold than toenails *click-click*ed across the rich mahogany floors. Two Plott bloodhounds raced toward them. Positioning himself behind the sheriff, Zeke let Merritt take the hit.

Resting their front legs on his uniformed chest, the red-and-white brindle dogs nearly knocked the sheriff down. But when one proceeded to tongue-wipe Merritt's jowls, it was a lick too far.

"Get these blasted dawgs off me, Anjanette," he growled.

Even if soaking wet, rail thin Anjanette Cozart wouldn't weigh a hundred pounds, but with a sharp clap of her bony hands, the dogs scrambled off Merritt and rushed to her side. "There's my good, good boys," she crooned.

She ran her palms over the dogs' velvety coats. The dogs tucked into either side of her wool trousers, whining with pleasure.

"You should lock up them killers when you're expecting company," Merritt fumed.

Anjanette's bloodless lips twitched. "I can't imagine why a big man like you would be scared of my babies." Her dishwater-blond hair fell forward as she lavished more love on her pets. "Pup and Runt wanted to say hello, didn't you, my darlin' sweethearts?"

"Can we get this meeting started, Mother?" Colin bellowed from the sunken living room.

Only one thing she loved more than her "babies" was her much-spoiled son. "Coming, sugar boy."

Colin's face flushed. "Mother . . ."

Anjanette shooed the Plotts out the door and closed it behind them. "Sorry, sweetie pie." She fluttered a bejeweled hand. "I forgot you've grown up on your mommy." She swept past Zeke and the sheriff, leaving them in the foyer.

Merritt did that thing he did with his mouth when he was beyond disgust. He didn't like his sister-in-law. But like the rest of the Cozart menfolk, he had enough sense to be scared of her.

The sheriff loped down the couple of steps into the high-beamed family room. Merritt was the middle brother. Ransom, the judge, the eldest.

Judson, the youngest brother who "conveniently" chaired the county commission, leaned against the massive river rock fireplace that dominated the open floor plan.

The entire back of the house was a sheet of glass with an incredible view of the Blue Ridge. Threaded by the silver glint of the river, their patchwork kingdom of farms and the town of Buckthorn spread beneath the Cozarts in the valley far below.

Merritt threw himself onto the brown leather sofa. Shirtsleeves rolled to his elbows, Colin slouched on the other end of couch, his full lips pushed out.

Dressed like she lived on Madison Avenue, Anjanette clattered over to Colin in her heels. She planted a quick kiss atop his curly black hair.

He made a face. Such a wuss.

"Don't pout, darlin'." Queen Anjanette seated herself in one of the wingback chairs flanking the fireplace. "Be glad you have a mama who loves you so much."

Zeke remained at the top of the steps—a physical metaphor for his association with this unruly clan. Separate and apart.

Sometimes they got so involved agitating each other, they forgot he was there and inadvertently dropped delicious tidbits of information into his lap. A trail of incriminating breadcrumbs he'd use against them in a court of law.

"Put another log on the fire, Judsy." Anjanette flipped her stringy blond hair over her shoulder. "I'm feeling a chill tonight."

With them, Zeke felt the chill day and night.

Her brother-in-law moved to do her bidding and poked the glowing fire in the hearth before adding a log. Judson ran the real estate development company responsible for laundering their ill-gotten gains.

Zeke's supervisor, Reilly, suspected their deep pockets had bought deep ties to influential North Carolina politicians. And so far, the Cozarts had been able to stay one step ahead of the law.

Above the fireplace mantel hung a portrait of the progenitor of the family's fortune and power—Old Mr. Cozart, dead about thirty years.

He ensured the Cozarts owned every strip of land when the Department of Transportation came calling. And in the eighties, when the new highway rolled through from Asheville, the family made a bundle.

Bad seed begat bad seed—and the stair-step brotherhood of Ransom, Merritt, and Judson was as vile a trifecta as ever lived.

Judson had built upon his grandfather's shrewd investments. A real estate mogul in his own right, he'd made sure the Cozarts—by hook or crook—held title to most land in the county not already state or federally owned.

A person couldn't be appointed dogcatcher in Roebuck County without Judson's patronage. Or get a fishing license, construction permit, or a teaching position . . . The list went on and on.

"For pity's sake, Merritt." Anjanette gripped the armrests of her chair. "Were you raised in a barn? Take that hat off in my house."

Ironic, coming from her. He'd done his homework on them. An undercover agent had to or die young.

He had it on good authority—Miss Dicy—Anjanette started life inside a shack within a particularly squalid holler. But as Judge Ransom's wife, Anjanette would like nothing better than for everyone to forget that unfortunate and inconvenient piece of personal history.

Crimson beneath the collar of his khaki shirt, Merritt did as he was told. He ran his beefy hand through his short-cropped, dark locks.

Like Zeke, the sheriff had started out in the military. He'd never married. Had no children.

Anjanette smoothed the front of her beige cashmere sweater. "Shall we begin?"

"How about let Sloane sit down first, Janette?" Seated in the other flanking wingback, the mild reproof came from the Honorable Justice Ransom Cozart. Her consort—and Colin's father.

A quiet, thoughtful man, he was the only one who ever shortened Anjanette's name. A term of endearment? It was hard to tell with this bunch.

But Anjanette blushed. For a second, her gaunt face filled with becoming color, and she was almost pretty. Her eyes flitted to her husband. A disturbingly intense look revealing an unusual vulnerability.

Yet gaze trained on Zeke, the judge didn't turn his head. Come to think of it, Ransom rarely looked at his wife. No wonder Pretty Boy was so screwed up.

With his patrician air, silvered hair, and Cozart-blue eyes, it was Ransom from whom Pretty Boy inherited his looks. The crazy most likely came from Anjanette.

Ransom Cozart had a long, if not distinguished, career on the bench of Roebuck County. His political cronies managed to "deliver" the election to him each and every time.

Apparently, they also possessed resurrection powers. It was rumored the ballot boxes were often stuffed with votes cast by citizens whose permanent place of residency was in the town cemetery.

Reilly had hinted he had someone on the inside looking into judicial wrongdoing. And the special agent practically salivated talking about nailing the judge for election fraud. Ransom Cozart was suspected of jury-rigging and witness intimidation too.

"What are you waiting for, Sloane?" Anjanette's lip curled. "An engraved invitation?"

He inched onto the matching loveseat across the glass coffee table from the sofa. A good position to not only listen, but also monitor body language and micro expressions.

Unbuttoning his suit coat, Judson eased down beside him. "Report," he barked.

Anjanette, who liked to be in charge of the family board meetings, flicked a glance at him but said nothing. Unlike Merritt, Judson was a favorite. Two peas in a pod.

Leaning forward, the sheriff rested his elbows on his knees. "Me and the boys raided a few of the farms today."

Scrolling through the feed on his phone, Colin didn't look up. "How much did you seize?"

Early October was pretty much the end of the illegal cannabis-growing season in North Carolina.

Merritt grinned. "Ripped out an acre. In full view of the public, of course."

Colin's mouth fell open. "Are you kidding me? An acre's worth what?" He angled his head toward his father. "Over a million dollars street value, right?"

An admission which solidified Zeke's suspicion that Colin was up to his highly educated frat-boy eyeballs in dirt. Like the rest of them.

The judge steepled his fingers on his chin. "Take the long view, son. Think how many acres remain now that we've satisfied the more curious of the state law enforcement agencies."

Judson stretched out his trouser-clad legs. "No one gave you any trouble, did they?"

Merritt snorted. "Not after last year, they didn't. My deputies made sure they toed the line, or else."

With the tobacco allotments gone, many of the local farmers had been convinced—aka strongly coerced—into switching to growing weed for the Cozarts. Serfdom was alive and well in Roebuck County. Every autumn come harvest, the sheriff seized a portion of the illegal crop and burned it for show.

The rest would be carefully sold to certain out-of-state "preferred" vendors. For their *protective* services, the Cozarts received a hefty cut of the proceeds. Zeke couldn't wait to nail Merritt on corruption and drug trafficking.

"My deputy got a sweet selfie of us with the weed piled in the truck bed. Front page in the *Sentinel*, tomorrow's edition." He rolled his hat between his hands. "Joker took one of me paying off one of the farmers too. Emailed it to the team."

"Have you lost your mind, Merritt?" Anjanette shrieked.

"It was a joke. He didn't mean any—"

"Get it off your phone. His too." A speck of malice peppered her pale eyes. "Unless you're no longer able to handle your end of the family business, Merritt?"

The sheriff's face darkened.

"Plenty of eager young bucks ready and able to step into your shoes, if you're considering retirement, Merritt." Judson's florid complexion intensified. "Maybe Ransom's thinking to run someone else in the next election for high sheriff."

For once, Anjanette gave Judson a scathing look. "The family business is for family." She cocked her head. "Or were you thinking of that boy of yours?"

"Pender run for high sheriff?" Merritt hooted. "I can't depend on him to do anything right. Though I've tried my best to learn him the proper ways." He lifted his hands. "Nothin' agin' you, Jud. We all know he takes his shiftless ways from his mother."

Defending neither his wife nor his son, Judson crossed one ankle over the other. Zeke had never met Judson's wife. From a prominent Asheville family, she now spent most of her time somewhere on the second story of the mansion in an alcoholic stupor.

Anjanette sniffed. "This is what comes from marrying outsiders."

The judge's eyes flickered. "Must we hash over that old ground?"

Merritt jutted his jaw. "Unlike my brothers, I've been too smart to make that mistake."

"Oh, is that the reason you've never married, *brother*?" Judson sneered.

Merritt half rose. "I'm flat out tired of cleaning up after Pender's—"

"Sit down, Merritt." Ransom pounded his chair.

Zeke's heart skipped a beat. What would the sheriff had said if the judge hadn't reined him in? Something about Kaci?

"And you mind how you speak to your kin, Jud." Ransom rubbed his temples. "We're family."

More like a nest of brooding, venomous vipers. Maybe if Zeke was lucky, they'd devour each other. Save the federal attorney the trouble of prosecuting them.

Anjanette cleared her throat. "It is precisely because of shoddy management that we've added Mr. Sloane to our enterprise."

Here it came at last. Why he'd been summoned.

But it was Ransom who gave him his marching orders. "Tomorrow you will accompany Pender on his rounds to distribute each grower's share of the profits."

This decision must have already been determined before the meeting convened, but it was clear Pender's father had been outvoted. A crack in the almighty Cozart ramparts.

They didn't trust Pender to get the job done. That explained the missing vehicle. And his absence from tonight's meeting.

Did they suspect he was shortchanging the growers? And yet who could the farmers complain to—another Cozart? Right or wrong, the family presented a united front to the world.

Was Pender taking a percentage off the top for himself and thereby endangering the entire chain of production? Zeke wouldn't put it past him.

Obviously, the family didn't either. Teeth clenched, Judson tapped his well-shod foot on the hard pine floor. But he didn't intervene.

Zeke leaned forward, locking his hands together. "I'll be happy to handle that for the family."

Brow furrowed, Ransom studied him for a moment but nodded. "Send him the information, Merritt."

Zeke would be absolutely thrilled to obtain a list of Cozart associates. Reilly would do handstands at the chance to add their names to the burgeoning case file.

And this would give Zeke an excuse to poke around their operations. Who knew what else he'd stumble upon? Some clue to Kaci?

"Will do, brother Ransom." Merritt laughed. "My advice to you, young Sloane, would be to keep Pender and his posse on a short leash."

"Mornings could be a problem." Thinking of Miss Dicy, Zeke bit his lip. "It's harvest season for apples too."

"What about the Mexicans Dicy Goforth hired?" Judson crossed his arms. "That's the trouble with depending on outsiders, like Sloane. Can't always rely on their loyalty."

Luis and Tonio were from Guatemala, not Mexico. Zeke would trust them with his life. But racism ran rampant among the Cozarts.

"Sloane's right." The judge fingered his chin. "We have to assume someone may be watching our activities. Someone not sympathetic to our interests. It wouldn't make sense for the orchard manager to leave the harvest. Colin, what do you think?"

The crown prince being groomed for the throne.

Colin's thumb darted over the keyboard on his cell. "Morning or afternoon, does it really matter? Sloane can figure it out." He looked up. "I try not to micromanage competent employees." He gave Zeke an oily smile. "You will prove competent, won't you?"

"I'm certain Mr. Sloane won't let us down." Anjanette fingered the strand of pearls at her throat. "As long as he remembers Pender isn't the only one on a short leash." She looked at him.

There was no danger of Zeke forgetting that.

Firelight flickered across her face, accentuating the hollow shadows of her cheekbones. Giving her more than a passing resemblance to a corpse.

The living dead. That's what he thought of when he chanced to look into her eyes, which was not something he liked to do too often.

She had sharp, hawklike features. Anjanette was only in her fifties, but her eyes . . . Her eyes were old. Feeling her gaze on him now, he fought the shiver of revulsion.

Among the sociopaths also known as Cozarts, Anjanette might just possibly be the meanest, most ruthless of them all. He'd encountered skinheads and Taliban extremists with less frightening eyes. Anjanette gave him the willies.

She rose. Meeting over. Everyone else followed suit.

It was with no small relief he stepped out into the open air, the door shutting firmly behind him. He took his first deep breath in an hour.

Dealing with the Cozarts was like walking across a minefield. He never knew when the next explosion was likely to go off underfoot. Or what would set it off.

He didn't linger as he hurried toward his truck. The "babies" were out here somewhere, roaming free on the grounds. It would be so like Anjanette to call Pup and Runt on him.

Just for fun, of course.

Chapter Four

It was dark when Tessa pulled out of the rehab center. After the unpleasant encounter with Judson Cozart, it had taken a while to get Aunt Dicy settled for the evening.

From the looks of the deepening twilight, she'd lingered in town too long. Her pulse ratcheted and beads of sweat broke out on her forehead. Her hands convulsed around the steering wheel.

She needed to get a grip on her emotions. Since the fire, she'd driven at night. Although she'd not yet been brave enough to venture out alone.

At sunset, she preferred to be behind lock and key—and several deadbolts—squirreled away for the night in her condo. Every light ablaze. But she hadn't felt safe in nearly a year.

She used to love the night. Standing before the stage lights, singing to darkened, packed opera houses on three continents, she'd come alive at night. Feeding off the hum of adrenaline and the anticipation vibrating in the air. Finishing an aria to thunderous applause, each note a personal triumph, heady and intoxicating.

But this was her new reality. Sadness. Fear. And confusion.

She passed through the stone entrance to the national forest. And when the trees shut out what light remained in the sky, her anxiety rocketed.

The gas light flickered. Too late she remembered she was supposed to refill the tank in town. But sidewalks in Buckthorn rolled up at sunset. So turning around probably wasn't an option. She half remembered a gas station on the other side of the park.

You got this. Time to stop being such a scaredy-cat. Biting her lip, she pushed on through the darkness.

She emerged from the primeval darkness into a broad valley not far from the orchard. Yet, because everywhere in the mountains took longer to traverse, it would be another ten minutes before she reached the farmhouse.

Tomorrow afternoon she had an appointment with a professor at the college in Mars Hill regarding her dissertation. And by the time she helped pick the cider apples, she'd be late if she didn't get gas now. There was no avoiding it.

Up ahead, the run-down station was brightly lit. Though she hadn't seen a car since leaving town, she turned on her blinker.

With relief—and a sense of personal accomplishment in overcoming the piercing anxiety—riding on fumes, she pulled alongside the row of pumps.

◆ ◆ ◆

By the time Zeke veered into the beckoning neon lights of The Honky-Tonk, the gravel lot was full of battered trucks and Harley-Davidsons.

Loud music blared from inside the rowdy establishment. Parking beside a mud-splattered Dodge, he let the engine idle. Inexplicably, thoughts of Tessa Goforth flitted across his mind.

Having her hang around the orchard had complicated things for him. She needed a lot of supervision during the apple harvest, which rendered him less free to pursue his operation unhindered and unobserved.

As much as he kept an eye on her proximity, he sensed she did the same with him. For reasons known only to her. Maybe she distrusted men. Perhaps she believed him to be exactly what he wanted everyone to believe about him.

Problem was her thinking so little of him bothered Zeke more than it should. This was his job. And he was good at it. Or he had been until . . .

He blew out a breath. Tessa Goforth was not his problem. He switched off the ignition. Finding Kaci, delivering justice for the others like her, and taking down the Cozarts *was* his business.

What Tessa did, where she went—was on her own head. She wasn't his responsibility.

He scrubbed his hand over his face, trying to shake the nagging sense dogging him about Tessa tonight. He wasn't fit company for anyone, much less someone like her. After the vicious consortium he'd just left, what he needed was another shower, but this time longer and hotter. Strong enough to scrape the stench of the Cozarts off his skin.

A slamming car door jolted him from his reverie. No rest for the weary. The Cozarts weren't the only ones who'd texted him. His informant, Brandi, was a waitress at The Honky-Tonk. And she'd asked him to stop by the bar.

He needed to check in with her on another line of inquiry. If only he could find a wedge past the Cozart defenses. A sliver was all he needed to divide and conquer. His angle into the weakest player in the pack was Gibson Bascombe.

Zeke thrust open his car door and slammed it behind him. His boots crunched on the pebbled stone. Music poured out of the low-slung dive.

From the packed parking lot, it was clear the bar was hopping with men and women seeking diversions. Spilling out of the bar, several Roebuck citizens dropped their chins, as if not wanting to make eye contact.

Setting his jaw, Zeke bounded up the steps. His reputation as a Cozart man preceded him. He didn't bother locking the truck. Nobody with any sense wanted to run afoul of the Cozart clan.

Inside, it took his eyes several seconds to adjust to the cavern-like darkness. He fought the urge to wrinkle his nose at the overwhelming odor of stale beer.

Glasses clinked. As his eyes focused, he realized every head had swiveled in his direction. The overblown laughter and conversation died.

Perched on barstools, three men nursed beers. His eyes stung at the miasma of cigarette smoke hanging in the air. But the No Smoking sign wasn't the only law violated here on a nightly basis.

A heartbeat later, the occupants of the bar, hardened with disinterest, returned to their libations. Conversation and laughter resumed. Several couples in an off-kilter two-step pounded out a tune about somebody done somebody wrong.

Pushing through the smoke-filled room, he spotted Brandi at the far end of the bar. The bottle blonde had her own role to play in his charade. Despite the coolness of the autumn night, she was clad in the usual low-cut, tight T-shirt.

Displaying her assets to maximum advantage was what The Honky-Tonk paid her for. And to deliver drinks. Few understood how much more there was to Brandi Murdock. He owed her big time. She'd paved his way into the sordid side of the little mountain community.

But she had as much on the line as he did. He intended for her sake, if nothing else, to see this through to the end. And to keep them both alive in the process.

He raised his hand.

Nodding, she said something to the bartender, Luther.

Zeke skirted the swaying couples on the sawdust-strewn floor, weaving his way toward her.

Taking hold of him, she yanked him onto the dance floor.

"What's so impor—wait. I don't . . . Brandi."

She steered him into a pocket of space next to one of the music speakers. "Dance with me. No one will overhear us."

"I can barely overhear us."

She threw her arms around his neck, pulling his head down to her face. "You're supposed to be into me, remember?"

"I remember," he grunted.

Like many country girls, she was way too fond of the tanning bed. But she was a naturally pretty woman, despite rather than because of the goop on her face.

"Then act like it." Her gaze darted. "You never know who's watching, who's listening."

Some Grand Ole Opry wannabe on the jukebox bleated about tight blue jeans, cold beer, and love in a pickup truck.

Who knew when they'd get another chance to confer without anyone suspecting? He still needed to locate Gibson. The night was young, the weather, mountain perfect.

And therefore, far too much mischief waited for a man like Gib without a moral compass to fall into out there.

But it wasn't Gib's hound dog image Zeke visualized. It was green eyes and the petal-pink blush on Tessa's face—

"Zeke," Brandi hissed in his ear. "Focus."

He jerked his attention to the petite woman. "Sorry. I got your message. What's up?"

"Gib drank up his rent money again this month."

Zeke stopped shuffling his feet. "And you know this how?"

She arched a highly plucked eyebrow. "You're questioning my sources? Keep dancing."

He grimaced. "I told you I don't dance."

She took firm hold of his forearms. "Gib came by earlier. Telling his sad tale and trying to finagle a drink from Luther."

"His lack of sobriety is what got him in this fix to start with."

She shrugged. "The Gibs of the world never learn. But it's the opening we've been waiting for."

"A chance to become Gib's new buddy and confidante." He made a face. "Lucky me."

"Luckier than my sister."

Remorse shot through him. "I didn't mean—"

She shook her tousled, blond mane. "It's fine."

But when she raised her gaze to his, her expression indicated she was feeling far from fine. They were about the same age, a little past thirty. Yet to look into the jaded depths of her brown eyes, someone would think her half a decade older.

What did someone like Tessa Goforth see when she looked at him?

Brandi's grip on his shoulders tightened. "We can't let those monsters get away with what they did to Emily."

He sighed. "We'll never get a first-degree murder conviction on the basis of Emily's case alone."

"They destroyed my sister." She bristled. "They as good as murdered her. You know it and I know it. Emily couldn't function after what happened. The noose was her way out of a never-ending nightmare."

"Brandi—"

"You've gotta make 'em pay." She fisted his shirt. "No one should suffer the way Emily did." Her voice trembled. "Th-the way your Kaci probably suffered too . . ."

"They won't get away with this, Brandi." He caught her face in his hands. "I won't let them."

"Where were you when I was stupid and sixteen?" She sagged into him. "Before my life went off the tracks. Maybe we could . . ." Her mascara damp with unshed tears, she probed his features.

This wasn't his first undercover investigation, but none had felt as intense as this operation. Or as personal. He'd seen it happen to other agents, though, the need to drop the pretense, to be real if only for a moment.

Yet was Brandi the woman with whom he truly wanted to unburden himself? He let go of her, and her face fell.

But she was nothing if not resilient. "Sorry." She swiped a quick finger under her eye. "It's been that kind of day."

For him too. He'd known many an agent—married ones, included—who wouldn't have denied her or themselves. And justified their actions as part of maintaining their cover story. But when this was over, where would that leave Brandi or him?

As empty as before.

Despite the loneliness and constant fear of exposure, he couldn't—wouldn't—do that. This way was safer for them both, on multiple levels.

"Be careful going home after closing." His voice was gruff.

Steel glinted in her eyes. "None of them are dumb enough to mess with me."

"Brandi."

She patted his arm. "Luther always makes sure I get home safe."

He glanced over to the hulking, bald man wiping off the bar. Poor Luther. Their playacting had to carve a hole in his heart.

During the aftermath of her sister's suicide, Luther had offered Brandi a shoulder to cry on. Even now, he was always ready to drop everything should she need him. From the covert glances Luther sent Brandi's way when he thought no one was looking, Zeke suspected the man had feelings for her. Feelings totally unbeknownst to the waitress, who considered the bartender just a dear friend. And despite Brandi and Zeke's "romance," Luther continued to pine for her, suffering in silence because he believed her way out of his league.

But she could do worse. Had done worse. After this was over, Zeke needed to give them both a shove in each other's direction.

"You better head out." Her voice went crisp. "Places to go."

"Scumbags to befriend," he smirked. He gave her a quick peck on the cheek for appearance sake. And to the sound of her gently mocking laughter, he exited the dance floor.

Pointing the truck out of the parking lot, he spared another useless, worrisome thought for Tessa Goforth. Where she was, what she was doing. Frustrated with himself, he pressed hard on the accelerator.

He didn't relish going all the way over to Bascombe's trailer. And then there was still the matter of his newest job responsibility with the Cozarts.

Maybe he'd cruise by a few of Pender's well-known hidey-holes. Kill—*didn't he wish*—two birds with one stone.

Where there was Pender, there was bound to be Gib. Wherever booze was flowing, there'd be Gib. Though, if surrounded by his crew, Zeke wouldn't make much headway with him tonight.

He'd have to be careful around the wicked-smart Pender. But the Cozarts had given Zeke a perfect excuse to infiltrate their group. Providing him more legitimacy when Zeke did finally catch Gibson alone.

Yet, like a dog with a bone, the thought of home wouldn't leave him. Home and Tessa. The feeling welled up that he needed to check on her. An urgency gripped him that he needed to make sure she hadn't come to any harm.

This was crazy. *He* was crazy. He had the go-ahead from the Cozarts. Intel from Brandi. He had no business—

Wrenching the wheel, he did a one-eighty in the middle of the deserted road. And for no sensible reason, he drove into the national forestland. To the road that connected the town to the orchard.

❖ ❖ ❖

Tessa got out of her car and headed toward the station to prepay for the gas. Stepping across the threshold, she spotted an old man behind the cash register. She also suddenly became aware of three men loitering inside the store.

Glancing through the plate glass window, only in that moment did she note the black truck parked beside the building. But by then, it was already too late.

Catching sight of her, their gangly, nonchalant posture shifted. Twenty-something, they looked the same as each other, which she knew couldn't be true. And yet somehow it was. Unshaven. Grungy ball caps and stained jeans. Razor-sharp features.

Their eyes frightened her. Feral. Alight with an emotion she couldn't pinpoint. But their gaze raked over her, leaving her feeling soiled.

Quivering, she paid the old man. Pinching his lips together, he took her money. Very deliberately, he closed the cash register and then walked to the back of the store. He shut the office door behind him.

She stumbled from the building toward her car. The men emptied out behind her. The stocky one stopped by the bench next to the ice cooler.

The youngest one paused by the jacked-up, pimped-out truck. The oldest of the men encamped to her right at the corner of the store.

Inserting the nozzle into the tank of her car, her hand shook. But she pressed the pump handle firmly. Her nose wrinkled at the pungent aroma of gasoline. There were gurgling sounds as the liquid sloshed into her tank.

Tessa's gaze darted between the men, keeping track of their where-abouts. Alert for any movement from them. Maybe she was being paranoid.

Her eyes cut to the meter. She willed the numbers to turn more quickly. Silently urging the gasoline to flow faster. Praying she hadn't made one of those life-altering mistakes.

This couldn't be happening to her again.

Alone. Vulnerable. Other than the night of the fire, more at risk now than in the crime-ridden, concrete Crescent City jungle she'd called home for the last five years. She swallowed hard.

This was a jungle of a different sort. Greener. Deceptively simple and placid. But with the potential to be as equally deadly.

She put both hands on the handle, pressing down with all her strength. She shouldn't have stayed in town so late. She'd forgotten how quickly the light winked out once the sun descended beneath the ridge.

Hurry. Hurry. She mustn't take her eyes off them. Not for one— The nozzle clicked off.

To replace the handle onto the pump, she turned her back to them.

In that fraction of a millisecond, the air changed. Fear raised the hairs on her neck. There was a pricking between her shoulder blades. The universal fear of prey stalked by predator in these ancient hills.

With menacing strides, they advanced, closing in like a pack of wolves.

She twisted the gas cap closed. Calculating the time it would take her to throw open the car door and, with one jab of her finger, secure the locks. Too much time. Time she didn't have to make an escape.

Her heart raced.

One mistake. One miscalculation. One misstep.

Sometimes that was all it took. The decisive difference between wholeness and brokenness. Wellness and injury. Life and death.

When everything that comes after can be irrefutably traced to this split-second decision. A seemingly innocuous impulse that on the surface appeared of no importance at the time. Easily forgotten, overlooked, ignored, but fraught with consequences reverberating with ever-widening ripples of destiny.

Like the first time Sandy innocently smiled at Anton. And later, in a gesture of goodwill, included him in their circle.

An irretrievable tipping point. When life irrevocably changed for good or bad. No going back. No do-overs.

Eternity in a moment.

When Sandy opened her dressing room door that night to Anton, had she a split-second cognition of what was to come?

Tessa gripped the car key between her index and third fingers.

The taller one threw down his cigarette, crushing it beneath the toe of his steel-toed work boot. "Haven't seen her before have we, Shel?"

Shel, the stocky one, grinned stupidly at her. After removing his ball cap, he resettled it on his head, but not before his shaven head gleamed in the security light. "Gonna have us some fun tonight, ain't we, Pen?"

Catching sight of his holstered sidearm, she fumbled for the door latch, but they were on her so quickly. The two of them rammed her against the side of the BMW.

She flailed with the intent to stab, but the younger one who'd been lurking in her blind spot caught her arm, grabbing her wrist. She screamed, trying to jerk free.

The trio crowded closer, trapping her against the car door. But she lashed out, the key making contact with one of them. There was an *oomph* of pain from the taller one, Pen.

"Get hold of her, Gib. You idiot," he yelled.

"I'm trying," the youngest whimpered.

The stocky one with a swastika tattooed on his forearm backhanded her across the face.

"Not so feisty now, are you, little hellcat?"

Seeing stars, she turned her face from his whiskey-soaked breath. The men pressed her against the Beamer until she feared her spine would split in half. Hands pulled at her clothing.

Pen grabbed a hank of her hair, pulling her upward, lifting her off her feet.

She cried out, reaching behind her head to relieve the pressure on her scalp.

"We're gonna have us a right good time, boys, with this little sweetheart."

She couldn't breathe. She was going to faint. But she couldn't faint. If she lost consciousness, she'd be on the ground. And once they had her on the ground—

From the direction of the road, tires squealed into the lot. A vehicle slammed on brakes, hard. She choked, gasping for air.

There were more of them?

She heard the sound of running feet. Someone was shouting.

Closing her eyes, she thought of that night at the opera house. What he'd done to her friend, Sandy. What he'd tried and failed to do to her. *Jesus, help me.* An unconscionable darkness yawned open before her—

"Get off her!"

Hands pulled at the men weighing her down. Her lungs expanded with room to breathe again.

She knew the voice. It was— Her eyes flew open.

The cords in his neck bulging, Sloane's face was a blaze of fury. Shoving away her tormenters, he inserted himself like a barricade between her and them.

Shel's hand fell to his gun. The younger one's chest heaved, fists coiled.

But Pen, obviously the one in charge, appeared coolly unruffled. If anything, only amused. "No need to push. Gotta take your turn, dude." His thin, cruel lips twisted. "There's enough to go around."

A muscle ticked furiously in the orchard manager's square jaw. "This is why the judge put me in charge tomorrow."

"What are you talking about? In charge of what tomorrow?"

Standing on her toes, over Sloane's bunched shoulder, she made out Pen's flushed face.

"You know what I'm talking about." Taking a wider stance, Sloane planted his hands on his hips. "They sent me to tell you."

Shel's fleshy, pale face scrunched. "You got no right . . ."

"Better call off your dogs, Pender." Sloane's voice dropped to a menacing gravel. "I've just returned from a family meeting to which you weren't invited. Merritt and the rest of them, including your daddy, are sick of cleaning up your mess."

"What's he talking about?" The younger one's voice rose in a shrieking falsetto. "How does he know about—?"

"Shut it, Gib." The look Pender threw Sloane was ugly. But palms raised, Pender backed away. "Looks like the party is over, Shelton." He ran his tongue over his bottom lip. "For tonight. First taste by rights belongs to the new boss man." Pender cocked his head. "Ain't that so, Sloane?"

He was part of their crew? Her skin crawled. Nausea roiled in her belly.

"Get out of here, Pender." Sloane's voice had gone scary dark. "While you still can."

A hoot of derisive laughter. Dinging of vehicle doors. A roar of an engine. Spinning tires.

Sloane held his ground until the engine noise faded into the deepening meadow mist. "Are you all right?" He pivoted. "Did they hurt you?"

Blood pounded in her ears. Rescuer or rapist? Which was it with him?

"First taste?" She raised her hand, the key still miraculously clutched between her fingers. "Don't you dare touch me."

Red-hot anger licked across his tanned cheeks. "I'll make sure you get to the farmhouse."

She'd misjudged him. Regret knifed through her. *Rescuer. Not rapist.* "A person is judged by their friends and associates. And if the Penders of the world are indicative of the company you keep, Ezekiel Sloane . . ."

"Get in your car, Tessa."

"What was I supposed to think?" She lifted her chin. "It's not like I know you."

Surprise blinked in his eyes. And then that disappointment thing again.

He swore and she flinched. He jerked open her car door, his tightly clamped jaw brooking no argument.

Without another word, she crawled behind the wheel.

His headlights followed her to the weathered Goforth Gap Orchard sign, but he didn't turn in behind her. Once she was safely under the crossbars, his truck accelerated past. Farther down the road, his red brake lights disappeared over the hill.

Despite her grave misgivings of his character, he had saved her. But if not at the small cabin, where did he spend his nights? She swallowed.

Probably nowhere good.

Chapter Five

Perched on the top gray-planked step of the covered veranda, Tessa sipped her morning coffee. Within the next few hours, the fog, curling like chimney smoke over the distant ridge of mountains, would burn away.

There was an apple-crunch crispness to the mid-October air. Jeans and sweater weather. Her favorite time of year in her favorite place, the Blue Ridge. She reveled in the riotous colors of the autumn foliage.

She loved Aunt Dicy's farm.

Gnarled apple trees, many rows still heavy with ripening fruit, lined the long, gravel driveway. The white farmhouse sat high on a knoll. River rocks lined the solid foundation and chimney, while the cherry-red door bade welcome to all.

Welcoming her every school holiday after her mother died, when her father hadn't wanted to be bothered with her. Even welcoming somebody like Zeke.

Oh, yes. Sometime in the wee hours of the night, while contemplating her near-fatal brush with disaster, his name had changed in her head to Zeke.

Not a change she welcomed.

Zeke—*stop it*—Sloane hadn't come home last night.

She knew this because her bedroom overlooked the rows of trees behind the house. And she hadn't heard his truck rattle across the small, plank bridge that spanned the creek in front of the cabin.

Not that she was listening for him, but because after what happened at the gas station, sleep had proven even more impossible.

Yet it could have been so much worse if Zeke—she sighed—hadn't come along. And she hadn't thanked him for saving her.

Her aunt would be ashamed. Tessa meant to rectify her lapse. As soon as he decided to show for work.

At the end of the drive, a cloud of dust signaled his return.

She glanced at her phone. Technically, he wasn't late. Cutting it close, though. No more than sixty seconds to spare.

Her back twinging from being slammed against the car, she rose off the step. The navy-blue truck barreled past the house, but he gave her not so much as a glance.

Vaguely affronted, she sniffed. Trust Zeke, without saying a word, to somehow manage to insult her. Or maybe that's what grated her the most about him—his lack of verbiage.

Taking her phone and the mug, she followed the truck around the side of the house. The wraparound porch allowed for incredible, three-sixty views. Sunrise or sunset, both were spectacular.

What was not spectacular was his truck screeching to a halt beside Tonio's seen-better-days Camaro. The orchard day laborer and the other hired hand, Luis, ventured out of the barn. Zeke jumped out of the truck, shirttail flapping in the morning breeze. The same shirt he'd been wearing last night.

She pursed her lips. It didn't take a Rhodes scholar to surmise what he'd been up to last evening. Up to something no good. And she'd just bet he hadn't done it alone.

The not knowing irritated her. Uncle Calvin used to say curiosity was her besetting sin. She preferred to think of it as an intelligent inquisitiveness.

Maybe if she'd asked Sandy more questions, the fire would've never happened. Her friends would still be alive.

Tessa ducked into the house. She rinsed out her mug and retrieved her travel tumbler from where she'd stashed it in the cabinet underneath the microwave.

She emptied the carafe of coffee into the insulated thermos. Owing Zeke more than caffeine, she pushed through the screened porch and outdoors again.

Toting a pair of aluminum tripod ladders, Luis and Tonio headed into the rows of Golden Delicious trees.

Just outside the barn door, Zeke bent over the green tractor, fiddling with the engine. He spent a lot of time babying the old John Deere. She had many fond memories as a little girl riding on the seat beside her late uncle Calvin.

At the slam of the screen door, he straightened. And when he looked at her, the look of disappointment from last night remained in his eyes.

Tessa's gaze fell to his blue-striped flannel shirt. The shirt he'd misbuttoned over the white T-shirt underneath. In his haste to return from wherever it was he'd been.

All night.

She thrust the thermos at him. "Not a morning person, Ezekiel?"

"What's this?" Taking it, he examined the script on the stainless-steel tumbler. "'It ain't over till . . .'" Glancing up, he cocked his head.

She shrugged. "Opera joke."

He unscrewed the lid and sniffed the contents. "Should I be worried?"

"It's just coffee today." She bared her teeth. "But there's always next time."

He took a cautious sip. As if he didn't trust her not to have put something lethal in the brew.

Seriously? She'd come out to apologize. But he was insufferable. He made everything so hard.

He frowned. "You made this in Dicy's coffeemaker?"

"I brought my own stash of coffee with me. It's not to everyone's taste."

He could make his own coffee next time.

Coffee, the silver lining in the loss of her singing career. Singers were as superstitious as sailors. Myth or truth—they never drank caffeinated beverages. No singer wanted to risk dehydration of the vocal cords.

There were other "rules" equally lacking in scientific evidence but just as religiously followed. Like no dairy products. And always eating bananas before a performance to calm the nerves. If she never ate another banana in her life, it would be too soon.

She folded her arms across the windbreaker she'd borrowed from the peg in the kitchen. She and her aunt were both tall, long-limbed women. Like all the Goforth women, Aunt Dicy had told her.

"Didn't say I didn't like it." He took another sip. "Chicory?"

"As a matter of fact, it is." She unfolded. "Not many people would recognize that. And I thought you'd prefer it black."

"Black, like my heart?"

That was not what she meant. Well, maybe she had. "You're determined to start an argument with me today, aren't you, Ezekiel? Or is your churlish mood on account of your late night?"

He gulped down another swallow. "Dicy mentioned you lived in New Orleans." He pronounced it the way the natives did—Nawlins. Impressing her, despite herself.

"Used to." She narrowed her eyes at him. "Sleep well?"

Throwing back his head, he chugged the remainder of the coffee.

And she was annoyed with herself when he caught her staring.

With a faint smile, he swiped his hand across his lips. "Are you wanting to know where I spent the night, Mother?"

She opened her mouth, but then snapped it closed. "No."

Yes, actually she did. None of her business, but when had that ever stopped her?

That penetrating blue gaze of his rested on her hair. Conscious of having looked better groomed, she smoothed a strand behind her ear. His eyes followed the movement of her hand. Lingering but, unlike the men last night, respectful.

She was discovering he was full of surprises.

When he caught her staring again, she flushed. "You didn't come home."

Something flickered in his eyes. His grip tightened around the mug. "Did they hurt you, Tess?" In the gravelly rasp and dragged-out drawl of his voice, her name became far more than just the one syllable.

It rolled between his lips like a musical caress. And a sensation, not unlike the sweep of dragonfly wings, fluttered within her rib cage.

This time, she found herself unable to look away. "I'm fine." Her scalp ached where Pender had yanked her hair. But that wasn't something Zeke needed to know about.

A silence fell between them, broken only by birdsong. She became fascinated with the pulsing vein at the hollow of his strong throat.

He hadn't clarified where he'd spent the night. Or with whom. The only thing that aggravated her more was how much she wanted to know.

Curiosity, her besetting sin. But as long as it didn't affect his work, what he did off the clock wasn't any of her business. Right? Right.

She took a deep breath. "Thank you for rescuing me, Zeke."

He gave her a crooked smile. "Same song, second verse."

Tessa wasn't sure what he meant. But the smile was a nice change from the usual scowl. She'd begun to believe maybe that's just what his face did when he looked at her. Yet the effect was transformative.

When he made the effort to be civil, there was a rugged appeal about him. Broad shoulders. A muscled chest that tapered to his narrow waist. Not her type, but Colin Cozart wasn't the only mountain man with charm to spare.

Zeke couldn't be bothered to exert himself often, but when he did . . . Her stomach somersaulted.

There was something not quite tame about him. An unpredictability. Making him more than a little dangerous.

And the result on her nerve endings—

She fanned herself with her hand. So what if he knew chicory from arabica? She was sleep-deprived. She was tired. She was having an emotional reaction because he'd saved her last night. Nothing more.

He handed her the mug. "Thanks for the coffee. As good as the Café du Monde, though minus the beignets."

She blinked. How in the world did he know about beignets? And the Café?

Unless he'd spent time in New Orleans. But that didn't compute with the facts—admittedly few—that she knew about her aunt's orchard manager. There were obviously uncharted depths to this man.

She didn't like pickup trucks or country music. Or the crazy effect he had on her pulse. Besides, if the hastily buttoned shirt was any indication, he was otherwise occupied.

He might not be particular about his romantic interests, or whatever a man like Zeke called those kinds of activities, but she was.

She wasn't into flings. She preferred expensive cars, opera, and erudite men. Tuxedos, not flannel and jeans. Although Zeke filled out his quite nicely.

"The guys are already in the orchard." His gaze swept over her, sending a flutter clear down to her toes. Apple picking was a labor-intensive process. Each fruit handpicked. "I'd best get to work."

So had she. However, neither of them moved. She bit the inside of her cheek. What was her deal with him this morning?

Not her type. Not interested. Tuxedos, not flannel, Tessa.

She snapped out of it. "I'll finish grading the apples we picked yesterday. Then I'll help you in the orchard."

He scraped his hand over his beard stubble. "Okay."

Soft or bristly? She curled her fingers into her palms. This was ridiculous.

Not her type. Not interested. Tuxedos, not—

Wheeling, she headed across the yard.

❖   ❖   ❖

Working the same row of trees, Tessa kept a sharp eye on his location the rest of the morning.

The Goforth orchard was more of a commercial operation than a retail one. Unlike some orchards, the orchard didn't cater to the tourists. Locally known as the leaf-peepers, they roamed the nearby Blue Ridge Parkway this time of year in search of epic autumn color.

Harvest months from Labor Day to late October were crucial in keeping the orchard afloat. Ninety percent of the crop would be sold to wholesalers of baby food, applesauce, or cider.

Family-owned and family-run for five generations, the orchard had as much business as her aunt plus a few hired hands could manage. Enough to keep them on the land the Goforths had farmed since the American Revolution.

She didn't like to think about what would happen to this place once Dicy passed. Her aunt and uncle had no children. Tessa was the last Goforth.

Not farm girl material, she liked the bustling city and bright lights. The orchard was great for the occasional vacation, as a place to run to when the world got to be too much.

But long term? She couldn't see herself sticking around Roebuck County. No reason to stay.

She frowned. That had sounded far too much like her father.

Leaning against the tree trunk, she pressed into the rung of the narrow-at-the-top tripod ladder and reached for the branch slightly above her head. Carefully maintaining her balance, she plucked the apple and placed it into the pick sack slung around her neck.

The chill of the morning had been replaced by a steady warmth from the noonday sun in an azure-blue sky. Picture perfect.

Standing at ground level near the wooden crate in the middle of the row, Zeke leaned against the tractor and rolled his sleeves to his elbow. His tanned, corded forearms were ropey with muscle.

By nightfall, the mountain air would once again bathe the orchard valley in a cold clarity. Coming down the ladder, she wondered, idly, if he'd spend another night away. Or perhaps tonight, the woman who occupied his evenings would come to his cabin.

Foot slipping, she wobbled. After catching herself, she stepped off the last rung onto the ground. Adjusting the padded strap of the sack on her shoulder, she strode toward the bin.

Gently, like he'd shown her, she unloaded the apples from her bag into the crate so as not to bruise them. "That's it for this row."

He climbed aboard the tractor, pulling his long, lanky self into the seat, his muscles bunching and releasing. "Great." The edge of his T-shirt rode up, exposing a smattering of dark hair. And a six-pack abdomen.

Cheeks burning, she cut her eyes away. "Where are the guys?"

"We finished the order. They've taken the flatbed with the crates to the processing plant."

She nodded. "I have an appointment this afternoon in Mars Hill."

His big hands went still on the wheel. "In Madison County?"

What made him think she had to answer his curiosity any more than he'd answered hers?

"I appreciate your help last night," she snapped. "But—"

He gave a drawn-out sigh, as if she tried all the patience to be had in the world. "It's different here than where you're from."

"Are you saying there's a different set of rules of behavior for women?" She could practically feel her eyebrows arching to her hairline. "I have a lunch date, if you must know."

"You've got a date?" His chin came up. "In Mars Hill? With whom?"

"Not that it's any of your business, but I have a meeting with a professor. About my graduate work."

"Oh. That. Right. At the college." He shrugged those broad shoulders of his. "Sure. Probably better you stay off the streets in Buckthorn."

"Not going to happen." She glared. "I will be filing a complaint for aggravated assault at the sheriff's office in Buckthorn."

"Uh, no, Tessa." Nimbly, he jumped down beside her. "That would not be a good idea."

She gritted her teeth. "Don't you dare tell me that boys will be boys."

"Not what I was going to say. I meant it won't do any good to file a complaint with the police. In fact, I'd advise you to lay low for a while, stay close to home. Let this incident die down."

"Till they attack another woman?" She went rigid. "I think not."

"You're not understanding what I'm saying to you. It won't do any good. It'll put a bigger target on your back."

She shook her head. "You rescue me from their clutches, but what is it with you? Can't bear to see your good ole buddies locked behind bars where they belong? You men are all alike. You stick together no matter what."

His face like steel, he towered over her. "I'm telling you jail is the last thing that will happen to them."

She jabbed her finger in his chest. "When I get through making my statement, that's exactly what will happen."

She winced as he caught hold of her wrist. "That's not how things work in Roebuck County. Not when you're a Cozart."

"Those apes were Cozarts?" She pulled free. "They can't be related to Colin—"

"You've met Colin?" He bristled. "Pender Cozart is Colin's first cousin. Judson's son."

"That resemblance I get," she muttered.

His mouth twisted. "Did you happen to notice the tattoo on Shelton Allen's arm?"

"You mean, when I was fighting for my life?" She whipped her hair over her shoulder. "Yeah, I did. A swastika."

"Shelton's into that white supremacy garbage, but he's not exceptionally bright. The skinheads didn't even want him. Gibson is a distant cousin to the other two. Not playing with a full deck either. Pender will be wanting revenge for you showing him up in front of his boys."

"Perhaps you ought to be the one watching your back." She rose on the toes of her running shoes, getting into his face. "Pender doesn't strike me as the kind of man who likes to have his urges thwarted."

Zeke's features darkened. "For now, he'll do as he's told."

"Oh, that's right. I forgot. You're his new 'boss man,' right? Whatever that means." She crinkled her nose. "Heads to bust this afternoon? Drugs to traffic to school kids? Or is it trafficking of a different kind you're into, Ezekiel?"

He opened his mouth. Closed it. Opened it again. "The majority of folks around here are good people. Unfortunately, there are also two other sorts in these mountains." He thrust his jaw out and forward. "Those who would as soon shoot you as look at you."

Rolling her eyes, she crossed her arms across her chest.

"Then there's the others." He raised his upper lip. "The ones who smile at you in the daylight, but who will ambush you in the dark. And when you least expect it. Don't ever turn your back to them. Of the two, I prefer the first. More honest."

"So which kind are you?"

Inhaling sharply, he pinched the bridge of his nose. "I'm the kind trying to . . ." He pressed his lips together. "I don't have time for this." He leaped onto the tractor and brought it to life. "Enjoy your date with the professor," he shouted. "And make sure you're at the farm before night falls." Rolling the tractor forward, he worked the gears of the forklift.

She stepped aside, giving him room.

The tines of the forklift caught the wooden pallet beneath the bin and hoisted it into the air. He shifted gears, and the tractor lurched toward the cooler.

Later, while putting the finishing touches on her makeup, she heard the bridge rattle. She poked her head around the curtain just in time to spot his truck roll past the farmhouse.

In this economically depressed region, many people worked second jobs to make ends meet. But whatever job he had with the Cozarts couldn't be on the up and up. Not if he was dealing with the likes of Pender and company.

Restless, she wandered into the living room and sighed at the mess she'd made last night. Vinyl record albums and empty sleeves covered the dining room table.

Used to traffic noises, she found the countryside unnervingly quiet. And after what almost happened at the gas station, she'd been more discombobulated than usual.

No surprise, when troubled, she turned to music. Her first night at the farmhouse, she'd discovered a treasure trove of folk music albums inside one of the cabinets next to the fireplace. The same albums she remembered Aunt Dicy playing when she came to visit as a child.

Over the past few evenings, she'd steadily combed through her aunt's collection. Classics by Woody Guthrie. Joan Baez. A virtual timeline of the folk music revival that began in the 1960s.

Folk music had flowed like rain across the byways of the nation, becoming the refrain of a generation. The anthem of movements, ranging from civil rights to war and peace. In the aftermath of a tumultuous decade of social change, the ballads shaped the fabric of modern America.

There was something hauntingly beautiful about the ballads. Something nearly indefinable about the wild, shrill melodies. With her Scots-Irish roots, something that held an intrinsic appeal and resonated deep within her.

Intellectually, her head knew the ballads were an interesting mix of modal scales—Dorian, Phrygian, Mixolydian. But her heart . . . her heart told a different tale. Her blood was stirred by music not unlike the wail of a bagpipe on a misty morn.

Yet too often, the ballads were about love gone awry. Adultery. Betrayal.

And a violence, to which young women in the hills were disturbingly prone. A violence she'd experienced firsthand. A violence not only confined to these ancient hills.

Last night, she'd searched in vain for something lighter to listen to until once again the sun eradicated the darkness of the night. At the back of the shelf, she'd pulled out an album by a female singer she'd never heard before—a Leota Byrd.

Tessa had found herself captivated by the lyrical quality of Byrd's voice. The young woman possessed an achingly beautiful tone that called to something in Tessa's own soul. Byrd's vaulting soprano contained that most elusive of elements—an indescribable joy in making music.

A joy Tessa had once known. Something about the stunning voice, even the selection of songs chosen for the record, intrigued her.

On the cover, there was only a small snapshot of Leota Byrd. Petite with wavy, dark hair and deep-set, sapphirine eyes, Byrd appeared to be no older than a teenager. The woman stood at the base of a high arching waterfall clad in a breezy broomstick skirt and peasant blouse. Very '80s.

She glanced at the clock on the mantel. A few more minutes wouldn't hurt. She couldn't resist the impulse to listen to the Byrd album again before she left the orchard.

Tessa had been searching for a twist on an old song—literally. A hook on which to hang her dissertation. A case study.

She pressed the switch on the circa-1960s record player—Dicy was old school. The arm lifted, swung, and dropped the needle onto the turning black disc.

The record, scratchy with age, found a groove. The woman's voice rang out, clear and pure as a meadowlark. There was something in the singer's voice. A quality that drew Tessa. Which she found impossible to ignore.

As she listened, she tidied the living room, returning the other records to their cardboard sheaths. The Byrd album came to the final song on Side 1. "Black Is the Color (of My True Love's Hair)"—one of Tessa's favorite ballads.

Made famous by the likes of Nina Simone and Celtic Woman. A classic. In the hands—in the voice—of this unknown young woman, it became extraordinary.

> Black is the color of my true love's hair
> His face so soft and wondrous fair
> The purest eyes
> And the strongest hands
> I love the ground on where he stands . . .
> I love the ground on where he stands.

An image rose in Tessa's mind of blue, blue eyes. And strong, tanned, fine-fingered hands. Zeke Sloane's hands. Heat flashed over her.

The record spun round and round on the turntable. Her senses reeled, still confused by the expression in his eyes when he looked at her that morning.

"Black is the color of my true love's hair . . ."

What was the matter with her? But, like her musical kinship with Leota Byrd, there was something about Zeke that felt familiar. Or was *safe* a better word? And that's what troubled her the most. After what happened in New Orleans, no one—no man—was safe.

Oh I love my lover
And where he goes
Yes, I love the ground on where he goes
And still I hope
That the time will come
When he and I will be as one
When he and I will be as one.

This thing with her and the brooding, darkly attractive orchard manager was further proof she shouldn't trust her instincts. What was so broken inside her that she was drawn to the wrong sorts of men, like Zeke?

"Wherever you go, you'll carry me with you," Anton had screamed at her in that final moment as the flames took him.

The song died away. The disc continued to spin. Until finally, the player's arm lifted the needle. With a click, the machine shut itself off.

Shuddering, she wrapped her arms around herself. Violence had followed her to the Blue Ridge. Anton had been right.

Even in death, she'd never escape him.

Chapter Six

No surprise—Pender and his gang failed to show that afternoon. Which left Zeke free to proceed with the payouts. Unaccompanied. And unsupervised.

Six area farmers grew the bulk of the product that provided a steady stream of cash flow to the Cozart coffers. Despite the legalization of marijuana throughout much of the United States, regulation wasn't a surefire fix to criminal activities.

There would always be an element of society that refused to go through the legal hoops. Like in the old days of Prohibition, the bootleggers, and now the weed growers, viewed themselves as entrepreneurs.

Supply meets demand. The American way. Without government interference, they could grow it cheaper, thereby undercutting sanctioned operations. Price followed demand. It was simple market economics.

By the time he'd distributed the third market "share," he noticed a pattern in the location of the pot farms.

He put in a call to the Bureau's satellite office in Asheville, updating Reilly on his sudden epiphany. "Like a horseshoe, all six farms form a semicircle on the southern, eastern, and northern boundaries of the Yonder Mountain wilderness area. Not a coincidence, I'm thinking."

"I won't bother telling you what I think of coincidences," Reilly said. "Why does Yonder Mountain sound familiar?"

Agent Reilly was a tough, take-no-prisoners kind of guy. They understood one another. But Zeke hadn't thought it necessary to read the special agent into his personal quest for Kaci. The man was too much of a Boy Scout, too by the book.

His supervisor's approach would eventually pay dividends on the official investigation into money laundering, drug trafficking, and a host of corruption charges against both of the elected members of the clan. But he now knew enough about how the Cozarts played the game to realize that approach would never work when it came to finding Kaci.

"The Yonder Mountain wilderness area has been all over the news in the last few years. Subject of a vigorous property dispute only recently settled—no surprise—in the Cozarts' favor."

"Interesting . . ." Reilly said. "Makes you wonder if the land grab is really about property development and jobs for the struggling Roebuck economy or—"

"Or if the proposed gated community will ever actually see the light of day."

"Real estate development for sure. But in all likelihood, more about developing acreage for illegal cash crops."

"That's what I was thinking."

"Keep on it, Sloane. We're nearly at the finish line. I'll look into tax records and title transfers. Someone in the state capital, or the courts too, made sure the verdict went their way. I'll let you know what I find out." He clicked Off.

Adolphus Robertson's farm was the last on the high sheriff's list. And the closest privately owned land to Yonder Mountain. The portion of the Appalachian Trail that ran through the wilderness area had been the last place Kaci was seen alive.

Zeke stepped out of the truck but remained by the clicking engine. He knew the drill. "Hello, the house," he called.

Robertson let him cool his heels a good five minutes before emerging from the brick ranch. The old man shuffled out onto the porch. A double-barrel shotgun rested casually across his arms.

Zeke kept both hands raised to show the old man he meant no harm. "I've brought your dividend on the harvest."

"I don't know you." His mountain-blue eyes were hard with suspicion. "You ain't one of the usual bums they send, and Cozarts keep the business in the family." The old man squinted at him. "Yet maybe that is a Cozart likeness I see in your face."

"No, sir. Just a hired hand."

"Like the rest of us." The old man spat a stream of tobacco juice over the railing, just missing Zeke's boot.

"My name's Zeke Sloane." He gestured at the gun. "If you'll allow me to approach, I can give you the money you're owed."

"Ain't no Sloanes in these parts." Robertson's grizzled features bunched. "But I knowed you . . ."

He shook his head. "I don't think so, sir."

"There's something familiar . . ." His brow clearing, Robertson bobbed his chin. "Virgil Alexander, that's who you belong to."

A cold sweat broke out between Zeke's shoulder blades. "I don't know you, Mr. Robertson."

"You may not know me, but I remember you. Though it's been a while." Robertson jabbed the barrels of the gun in the air. "Goforth orchard."

A sick, sinking feeling seized hold of him. It couldn't be true. Until he'd come in search of Kaci, he hadn't set foot in Roebuck County since he was a boy.

Robertson lowered the gun. "You were skinny as a tadpole. Nothing like ole Virgil." He cocked his head. "Reckon he's long gone. Now I'm the old man. I knowed who you are, son."

"You have me confused with someone—"

"Virgil preached at the little chapel outside town." Robertson settled himself in one of the hickory rockers. "Made my missus sad when he retired. A good man. Best I ever knew."

He opened his mouth, ready to launch into some sort of plausible deniability. Anything to protect his cover, but Robertson spoke the truth. Virgil Alexander had been a good man. The best Zeke ever knew too.

"You're an apple fallen far from the old man's tree if you've taken up with the Cozarts."

Shame smote Zeke. The same kind of shame that sent him spiraling off last night when he beheld the fear and loathing in Tessa's eyes. Averting his gaze, he scrubbed the back of his neck.

But he hadn't headed to Brandi's nor anywhere similar to what Tessa implied this morning. He'd parked his truck in the deserted parking lot below the bridge at the put-in for the rafting company, then overslept.

Yet a perverse contrariness caused him to let her believe the worst about him.

"I never forget a face. Ain't no Cozart I ever seed felt no regret for nothin' they ever done. You're one of them feds, aren't you?"

Zeke never remembered going anywhere during those summers with his grandfather but to the orchard. Not to town. Not anywhere. Therefore, he'd thought he'd be safe to take the assignment. And now it came down to this? An old farmer remembering a young boy from a chance encounter decades ago? One loose thread threatened to unravel everything, to nullify the dirty work he'd been forced to undertake to expose the truth.

"Does this mean somebody's going to finally bring them Cozarts down?" Robertson set the rocker in motion. "Or is there something else going on?"

Think. Think.

He couldn't allow the entire investigation to be derailed because of him. Perhaps he could divert the old man. Satisfy his curiosity. Avoid disaster. "Don't know if you heard about a girl who disappeared not far from here."

"Yep." Robertson laid the gun across the armrests, still within easy reach. "A year and a half ago, the woods were crawling with forest rangers and other law enforcement types."

Zeke opened his palms. "I don't care about your land use practices, Mr. Robertson."

At the cry of a red-tailed hawk, the old man's gaze swept toward the patch of sky above the trees.

"I'm looking for any information you might have that could lead me to her."

Robertson's rheumy eyes followed the swirling loops of the bird, borne aloft on a wind current high above the valley.

"She's never been found. There's people who miss her . . ." His voice hoarsened.

The old man's eyes dropped to his. "My people have farmed for two hundred years. I don't know no other life. Old Man Cozart didn't give my daddy a choice. Bootleg for them or lose the land. Not dissimilar to the choice they gave me. I won't be the Robertson who loses the farm."

"Did you see something that night? Did they pay you to look the other way?"

"You got it wrong, boy. I'm paid to grow pot." His liver-spotted hand caressed the wooden stock of the shotgun. "I got enough sense not to stick my nose into places it could get blown off. And if you're half as smart as you think you are, you'll steer clear too."

"I'm afraid I can't do that."

Robertson blew out a breath. "You sure that gal ever came off the mountain? Cause I ain't."

"What do you mean?"

Robertson smacked his gums together. "Plenty of places on that mountain to hide misdeeds."

"Won't you tell me what you've seen? What you know?"

"You is on the right track, but I ain't pointing no fingers. Fingers can be chopped off. Stuff like that don't just happen in Mexico, you know."

"You've got granddaughters." Zeke's voice rose. "What if it had been one of them?"

"Why do you think so many tolerate their ways? Cause we like 'em?" Robertson snarled. "You're either for 'em or agin' 'em. You work with 'em or your people suffer for it."

"So they're going to get away with it? Every hellish thing they've put this town through in the last fifty years." He struggled to rein in his temper. "Give them an inch, they'll take a mile. And another. Until one day, it's your family they've hurt."

"Much as I respected your granddad, I can't." Robertson sighed. "But I will tell you where you should start to look."

Zeke went still, very still, afraid to breathe lest the old man change his mind.

"Nothing on the mountain, except that crazy old woman still living up there. But at the eastern base of Yonder, there lay the original Cozart homeplace."

Zeke scrounged in his pocket. Found a pen and the blank side of a receipt from the hardware store. "Draw me a map to it."

Robertson took the pen with reluctance. "I'm telling you to be careful. And leave me well out of it. For a place nobody but ghosts have lived for nigh on eighty years, I see a lot of dust swirling on the back road to

Yonder. Somebody keeps the barn in good repair. Probably for no good reason."

No good reason—like murder.

But proving it was another matter entirely. Pender Cozart, Shelton Allen, and Gibson Bascombe were neck deep in everything rotten in this county.

It was too late in the day for a trek into the mountains, but he promised himself soon. Between his cover at the orchard and doing the Cozarts' dirty work, he'd have to find the time to conduct a proper search.

He gave Robertson his share of the cut for this year's harvest.

"I won't be telling your secret, boy."

There were few people whose word he actually trusted. Three of them were forever dead—his grandfather and his parents. The fourth, Kaci, might be forever lost.

Robertson sagged. "The girl must mean something to you."

"She does."

"Family or girlfriend?"

There'd been a moment when one had almost become the other. If he'd ever taken a milli-step in that direction, Kaci would've been thrilled.

But he hadn't. For reasons even now he didn't fully understand.

"Family." Despite the guilt of not reciprocating his foster sister's teenage crush, it was the only answer he could offer the old man.

At the time, he'd believed Kaci at an impressionable age. That with maturity, her interests would broaden. That someone better, that deserved her more, would cross her path.

What crossed her path had been Pender Cozart and his crew.

After what almost happened to Tessa last night, he was forming a clearer picture of the night she went missing.

Kaci never got the chance to fall in love with someone else. He'd probably carry the burden of his guilt to the day he died. For not loving her the way she wanted him to. For not protecting her. For not being there in every sense of the word when she needed him most.

The ache never left him. He'd about convinced himself only one thing would ever help—spilling the blood of those who'd spilled hers.

Robertson chewed his cud for a moment. "What we will do for family, eh?"

What, indeed.

"No love lost for the Cozarts here." He spit another stream of tobacco. "And I'd not be the only one wishing you happy hunting."

Zeke moved toward the truck. Would Robertson keep his identity secret? He'd only know for sure if next time he was with the Cozarts no knife plunged into his back.

One other person he trusted . . . Dicy Goforth. But he'd not told her about Kaci. Only about the official investigation into the Cozarts.

Dicy had become a moral anchor for him. And he'd be glad when she returned to the little white farmhouse where she belonged.

He needed to give her a call. See how she was feeling. She was getting out of rehab soon.

Which gave him an idea. Something that would help him feel more like himself. Or at least the self he used to be.

He headed toward the local lumberyard.

A scenic little town surrounded by the Appalachian Mountains, Mars Hill was only twenty minutes via I-26 to Asheville, but the eleven miles to the Tennessee border took forty-five.

She'd picked a clear day to venture into the small mountain community. In the distance, she could just make out Mount Mitchell, the highest peak east of the Mississippi. And also Old Bailey about a mile northwest.

One of the university's main claims to fame was its dance team—the Bailey Mountain Cloggers, who had won twenty-something national championships and performed all over the world.

The university's other claim to fame was the center dedicated to the preservation of the heritage of the Southern Appalachians. Once she made the decision to help Dicy with the orchard, Tessa had emailed the center, seeking assistance in finishing the research she'd begun on Southern Appalachian folk music. And to gain access to the center's extension collection of artifacts.

Climbing the stone steps from the parking lot to the brick administration building left her puffing slightly. She was still getting used to the higher elevation.

While Mars Hill was over 2,300 feet above sea level, New Orleans essentially lay at the bottom of a big earthen bowl. Hence, the devastation of Hurricane Katrina.

Professor Ruth McClaine waited for her beside one of the white columns on the broad veranda of the venerable old building. Over the last few days, they'd exchanged email messages. But somehow Tessa had expected the musicologist to be older.

Appearing to be in her early forties, the professor was an angular, spare woman like so many Tessa had met in the Blue Ridge. Like Aunt Dicy. Like herself.

She had dressed for their meeting in a blue jean skirt, black long-sleeved T-shirt, and olive-green tied scarf, but Ruth McClaine was mountain casual. Her oversize beige cardigan reached to the holes in her acid-washed, ripped jeans.

Tessa felt decidedly overdressed.

"Welcome to you." The professor waved and then pushed her black cat-eye frames higher on the bridge of her nose.

"Dr. McClaine."

"Ruth, please. You must be Tessa. My office is on the second floor." She paused at the bottom of the marble stairs. "Unless you'd rather walk a few blocks to the coffee shop." The professor fluttered her hand again. A metallic gray color glimmered on her nails. "Fine by me if we schedule all our meetings at The Grind."

A memory of early morning coffee with Zeke flashed through her mind. Her pulse did a staccato beat. She'd stick with the chicory. "Perhaps next time."

Leading the way up a sweeping staircase, Ruth gave her a rundown on the center's collection. "Bascom Lamar Lunsford—you've heard of him, right?"

She nodded. "Minstrel of the Appalachians."

Reaching the second story, Ruth paused. "Born in Mars Hill, he was best known for the jingle 'Good Ole Mountain Dew.'" She threw open a door. "He sold the rights for the price of a train ticket home."

Tessa stepped inside. "Musicians don't always make the best business decisions."

Ruth's office was lined with overflowing bookcases. From the most prestigious of ethnomusicology programs, her diplomas were framed and tacked to the wall behind her desk. Undergrad at UT-Austin. MA at Indiana U in Bloomington. PhD—UCLA.

Slipping behind her desk, she gestured for Tessa to take a seat in one of the padded chairs. "You've enjoyed quite the career in music performance. Opera?"

Pursing her lips, Tessa nodded again.

"If I may ask, what led you to leave a promising career"—Ruth propped her elbows on the desk—"yes, I looked you up—to pursue finishing your PhD in folk music?"

She wasn't the first to wonder.

"If you've looked me up, then you also read about the fire, I assume."

Ruth's dark brows drew together over the frame of her glasses. "Were your lungs scarred in the incident?"

Tessa smoothed a hand over her skirt. "Smoke inhalation only, but . . ." She shrugged.

"I listened to a recording of you singing the aria from *St Matthew Passion* by Bach. 'Erbarme dich.'"

Which translated to—*have mercy on me.*

But there'd been no mercy the night of the fire.

Her stomach tightened at the memory of the live recording with the German symphony. As usual, Anton performed the principal violin solo. In her head, she could hear it now—every note pure and true.

"You're a contralto."

"I *was* a contralto." She put a hand to her throat. "Do you not hear how I sound now?"

"You are still a contralto." Ruth half turned toward the window. "I'm not a medical specialist, but to the ear your voice reminds me of the river. A deeply grooved river."

She shook her head. "My voice lacks buoyancy, flexibility, and fluidity."

That wasn't exactly true.

She'd long ago recovered from the effects of the smoke inhalation. But something had been laid waste in her mind, in her nerve.

Tessa could no more go out on stage to sing than she could fly to the moon. Liquid sound no longer poured effortlessly from her throat. The sound—when she could make a sound at all—wasn't the music she heard in her head. Not the music she'd made all her life. And she wasn't willing to settle for anything less.

"Your people, the Goforths, are native to this region."

"I heard the ballads as a child, so I decided to conduct my research on the topic. To analyze the surge of interest in the folk music that occurred after the Bicentennial."

Ruth stared at her for another moment, her focus intense, shrewd. Finally— "I guess you know best. Such a shame, though, that you no longer perform."

Yes, it was.

"Your performance is possibly the most powerful rendering I've heard of that particular aria. Your voice has a mysterious, melancholic quality."

Had. Tessa forced a smile. "So, about the Lunsford Collection?"

Ruth exhaled and, thankfully, moved on. "The collection contains photos, sound recordings, transcribed ballads, and other memorabilia Mr. Lunsford acquired over the course of his lifetime. Previously unknown ballads that, if not for his efforts, might have been lost."

Tessa took out her notebook. "I've been told the center also contains collections featuring the work of Dellie Norton and Obray Ramsey?"

"You will have access to all of it." Ruth flipped through a file on her desk. "From the notes you sent me, I see you've already thoroughly explored the history of the songcatchers."

The ballads not only migrated from the British Isles, but also mutated according to the singer's preferences or memory of the oral tradition. Between the world wars, an Englishman—one of the first songcatchers—had traveled extensively throughout the Southern Appalachians collecting and preserving the ballads.

She edged forward on the seat. "Across an ocean and across the centuries, the connection to traditional Irish, English, and Scottish music is amazingly unbroken."

Ruth leafed through the pages in the folder. "Since the Scots-Irish first settled these mountains, songs have passed from generation to generation."

"I'm also interested in the ballad singers." Tessa handed her the paper where she'd written Leota Byrd's name. "The album bio said she was from Roebuck County."

Ruth examined the paper. "I've never heard of her. How odd."

"The album had a copyright date of 1988. I googled her. Apparently, there was only the one album that she ever recorded."

Ruth lifted her head. "I wonder what happened to her."

Feeling an unexpected kinship with the long-ago balladeer, she had wondered the same. "The logical thing to do seems to start with the information on the album cover and work forward."

"Was Byrd her married name?"

"I'm not sure."

"That will make it harder. In these parts, many local women marry young." Ruth nibbled at her lower lip. "But there's bound to be old-timers around here who remember her. Before we were invaded by the Floridians, everybody who was anybody in folk music knew one another. It will take some digging . . ."

She felt a stir of excitement. "But that's the thrill of the chase, isn't it?"

Ruth laughed and sat back. "On this album, there weren't any 'new' ballads"—she made air quotes with her fingers—"were there?"

The holy grail of ethnomusicologists.

"If only."

"Stranger things have happened. These mountains are old. Some of the oldest on the planet." Ruth's face grew pensive. "There's no telling what secrets they may yet reveal to someone who knows where to look and the right questions to ask."

Tessa had experienced more than enough strange for one lifetime. Thanks, but no thanks.

Ruth came around the desk. "I'll take you over to the archives."

The compassion she beheld in the professor's eyes was unexpected. And took her aback.

"Don't only write about these songs, Tessa. Listen to them. Let them soak into your soul."

She couldn't help but smile. "Doctor's orders, Dr. McClaine?"

"There are worse ways to spend your time."

An image of Anton drawing his bow across the strings rose in her mind. That last exquisite note, hovering in the air between them, amidst the searing flames.

Yes, there were.

Chapter Seven

Tessa spent the rest of the afternoon buried in the archives in Mars Hill. Once back at the farmhouse, she did an internet search for the Nashville studio where Leota had recorded the album. Now defunct, Stargazer Records had gone out of business in 2008 with the onset of the Great Recession.

However, she found contact information for several former employees. Perhaps one of the studio employees could provide a clue as to Leota's whereabouts since 1988. She sent out emails, hoping one of them would remember the teenage mountain girl. But thirty plus years ago was a long time.

It was dark when Zeke returned to the cabin. Yes, some perverse instinct had her listening for him. Of course, she had no way of knowing if he returned alone or not.

The next morning, Luis and Tonio were busy working in the orchard. Yet Zeke was emphatic—and churlish—about not needing or wanting her help.

Standing just inside the barn, she folded her hands inside her sweater against the morning chill. "What is your problem today, Ezekiel?"

He rummaged through a toolbox and didn't bother looking up. "Other than you?"

And here she believed they'd achieved a sort of détente. Or at least a peaceful coexistence.

Fine. She had plenty of other things she could be doing. The dissertation wasn't going to write itself. "I'm going out." She waited for the usual bossiness.

He picked up a handsaw only to lay it aside. He sorted through a bunch of screws.

She exhaled. Loudly.

"No one's stopping you, Goforth." He bent over the workbench. "Knock yourself out."

She narrowed her eyes at the back of his hard head. "You first," she muttered.

"What?" He looked at her then. The man had the ears of a bat.

"Nothing." She exited before she gave in to the impulse to grab a hammer and brain him.

It grated that he didn't seem to like her. Which was ridiculous. Why should she care whether he liked her or not? She didn't like him either.

Tessa arrived at the university earlier than she'd anticipated and finished sooner than expected, so she decided to share lunch with her aunt at the rehab center. But not finding Dicy in her room, she inquired at the front desk.

"She's had a string of visitors this morning. Lots of calls too." The aide waved Tessa toward the lounge. "Folks from her church and such."

Hopefully, the such did not include the odious Judson Cozart.

Speaking into her bespangled, pink cell phone, Dicy's eyes lit when Tessa strolled into the sunny room.

There hadn't been many people in Tessa's life glad to see her, much less that loved her. But her aunt was one.

Dicy spoke into the phone. "Thanks so much for checking on me." She motioned Tessa closer.

She maneuvered around the overstuffed, chintz-covered sofas.

"You come see me soon, dear heart." Dicy clicked Off and stuck the phone in the pocket of her velour robe.

Tessa dropped a kiss on her aunt's paper-thin cheek.

Her aunt patted the seat beside her. "Look who the cat dragged in."

"Aren't you Miss Popularity today?"

Dicy's blue robe matched her eyes. "Such is the life of us social butterflies." She smiled.

"And the therapy yesterday?"

"Doctor says my leg is healing ahead of schedule."

"That's good news." Tessa laughed. "Always such an overachiever."

"I've talked them into releasing me early."

Tessa squeezed her hand. "That's wonderful. When?"

"How about late this afternoon after my last therapy session?" Dicy's brow furrowed. "Though I hate to ask you to hang around town waiting on me."

"Don't worry about me. I'll find something to keep me occupied. I'm just so happy to get you home."

"It seems a century since I slept in my own bed." The old woman leaned against the cushion. "How are you and Zeke getting on? He called to check on me yesterday. Such a thoughtful young man."

Remembering their latest clash, Tessa didn't see it. But whatever.

"He told me about the work y'all have done on the harvest so far. He's a born farmer, don't you think?"

Zeke was a born something all right.

He had the social skills of an ox. But obviously, Dicy was a card-carrying member of the Zeke Sloane fan club. As would be the woman with whom he'd probably spent the night.

Tessa grimaced.

"What's wrong, Tessie?" Dicy was no one's fool—except when it came to Zeke. "Nothing's happened, has it?"

She hadn't told her aunt about the incident at the gas station. Dicy needed to concentrate on getting well. But Tessa planned to file a complaint before she left town today.

Tessa adjusted her expression. "Just wondering if I need to make a quick grocery run before you get home." Thank goodness she'd straightened the house before she left this morning.

Her aunt folded her hands over the crocheted throw on her lap. "How was your visit to Dr. McClaine?"

"I've had this great new idea to include in the dissertation. I'm going to do a case study on a local ballad singer from the 1980s."

"Someone Dr. McClaine knows?"

"Actually, I discovered her from an old album in your collection."

Dicy tilted her head. "There's not many around here who sing the old ballads anymore . . . There's a lot of talent around Madison County, though."

"I'm hoping a social butterfly like you might help me track her down." She touched her aunt's arm. "Or point me to a relative of hers."

Dicy pursed her lips. "The young people with talent usually went to Nashville. Not much to keep them, then or now, in Roebuck County."

"She only made one album. Unless later she recorded under a stage name."

"Could've gotten married. Or wasn't able to continue as a solo act but found work doing background vocals." Her aunt wagged her finger. "A lot of young people leave seeking fame and fortune only to find disappointment."

"This woman's voice is exceptional. I can't believe the music industry wouldn't have taken notice. She should've enjoyed a long and illustrious career."

Dicy rapped her fingers on the padded armrest. "I'm racking my brain—feeble as it is—trying to remember what album, what singer, you found in the cabinet. I haven't foraged in there for so long."

"On the cover, she looked young. But she has the most powerful, moving voice . . ." Tessa leaned forward. "Her name is Leota Byrd."

Dicy's face fell. "I'd forgotten about that album."

She frowned, unsettled by the old woman's reaction. "You didn't like her voice? Or the songs?"

Dicy dropped her gaze. "After she went to Nashville, folks that loved her never heard another word from her."

"You're telling me this incredible singer just dropped off the face of the earth?"

Dicy fretted one of the cushion tassels. "Leota was often impetuous. She excelled at running away. Her family wasn't keen on her music. I don't believe any of the Byrds are still alive. And if they were, they wouldn't talk to you about a black sheep like her."

Tessa threw out her hands. "How could they not appreciate a voice like hers?"

"Leota's people held extremely conservative religious beliefs. They had strict ideas on what holiness meant. Being set apart to them meant rejecting all forms of worldliness."

Tessa's eyebrow arched. "Singing is worldly?"

"She attended high school in Buckthorn during the years I was a school nurse. She had a way about her . . . Local boys were drawn to her like bees to honey."

"But most churches include music. How could they view Leota's songs as wrong?"

"Other than the voice itself, her family's church didn't hold with musical accompaniment. The list of don'ts only made Leota long to do them more. Her senior year, as soon as she turned eighteen, she ran away to make the album."

"She had a voice that wouldn't be denied."

Her aunt arched her brow. "Like you."

Under her scrutiny, Tessa fidgeted. Dicy could be like a dog with a bone. Her great-aunt's current bone of contention was that Tessa needed to return to making music. Not just writing about it.

"Neglect not the gift that is in thee," Dicy admonished.

"I can't sing. I've tried. But I just—" She looked away.

"The problem lies not in your vocal cords but with your heart." The old woman's face clouded. "I'm praying you will truly come to know what it is to make melody in your heart to the Lord."

Dicy spoke of her Lord as a close friend, near at hand. And during those long-ago summers, she taught Tessa His ways too. But after the fire, Tessa wasn't sure she even believed God existed. Or if He did, that He cared.

"Every good and every perfect gift comes from above and comes down from the Father of lights with whom there is no variableness, neither shadow of turning."

Dicy had a habit of quoting Scripture. With anyone else, Tessa would've viewed it as self-righteous and condescending. But her aunt was a woman of great humility and faith. Her only desire was for Tessa's good. Dicy meant well.

"So you're telling me the odds of finding Leota Byrd are zero to none?"

Dicy sighed. "If there's anyone who would've heard from Leota, it would be Ouida Kittrell." Her mouth flattened. "One of the ones most hurt by Leota. But speaking of Ouida actually brings me to a favor I wanted to ask of you."

"Of course I'll do it."

Her aunt eyed Tessa over the rim of her glasses. "You don't know what I'm going to ask yet."

She gave the elderly woman a gentle hug. The comforting aroma of roses enfolded Tessa's senses. "It must be important or you would never ask."

"I realize you two have never met, but I need you to check on Ouida for me."

"Okay . . . sure."

"It won't be as easy as I've made it sound. Ouida and I are distant relatives. There's a twenty-year age difference twixt and tween us. She lives over on Yonder Mountain. Since the trouble, I've trekked over there at least once a week to check on her. She'll be wondering what's happened to me."

"Trouble?" Tessa frowned. "Is she sick?"

"Mind your manners when you go. Ouida is ninety if she's a day. She's set in her ways. And can be contrary if she takes against you."

This was sounding more and more like fun. Except not really. "Why would she take against me?"

Dicy removed a scrap of paper from her pocket. "I've sketched a map. Her place is in the back of beyond."

Tessa studied the drawing. "I see the highway. But what's the name of the road that runs by her house on the mountain?"

Dicy laughed. "Bless you child for the millennial you are. There is no road that runs up the mountain by her house. Not since before my time."

Tessa pulled up a map of Roebuck County on her phone and compared it to her aunt's rendering. "It says here that this is government forestland."

"When I was a girl, that whole area was full of folks. The Cane Creek community. But everybody was forced to come off the mountain after the land was made into the national park. Ouida's the only one left now."

She gaped at her aunt. "Ninety years old and she lives on the mountain by herself?"

"Ouida was born on the mountain. She's vowed to stay till one day she rests with her people on the mountain."

"I never realized the land belonged to someone before it became a national park."

"The national park was supposed to bring jobs and put food on the table for men able to build a great roadway at the height of the Great Depression. Nobody cared there were communities like Cane Creek, farms, and people already on Yonder Mountain."

She frowned. "I can't imagine people in Roebuck County leaving their homes without a fight."

"Little good it did them." Dicy sniffed. "Then as now, you get about as much justice as you can pay for. Those that didn't go along with the government's plan—the land having been in their family for generations—were foreclosed upon. Deputies forcibly evicted them."

Tessa began to understand why mountain folk remained suspicious of outsiders and government authorities.

"I was only a slip of a girl when the scattering commenced. It was a sad sight—the trucks piled high with everything a family owned, wide-eyed children clinging to the sides, not sure what the future would bring."

"Were the Goforths or your family scattered too?"

Dicy shook her head. "The Kittrells first settled on the mountain, but my branch drifted to town long before the scattering. The Goforths, Calvin's people, settled in the valley to grow apples." She chuckled. "Ouida would say we've always been soft."

"That was so long ago. Why does this matter now?"

"In these mountains, we've inherited a bitter legacy. Folks like Ouida only want to be left alone, but people like the Cozarts won't let them be."

"Ouida's been living there all this time. What changed?"

"Because they're strapped for cash, the National Park Service handed the wilderness area over to the state Forest Service. Then, in the midst of the worst economic downturn since the Great Depression, the state government invoked an obscure eminent domain clause. Touting redevelopment for the public benefit, they transferred the land including Yonder Mountain to a private party. The Cozart Development Corporation."

Tessa wrinkled her forehead. "So earlier this week, Judson was threatening Ouida?"

"Judson Cozart claims they want to increase the tax base by putting in a high-end gated community for the snowbirds who migrate here every year."

She probed Dicy's expression. "But you don't like the idea of new-comers? Or you think this is another land grab?"

"How do you know when a Cozart is lying?" The old lady glowered. "When their mouth is moving."

"But if the planned community is real, wouldn't that be a good thing for the county?"

Dicy shrugged. "The Cozarts are not without their supporters. The project would bring jobs and improve the infrastructure. In light of that, what's the plight of one very old woman clinging to a way of life long past?"

Tessa scanned the map again. "What about environmental concerns? Loss of habitats?"

"A fair point, and folks are divided." Dicy waved her blue-veined hand. "None of that has ought to do with you. Yet I wanted to give you a heads-up. Her friends—and Ouida does have some—have been appealing the verdict. They lobbied to get the ruling overturned, but the attorney has exhausted the last appeal."

"So that's an end to it."

"Ouida has just a little over two weeks to vacate." Her aunt sniffed. "She won't go without a fight. I was hoping you could persuade her to come stay with me. I'm rattling around in the house all by my lonesome."

It was the first time she'd ever heard her widowed aunt voice an objection to the solitude of her life since Uncle Calvin passed. It'd been five years since Tessa's last visit. She'd meant to come, but there'd been no opportunity for an extended trip to the orchard. A flurry of international concerts had followed each opera season. There was always another part for which to train. Another rehearsal. Another fitting.

Until there wasn't.

Then, shattered by the trauma she'd endured, she'd been too scared to venture much beyond the carefully regulated new routine she established for herself. Trips were limited either to the grocery store or to work on her dissertation with the university advisor and back again to her condo. She'd been consumed by an overwhelming need to control every aspect of her environment.

Tessa shifted her weight. "Why do you think Ouida will listen to me?"

Dicy brushed her finger across the shiny grain of the cushion fabric. "You two have a lot in common."

She stared at her aunt. What could she and a ninety-year-old recluse possibly have in common?

"Back in the day, Ouida had a right fine voice. She traveled the circuit round here when she was a girl, singing with her family. She mentored Leota Byrd." Dicy gave her a shrewd look. "Ouida could tell you a thing or two about making a new life after loss."

She slumped. "I'm trying, Aunt Dicy. I'm working on this dissertation."

"If that's what you think will make you truly happy, cinnamon bun."

She didn't buy Dicy's wide-eyed look of innocence. "I'm not abandoning my gift." She dropped her chin. "The gift abandoned me."

Dicy rested her hands in her lap. "I'm praying you two will form a connection, and you can persuade her to reinvent herself one more time. But be gentle with Ouida. And careful."

"What do you mean *careful*?"

"That branch of the family—the Kittrells—always seems to know things."

"I don't get what you mean."

"Ouida's people called it a gift." Dicy reached for a well-worn Bible tucked underneath her arm. "My mama didn't hold with it. And with everything that happened to the Kittrells, I've wondered if it wasn't so much a gift as a curse."

"Are you saying Ouida's not right in the head, Aunt Dicy?"

"I thought you should know what you're getting into before you traipse over there. Folks say she has the Sight."

"That's crazy."

Dicy gave her a look. "God is a whole lot bigger than the box most folks try to keep Him inside, missy."

"Surely you don't believe in that mumbo-jumbo stuff?"

"All I know is once she came to help my first cousin deliver a baby and brought a hand-sewn shroud with her." Dicy shivered. "The baby only lived six hours."

◆ ◆ ◆

It surprised Zeke how much he enjoyed the slower pace of life in the country. The satisfying connection he felt to the soil. Working with his hands.

Orchard life sure beat lying for a living and consorting with the lowest forms of humanity.

It had been a busy morning. One of the things he loved most about working in the orchard—every day was different, had its own challenges. Unlike with the ambiguities of life undercover, he could reflect back on a day and take stock of what he'd accomplished.

Apple harvest was winding down, leaving him free to pursue his great idea for Dicy. Cordless drill against the pine board, he ratcheted the screw into place. The sun felt good on his neck. Bees hummed in a patch of clover near the porch. He reached for the hammer.

He'd been rude to Tessa this morning. It rankled him how his pulse leaped at the sight of her. With everything else going on, she ought to be the last thing on his mind.

Ought to be.

But when she sauntered into the barn today, without even turning, he'd somehow known she was behind him. He felt an almost visceral connection with her. A connection he'd never experienced with anyone else.

Framed by the light of the open barn, her hair had waved about her shoulders, red gold in the dewy light of the day. One quick look and he'd had the good sense to keep his head down before he said something to betray himself.

So he fell back on what he did best with Tessa—animosity.

He hammered the protruding nail with more force than necessary. He shouldn't be thinking about her. He should be focused solely on finding Kaci.

Yet some instinct—GrandPop would've said God—had gotten him there in time to save Tessa at the gas station. His gut went hollow. She could have so easily been a repeat of what happened to Brandi's sister, Emily.

And what must've befallen Kaci the night she went missing.

He squeezed his eyes shut and swiped his forearm against the sweat on his brow.

The Bureau interviewed other hikers on the Trail that week. Several remembered the bubbly, young woman. The witnesses enabled the investigators to sketch out a rough timeline of events.

Her deserted campsite was discovered in the remote wilderness area. Her backpack containing money and her cell phone had been untouched. Robbery hadn't been a motive. The agents assigned to the missing person case discovered a ripped sleeping bag in the underbrush.

Reconstructing the events of that evening, Zeke could now put faces on her abductors. Through-hikers were up with the sun and in bed by sunset. Kaci would probably have already been asleep when they came upon her.

Zipped in the sleeping bag to ward off the chill, she would've had no chance to escape before they encircled the campsite, before they were on her.

An old friend in the agency had let him see the official report. There'd been deeply gouged drag marks in the dirt. Broken tree limbs. Scattered bracken.

Streetwise tough, Kaci would not have gone gently into the night.

There'd been lost hours before another hiking couple came upon the abandoned camp. And hiked down the mountain for help. Thank God they'd hiked into Madison County, not Roebuck.

Unfortunately, in the intervening hours between her disappearance and the report, there'd been weather on the mountain. It kept the SAR team at bay, and rescuers had lost even more precious hours. The evidence trail went cold. It was as if she'd vanished into the mist.

The investigation stalled and theories abounded. Speculation went that Kaci was taken off the mountain to a waiting vehicle. Closest road to the Trail—he'd checked—was an old, gravel logging road.

He'd worked the route forward and backward. The logging road dead-ended in one of the last true wilderness regions in the Appalachians. An untamed, isolated area accessible only with a great amount of grit and bushwhacking.

From the other direction, the log road fed into the Pisgah, which was comprised of heavily forested slopes, huge whitewater rapids, and eagle eyrie gorges. From the Pisgah, the paved road eventually opened into a handful of North Carolina counties straddling the border of Tennessee.

To Zeke, it was no longer a question of who had taken Kaci. But two crucial questions remained—What had they done to her? And where was she now?

Brandi had filled in some of what was lacking from the official file. Information he could have only acquired through a local. They both suspected Pender and his gang of being responsible for repeated acts of abduction and rape. People were afraid to talk, but someone high in the "Cozacrat kingdom" had helped Pender get away with it.

High Sheriff Merritt Cozart was at the top of Zeke's list.

Finding Kaci's body was crucial. If what happened to Emily was any indication—and it turned him inside out to think about it—there'd be DNA evidence to nail those sons of—

He sank down heavily on the ramp he'd fashioned for Dicy. At the gas station, he'd seen himself reflected in Tessa's eyes. She'd believed he was one of them . . .

But why wouldn't she think he was like them? He'd spent the better part of a year convincing everyone he was exactly like them. Unprincipled. And worse.

Yet it had shaken Zeke, seeing himself like that in her cool green eyes. He didn't know how much longer he could continue in this line of work. It was eroding everything he was inside. He disgusted himself.

But what else was there? Whatever it said about him—and what it implied wasn't to his credit—he was good at being a chameleon. Good at faking. Good at deceiving. Good at manipulating.

If not for GrandPop and his parents, could he have been just like the Cozarts? Like Pender?

He swallowed the bile rising in his throat. Grace of God. Better genes. Nurture versus nature. Whatever Zeke called it, he wasn't like Colin or Pender. Not yet.

Though one day when, not if, he found Kaci and uncovered the despicable thing they'd done to her, he was afraid of what he'd do to them. Afraid of himself.

He chucked the hammer. It landed with a clatter in the toolbox. Maybe tomorrow he could make the expedition out to the old Cozart barn. Tonight, he should check in with Brandi.

Rising, he gave the handrail a shake, testing it. Sturdy. Every nail in place.

The Cozarts didn't know it yet, but he was getting ready to put the final nails in their coffins too.

Chapter Eight

After lunch in the cafeteria, her aunt was bundled off to the physical therapy wing. Tessa checked her phone, hoping one of the Stargazer employees from the recording studio had contacted her. There was nothing. Not yet.

But Dicy's remark about Leota Byrd attending Roebuck County High School gave Tessa an idea. The town library was an easy stroll from the rehab facility. Maybe she could find additional info regarding the elusive ballad singer there.

Inside the old library building, a group of children sat crisscross applesauce as a young woman read aloud from an oversized picture book. *Crisscross applesauce.* She smiled.

One could take the girl out of the orchard, but maybe not the orchard out of the girl.

During rainy summer days, she and her aunt would sit crisscross applesauce on the old rag rug in the farmhouse living room, happily singing along to Dicy's album collection.

An older woman looked up expectantly from the checkout counter.

There were many things a teenage girl might not tell her family or even a respected mentor like Ouida Kittrell. But friends, especially girl friends, were a different matter.

At her request, the librarian brought Tessa a handful of yearbooks spanning Leota's high school career. In the alcove, Tessa scooted the chair closer to the table and flipped open the 1987–1988 yearbook.

Leota's senior picture revealed a wistful, lovely girl on the brink of great things. It seemed incredible to think someone so young could record with such a mature sound. And so unbelievably sad that such talent failed to produce another album.

Driven by a compulsion she didn't altogether understand, Tessa flipped through the pages, searching for other photos of Leota. Why had Leota stopped singing?

Once Leota left music, what did she do with the rest of her life? Leota Byrd was no more than an obscure musical footnote in the history of folk music. And yet Tessa couldn't shake the urge to learn more. To uncover the truth. And in so doing, maybe she'd also stumble across answers to her own future.

Because, after she finished the dissertation, what was she going to do with the rest of *her* life?

She stopped turning pages and gazed out the window overlooking Main. Hanging around the orchard forever wasn't an option, was it? She frowned, recalling the curt exchange with Zeke. Staying wouldn't be a good idea.

For more than one reason.

He didn't like her. That much was clear. She set aside Leota's senior yearbook.

Without knowing her, he had jumped to a host of conclusions about her character. Believed her snobby, vain, and worse. He hated her hair. Almost every day he would stare at it and then frown.

She bit her lip. Hadn't she done the same to him? Prejudged him. On the basis of what?

It wasn't as if she knew him. Knew anything about him really. They had only met a few days ago. Yet he consumed her waking thoughts. He addled her, his moods swinging from cold to hot.

Or was that just how he made her feel?

She chewed the inside of her cheek. Cold? Not so much. When she was with him, she forgot to breathe. She couldn't think, couldn't seem to do anything.

Like now? *Get out of my head, Zeke Sloane.*

She paged through Leota's junior yearbook. Leota hadn't been involved in any clubs or activities. Therefore, she'd left no clues to her friends. Or if she'd had any.

Back on the senior class spread of the yearbook, Tessa ran her fingertip across the individual pictures. *Akins. Allen. Bascombe. Byrd. Caldwell. Clancy. Cozart.*

Cozart, Merritt.

A grainy color photo revealed an earnest lug of a boy. With a neck as big as her thigh, Merritt Cozart had the build of a football player. He obviously worked out. A lot.

Keeping her thumb inserted on the senior class page, she scrolled to the athletic section. *Merritt Cozart. Defensive tackle.*

Dark-haired, he wasn't exceptionally good-looking like Colin, but he had what she was coming to recognize as the Cozart eyes. He and the uncouth Judson must only be a few years apart in age.

She scanned the photos in the junior class . . . sophomore class . . . and found a younger but equally arrogant version of the real estate developer. Judson must be Merritt's brother. And Dicy mentioned something about another brother, handsome Colin's father.

But in the years when Leota would've been in high school, she found only Merritt and Judson. Merritt had been in Leota's graduating class. Considering them friends might be a long shot, but odds were—the school was small—they must've known each other.

Using her phone, she took a quick photo of the senior class pages. Dicy would know if any of them were still around. If she had to, she would interview them all.

And tomorrow, when she visited Ouida Kittrell, she'd ask the old woman about her young protégé.

Tessa put away her notebook. She slipped the strap of her purse over her arm and returned the books to the librarian.

"You must be Dicy Goforth's niece." Looking over her reading glasses, the older woman smiled. "We attend the same church. It's so wonderful you've come to help with her recovery after she returns home."

Tessa's gaze cut toward the children on the rug. "There's no place I'd rather be than with Aunt Dicy."

The volunteer transitioned the kids into a preschool nursery song. "Down in the Valley" was an Appalachian ballad.

"Dicy loves story time with the little ones. She comes every week." The librarian hefted the yearbooks off the counter. "We've missed her."

A lump swelled in Tessa's throat. Her aunt had flown to New Orleans immediately after the fire and begged Tessa to return to the orchard with her. But she'd been caught in an emotional stupor, paralyzed by survivor guilt.

The librarian came out from behind the counter. "Your aunt is so proud of you." The green-beaded chain of the librarian's reading glasses gently swung, almost in tempo, with the children's song.

No one, not even Dicy, knew the truth about that night at the opera house.

Like Leota, Tessa was a runaway. She'd run the night of the fire. And she'd been running ever since. She'd left her friend to die. With Anton.

The librarian cradled the books in her arms. "Was there anything else I can help you with?"

"Maybe just some information." Tessa pulled herself from the ashes of that night with effort. "Do you know where I might find Merritt Cozart?"

Was it her imagination or did the librarian's friendly gaze cool several degrees?

"Go to the law enforcement annex next to the courthouse." The woman's lips thinned, all but disappearing. "And you can talk to the high sheriff himself."

So the gentle-faced linebacker had become High Sheriff of Roebuck County. Tessa headed toward the gleaming copper dome of the county courthouse.

No matter what Zeke Sloane said, she intended to file charges. If Sandy had reported Anton's harassment sooner, perhaps he would've been stopped before he escalated his behavior. Before lives were lost.

Inside the annex, shoulders squared, she went straight to the desk sergeant. "I'd like to report a crime."

The fortysomething deputy didn't bat an eye—or quit scrolling through his phone. "What crime?"

"A physical assault. I believe they also intended to sexually assault me."

The deputy stopped scrolling. "Where did this happen?"

She gave him the particulars.

"You're not from around here, are you?"

She was getting sick of hearing that. "Where I'm from, sexual assault is taken seriously. Shouldn't you be writing this down?"

The deputy pulled a face. "Can you give a description of the alleged perpetrators?"

"I can give you their names."

"Well, that will certainly save time." He made a point of plucking a triplicate form from a basket on top of his desk. "Shoot."

She took a breath. "There were three of them. Shelton Allen. Pender Cozart. And a Gibson."

The deputy's entire demeanor changed, and he stopped writing. "Why should I take the word of a newcomer over theirs?"

"How about because I'm the victim?" Her voice rose.

The deputy stood. "No need to get hysterical, ma'am."

"I'm not . . ." She lifted her chin. "I have a witness who can corroborate what happened."

"And who would that be?"

"Zeke Sloane."

The deputy raised his brow. "Are you sure Zeke Sloane will verify this story of yours?"

"It's not a story. It's the truth." She gripped the strap of her purse. In actuality, she wasn't sure about Zeke. He'd told her not to report it in the first place. She jutted her chin. "You have a duty to investigate."

"And how much had you had to drink during this alleged incident? Maybe you'd given them a reason to think you were more than willing."

"How dare you—"

"You sure you want to go through with this, sweetie pie?" The deputy leaned over the counter. "The law takes a dim view of frivolous charges."

"Are you insinuating I asked for it?"

"What's going on here?" A tall, strapping man in uniform ambled into the reception area. "Deputy Perkins?"

"Sheriff, this lady here claims Pender and his boys got a little too friendly the other night. Wants to press charges."

High Sheriff Merritt Cozart was an imposing man, who hadn't allowed himself to degenerate into flab. Only a fleeting hint of gentleness remained in the face of the boy in the senior class photo. In the intervening years, a hardness had overtaken his features.

Cozart rested his meaty fists on his gun belt. "And who would you be?"

"My name is Tessa Goforth. I'm within my rights to file a complaint."

He pushed the brim of his regulation hat back a notch off his fore-head. "Dicy Goforth's niece. I'm sure the incident was very upsetting to you, Miss Goforth."

She nodded.

"Perhaps when you've had time to think things—"

"Those scumbags tried to rape me, Sheriff."

"But they didn't, did they?"

She threw out her hands. "Only because Zeke made them leave me alone."

An interesting look crossed the high sheriff's face. "Zeke Sloane?" Merritt Cozart rubbed his chin. "I'll have a chat with him. See what we can do to settle this matter to everyone's satisfaction."

"Is this the kind of protection that you offer all female citizens, Sheriff Cozart?" She sneered. "Or just me, because I'm not from around here?"

Cozart squared his broad shoulders. "I told you I'd look into it. And I will. Now, if you'll excuse me . . ."

"There was one other matter, Sheriff."

He paused behind the counter. The look on his face said, *now what?*

"I have a question about a girl from your senior class that I'm trying to locate."

Perkins grinned. "Ancient history, eh, Merritt?"

Cozart looked at her, eyebrows nearly to his hat. "You a genealogist?"

"No. I'm doing research on folk music. The girl in your class became a ballad singer of some renown."

Cozart's ruddy complexion paled. "Leota Byrd."

"Did you know her?"

His hand shook as he removed his hat, but he clamped it to his side. "Won't do you no good to look for her."

"Why's that?"

"She's long gone. Left during our senior year. Didn't come back to graduate." He swallowed. "Seeing as you're a friend of Sloane's, it's only right I tell you that asking questions about Leota Byrd will merely bring trouble on yourself. Trouble best left where it belongs. In the past."

And then she was unceremoniously shown the door.

Out on the sidewalk, Sheriff Cozart replaced his hat on his head. "What allegedly happened to you the other night should never have happened, Miss Goforth."

She gritted her teeth. "Allegedly?"

"Certainly not on my watch." The lines deepened around his eyes. "But I promise you, no one else will threaten you. Pender Cozart or no Pender Cozart." With that, he stalked toward his parked cruiser.

She watched him peel away from the curb. He'd been so jaded and indifferent until . . .

Until Leota's name rattled him. What had Leota Byrd meant to Merritt?

"Tessa?" With a pleased smile, Colin Cozart stepped lightly down the broad granite courthouse steps and over to her.

After this morning's less-than-stellar encounter with Zeke, it was gratifying to see admiration on a man's face.

"I'm so glad I ran into you. I was going to call you. See if you were free for dinner."

He really was such a handsome man . . . pretty as a girl with those long, thick black lashes of his.

Like the ballads, blue eyes must be a cultural carryover in Appalachia. Eyes the same color as surly, darker-complected Zeke. But there the resemblance ended.

Because Colin apparently liked her company.

"I'd love to, Colin, but my aunt is being released this afternoon. I have to get her home."

He smiled that electrifying smile of his. "Local musicians are congregating for an autumn jam session. Surely your aunt could spare you for a few hours. I hoped you might be interested."

"You googled me."

"Guilty as charged." He threw her a lazy grin. "The old-timers come out. Singing, fiddling, dancing. Not as high-toned as what you're used to, but well . . ." He spread his hands. "We country bumpkins do our best to please."

She was interested. The added incentive of being escorted by the attentive Colin didn't hurt either. "You, Colin Cozart, are hardly a country bumpkin."

He grinned. "Aw shucks, ma'am." Charm practically oozed out of his pores. "You noticed."

"Do you sing too?"

Colin laughed. "Afraid not. Got my mother's musical ability. Which is to say, I have none. My dad sang in his college chorale. Played the guitar when he was a boy too."

"Your dad?"

He nudged his head to the courthouse. "Judge Ransom Cozart. And my uncles aren't too bad at carrying a tune."

She pursed her lips. "I've met your uncles Merritt and Judson."

"Uh-oh." He winked, unfazed. "Don't let their 'charms' put you off the rest of us."

"I'm still trying to untangle the Cozart family tree."

He laughed. "It's a crooked tree I'm doing my best to right. What do you say?" He leaned closer. "Will you give this Cozart the benefit of the doubt? Give me a chance to impress you with a taste of our rural delights?"

Despite warnings to the contrary—mainly, because she was peeved with Zeke—she found herself agreeing. They made plans for Colin to pick her up later at the farmhouse.

She returned to the rehab center. The nurse gave her a printout of instructions and a brown paper sack containing a medication to alleviate any bouts of pain.

Dressed for company, Dicy sat in the hospital wheelchair, a small canvas bag of belongings in her lap. "I cannot wait to get home."

"I can't wait to have you home."

Tessa blew her a kiss and went out to get her car. She pulled up outside the lobby as the aide unlocked the wheelchair and rolled it to the curb.

She got out, came around, and stood back, unsure and awkward. The aide, however, quickly transitioned her aunt into the front seat. Then the aide showed Tessa how to fold the wheelchair and stow it in the trunk of the car.

Dicy was in bright spirits as they drove down Main. "River looks low. Could use rain." She waved to someone outside the hardware store standing by a cluster of vivid burgundy chrysanthemums and a stack of pumpkins. "What have you been doing, Tessie, while I was waiting to be sprung this afternoon?"

Passing the library, Tessa gave her a rundown on what she'd discovered in the yearbooks. Turning left at the courthouse, she told Dicy about her meeting with the high sheriff. But she left out the part about her failed attempt to file charges. The gas station incident was on a need-to-know basis. She'd have a word with Zeke to make sure he understood her aunt didn't need to know.

At the mention of running into Colin, Dicy's lips compressed. To save herself from the argument she knew would ensue with her aunt, Tessa put off announcing her concert date until later. Way later. Like when Colin's car pulled up to the house.

They left town and drove through the forestland. The trees were at their peak. Crimson reds, golden yellows. A few of the leaves were an eye-popping orange, so beautiful it almost hurt to look at them.

As the little white farmhouse on the knoll came into view, Dicy let out a sigh of contentment. "There's no place like home . . ."

"Well said, Dorothy Goforth." After parking next to the house, Tessa popped the trunk. She struggled to lift the wheelchair out. Gritting her teeth, she finally wrested it to the ground. Now what?

The aide made collapsing the chair look so simple. But how did she get it to unfold . . . Bottom lip stuck between her teeth, she figured it out. She brought the chair around to the passenger side, opened the door wide, and released Dicy's seatbelt. "Let's get you in the house."

Her aunt swung her right leg out of the car, feeling for the ground with her shoe. Bringing her weight to bear on her good leg, she winced as she inched off the seat.

She took hold of Dicy's arm. "Not too fast. Take your time. Let me do the work."

The older woman's face crumpled. "I feel so clumsy and useless."

Hand under her elbow, she gingerly pulled her aunt out of the vehicle. "You're neither."

"I 'clare I didn't see what I tripped over. Guess my eyesight's going too." Dicy's mouth quirked. "Probably only a matter of time before my brain's shot as well."

"You liked to worried me to death the first time I saw you lying so pale on those white sheets at the rehab, Aunt Dicy."

"Liked to worried you to death, huh?" Her aunt's blue eyes twinkled.

"Didn't take long for you to lose the big city talk." She patted Tessa's cheek.

And Tessa was glad she'd come. Nothing and no one was forever. Dicy wasn't getting any younger.

She'd been Tessa's rock when her world had fallen apart. As a child when her mother died and again last year. She'd taken for granted that this peaceful mountain haven and her Aunt Dicy—synonymous in her mind—would always be there.

"I've got the chair, Miss Dicy," Zeke's gravelly voice rumbled.

She and her aunt both startle-jerked.

Dicy placed her hand over her bosom. "You a-going to give me a heart attack too."

Clad in his usual jeans, work boots, and flannel shirt, he stood behind the wheelchair. "I was at the cabin, or I would've come sooner." His large, work-roughened hands rested on the handles of the chair.

Tessa planted her hands on her hips. "Must you sneak around like some backwoods ninja?"

A lopsided smile crept across his lips. "Backwoods ninja? I like it." He cocked his head. "You have quite the way with words."

She placed her arm around Dicy's waist. "I'd like to give you a few choice words . . . sneaking up on me like that after—" She clamped her lips sealed.

"After what, cinnamon bun?"

She shot him a warning glare in the space above Dicy's head.

"You need to maintain more situational awareness." He pushed the chair closer to her aunt. "I could give you a few pointers on how to rectify that." He held the chair steady as the older woman carefully lowered herself into the seat.

Tessa raised Dicy's casted leg onto the footrest. "And I'd tell you to mind your own business." She nudged him aside. "I got this."

Scowling, he let go of the wheelchair. "Just trying to be helpful."

"Isn't there some bimbo waiting to be dazzled by your roughneck charms? Some beer to guzzle? Some lowlife friend needing you for mischief and mayhem?"

"Tessie, what a thing to say . . ." Her aunt *tsk*ed.

But he smiled, an easy curve to his lips. "You think I'm charming."

"I do not." Her mouth snapped shut. "That's not what I . . ." She pulled at the chair.

Nothing happened.

She tried again.

Leaning forward, he released the lever behind the wheel. "The foot brake. Try it now."

She yanked the chair, and he hopscotched backward when she almost ran over his boot. Almost on purpose.

"Nice." He grunted.

Tessa fluttered her hand over her shoulder and headed for the screen porch at the back of the house. "Sorry about that."

"Sure you are." The car door slammed behind her.

"Temper, temper," she smirked.

She pushed Dicy around the corner of the house and passed the clump of hydrangeas with their dried flower clusters.

"I don't know why you children can't get along." Her aunt gripped the armrests as they zipped along. "And he's not the only one with a temper."

Tessa slowed her pace. "Why are you letting him live on the farm? He's hiding something. I know it."

"Not every man is untrustworthy." Dicy shifted in the seat. "They are not all like your father."

She ground to a halt. "Not everything is about my father."

"Isn't that where your distrust began?" Twisting around, Dicy reached for Tessa's hand. "But you don't have to be afraid of Zeke. He's not like that terrible Russian violinist who murdered your friend."

Tessa let go of the chair. "I don't want to talk about Anton. I'm not scared of Sloane. He's just . . ." She was no longer sure what Zeke was or wasn't. Full of contradictions, he confused her.

"Without his help this last year, I wouldn't have been able to keep the orchard going. He comes from good people, Tess. What is it about him that riles you so?"

She folded her arms. "How about his bad attitude? Or that cocky swagger of his? Or-or . . ." She unfolded and fisted her hands.

Or the fact that when he looked at her, her insides turned to liquid.

Dicy waved her hand. "The boy's got a good heart."

"He's not a boy."

Dicy's mouth twitched. "You've noticed that, huh?"

She blinked. Twice. "That's not what . . ." What had she meant?

Of course, she'd noticed he wasn't a boy. Anyone with eyes could see that. He was a man. A very manly man.

Beneath the beard scruff and flannel, a lot of testosterone tied up in one very attractive package. He wasn't classically handsome like Colin, but Zeke might have the more interesting face.

Gripping the handles again, she pushed her aunt the remaining distance. And came to an abrupt stop. In a series of switchbacks, a wooden ramp sloped over the concrete steps to the door.

Her aunt clapped her hands together. "If that don't beat all. Look what Zeke's built for me. How thoughtful. How considerate."

Very thoughtful. Very considerate. She could feel the flush mounting from her chest to her neck. The ramp hadn't been there this morning. He'd been busy while she was out today.

She hadn't thought through how she would've gotten her temporarily immobile aunt into the house. Good thing he had.

The screen door at the top of the ramp squeaked. Zeke held the door open for them. He'd come through the front. He lifted the chair over the door jam and into the house. A task with which she would've struggled.

Dicy was effusive with her thanks.

He glanced Tessa's way, his face like a thundercloud, and she felt about two inches tall.

"The ramp was kind of you." She swallowed. "Thank you, Zeke."

His stormy eyes flickered.

Their gazes locked. Her heart slammed against her breastbone, leaving her feeling slightly out of breath, pulse zinging.

"No problem." He stuffed his hands into his pockets. "Gotta go." He planted a quick kiss on Dicy's silver head.

"Be careful of the darkness, dear heart."

She stared at her aunt. A strange thing to say.

Already halfway out the door, he poked his head back around. "Always am."

Suddenly, she was reluctant to see him go. "We've got a ton of church-lady casseroles in the fridge if you want to eat dinner with us." Why on earth had she said that? She ought to be glad to see the back of him.

He hesitated. "Some other time, okay?" His eyes found hers again. Like a bobblehead fool, she nodded.

Dicy stretched out her hand. "You're sure you won't stay?"

"Can't." He winked and rapped his hand against the doorframe. "Bimbos to dazzle."

He was gone before she could find something to throw at him. Anything to wipe the self-satisfied smirk off his handsome face.

Whoa. Since when had she started thinking of him as handsome? Setting her jaw, she propelled her aunt into the downstairs bedroom.

If she was starting to see Sloane as appealing, she'd been without male companionship way too long.

But a secret part of her wished she were going to the concert with a charming, backwoods ninja named Zeke instead of with charming Colin.

Chapter Nine

Pretending to be Brandi's boyfriend was getting old. Harder on poor Luther too. Huddled into the corner booth at The Honky-Tonk, Zeke glanced over to the bar.

Bald head down, Luther stood, morose, drying shot glasses with a cloth.

A different clientele from the usual sort slowly filled the surrounding tables. The monthly jam sessions with local musicians was extremely popular in the community. Like with grandmas, who otherwise wouldn't be caught dead in a place like The Honky-Tonk. In the crowd, he spotted several aspiring teenage musicians. Lots of townsfolk.

Folk music remained one of the finer Roebuck County traditions. The old-time balladeers and fiddlers had been gathering here once a month since the days of Prohibition. But on jam nights, less alcohol was served and other heartier fare became available.

Merritt Cozart swept in with the first of the banjo players. He made a beeline for Zeke.

A spark of fear ignited in his belly. Had Adolphus Robertson ratted him out?

"Been looking for you."

Were the Cozarts on to him? Sweat peppered his forehead. Was he blown?

"I had me a talk with the Goforth girl this afternoon."

Zeke wrapped his hand around the beer he'd been pretending to drink for the last half hour. "Oh, yeah?" If he'd been made, though, he reckoned his throat would've already been slit, his truck burning in a remote holler.

Cozart's eyes narrowed. "You didn't tell me about your run-in with Pender the other night." Merritt didn't bother to sit down.

Poker-sharp vexation sizzled his gut. He'd told Tessa not to . . . "I handled it, Sheriff." He raised his shoulder an inch and let it drop. "Figured the family wouldn't want any publicity about a well-known opera singer being attacked in your county."

The sheriff snorted. "Pender needs to be muzzled."

Pender Cozart needed to be put down like a rabid dog. But Zeke let that go. For now.

"Not many people would've stepped in. Much less crossed him." Merritt's jaw clenched. "Were you drunk, or feeling suicidal?"

"I like to think there are things no real man would tolerate, Sheriff. Abusing a woman happens to be one of them. At least for me."

Merritt's face turned to stone.

Zeke tugged at his neck. What had gotten into his mouth? He'd as good as implied the sheriff was the kind of man who countenanced such behavior.

Yet if the sheriff had done his job when Brandi reported Emily's attack, Pender would be serving time in some dark hole like the one he'd crawled out of. And Kaci would still be alive.

"I told the girl, Tessa, she need not worry." Merritt's eyes hardened. "I'll be making sure Pender won't bother her again."

Zeke took a real sip this time. "I owe you one, then."

Giving him a strange look, Merritt pushed off from the table. "Son, you owe me more than one."

The sheriff exited as band members tuned their instruments. Guitars, banjos, fiddles, a mandolin, and an upright bass. A sound engineer ran around hooking wireless mics onto black stands.

"Whew!" Brandi dropped into the seat beside him. "Finally, a break." She plopped a kiss on his mouth.

Masking his surprise, he hoped it was for the benefit of onlookers.

The perfume she favored was a cloying department store variety. He preferred Tessa's clean, lavender fragrance. He wasn't sure if the scent came from her soap or her shampoo. But it wafted through the air, teasing his nostrils, on the waves of her hair.

Now he'd reek of Brandi all night.

His gaze cut to the bar.

Luther had wandered to the far end of the bar, putting his back to them.

She pouted. "You need to learn to relax a little."

"I relax, I die," he growled. "What was it you wanted to tell me?"

The band went into a rousing rendition of "Squirrel Hunters."

She snagged his arm. "I feel like dancing." She tugged at him.

He didn't budge. "Well, I don't." Especially not to a heel-kicking, foot-stomping bluegrass tune.

She went without him. She grew up clogging. Like Irish step dancing, the Appalachian variation didn't necessarily require a partner. Arms rigid at her sides, she went to town, stomping the floorboards.

Once Luther realized she was dancing alone, he dropped the cloth and headed straight for her. Puffing and clomping, he matched her jig for jig. The fiddler's bows slid faster and faster across the strings.

Zeke wouldn't have guessed the bartender had it in him.

Heels keeping time with the downbeat, they pounded the wooden floor.

With a final, triumphant flourish, the fiddlers sawed to a close. Out of breath, Brandi and Luther laughed. There was a joy in her brown eyes Zeke hadn't seen since they met.

Returning to the table, she fanned herself with her hand. "I need air after that workout."

Luther leaned close to his ear. "You hurt her, Sloane," he snarled, "and I'll hurt you." He stomped toward the bar.

The gathering cheered when a woman with flowing black hair stepped to the mic, a mandolin balanced in her arms. "The Gardenia Waltz," she called to the others.

"You would pick a hard one." The bass player groaned. "Full of double stops." But he and the rest of the pickup band effortlessly followed her lead.

Originally from Roebuck County, the woman was as unassuming as the rest of the musicians, yet she had several Grammys to her credit.

Zeke wasn't musical, but he had a CD of her latest bluegrass recording. And he appreciated those like Tessa who had the gift. He drummed his fingers on the table. He needed to stop thinking about the redhead.

Brandi floated over to him. "It's not a fast one, Zeke. Dance with me." She held out her hand.

Might as well get this over with. She'd never give him any peace until he did.

He followed her onto the floor and tried not to inhale too deeply as he wrapped his hands around her waist. He concentrated on moving his feet from side to side and swaying. "What info do you have for me?"

"Such a killjoy." She play-slapped his shoulder. "Gib's alone tonight."

"On a Friday night?"

"Pender was here earlier for a quick drink, complaining about his uncle sending him over to Tennessee. Deputy Perkins too."

Merritt had been as good as his word. They must be meeting with another link in the Cozart supply chain. Intel he hadn't yet managed to weasel out of the family. "What about Shelton?"

"Shelton got into a knock-down-drag-out with his ex in Asheville over child support. He's spending the weekend as a guest of the Buncombe County Sheriff's Department. The coast is clear for phase two in the Gibson operation."

"This could be the break we've been waiting for." He gave her a gentle squeeze. "Once I get Gib to spill his guts, the end could be in sight."

Her gaze wandered over his shoulder to the entrance. "Would you look at who's decided to pay The Honky-Tonk a visit?"

Zeke swung her around and froze as Tessa glided through the door on the arm of Colin Cozart. Her eyes immediately met Zeke's, and he dropped his hold on Brandi so fast she stumbled.

"What's wrong with— Oh." Brandi chuckled. "So that's how it is with you, huh?" She mock-sighed. "All the good ones . . ."

He lurched forward.

She caught his sleeve. "Where are you going?"

"Tessa has no idea about the snake she's dealing with over there."

"She wouldn't believe you about Mr. Charming. And you don't want to get in Colin's sights. Not yet anyway."

This wouldn't be the first time this week he'd crossed the Cozarts. Pender was a ne'er-do-well embarrassment to the whole clan. However, Brandi was right.

Colin, beloved son and heir, was a different story.

Tessa Goforth had an unusual ability to attract trouble. Zeke was beginning to suspect she went looking for it.

"You're not going to let this go, are you?" Brandi rolled her eyes. "Who am I to stand in the way of raging testoster—"

He stalked away.

Tessa was taking a seat at one of the tables on the perimeter of the dance floor.

At Zeke's approach, Colin's eyes narrowed, and he placed a proprietary hand on her slim shoulder.

"Colin."

"Sloane."

Defiance flashed in Tessa's green gaze, but she said nothing.

Zeke stabbed his fingers through the short ends of his hair. "Slumming, Miss Goforth?"

Her eyebrows hitched.

Tightening his jaw, Zeke turned to Colin. "Didn't realize you were a bluegrass fan."

"I'm a connoisseur of many musical genres." Colin pulled out the chair next to Tessa. "My tastes are diverse." He moistened his bottom lip.

Bile rose in Zeke's throat.

Colin placed his hand over Tessa's. "I hoped I might persuade this lovely creature to favor the local yokels with a song. What do you say, sweetheart? Will you sing for me?"

She slid her hand from his and put it in her lap.

Mine. He wanted to rage. *Since the beginning, she's been—*

"I don't sing anymore, Colin." She bit her lip.

Last winter, when he first arrived at the Goforth orchard, Dicy had shown Zeke a recording she'd taped—some PBS special—of Tessa singing as the featured soloist with a New York City symphony. He clenched his jaw so tight his molars ached. *What happened to you that you'd even consider a piece of filth like Cozart?*

Colin smirked. "You're here a lot though, aren't you, Sloane, with your little blond bombshell? What's her name? Sherry Something-or-other?"

He ached to put his fist in Cozart's snarky face. But he couldn't. Not yet.

"Colin, don't." Cheeks pink, Tessa's gaze dropped. "Leave him alone."

Did she think he needed her to fight his battles for him? "Her name's Brandi," he snarled. But Cozart already knew that.

"Very apropos." Colin sneered. "Brandi, the bar maid."

"Tess . . ."

Her eyes lifted to his. "Yes, Zeke?" She scanned his face, searching for an answer he wasn't free to give.

Something tore in his chest. It had almost been easier when her insistent use of Ezekiel kept them at arm's length.

The idea of her spending the evening in this jackal's company made him want to puke. But Brandi was right. Until he had proof, what could he say that wouldn't sound ridiculous? "How is Miss Dicy?"

Scrubbing at some residue on the table, Tessa grimaced. "She's settled in bed. Colin promised we wouldn't be out late."

"Was there something else, Sloane?" Colin squared his shoulders. "If not, then don't let us keep you from your girlfriend."

"Brandi's n—" He bit his tongue. He couldn't afford to show his hand. But one day Colin and the Cozarts were going to get what they so richly deserved.

And he was determined more than ever to make sure their day of judgment came sooner versus later.

His throat constricted. "I have to go."

"I'm sure Margarita will miss you." Colin raised his lip. "Although she isn't noted for being too particular with her favors."

He balled his fists.

The weasel smirked. "Just stating a fact."

"Zeke . . ." Tessa's husky whisper nearly undid him.

He needed to get out of here. Before he went and said something— did something—stupid.

Like give Cozart exactly what he'd been begging for his whole over-privileged, over-entitled life.

He had important work to do. Killers to catch. Evidence to uncover.

The band eased into "The Lover's Waltz," a particular favorite of his. But Zeke slammed out, wondering what it would feel like to hold Tessa in his arms. To dance with her.

Colin would surely know sooner than he would.

You like hanging with sociopaths in your free time, Tess? Have at it.

He kicked up a cloud of gravel as he stomped to his truck. He'd figured her for better sense, if not better taste.

Was she too shallow to see beyond the fawning smile? Scratch beneath the tailored suit, and Colin was no different than his cousin, Pender.

If she couldn't see through Cozart, then maybe they deserved each other. No skin off his nose. It wasn't as if he cared one way or the other when it came to Tessa Goforth.

Right.

He jerked open the truck door. *You keep telling yourself that. Whatever helps you sleep at night.*

Something he hadn't been doing much of lately. Not since Dicy's flame-haired niece arrived at the orchard. He threw himself into the truck and cranked the engine. Tessa Goforth wasn't any of his business.

And what she chose to do or not do with her time, none of his concern.

Tires squealing, he peeled out of the parking lot. Gravel sprayed the undercarriage. He deserved a medal in self-restraint for not giving into the impulse to knock Cozart's arm off her silk-clad shoulders.

After crossing the bridge over the river, he took the fork to the right. Like a stripe on a candy cane, the road spiraled around the mountain for a half mile. Sharp, braking curves.

Following the contours of the terrain, he took a series of loops. Rising, dipping, swelling, cresting ridges. The bumpy secondary road wound down the opposite side of the mountain.

He veered off the highway, edging farther into the Deep Holler community. Not so much a community, actually, but more a trailer park. Respectable people didn't live in Deep Holler.

Like fallen toy soldiers, a row of mailboxes lay in the drainage ditch. He'd heard Buckthorn postal workers refused to deliver the mail here. He didn't blame them.

Backlit by the yellow glare of a lone exterior light, a few hardy souls squinted at him from shabby porch recliners. In the descending twilight, the preferred form of evening exercise consisted of tipping beers to their lips.

Some kids kicked a deflated white ball in the packed earth of a yard.

They stopped to watch his progress down the street. House after house, the children were the same.

He kept his gaze averted. It hurt to look too closely. Their eyes were old. Lost. Their future, stark.

The girls would get knocked up young. Later, just knocked around, period, by boyfriends or husbands. A habit first wielded by their fathers.

Anger would engulf the boys, leading to a life of petty crime. Prison awaited them.

Boy or girl, addiction or alcoholism would consume them. Maybe both. Violence, early death, and wasted lives were their destiny. Like nearly all the child victims of abuse.

He blew out a breath, fogging the window.

Most people in Buckthorn lived in nice, if modest, brick or white-framed homes. This pocket of despair went deeper than rural poverty.

There were places like Deep Holler in every American city, in the best and worst of neighborhoods. Wherever there was a bankruptcy of soul, this kind of hell flourished.

His parents had hoped by fostering Kaci to save her from such a fate. And she would have been safe. If he'd been a better man.

The light-starved cove—light-starved in more ways than one—made him vaguely uneasy. But it wasn't only the people or the broken-down trailers lining the road. The surrounding overhang of the mountains blocked the sun even on the brightest of days.

It didn't get any better the farther into the cove he ventured.

The truck lurched, bouncing from pothole to pothole. His head hit the roof, so he slowed. Like a bunch of turkey vultures, a cluster of modular units in varying degrees of disrepair hunkered ahead.

Cannibalized for their parts, rusty automobiles rested atop cinder blocks. A toilet sat in the middle of a semi-derelict property. The lid yawned open.

He tapped his thumbs against the steering wheel. Hip-hop music pulsed from the trailer he passed, and the occasional angry tirade came from another of the mobile homes. He pulled into the last rutted driveway.

If anything, Gib's abode was the worst. And that was saying a lot considering the area was unofficially known as Bascombe Catacombs. A place fit only for the dead.

Or those who ought to be.

Among the honest, hard-working citizens of Roebuck County, the Bascombes were renowned for their laziness and self-inflicted ignorance. Mean as junkyard dogs, they kept to themselves and married among themselves.

Nobody with any sense drove over here at night.

And that was the long and the short of it, Zeke reckoned. He lacked good sense. Who else would associate with the likes of a lowlife like Gib? Poking his nose into stuff that could get him killed?

Or hanker after a red-haired gal with a golden voice.

He killed the engine. Stepping out, he pressed on the horn, giving one brief, sharp retort. Mountain etiquette.

Sure enough, Gib poked his greasy blond head out the storm door.

At the base of the cracked cement stoop, Zeke's nose twitched as the wind brought the scent of something illegal past his nostrils. Gib was drunk and probably stoned too. But his befuddled state might move Zeke more quickly into the next step of this operation.

He was for anything that brought him to Kaci.

"Gib!" He threw up his hand. "Buddy . . ."

Bascombe's piggy small eyes squinted through his smoke-induced haze. "Whatcha doing here, Sloane?" Gib's squeaky high voice snarled.

That was the Bascombes for you. Didn't trust anyone as far as they could throw them.

Feeling is mutual. But he didn't voice his thoughts out loud. Instead— "Heard you're in a pure-D mess today, Gib."

More like self-imposed idiocy.

Gib slouched out onto the top step. "Where'd you hear that?" He threw back his scrawny shoulders, weedy in more ways than one.

"I heard that low-down dog of a landlord refused to float you an extension."

The low-down dog of a landlord also happened to be Gib's stepmother. That was the Bascombes for you.

Gib folded and refolded the brim of the Cozart Auto Repairs ball cap. "That stupid witch! After what my daddy done for her—"

Done *to* her, if the stories Brandi told were to be believed. And Zeke didn't doubt they were.

"Gave her a roof when her own pappy kicked her out—"

For the dubious pleasure of finishing the rearing, such as it was, of Gib's motley siblings.

"My daddy up and dies and then she's lordin' it over—"

There were no-account good-for-nothings everywhere, not only in the mountains. The typical stereotype of people in Appalachia being nothing more than inbred white trash was totally false. In Bascombe's case, however, it wasn't.

"I'll show that jumped up piece of—"

Not if Zeke got to Gib and his pals first.

But if nothing else, the Bascombes were a classic example of why survival of the fittest wasn't always a sound theory. More like survival of the most cunning. They had an innate sense of self-preservation.

"Gib."

Zeke's authoritative tone cut the venomous rambling short. Gib had spent a lifetime doing what other people told him. He was good at it. Perhaps the only thing Gib was good at.

"I came to take you to pay your stepmother. Get her off your back for another month."

Gib's head reared. "You want to pay my rent? Why?"

He had Bascombe's attention. "Just because." He took a step toward the rickety steps. "Because that's what friends do."

Gib peered at him suspiciously. "We're friends?"

He made a show of placing his hand over his heart. "Dude. You wound me. We closed down The Honky-Tonk together last weekend, remember?"

Gib pushed up the brim of his cap. "Kind of? Sort of . . ."

"We practically drank each other under the table, man."

Gib had been under the table. Zeke had long ago perfected the art of nursing one solitary beer.

Thanks to a heads-up from Brandi, a rendezvous long in the making. Culling Gib from his usual herd wasn't easy. It wasn't often Gib was left alone to fend for himself.

He suspected the others didn't trust Gib alone.

"You-you brung me home." Gib made a sweeping gesture, unsettling his carefully contrived balance. He fell against the railing.

Zeke winced, hoping the wood would hold. "Why is your stepmother so hard on you? It isn't fair."

Gib shook his shaggy head. "Not fair."

Zeke placed his boot on the bottom step. Dealing with a feral creature, it didn't pay to rush proximity. "Can't she see you're doing the best you can?"

Gib's lip protruded. "Best I can."

"After you got hurt working, where's her compassion?"

Gib spit at the ground. Narrowly missing Zeke. "Heart like granite stone."

"It ain't right, man. It just ain't right." He shook his head, slow, in a show of solidarity. "So I decided to come by. See if I could help."

Gib leaned forward. "You'd do that for me, Sloane? Pay my wicked stepmother this month's rent?"

He rested his elbow on his knee. Close but not too close. "We're friends, right? Buddies."

At the notion of free money, Gib frothed at the mouth. "Friends. Buddies. Cohorts."

Bascombe ought not to use words he couldn't spell.

He honed in for the kill. "Unless . . ."

Gib's head shot up. "Unless what?"

He made an elaborate shrug. "Unless you think the workman's comp—"

"I don't get no worker's comp."

And if he had, Gib was bad to drink. He wouldn't have paid his rent with it. "But you were working for the Cozarts at the time of the accident. And everybody knows they are as rich as Midas."

"Who?"

Remember who you're dealing with . . . "As kings."

Gib nodded emphatically. "Yeah."

"I thought you and the Cozarts were tight." He let the silence draw for a moment. "Friends. Buddies. *Cohorts.*"

Gib puckered as if to spit again.

He moved out of the line of fire. "I reckon them Cozarts don't care nothing 'bout anybody except Cozarts." He shook his head like it was a sad but new revelation.

Gib folded his arms against the rising chill of the evening. "Truer words, Zeke, my friend. Truer words."

"And after all you've done for them . . ." He held his breath, willing Bascombe to take the bait.

"Me, a poor crippled man. Crippled doing their dirty work."

A career consisting of money laundering, trafficking, and intimidation. Almost there . . . He moved up a step. "You and me, we're dirt under their feet."

Gib's eyes took on an inebriated blaze under the glare of the porch light. "No 'preciation for Bascombe keeping their dirty little secrets."

"What about when it's your turn to need something, Gib?"

Gib's voice took on a singsong, mocking quality. "They be saying, 'Don't bring that trashy Bascombe mud to my doorstep, boy.'"

He pretended shock. "They don't never talk that way to you."

"They surely do, Zeke, my buddy."

He hung his head. "Gib, I had no idea how low they treated you. I'm rightly ashamed for you."

Bascombe sniffled.

Gotcha.

The Bascombe family pride, twisted though it be. Easily enough manipulated if you pushed the right buttons.

"Grab you a jacket, son, and let's hightail it over to your stepmom's house." Zeke grinned at him. "I can't wait to see her face when we flash the cash."

Bascombe chortled. "Another month she won't get to toss me out on my—"

"Exactly."

"Iffen you're driving, let me quick drink a little liquid." Smiling to beat the band, Gib seized hold of the door handle. "All this jawin', I'm 'bout parched to death."

Climbing the remaining steps quickly, he touched Gib's sleeve. "You've had a hard row to hoe. And if there's anything else you ever need, man, please don't hesitate to call. You can count on me."

Gib's bleary blue eyes suddenly got blurrier. "I ain't ever had me a friend like th-that. A best friend."

He stuck out his hand. "Best friends, Gib."

Gib shook his hand.

Zeke's conscience didn't even twinge. After what Gib tried to pull on Tessa, and if he'd been a party to what Zeke believed had been done to Kaci . . .

The end did justify the means.

Chapter Ten

Colin had caught Tessa staring after Zeke as he angrily strode from The Honky-Tonk. From there, the evening went downhill fast. As the night wore on, she just wanted to go home.

An underlying tension she didn't understand had pulsated between the two men. A vibe that went beyond her. She had been merely the unfortunate spark that lit the tinder.

Tessa refused to sing, and Colin wasn't used to being told no. He became petulant and even more out of sorts when she repeatedly declined his invitations to dance.

Sulky, he swanked to the bar to lord over the bartender, a man who looked like he'd done hard time. With the kind of face only a mother would love.

The bottle blonde—Brandi?—ventured over to the table. "If he's making you uncomfortable, Luther or I can take you home, Miss Goforth."

"You know my name?"

"Zeke reveals more than he realizes of himself. About what he thinks." The woman gave her a bittersweet smile. "And about who he cares for."

Brandi's boyfriend cared about Tessa?

When the band finished with their signature song, "We'll Meet Again, Sweetheart," Colin took her home, loudly declaring her "no fun."

She should've listened to Dicy—and Zeke—about Colin. She'd only agreed to go out with him because Zeke had spurned her overtures of whatever their relationship was—mutual toleration?—at the barn that morning. The realization did her character no credit.

Her aunt and Zeke were right. The Cozarts, the whole lot of them, were no good. In her haste to be rid of him, she got out of Colin's car outside the barn.

The Corvette roared off into the starry night, and she walked halfway across the bridge before she realized Zeke's truck wasn't parked outside the cabin.

She'd hoped to apologize for Colin's behavior, for keeping company with a creep like him. Zeke must think her the most shallow fool he'd ever met. And suddenly, his good opinion of her mattered more than a lot.

The next morning, she rose to an overcast sky. Not the best of days to hike into the mountains, but she'd promised Dicy she'd check on Ouida Kittrell. Maybe she could beat the weather. Shivering against the chill, she donned a baggy gray sweater and jeans.

Brushing her hair, she glanced out her bedroom window, beaded with condensation. Zeke hadn't come home last night. The bristles of the brush bit into her scalp. She'd listened for him. Maybe he'd spent the night with Brandi.

Not a comforting thought. Filled with a strange restlessness, she gave the brush a savage yank through her curls.

Today wasn't about Zeke. Today was about persuading a crazy old woman—the tales of which filled Tessa with more than a little trepidation—to come off the mountain.

She tiptoed downstairs, but Dicy was already in the kitchen. "Why didn't you call me? You could've fallen and hurt yourself."

Leaning against the crutch, her aunt popped bread into the toaster. "I'll let you make the coffee since you're so particular."

After breakfast, Dicy "supervised" while Tessa loaded a split oak basket.

She ducked into the pantry. Aunt Dicy's flowered apron hung from the hook inside the pantry door. The blue stool that enabled a younger Tessa to reach the faucet at the kitchen sink still sat in the corner, tucked away for the next visit.

She'd outgrown the stool long ago. Aunt Dicy and the farm, never.

Row after row of canned produce in Mason jars gleamed on the pantry shelves. Purple-red beets. Blackberry and blueberry jams. The greens of pickle relish and chowchow.

"Ouida purely loves my pickled peaches," Dicy called from the kitchen. "Get those bread and butter pickles too."

Tessa emerged, a jar in each hand.

Dicy's blue eyes sharpened. "Not that one, cinnamon bun. That's the dill pickle batch."

She returned with the correct pickle jar. It didn't seem right not to catch Uncle Calvin in his usual denim overalls trying to sneak freshly baked cookies from his bride.

Tessa set the jars inside the gingham-lined hamper. The work of farming the orchard without Uncle Calvin must've been overwhelming. Not that her stubborn, fiercely independent aunt would have admitted to that. But considering the timing, maybe it did explain why Dicy finally hired Zeke. So she could fly to New Orleans to be with Tessa after the fire.

"Ouida's got a sweet tooth. Don't forget the sugar you bought at the Piggly Wiggly."

She tucked in other sundry items, including brightly colored spools of thread.

"Ouida, like generations of Kittrell women, is a world-class quilter. She'll probably show you some of her family's treasures." Dicy smirked. "If she decides she likes you."

"Why wouldn't she like me?"

Her aunt concentrated on ironing out a crease in the tablecloth with her hand. "Ouida doesn't like people on her mountain."

"You'll tell her I'm coming, though."

"Can't." Dicy straightened the placemat. "Ouida doesn't hold with newfangled conveniences."

"Like cell phones?"

Dicy's lips twitched. "Like electricity."

Tessa must have worn a shocked expression because her aunt laughed.

"Ouida's old. Too old to change her ways." Dicy surveyed the spotless kitchen. "Reach me the dish drainer. I reckon I could dry the breakfast dishes."

"Or they could air dry?"

Her arched brow let Tessa know exactly what she thought of that.

"Idle hands are the devil's playground. And there's far too much devilry in this world already."

She placed the dish drainer and its contents on the table in front of her aunt, then handed Dicy a drying cloth. "Is it too hard for Ouida to come off the mountain anymore?"

"At her age, we should all be as agile as Ouida Kittrell." The older woman set the dried plate aside and reached for another. "Since the ruling, it's not a matter of *can't*, but *won't*. She was the county midwife for years. A godsend to the folks who couldn't afford a doctor."

Tessa closed the hamper lid.

"Out kind of late with that no-good Cozart boy."

She recalled the dislike in the librarian's eyes at the mention of the Cozarts. Like an electric wire, an unspoken resentment of the clan thrummed through the rural community.

"You best be careful with that one, Tessie."

She wrapped her hands around the spindles of the ladder-back chair. "I won't be going out with Colin Cozart again."

Dicy threw her an I-told-you-so look. "Even before the scattering, you couldn't trust a Cozart far as you could throw them."

"I didn't realize the Cozarts were originally from Yonder Mountain." She drifted to the window over the sink. "What became of the people in Cane Creek, Aunt Dicy?"

"Resettled in government housing. It meant a chance for a better life. Closer to schools. Closer to a wider variety of opportunity. The Cozarts took to it."

Tessa moved aside the fluttery, red-checked curtain. "The Cozarts have done well for themselves." For the umpteenth time, she peered across the meadow.

"Usually at someone else's expense."

Letting the curtain panel drop, she angled around to her aunt.

"Others, like the Bascombes, never could adjust to the flatter lands." Dicy's lips pursed. "They couldn't breathe. The air wasn't thin enough."

Tessa had seen the name Bascombe somewhere . . .

Dicy's mouth puckered. "There was a soul hunger for the vistas of the sky land. And knowing they'd never live another of their born days in the high country, they drank too much. Despaired of life, they gave up long before their bodies gave out."

To ease the ache in her back resulting from the attack, she pressed the curve of her spine against the rounded edge of the counter. "How is Ouida Kittrell still on her homeplace if the others were moved out so long ago?"

"With the onset of the Second World War, construction on the parkway came to a stop. The Kittrells got a temporary reprieve. Time enough for Ouida's parents to be buried on the ridge above the cabin. After the war, she met Foley Reaves."

"Since Ouida's still called Kittrell, not Reaves, I'm guessing it didn't work out."

Dicy shook her head. "They were fixin' to marry. Her life would've been so different. Instead, she's been alone all these years with only the past for company." Her aunt wagged her finger. "A lesson to us all."

Tessa dropped her gaze. "Maybe it's only when we truly understand the past that we can move forward into the future."

"Or the pain of the past becomes an excuse not to enter the joy of the present." Dicy's tone became crisp. "Which is it with you, cinnamon bun?"

She crossed her arms. "I thought we were talking about Ouida."

"Were we just?" Dicy arched her brow. "Anyway, because of Foley, Ouida opened her heart to Leota Byrd. Course by then, he'd been dead for decades."

She sat down next to her aunt.

A smile fretted across Dicy's thin lips. "He was a handsome thing. During the war, he'd been treated well in Europe, and back home, he wasn't content to allow things to go on the way they'd always been. But there's plenty of folks who'll commit unspeakable acts before they'll change."

"I don't understand."

"Leota was kin to Reaves." Dicy sighed. "They were Melungeon."

Tessa frowned. "What's a Melungeon?"

"White, black, and Indian." Dicy shrugged. "Who knows where they came from originally. His skin was the color of a Cherokee. His eyes were bright jay-blue. And his hair—his hair was full of crinkly curls."

"I've heard of other triracial isolate groups. Was that why they didn't marry?"

"No . . ." Dicy folded the drying cloth. "His car was found burning in the woods. His body, swinging from a tree."

She gasped. "They lynched him?"

Her aunt dropped her gaze. "The Cozarts had started to become powerful. Everyone knew the noose would never have been put around his neck if Old Man Cozart hadn't given the go-ahead. Ouida never sang again."

Tessa put her hand on her throat.

"A state senator heard about the lynching. That was before the Cozarts got their hands in the General Assembly's coat pockets. The senator made sure Ouida got a life tenancy on her mountain when the range was declared a designated wilderness area."

Tessa nodded.

"With the recent ruling, however, the entire mountain will revert to them. Cozarts have been waiting for that day for decades." Dicy lifted her chin. "But Ouida may outlast them just for spite."

Later in her car, Tessa followed her aunt's directions into the forestlands. Thickets of rhododendron shadowed both sides of the winding road. Dark evergreens loomed on the ridge.

Sunshine dappled the lower slopes. Brilliant flashes of crimson, saffron, and orange pulsed with a vibrant vitality.

Higher and higher she wound around the mountain until the valley was but a misty shadow below. The paved road became gravel. The world fell away, as did her cares. And for the first time since the fire, she felt . . .

Free? Calm? Happy?

The road abruptly ended. A backhoe and bulldozer sat parked in front of a sign.

No Trespassing, Violators Will Be Shot.

Okay . . . not good.

After getting out of the car, she hefted the basket from the back seat. From force of habit, she pressed her key fob, locking the car. The clicking beep sounded incongruous in a place so untouched by the modern world.

She skirted the equipment. Ignoring the sign, she stepped through the gap of trees. Beyond, the forest closed around her as if here time had stopped.

Tessa followed the steep path, overgrown with weeds. By the time she reached the top of the incline, her arms ached from the weight of the basket.

A smell of woodsmoke hung in the air. A metal roof gleamed, beckoning her forward. The unpainted, board-and-batten farmhouse perched precariously on the side of the mountain. The house appeared either ready to take flight or to tumble into the valley below.

In a faded flower-print housedress, an old woman with deep-set dark eyes and equally deep wrinkles stepped out onto the long, low-fronted porch. "Who you be? You one of them government people?"

Of more concern to Tessa was the shotgun clasped to the woman's sagging bosom. "No, ma'am. I'm Tessa Goforth." She lifted the basket. "My aunt Dicy sent you this."

The old woman lowered the shotgun. "I expect you best come in then. I knowed somebody was a-coming today. I made cornbread." Ouida Kittrell stepped inside the house, leaving Tessa to follow.

Dark clumps of laurel framed the porch. It felt to her as if she stepped across more than a physical threshold. As if somehow she'd stepped back in time, circa 1940.

It took a moment for her eyes to adjust to the large front room. Only the cozy, orange flames in the giant stone-studded hearth relieved the dim light. A rocking chair and a high-carved wooden settee flanked the fireplace. Beyond the great room lay a smaller room.

The old-fashioned kitchen smelled of recent cooking. Catching a whiff of herbs, she glanced at the dried bunches of flowers hanging from the ceiling. A red dishcloth lay spread to dry over a scarred, wooden counter.

"My pa run water to the cabin afore he passed." The old woman tucked the shotgun onto the pegs protruding above the mantel. "He was a clever one."

Tessa placed the basket on the farm table.

"You'll tell Dicy thank you kindly for me, won't you?" Ouida bustled about, removing the jars from the basket. "Set yourself." She gestured. "I'll get these put away, and then we'll have us a treat." The old woman shuffled across the puncheon floor to the black cookstove, opened a door, and removed a cast-iron skillet. When she lifted the lid, a delicious aroma filled the air. Ouida talked as she worked. "You're wondering why anybody chooses to still live this way."

She opened her mouth to speak.

Ouida continued without a pause. "I like the quiet. Too much noise in your world below."

"There is something to be said for silence."

"More like a hushed stillness here." The old woman sliced the cornbread into quarters. "Not sure your generation knows what it is to be still. To really listen."

"What is it you hear up on the mountain all alone?"

"Give me the cadence of the crick or the melody of birdsong any day over your buzzing, clamoring modern world." Ouida pulled out a blue porcelain plate from the mint-green Hoosier in the corner. "The wind itself says a hundred different things to the leaves if you've ears to hear."

"The trees talk to you?"

Ouida took a butter dish from the oaken icebox. She layered a pat of butter on top of the steaming slice of cornbread. "The Lord God speaks in many ways." She handed Tessa the plate.

"Thank you, Miss Ouida."

"Iffen you like it, I can give you the recipe to make for your man."

She flushed. "I've no man to make it for."

"Not yet." Ouida cocked her head, resembling a small, pert black-eyed robin. "But I know you soon will."

Unsure how to respond to that, Tessa sat on the settee near the fire and nibbled at a small piece. The warm, melted butter softened the cornbread, leaving a rich taste on her tongue.

Ouida settled herself into the applewood rocker. "I trust Dicy's on the mend."

"How did you—?" Maybe it was better not to ask. "Yes, ma'am. I came to help her. I'm also working on my dissertation."

"And after that?"

Tessa didn't say anything.

"I done heard you've had your own troubles."

She bit back a sigh.

"Don't be put out with Dicy. The Lord laid it on her heart to tell me. It's no small thing to lose someone." Her wizened face scrunched. "Especially to violence. A different slice of pain altogether."

"I'm so sorry about what happened to your Foley, Miss Ouida."

"Foley stood right there in the doorway you come through." Ouida's eyes took on a faraway gaze. "I try to remember him the way he was that last time."

Tessa set the empty plate on the settee.

"I told him to be careful—Cozarts wouldn't like him refusing to run their 'shine. Like men do, he laughed at my fears."

Her heart hammered. That's exactly what she'd felt after witnessing the angry exchange last night. Fear for Zeke.

"Foley told me he'd see me by and by." Ouida's gaze wandered to the door, seeing something—someone—far beyond the barrier of the walls. And the years. "I'm still waiting for that by-and-by." Her attention returned to Tessa. "Folk used to come for my remedies. Now the Cozarts got most of them scared of their own shadows. Too skeered to cross the invisible boundary they've drawn around my mountain."

"Aunt Dicy would love for you to come live with her at the orchard." Tessa worried her bottom lip. "She doesn't let on much, but I think she'd be glad of the company since Uncle Calvin died."

Ouida made a shooing motion. "I done told you I have to be here when my time comes. For the by-and-by."

"But the eviction date is approaching, Miss Ouida. They'll turn you out if you don't go."

The old woman didn't blink. "They can try."

Okay . . . Next topic. "I'm working on a project about a folk singer. Aunt Dicy said you knew her."

The fire crackled and hissed.

"Leota Byrd." Tessa laced her hands together. "Do you remember her?"

"My mind isn't gone yet," Ouida snapped. But her wrinkled, old mouth trembled. "I remember her."

"The ballads on her album were old tunes, but some had different words from anything transcribed in the Folk Center archives."

"In my Foley's day, nobody was interested in the Melungeon songs. By the time Leota came along, people were more tolerant." The old woman's coffee bean eyes cut to hers. "There were other songs she didn't have room for on the album."

A tingle of excitement frolicked like ladybugs on Tessa's skin. Ruth McClaine would do cartwheels if she uncovered previously unpublished ballads.

To the best of her knowledge, there'd been very little scholarly research done on the triracial isolate group. A neglected field of study? Literally, music to an aspiring ethnomusicologist's ears.

"Leota didn't only have the gift of the song," Ouida's double chin wagged. "She had the gift of framing words too."

Tessa leaned forward on the edge of the settee. "Musical composition is a separate skill."

"God gives good gifts to us all. That child could sing sweeter than a bird—well, you've probably heard her yourself." Ouida's gnarled fingers plucked at the cuffs of her dress. "Your uncle Calvin brung me a battery player to listen to a cassette."

"From Leota's album?"

"It didn't come close to capturing the purity of sound that poured from the girl's throat. A rare and beautiful thing." The old woman's face softened. "Puts me in mind of a song Dicy played for me a few years ago. A song you sang in Paris, France."

She looked away. "I no longer sing."

"I hate to see the good Lord's gifts wasted."

Tessa stiffened. "Yet you stopped singing a long time ago."

Ouida shrugged. "I didn't have the passion it takes to hone a gift like yours and Leota's. But God brought Leota into my life. And I like to think I was the Lord's gift to her, encouraging her talent when no one in her family would." The old lady's eyes drooped. "But in the end, I failed her."

"What do you mean?"

Ouida tapped her fingers on the armrest. "Not too many escape from life unscathed from sorrow."

Thinking of Sandy, she lifted her chin. "And some get more than their fair share."

Knees creaking, Ouida pushed up from the rocker. "'I will lift up mine eyes unto the hills, from whence cometh my help. My help cometh from the LORD, which made heaven and earth.'"

Tessa rose too. "Your faith is strong."

"Not always."

"I'm afraid I've lost mine."

"Can't lose something, if you know where you laid it last." Feet planted wide, Ouida steadied herself for a moment before shuffling toward the back room. "Foller me."

Tessa set the plate on the table and then hurried after her. "What happened to Leota? Why do you think you failed her?"

A pine trunk stood at the foot of the bed, covered in a very old red-and-yellow quilt. The window provided a spectacular view of the entire valley. Ouida might even be able to see the orchard from Yonder. Against the far wall, another quilt lay draped over a rustic wooden rack.

Tessa ran her hand over one of the interlocking floral circles at the top of the fold. "This is beautiful."

"Feed-sack squares." Ouida pulled open a drawer in the walnut dresser. "I made it for a bridal bed never to be."

"I'm sorry." She removed her hand. "I shouldn't have—"

"Later, I knowed it weren't never meant to be used by me. Meant instead for another. After my by-and-by."

A shiver crawled up Tessa's arms. Disarmed by the old woman's ordinary appearance, she'd forgotten Dicy's warning. "How is it you claim to *know* the things you do?"

Ouida rambled through the drawer. "You've got your gift. I got mine."

"Do you see things in a dream or a vision? Are you awake or asleep?" She planted her hands on her hips. "How does it work?"

"Sometimes I'm awake. Sometimes I wake up from a dead sleep, and I just know things." Ouida seemed amused, as if she were Einstein trying to explain quantum physics to a child.

"The music in me died that night, Miss Ouida. But if I'd known what Anton planned . . ."

Ouida stopped rummaging. "It's not like a faucet you turn on and off at your convenience."

She threw out her hands. "What's the point in the gift if you can't stop bad things from happening?"

Ouida sighed, the sound like the rustling of autumn leaves. "Knowing is a far different thing than having the power to stop it. Such power is reserved for God Himself."

Tessa took a ragged breath.

"You should stop blaming yourself for not saving her." Ouida's dark eyes became opaque. "When the fire commenced, she were dead already. Your friend wouldn't want grief to rob you of the music."

The hair rose on the nape of Tessa's neck. "How did you . . . ?" She'd never told Dicy about her guilt over not saving Sandy.

"Leota's album made Nashville take notice." Ouida pulled a manila folder out of the drawer. "She compiled a batch of songs to include on a second album."

Tessa nodded, relieved to steer the conversation away from herself. "One music critic called her the Songbird of the Blue Ridge."

Ouida sat down heavily on the side of the bed. "That is exactly what my Leota Song-Byrd was like."

"I've tried to contact her record producer at Stargazer. No word yet. In a few weeks, once I'm able to leave Aunt Dicy, perhaps I'll head to Nashville."

"You won't find Leota there." Ouida patted the mattress. "Give your feet a rest."

She sank down beside the old woman. "Is this one of those *knowing* things again?"

Ouida squared her shoulders. "I'm neither daft nor senile, but that's not how I know she isn't in Nashville. The trail runs closer to home. The album released in the spring. That May, Leota just showed up on my doorstep."

"Leota returned to Roebuck County?"

"She spent a few days with me. Giddy with a peculiar energy. Hoping to reunite with her young lover."

Tessa's mind flew to Merritt Cozart's odd reaction yesterday. "I didn't realize Leota was involved with anyone in Roebuck."

Ouida grimaced. "You and me both."

The fact that Leota kept secrets obviously still bothered the old woman.

"She sat on the porch." Ouida motioned. "Singing one tune from her album over and over again."

"'Black is the Color of My True Love's Hair,'" Tessa murmured. Leota's signature song.

Ouida got off the bed. "And then . . ."

Tessa held her breath. "Then what?"

"She was gone. She wouldn't have left without saying goodbye." Ouida extracted a handwritten musical score from the sheaf of papers. "Nor left her songs behind."

Could Tessa have somehow stumbled upon a treasure trove of hitherto undiscovered ballads?

"You're a smart girl, I hear tell."

Tessa gave her a slow nod. Where was this headed?

"How about we do an exchange of services?"

What could Ouida Kittrell possibly want from her?

"Sing Leota's songs for me. They deserve to be sung by someone of your quality."

Tessa shook her head. "I don't sing anymore, Miss Ouida. I told you."

Ouida removed a batch of pages from the portfolio and held them out. "Some things we don't get choice of. Some things we do."

No more able resist the siren call of the music than she could force herself not to breathe, she took the songs from the old woman.

Ouida lumbered over to the dresser. She slammed the drawer shut. Tessa jumped.

"My jaws are plumb wore out from the unaccustomed exercise. That's enough for today. Those of us that ain't Cozarts got honest work to do."

She followed Ouida onto the porch.

"There's something else I could tell you of Leota." A wily look flashed across the old woman's features. "Mayhap, you sing pretty for me, I'll trust you with more of her songs."

Ouida Kittrell wasn't crazy like a lunatic. Just crazy like a fox. Tessa saw now that she'd fallen into a conspiracy. An intervention cooked up by Aunt Dicy and the old hermit. A backwoods cure for what ailed her.

Tessa debated returning the songs and leaving the cantankerous recluse to her ghosts. But she didn't. The lure of the music wasn't to be denied.

Something dear Aunt Dicy had no doubt counted on.

A sudden, strange, alert expression passed over the old woman's face. "Did you hear that?" Ouida whispered.

Foreboding tightened in the pit of Tessa's belly. She shook her head so violently tendrils of hair escaped the ponytail and fell about her ears. "No." She gulped.

"Sometimes . . ." The old woman cocked her head. "If I tune my ear just right, it's as if I can still hear her singing in the music of the river."

Chapter Eleven

Sleeping in the truck was getting to be a bad habit.

Last night, Zeke took Gib to pay his rent. Bought him groceries. Fixed him dinner too.

Though he drew the line at eating in the less-than-sanitary conditions of the trailer, Gib didn't notice that Zeke skipped dinner. Too busy blubbering over his beer, whining.

All that was required was the occasional murmur of sympathy. No useful information came of it, but it was a start toward building trust. Gib finally drank himself into unconsciousness. And Zeke had no intention of bedding down anywhere in the cockroach-infested dump.

But needing to be there when Gib awoke the next morning, he decided to crash in his truck. He hoped Gib would be appropriately grateful and forthcoming to his new best friend.

His phone buzzed on the console. He jerked on the seat, instantly alert. His gaze cut to the dashboard clock.

Six a.m. He clicked On. Had to be either a Cozart or—

"Zeke? How did it go with Gib last night? Where are you? We need to talk."

Or Brandi.

He swiped his hand over his face. "I'm still at Bascombe's. This couldn't wait until the sun is higher in the sky?"

"Did you get anything out of him? Do you know what they did with Kaci? Is this ever going to end?" The last part turned into a wail.

He let his head fall onto the seat. "The tension is getting to all of us, Brandi. But we're getting close to finding the answers we both want."

"Sometimes I just get so . . . The nights are the hardest . . . When I think about Emily . . ."

Brandi had been a trouper. With steelier nerves than some agents he'd worked with. But she was falling apart on him.

He gripped the cell. "Where are you?"

"I'm with Emily."

A preternatural chill ran over him.

"I'm at the cemetery. Closest I can be to her unless—" She bit off a sob.

"Don't you bail on me, Brandi. You've got to hang in there a little bit longer. Give me more time."

She quietly sobbed into the phone.

"Emily would want you to live. You've got to see this through."

"Why should I?" she moaned. "It will always be the same—the Cozarts winning."

"You've got to go on because Emily didn't get a chance to live. Because she didn't get to see this through. Because we can't let the Cozarts win again."

"I'm so tired of fighting them, Zeke."

"Stay where you are. I'll meet you at the cemetery. Promise me you won't do anything foolish."

"I-I promise."

He wrote Gib a note, promising to check on him later. He left it where Gib was sure to find it—under the bottle. There were a few swigs left in the bottom, and Gib wasn't one to let good or bad liquor go to waste.

It was a bleak, forbidding day. The mountains in the distance were wreathed in clouds. Rain was forecast.

He retraced the route through Deep Holler. No better in daylight than the night before. After forking left, he drove the serpentine road that snaked along the river.

At the top of the hill overlooking the steel girders of the bridge and the town, he parked beside Brandi's white sedan. Outside the old white-framed church, under the massive oak, a carpet of brown leaves gleamed with frost, which crunched under his boots.

GrandPop had pastored here and raised Zeke's mother in this

mountaintop congregation. But she'd married away, and after Zeke's birth, GrandPop moved to the flatlands to be closer to his family.

Zeke paused for a moment to gather his thoughts before facing Brandi. It was pretty up here. And peaceful.

Despite having loving parents, he'd always felt a little lost and never really understood why. Perhaps it was why he and Kaci had hit it off. After his parents fostered her, he sensed in Kaci another lost soul like himself.

Far below, the silvery twist of the French Broad ribboned its way across the valley floor. On the wind came the faint sound of a train whistle.

Once around the corner of the church, he stopped outside the rusty iron fence of the graveyard. Many of the granite pillars were weathered from exposure to the elements. Some of the headstones were broken or tilted. A few inscriptions were so old as to be unreadable.

He wondered what lonely grave Kaci occupied. If her killers even had the human decency to return her body to the earth. Or had they left her to the animals?

The burying ground mocked his failure to bring the guilty to judgment. He glanced at the bronze plaque on the gate.

A fitting echo of his thoughts, it read, "Remember me as you pass by. As you are now, so once was I. As I am now, so you must be. Prepare for death and follow me."

"I do remember you, Kaci," he whispered to the wind.

The restlessness had begun to plague him about the time his grandfather died. As a teenager, he'd dodged his parents' loving attempts to include him in the family's heritage of faith.

But Kaci had soaked it in like rain on desert-parched ground. She carried the small blue New Testament with her everywhere. GrandPop would've loved her. And sorrowed over Zeke.

He was the only one who didn't buy into the legacy. Who didn't—wouldn't, couldn't—believe. He wasn't sure why. He'd always had more questions than answers.

Some things never changed.

"I found Him, Zeke," Kaci told him that long-ago day after attending a youth retreat. "Found what I somehow knew had to be there all along."

She'd tried to share her joy of discovery with him. He'd been on his way to Basic. He was glad for her but not interested for himself.

"I'm going to pray for you," she told him. "Pray you into heaven. Next time, you must come to the mountains with me. Someday I want us to hike the Appalachian Trail together."

Someday had come, but not for him. His parents died in a car accident, and he survived several tours of duty only to be recruited by the Bureau.

Kaci worked through her grief by setting off on a quest to climb North America's grandest peaks.

But after everything he'd seen, he was even less interested in God. And he didn't have the time. He was preparing to embed with the white separatist group when she texted him she was going on the Trail. By the time he emerged from deep cover, she'd gone missing.

Had Kaci been prepared for death? He scrubbed his hand over his beard stubble. Yeah. He believed she probably had been. Would he have been as prepared?

Zeke glanced at the plaque. No, he thought not.

A blue haze—the blue jon, locals called it—hovered over distant peaks. There was a timeless quality, an eternal aspect to the view. Yet surrounded by graves, he felt as fleeting and ephemeral as the mist floating like cotton batting along the ridge.

Brandi stood in front of a large headstone.

Zeke entered through the gate and came alongside her.

The granite epitaph read, "Enter into My Rest."

"Emily can never be at rest until those vile monsters are held accountable for what they did to her," Brandi spat, breaking the silence. "I couldn't get the deputy to look for her. He said she'd come home eventually. Probably out partying, the usual high school hijinks."

Her young sister missing, Brandi had been frantic.

Then after three days, she'd found Emily huddled in her car in their driveway. Bleeding and half naked. Emily Murdock was sixteen years old.

Of course, he'd already heard the story. Brandi told him after they joined forces. But it festered like a sore inside her soul. He knew she needed to let out some of the pain, needed to speak it again.

"They ran her off the road on her way home from working at the dollar store."

When her abductors let Emily go, somehow she had managed to drive herself home.

"She never would tell me their names. Only that there were three of them. One held her down while the others . . ." Brandi swallowed hard. "Why not me? I would've fought them. They'd had to kill me before . . ." Tears rolled across Brandi's cheeks. "Why her?"

Feeling helpless, he took her into his arms. With the premature death of their parents, Brandi had always been more mother than sister to Emily.

"She never returned to school. It got to be I was scared to leave the house. As soon as she fell asleep, the nightmares would come."

"You had to go to work, Brandi." His response was automatic and the same as the last time she'd needed to say the words out loud.

She nodded, not so much to him as to herself. "Or how else could I pay the bills that kept a roof over our heads?" She buried her face into his shoulder. "Emily wouldn't let me take her to a doctor." Brandi lifted her tear-streaked face. "They'd said terrible things to her. Beaten her into believing their shame was hers. That she was to blame for what they did. And weeks later we realized she was pregnant . . ."

The images she'd painted of Emily's attack replayed themselves in his head each night, when he ought to have been sleeping. But instead of Emily, he saw Kaci's face.

"I should've insisted we seek medical help. But she was terrified. Halfway through my shift that day, I got this feeling I needed to go home. But I was too late."

He tensed, knowing the part that came next.

"She hung herself, Zeke, on Christmas Eve. The note said she couldn't bear to bring a child with the Cozart's evil blood in its veins into the world. That's when I knew it had to be one of them. And then you came to town, asking questions about Kaci. It had to be connected to what happened to Emily." Brandi removed herself from the shelter of his embrace.

A stiff wind sprang up.

"Justice is taking too long. Maybe I should just buy a gun."

"Don't talk like that." He seized hold of her upper arms. "You're not the one who deserves to rot in prison."

She glared at him, her eyes bloodshot with grief. "Prison's too good for them. They ought to suffer like Em—" She broke off with a sob.

He pulled her into his chest again. "We didn't start this for revenge."

"Revenge?" she choked out. "Knowing they probably did worse to Kaci, you can stand there and tell me you think their punishment should be a few years behind bars?"

"Not a few years, Brandi. Life."

She shoved him away. "Who are you kidding? Common variety criminals get out for the most unspeakable crimes after a few years of good behavior." She cocked her head at him. "What does justice look like to you these days?"

He held his ground. "Real justice isn't the same as mountain justice."

"Maybe it should be." Bitterness twisted her features. "We know Gibson was involved. And where Gib is, Pender and Shelton are usually four steps ahead. We can end this now, Zeke. Put an end to them."

"I can't do that, Brandi. It would make us no better than them. Don't you see? We can't move on them until we find Kaci."

She pulled her jean jacket tighter around herself. "I ain't no better than them." When she looked at him, her eyes mocked him. "And if you're honest, you ain't either."

That was the truth that kept him awake at night. Right alongside the emptiness of not knowing what happened to Kaci.

"Or maybe you didn't love your foster sister like I loved Emily."

"I loved her." His voice was gruff.

But it hadn't been enough. Would it be enough now?

He raked his hand over his head, combing his fingers through his hair. "We probably shouldn't be here."

"Who's to see us? Nobody but us and the dead." She fumbled in the purse slung around her waist. "I need a smoke. And a stiff drink."

"I need a good night's sleep."

She stuck a cigarette between her lips. "Sleep when you're dead."

Was that all that awaited Kaci when she closed her eyes for the last time? All that awaited any of them?

"Got a light?"

"You told me you were going to quit. New Year's resolution, Brandi."

The unlit cigarette dangled from her lips. "Is that all this investigation is to you? A quickly faded resolution?"

He scuffed the ground with the toe of his boot. "You know better than that."

She plucked the cigarette from her mouth and cast it down. She ground it with the heel of her shoe. "I was climbing the walls in the house all by my lonesome."

"Luther—"

"What about Luther?" She glanced at him sharply. "He said something to you about me?"

"Luther's a good guy."

She smiled for the first time. "He may be the only man in the county besides yourself not in cahoots with the Cozarts."

"You should give him a chance to be more."

"That your way of giving me the kiss-off?" She narrowed her eyes. "I'm thinking you got a thing for redheads these days."

"Don't wig out on me." Stability wasn't her middle name. "Stick to business."

"You should take your own advice." Her lips flattened. "Aren't you dying to ask me how the rest of the redhead's date went with Colin Cozart after you stormed out?"

He wasn't going to ask. Yet while Gibson had rambled meaningless trash about the unfairness of life, thoughts of Tessa with Cozart had twisted like a knife in his gut.

A bank of dark clouds had settled low on the horizon above town.

"They probably danced to every tune. Lots of laughter. A good time had by all."

Brandi rolled her eyes. "You got it bad, Zeke Sloane. And all wrong. They didn't dance. She didn't look like she was even remotely dazzled by the legendary Cozart charm. Got more sense than I credited her for."

"They still left together, didn't they?"

"He got mad when he called her to the mic in front of everyone, and she refused to sing."

Good girl. His notoriously precarious faith in humankind—in

Tessa—rose a notch. "Tessa used to sing all the time. That's what I remember about her the most." And the hair.

Brandi gave him a funny look. "What are you talking about?"

He shook his head. "It doesn't matter."

"Mama Cozart's spoiled baby boy didn't take too kindly to being publicly rejected." Brandi stuck her hands in her coat pockets. "Tessa Goforth has no idea what you're really doing here, does she?"

"No. She doesn't."

Brandi's plucked brow rose.

He dropped his gaze to the headstone. "She's come here seeking refuge, not complications."

"Some refuge." Brandi blew out a breath. "Roebuck County—out of the frying pan and into the fire. Colin won't allow the humiliation to go unpunished."

As the first droplets of rain began to fall, he walked Brandi to her car.

"Those shoulders of yours are broad." She nudged him with her elbow. "But while you're watching Ginger's back, don't forget to protect your own."

❖   ❖   ❖

When Tessa returned to the orchard from Yonder, she gave her aunt a rundown on her conversation with Ouida. Then, spotting Zeke by the barn, she wandered out. He worked as if a dragon rode his back. Apparently, tinkering with the tractor had become his personal mission in life.

An unusual flush beneath his tanned cheeks, he wouldn't look at her. She didn't miss the bickering so much as the sound of his voice. He seemed almost shy around her. Or nervous.

So she stood there, working up to apologize for not listening to him. For ever giving Colin the time of day.

To fill the silence, she told him stuff he probably had no interest in hearing. About Dr. Ruth McClaine, the near-mythical quest for Leota Byrd, and her weird morning visit with Ouida Kittrell.

True to her verbally inclined nature, she babbled. And true to his pay-for-every-word demeanor, he said nothing. Head down over the motor, he kept working.

She stood at his elbow like a surgical nurse, ready to hand him the next tool.

"Phillips," he growled.

One word, but a start.

Yet who knew the cute screwdriver with the star-shaped head wasn't the same thing as a Phillips?

He scowled. "Why don't you go help Dicy?"

Tessa's smile faltered.

"For the love of John Deere, please . . . go. Bother someone else."

So much for her apology. Lips pinched, she drifted inside the house.

Her aunt sat at the kitchen table, a laptop open to an agricultural software program.

"I had no idea you were online these days, Aunt Dicy."

Her aunt keyed numbers into a row of columns. "Zeke set up the spreadsheet for me." She fluttered her hand at Tessa, never glancing up. "Can't talk right now. Got to concentrate or I'll lose my place."

No one wanted her company today.

Seated on the round oak pedestal at the old upright piano in the living room, Tessa plucked at the musical notes on one of Leota's hand-written scores. An old ballad.

Hush-a-bye, don't you cry,
Go to sleep, little baby.
When you wake, you shall have
All the pretty little horses.
Blacks and bays, dapples and grays,
All the pretty little horses.
Hush-a-bye, don't you cry,
Go to sleep, my little baby.

Out the bay window, she could see Zeke bent over the tractor. He'd sent Luis and Tonio to finish picking the Winesaps while the weather held.

She fingered the tune to "All the Pretty Horses," singing under her breath. "Hush-a-bye, don't you cry. Go to sleep, my little baby . . ."

"You don't know how good it is to hear you sing again, cinnamon bun."

Jolted, her hands crashed on the keys. "Aunt Dicy! You scared me."

"I had to come listen." Her aunt leaned on the walker. "Your voice isn't the same."

Her heart squeezed. "I tried to tell you—"

"Different doesn't mean bad. There's a mature beauty in your tone. A depth that wasn't there before." Dicy smiled at her from the doorway. "The best way to process your grief isn't by locking the music inside you. Writers write. Singers sing. I grow apples."

"Fish gotta swim?" Tessa tilted her head. "Birds gotta fly?"

"Something like that."

"Listen to this last verse about a poor little baby crying momma." She turned the page. "While birds and butterflies fluttered around his eyes. Ugh."

Dicy stumped over to the piano. "Southern gothic at its finest."

"I ran across this ballad during my research in Louisiana. The song predates the Civil War. It's really a slave song about a mammy busy tending her master's child while her own lies dying of neglect." Tessa grimaced. "One of those happy, happy songs for which this region is infamous."

Dicy rifled through the other two songs on the piano rack. She held the sheet to the light of the window and read the words aloud. "When the honeysuckle's climbing 'round the door, the music is a chiming soft and low. And the twilight skies are gleaming with the colors that are streaming. It's like what you see in dreaming."

Her aunt lowered the page. "My mama used to sing this song. I forget its name."

"It's called 'A Southern Lullaby.'" She ran her hands over the keys, stroking out the simple melody. "Written during World War I by a popular composer."

Dicy flipped the sheet music to the last song Ouida had given Tessa. "I don't recollect this one. 'Moonstone Lullaby.'"

"The three songs are in a six-eight meter, a traditional tempo for lullabies. Was Leota planning a second album composed entirely of folk lullabies? And why?"

"An unusual choice for an eighteen-year-old. Unless the eighteen-year-old was expecting a child herself."

Tessa swung around on the pedestal stool. "I can't find any record of this 'Moonstone Lullaby' being published anywhere." She swallowed against the excitement building in her chest. "I'm nearly afraid to hope. It's too fantastic to believe, but I think this is an original composition by the Songbird of the Blue Ridge."

Dicy placed the music against the rack again. "Ouida would know."

"Ouida knows . . ." She made a face and rephrased. "Ouida has a lot of facts in her possession that she may or may not be willing to share."

"If you want answers, you'll have to sing the songs for her."

"What do the both of you imagine will happen?" She slammed her hands upon the keys in a discordant crash. "That my throat will suddenly open and I'll return to the stage? Do you want rid of me so badly?"

"I don't want rid of you at all, Tessa. And I don't care if you ever sing another opera again."

Tessa gaped at her aunt. "How can you say that?"

"Singing is the mechanism that unlocks what's in your soul. It's your heart I'm worried about. And whether you believe it or not, so is Ouida."

Tessa banged the piano lid shut. She wasn't ready. She might never be.

Chapter Twelve

Zeke stayed behind when Tessa drove Dicy to church the next morning. It never did rain yesterday.

Today, the orchard lay quiet in the early morning dew. Luis and Tonio wouldn't be here again until Monday. Sunday was supposed to be a day of rest.

But not for Zeke. Nor the wicked either. Although which category he fell into these days . . .

He bypassed the town. There weren't many cars on the road nor many folks stirring. Veering off beyond Robertson's farm, he lurched down the washed-out gravel road to the old Cozart homeplace inside the Yonder Wilderness area.

The remains of a stone chimney lay tumbled and broken off to one side, but the barn appeared to have weathered the years more or less intact. He got out of the truck.

According to Robertson, the homestead enjoyed regular visitors. Since there'd been no rain for a while, Zeke could just make out tire tracks. He pulled out his cell and snapped a few pics.

The barn door hung on rusted hinges. A strong breeze sprung up, swinging the door wide. As if welcoming him.

His skin prickled. Fighting his unease, he strode forward across the low threshold.

Inside, the air smelled musty and stale. The structure felt cavernous. Light trickled in through gaps in the boards where the hundred-year-old chinking had fallen away. From holes in the gambrel roof, dust motes danced in the beams of filtered sunlight.

Four wooden posts stretched from the splintered wooden floor to the empty hayloft above. He crouched beside a remnant of blue cord, knotted around the farthest column.

Dots of some aging stain splattered the splayed woven threads. Probably blood that grayed over time. He imagined the rope chafing and scraping tied-together wrists. If the sample wasn't too degraded, the lab might be able to extract DNA.

Perhaps they'd get a better idea of what had taken place here with Emily. Maybe Kaci too. To the other women Pender had also brought here to torture and rape. Zeke didn't for a second believe Pender's crimes were confined to only two victims.

As he hunkered close to the ground, all at once an unseen yet palpable sensation slammed into him.

Gasping, he rocked onto his heels. His overactive, overwrought imagination? Or was he picking up the latent undertones of something beyond his ken?

A memory of sorrow permeated this building. An atmosphere lingered. Was that possible?

Sensations. Fragments. His head spun with sounds of pain. The smells of fear. A feeling of joy.

A melody. No, that couldn't be right. Not if what he suspected had occurred within these creaking walls.

The barn around him blurred as if he were seeing the world through a smoky, dark veil. In the darkness of night, the pitch black would've been unrelieved by the moon.

Wait. How did he know that?

Jerking to his feet, he backed away from the rope. "Kaci?" he whispered. His gaze searched the dark space over his head. "Are you trying to tell me something? Are you here?" His voice rose, echoing.

This couldn't be happening to him. He didn't believe in ghosts and spirits, no matter how unhappy or cut short the life. If what GrandPop believed was true, Kaci was in a place from which no one would ever want to return.

Shaken, Zeke grabbed hold onto who he was—a federal agent. And to what he was supposed to be doing—hunting for evidence. Not haints.

He took photos of what he suspected was a crime scene. From every angle of the deserted barn. Doing the best he could with the light he had.

Good advice for life. Though not exactly the Light his family had encouraged him to embrace. He retrieved an evidence bag from the truck, cut the rope free, and placed it inside.

He wandered over to the three stalls subdividing the barn.

Two were empty. The last one held a ragged, dirty mattress. Dark-brown stains. Blood? Other stains too . . . Semen?

White-hot fury shook him to his core. At what those animals had done. At what Emily had suffered in their monstrous clutches.

He took more pictures before dragging the abomination from the stall and outside to the truck bed. After slamming the tailgate, he speed-dialed Reilly's number at the Asheville office. "Can we meet?" he barked.

"Where are you?" Reilly's voice crackled in and out. "I can barely hear you."

He glanced around the clearing.

Reception was spotty in remote sections of the mountains. He was lucky he'd gotten a signal at all.

"I've collected some physical evidence that forensics needs to take a look at." Zeke gulped. "I need your help. I also need to read you in on why I really accepted this assignment. Oh, and Reilly, bring a truck."

The little white-framed chapel sat on an overlook above town. Dicy had been welcomed as if she'd been away for months instead of a couple of weeks.

"Let me hug that Dicy Goforth's neck." A large woman swooped toward them. "It sure is good to see you, Miss Dicy. Right where you belong."

Her great-aunt was greatly loved.

It was quiet inside the church with its hand-hewn wooden beams. A simple place of worship filled with the warmth of community.

She was surprised by the number of young families in attendance. As everywhere else in Roebuck County, church attire was mountain casual. The usual jeans, though pressed for go-to-meeting day. Polished boots.

From outside filtered the sounds of children playing under the oak.

Young women called the kids to come inside. She recognized several people who'd dropped off casseroles.

"We can get plumb rowdy with the joy of the Lord," Dicy whispered. "But it's a happy place we're going to in the by-and-by. So no point in not practicing the happiness in the here and now."

Tessa had spent many a summer Sunday on the same red pew cushion between her uncle and aunt.

Dicy patted her hand. "Zeke's grandfather pastored here a long time ago. Before either of you was born."

"I didn't know that about Zeke." She tucked a strand of hair behind her ear. "A preacher's kid."

Her aunt shook her head. "Preacher's grandson. Police detective's son."

Tessa straightened as a man in his forties mounted the platform. The singing was of a nature she'd never heard before. Dicy had mentioned the congregation hadn't had an accomplished pianist in several years.

But ever resourceful, the older mountain folk had retaught the younger generations to sing with the old-time traditional shape notes. There were seven individually shaped notations for the songs in the green hymnal, each shape note with its own easily memorized tone.

Do, re, mi, fa, sol, la, ti.

Tessa didn't sing, but she basked in the musical blend of voices. The harmonies were surprisingly intricate, accomplished not by professional musicians, but by those with a melody in their heart. Singing praise to their Maker.

"Lest the rocks cry out," Dicy whispered.

The outside world fell away. Like when she'd been on the mountain yesterday. As vibrant as the stained-glass colors in the windows, the notes shimmered in the air, coming together to form a glorious whole. Lasting even as the final notes floated into the rafters above.

After the service, she helped her aunt into the car, and they headed down the road toward home. "That was nice, Aunt Dicy. I'm glad I went."

"Music, it does restore my soul. How about you, cinnamon bun?"

Hands on the wheel, she glanced at her bright-eyed aunt. "It's getting there."

Dicy pressed a button to lower the window. And stuck her head out into the breeze. Laughing, the older woman let the wind buffet her face. Joy bubbled out of her.

Tessa got a glimpse of the young girl she must have been. The young woman her uncle Calvin had loved so long and so well. Still there, beneath the trappings of her aging, wearing-out body.

A glimmer of the human spirit. A spirit that was meant to be eternal. Which one day would fly free to her real, forever home. To the true lover of her soul. In the by-and-by.

For the first time, Tessa wanted to know the wonder of that kind of love. That kind of joy. A time or two caught up in her music, she'd come close. Felt the tingling of an exquisite, rapturous note which left her hungry for more. Though not for more music. Or words.

But for the only One able to satisfy the yearning of the soul.

For those with eyes to see, ears to hear, the music was but a shadow of what was to come. For those with hearts to sing, the music was a dim reflection of the eternal Glory.

Cheeks rosy with color, Dicy pulled her head inside the car and raised the window.

Tessa wanted time to ponder this new awakening for God inside herself. "If it would be all right with you, Aunt Dicy, I think I'd like to do some exploring this afternoon."

Dicy smiled. "I think that would be a grand idea. There's a shortcut into the Pisgah on the other side of the meadow. If you don't mind getting off the beaten path."

"The road less traveled?"

"Not even a road." Dicy grinned. "But oh, my darlin' girl, the view will take your breath."

◆   ◆   ◆

They met at the usual rendezvous point halfway between the orchard and Asheville. Reilly took one look at the mattress lying in Zeke's truck bed and swore.

After Zeke explained his personal connection to the county, Reilly cursed him long and hard.

"Every agent's background is thoroughly investigated. How did this foster sister not show up in your file?"

"My parents fostered Kaci, but she never adopted our surname."

Additional cussing ensued. "Do you have any idea how this could've jeopardized our case? Compromised our ability to prosecute? Not to mention gotten yourself killed." The fifty-something special agent appeared apoplectic. "If the Cozarts don't kill you, I still might." More ranting. Eventually, however, the special agent ran out of steam.

Zeke lifted one end of the mattress.

Reilly obligingly took the other side and helped him transfer it to the unmarked, federal property truck.

"And there's this." He passed Reilly the evidence bag. "Kaci's DNA was taken off the items left behind on the Trail. I'll have Brandi provide you with some of Emily's things so you can get a good sample."

Reilly wagged his balding pate like a doleful hound dog. "You've stepped in it now, Sloane. After this stunt of yours, you can kiss your promising career goodbye."

Leaving Reilly to fume, Zeke left the rolling, open land and returned to Roebuck County.

Somewhere along the line, he'd lost the taste for the thrill of the chase.

But he didn't possess a great many marketable skills. He wasn't sure what he'd do with his life after the Bureau. An adrenaline junkie lurked in every undercover agent. The danger, the risks, fed something inside him. Could he ever be content with a normal routine? A normal life?

And what was he supposed to do about his confused feelings for Tessa?

Reilly wasn't the only one with whom he needed to come clean. He hated the secrets that stood between them. Perhaps if he told her the truth about what he was really doing in Roebuck, she wouldn't be so guarded around him. Maybe she'd open up.

But more importantly, for her own safety, she needed to know exactly the kind of man she decided to keep company with last night. And about his crazy, murderous family.

At the farmhouse, her Beamer sat parked under the pecan tree.

Dicy came out onto the ramp as he opened the truck door. "Just missed her," she called.

He sighed. When were he and Tessa going to stop missing each other? Would they always find themselves at cross-purposes?

Dicy had asked no questions when he came looking for a job and a place to stay. She'd trusted his intentions, based on her unshaken confidence in his long-dead grandfather. It was time to let her in on the rest of the secrets he'd been keeping.

To justify her keeping faith with him.

He got out of the truck.

"If you hurry, you could catch her." Dicy waved a cane. "She's gone exploring up to Cane Creek."

His gut seized. Close to the Cozart barn. And far too close to where Kaci disappeared, never to be seen again.

Since Tessa was skipping lunch, Dicy had insisted she take food with her on the hike. Fortified with a blanket and a bottle of water stashed in Uncle Calvin's canvas knapsack, she set out on foot across the wildflower-studded meadow.

In the knee-high grass, goldenrod and purple asters sashayed under the influence of a gentle breeze. Zeke's truck was missing from its usual spot, and the cabin had a slightly empty feel.

Disappointment welled. Subconsciously, had she been hoping to find him here? And if she had, would she have invited him to go with her to the mountain?

He'd been there earlier when they left for church, so where was he now? With the curvaceous Brandi? Shading her hand over her eyes, Tessa made a face at a cloud overhead.

Beyond the cabin, she sighted the faint outline of a well-trod path through the brush. Maybe a favorite hike of Zeke's too. Had he ever brought his girlfriend here? Like air from a hole in a balloon, some of her happiness leaked out of the day.

Climbing the steep, wooded slope, she left the valley behind and strode toward the trees.

She hated the discord between her and Zeke. And yet there were times it felt so easy between them. More than their brief acquaintance should warrant.

A seemingly familiar camaraderie that went beyond the need for words. When she was with him, an almost tangible if elusive thread of happiness felt nearly within her grasp.

Get a grip. She was so . . . so ridiculous. Ezekiel Sloane was about as interested in her as a—

As if she'd crossed an unseen barrier, the trees closed around her. Mist enveloped her and she was suddenly afraid. Going off by herself didn't seem such a good idea anymore.

The absence of sound wasn't natural. There ought to be birdsong this time of day. But it was quiet, too quiet. As if nature knew something she didn't. As if the creatures of this kingdom held their breath, feeding off her disquiet or, perhaps, sensing something dangerous.

Was she the intruder? Or did someone lurk, waiting? Watching—

A twig snapped behind her.

She whirled.

The foggy silhouette of a man emerged from the trees.

She tightened her grip on the strap of the knapsack, preparing to take flight. To run. But where?

He stood between her and the sunlit safety of the meadow. "Tess . . ."

She sagged in relief. "I ought to brain you with this backpack, Zeke Sloane."

"What's with you coming up here alone?"

She rolled her eyes. "This may come as a complete surprise to you, but I can manage a walk through the woods all by myself."

"It isn't you I'm worried about." His tone was clipped. "It's the maybe-not-so-alone part."

"How did you know where to find me?"

"Dicy got to thinking you might get lost, wandering this side of Yonder."

She frowned. "All who wander aren't lost, Ezekiel."

"It's the story of my life. And with my unerring sense of direction, I thought I'd show you the way to the old Cane Creek community." He raised an eyebrow. "Unless you've got an objection to my company?"

She sniffed. "Funny, after yesterday I figured it to be the other way around."

He looked sheepish. "I was out of sorts, Tess. A lot on my mind. My fault, not yours." He cut his eyes at her. "Say you forgive me, please? Will you keep me company this afternoon?"

She didn't have an objection—not a valid one—to his company. Unless she counted how he looked at her out of those half-lidded, swimming pool eyes of his.

The exact way he was looking at her now. Her knees went weak. But she wasn't about to go admitting to that.

Yesterday, she'd tried to get him to talk with her so she could apologize. To explain about being out with Colin Cozart. But now that she could . . . Her nerve deserted her.

Her temples thrummed. No, wait. The thrumming came from outside herself.

Tessa cocked her ear toward the hammered, staccato *brrr*. "Listen, listen. What do you hear?"

Something seemed to loosen in Zeke. "I hear a pileated woodpecker. It sounds like rapid machine gunfire." He motioned toward a pine. "One point for me."

In a steady drumbeat, the red-crested black bird jackhammered the tree trunk.

"Listen, listen. What do you hear, Tess?"

"I hear a gray squirrel chattering." Her lips twitched. "That's worth at least two points."

He gave her an endearing smile. "An old game."

A very old game. And for a second, a memory floated across her consciousness. But elusive as the thinning mist, it was gone before she could capture it.

She took a breath. "Well, since you have an unerring sense of direction . . ." She swept her hand toward the trail. "Lead on."

His posture altering, he dropped the defensive stance he wore with her. "Okay then, Red." He grinned.

She glared at him as he'd probably known she would.

The smile made its way to his eyes. "Let the adventure begin."

Suddenly breathless, she had a feeling it already had. An adventure she'd somehow never seen coming.

Yet like a vaguely remembered dream, one she'd been looking forward to for a long time.

Chapter Thirteen

Zeke held back the branch to keep the blackberry brambles from digging into her clothes. "It's this way."

Across a carpet of fallen leaves, a ghost of a trail curled along the slanting slope and disappeared. The sky was a cobalt blue.

She passed through unhindered. "You've been to Cane Creek before?"

"A long time ago with my grandfather."

"But you didn't grow up here." She stepped over a moss-covered log. "Aunt Dicy said your dad was a detective."

"With the Greensboro Police Department."

Her lips parted as if she meant to ask him about that, but instead she said nothing. Why shouldn't she wonder how the son of a police detective came to be working for the Cozarts?

"Every June when I was a boy, my parents attended a weeklong law enforcement convention in Myrtle Beach. As soon as they were out the door, my grandfather would announce we were heading to Roebuck County." He took a deep breath of cedar-scented air. "I looked forward to coming every year."

Gazing around the wilderness, she planted her hands on her slim hips. "It's hard to believe an entire community of people used to live here."

Once the native inhabitants were moved off the mountain, the land had been allowed to revert to its natural state. "If it's too tough a climb for you, Red, we can turn back."

Her green eyes flashed.

Zeke bit back a smile. It was always so much fun to wind her up, then watch the flame-haired opera diva go all hula girl on a dashboard.

She arched her eyebrow. "If you don't think you're up to the challenge, Ezekiel, please don't strain yourself on my account."

He stuck his tongue in his cheek. "Thought you might be feeling tired after your late date with Colin."

Blushing, she caught his gaze. "Colin was a mistake. I know you think I'm a big-city snob, but I didn't like the way he talked to you."

He hadn't expected this from her. "I haven't thought you were a snob." He tossed her a grin. "At least, not in the last few minutes."

She threw a pine cone at him.

Laughing, he ducked. "You're sure you want to head to Cane Creek? It'll only get rougher from here."

"I'm tougher than I look, Ezekiel." She batted her eyes.

He rolled his.

The wind murmured through the pines, setting the boughs to dancing. They continued down the trail.

"So tell me about your annual trip to Roebuck with your grandfather."

"It was our secret, just mine and GrandPop's." He strode after her. "This was before Kaci came into the picture."

"Kaci?"

The mention of Kaci threatened to overshadow what promised to be a good day. He could use more good days in his life. Days like this. On a mountain. He was not a man meant for interior spaces. But with Tessa, anywhere had the potential to become a good day.

"Why was coming here a secret?"

"Good question." He shrugged. "I never asked my grandfather. Nor told my parents we came."

"Your mother grew up here, though."

"But, to the best of my knowledge, she never returned. She preferred the wide, open spaces of the ocean for vacation."

Tessa looked at him, but she didn't push him to explain. She was a person with the rare ability to hear, to really listen to what another person said.

And he knew this was the moment he needed to tell her about himself. He could trust Tessa. Somewhere inside him he'd always known he could trust her. He'd just needed to be reminded.

She peered up to where the deer trail wound over a boulder. "Aunt Dicy said the journey would be worth the view. What do you think?"

"We'll have to keep going to know for sure, but I think she's right."

Tessa touched the rock face. "She usually is. But maybe I could use your help. The first step is the hardest."

Yes, it was. He wanted her to know everything. He wanted to know everything about her. But he wasn't sure she'd ever tell him about what happened to make her so brittle, so wounded.

Zeke wanted her to trust him. Yet words had never come easy for him. He'd need to work into telling her about Kaci.

He clambered up the rock ledge and leaned to take her hand. Bracing, he pulled her beside him. His pulse raced when she didn't let go.

"Was your childhood a happy one, Zeke?"

"It was." He guided her over the rocks to a place of easier ascent. "It was only later I realized how many don't get that. Did you, Tessa?" Like tossing the proverbial football, he lobbed the question out there to see what she would do with it.

"Until my mother died." She kept her eyes trained on where she placed her feet.

Given the climb, part physical necessity. But part emotional reticence too?

"I like the ocean." She panted as the elevation increased. "But there's something special about here."

"There's something old about here." He waited for her to catch up. "GrandPop liked to visit his best friend, Calvin Goforth, at the orchard. We would stay at the cabin, and GrandPop and I would hike to favorite lookout points. Every spot had a story to tell. And a lesson to learn."

She took a deep draught of air, as if trying to acclimate. "That explains so much. Why Dicy hired—" She bit her lip.

He cocked his head. "Why Dicy would hire a ne'er-do-well like me."

She touched his arm. "You've done a wonderful job with the apple harvest. The orchard is in the best shape since Uncle Calvin died."

He gave her an oddly bashful smile. "I didn't realize when I took the job how much I would enjoy working on the farm. An added bonus."

"Why did you return here, Zeke? Why now?"

"Do you want to know another odd thing about our annual trips to Roebuck?" He dodged her question.

She pursed those beautiful lips of hers. "Sure. Tell me."

He had no business studying her mouth. Zeke stuffed his hands in his pockets. "GrandPop never, not once, took me to town."

"Your grandfather was full of secrets, wasn't he?"

"As mysterious as the hills themselves, I reckon. But good training for the work to which I've given a large chunk of my adult life. Maybe keeping secrets are in my blood."

The moment had come. There could be no turning back. She'd either accept what he had to say, accept who he was, or shut him down.

"I'm an FBI agent, Tessa. I'm working undercover to bring charges against the Cozart empire. An empire built on the sale of illegal substances, corruption, and money laundering."

Eyes wide, for a second she stared at him. Then she threw back her head and laughed. "Oh, thank God."

Zeke furrowed his brow. "Thank God, I'm taking the Cozarts down?"

Her smile was as brilliant as the sun. "That, but mostly thank God you're only pretending to be like them."

Zeke wished he were as sure of the pretending part as she seemed to be. And there was one other point he needed to make crystal clear. "Brandi and I . . ."

Tessa's face clouded. She stumbled back, a misstep too close to the edge. Pebbles slithered down the side of the mountain. She flailed.

He got hold of her arm and jerked her against him. "You're going to give me a heart attack." Holding her close, he could feel the too-rapid beat of her heart through the fabric of his shirt.

For a moment, she clung to him, her head buried in the hollow of his shoulder. Then, she stiffened, and tried pulling away.

"Brandi is part of my cover story. We're not . . ." He moistened his lips. "Intimate in any way."

"The nights you don't come home . . ." She blushed.

"I'm not with her." He liked the sound of home on her lips. "There are other aspects of my investigation that involve Pender Cozart and his gang. Brandi's helping me get to the truth about what they did to her sister." He exhaled. "And to Kaci."

❖　❖　❖

Clearing the knob, they emerged out of the trees into what was left of Cane Creek.

It seemed to Tessa like a place apart, where the past lingered in a moody blue haze over the land.

She waited for him to continue the conversation about Brandi and the Kaci he'd mentioned, but as if taking its cue from the abandoned hamlet, a heaviness settled itself like a mantle upon his shoulders.

Once a community had thrived in the hollows and glens on this mountain. Nothing remained except for a near impenetrable wilderness of laurel hells, broken stone foundations, and the graves of those gone before.

"What do you think happens when you die, Zeke?" It was that kind of place. "Is this all there is?"

He sat down on a slab of rock that might have been the front stoop to a long-vanished cabin reclaimed by the wilderness.

"Nonexistence is too easy." He raked his hand through his hair. "What justice would there be if, after all the evil some do, they get to simply cease to exist?"

She nodded. "And if there is a place for evil, there ought also to be a place for good."

"All the loved ones I've lost . . ." He took a breath. "I'd like to think they are somewhere good. Together and happy again. What do you think?"

"I think this can't be all there is." She gestured. "There has to be more. Beauty, love—the bright essence of being can't just end. It must go on."

"Just somewhere else?" He rested his arms on his drawn knees. "I wish I could know for sure."

"Faith is a risk. But then so is life." She looked at him. "The leap of faith ought to appeal to someone in your line of work. Dicy says God isn't afraid of our questions or doubts."

Zeke scrubbed his forehead. "I guess there comes a point when everyone has to decide what they're going to believe."

"Have you?"

"I thought I had." He looked at her. "But recently I've come to the realization my conclusions might've been premature. About a lot of things."

Her pulse accelerated. "Did you eat lunch?" She slipped the knapsack off her shoulders and unzipped the pack. "Dicy made me pack enough for an army."

"Your aunt has a gift of food. Like a lot of Southern women, it's how she shows her love." He peered into the bag. "What did you bring?"

She held up two paper-towel-wrapped sandwiches. "Pimento cheese or chicken salad?"

"You pick. I'll eat anything that comes from Dicy's kitchen."

Concentrating on the food, they fell silent for a while.

She unscrewed the cap on the water bottle. "Mind sharing?"

Catching her eye, he threw her a lazy grin. "Why, no, Red. I'd love to share spit with you."

Her heart stutter-stepped.

For the love of Mozart, it ought to be against the law to have eyes like his.

She felt a tidal wave of pink surge in her cheeks. But the drama-laden world of opera was not for the faint of heart. Feigning a nonchalance she was far from feeling, she tore her gaze away. And took a swig of water before she passed it to him.

His mouth quirked as he pressed the bottle to his lips.

"I'm glad you're not what I believed you were." She tilted her head. "It was getting harder to rationalize liking someone who associated with a scumbag like Pender Cozart."

He sputtered and wiped his mouth with his sleeve. "Is that so? You've decided to like me."

She shoulder-butted him. "Don't let it go to your head. I like old people and babies too." She fluttered her lashes. "Here's the part where you say, 'Tessa Goforth, I like you too.'"

"You are a very likable person. For a redhead."

She gave him a death glare.

"You know what they say about freckles on a redhead?"

"No." She jutted her jaw. "What do they say, Ezekiel Sloane, about freckles and redheads?"

"There's a freckle for every soul they've taken."

She touched her hand to the bridge of her nose. "I don't have freckles. And I don't take souls."

"You do when you sing." Letting his head fall back, he took a long chug of water.

And watching the cords of his neck convulse as he gulped liquid, she got a little lost. When he came up for air, so did she.

"No freckles." He winked. "Only reason you and I could ever be friends."

"Any more comments about my hair and I'm going to take it back about liking you."

"I call 'em like I see 'em, Baby Red."

For a split second, time went sideways. To another meadow. Another day. Once again, the memory evaporated before she could capture it. She handed him the bottle cap. "I won't tell anyone about your real purpose here. Your secret is safe with me."

Zeke repacked the trash into the knapsack. "If I hadn't known that, I wouldn't have told you."

He'd been so honest. It was time she trusted him.

Zeke zipped the bag closed. "We're nearly to the top. Seems a shame to stop now, doesn't it?"

She lifted her chin. "It does seem a shame."

"I want to show you the lookout point." He gave her that lovely lop-sided grin of his. "From there you can almost see forever."

When he offered his hand, she took it and together they left the ghost village behind. He refused to let her carry the knapsack.

And having once established her ability to carry the load this far, she saw no further reason to continue to prove her independence. Chivalry wasn't dead. So why not let him lug the extra weight?

He veered off the main branch of the trail to a precipice that jutted into the nothingness of the deep-plunging gorge.

Gasping, she shrank against him. "What is it with you and needing to live life on the edge, Ezekiel?"

"That's Tennessee." He pointed. "Over there to the northeast, Virginia."

"And on the other side of the mountain is Ouida Kittrell's home-place?" The wind buffeted her face, stinging her cheeks.

He nodded. "Never been there, but I suppose so. That side is easier reached by the road."

She huffed. "Some road."

"Not up to New Orleans's standards, I'll grant you." He pulled her toward safety in the shade. "My last case before this one was working a white supremacist enclave in the bayous of Louisiana."

Her mouth opened. She closed it.

"What?"

"Just trying to envision you as a skinhead."

"I'll have you know I made a convincing skinhead."

"You make a convincing good-ole-boy waste of space."

"Thank you."

"You're welcome. Louisiana. Is that how you know about the Café du Monde?"

Zeke removed the red tartan blanket from the backpack. "Great place to meet my case officer." He billowed the blanket over the dry, brown leaves. "And get pastry. The donut thing with law enforcement is true."

"How long were you undercover?"

Zeke shrugged. "Six months. Felt longer." He flopped down on the blanket.

"How did you go from what sounds like a fairly normal childhood to . . . to . . . ?"

Zeke grinned. "Opera isn't the only career that demands acting skills. That, and the sheer weight of my vast intelligence—"

She groaned. "Please . . . Tell me another one." She lay on her side, hand cupping her head, propped on her elbow. "Why do you risk your life?"

"If somebody like me doesn't, who will?" He rolled over, facing her. "I like the thrill. I can handle myself. I'm careful not to get in over my head, and I always remember I'm playing a part."

She narrowed her eyes. "So this isn't the real you."

He frowned. "I imagine it's like when you sing. You temporarily step into someone else's shoes. But the mannerisms, the experiences you draw upon to play the character, those are yours. You bring it with you to the role."

"I don't sing anymore." She angled away, lying on her back. "Which Zeke is with me today?"

"The me when I'm with you is the real me." He touched her face. "As real as I've ever been. How about you?"

And like that, he gave her a place to begin. She sat up. "I expect Aunt Dicy told you what happened to me in New Orleans." She leaned over the edge of the blanket, twisting a pine needle around her finger.

"Dicy started to tell me, but I stopped her."

Tessa stopped mauling the clump of grass and looked at him. "But you know, don't you? It was a media circus for weeks afterward."

"No, I don't know."

"You didn't google me?"

"I preferred for you to tell me yourself." He swallowed. "When you were ready."

Did she feel ready? She'd never told anyone everything that happened that terrible night, not even her beloved aunt.

Yet for some strange reason she found herself yearning to tell him. Maybe it was easier because he was a relative stranger, because he didn't know her before—the Tessa she used to be. Because their lives were only for this brief autumn at an intersection, and soon they'd each be on their separate paths to different destinies.

Or . . . perhaps, because somewhere deep inside, she knew she could trust him with her life. With something heavier than her life—her darkest secret.

"My best friend and roommate in New Orleans, Sandy, had the most amazing coloratura voice."

"Am I supposed to know what that means?"

"It's like a high-arching fountain." She demonstrated with her hands. "Light, bubbly."

He smirked. "Is this where I'm supposed to break into 'The Hills are Alive'?"

"You, Ezekiel, are a musical cretin."

"Big words," he crowed. "And me just a poor, country—"

She shoved him.

He fell over on the blanket.

"I'm trying to learn you something, Ezekiel. Listen up."

He lifted a corner of his very attractive lips. "Yes, ma'am."

She touched her hand to her throat. "My voice is lower on the scale. Like—"

"Like Etta James in 'At Last.' Like the deep, rich grooves of a river current."

She blinked. "Excuse me?"

"I never said I hadn't heard you sing." He suddenly became fascinated with a small pebble, moving it from hand to hand. "That's what your voice reminded me of." He glanced up, brow creased. "Was I wrong?"

She smoothed a strand of hair behind her ear. A gust of wind undid her efforts.

"The wind . . ." He caught her hand before she could try again. And wrapped the tendril around his finger. "Same as at the ocean. Always blowing. Maybe that's why my mom liked it there."

Her heart squeezed in her chest. They were sitting close, very close. If she inched forward . . . if he exhaled . . . Their mouths could be touching.

Did she want their mouths to be touching?

Yes. Her pulse raced. Yes. She did.

But apparently he didn't. He tucked the hair behind her ear, then moved away, inserting space where there'd been none before. "My parents liked Etta James. She was a—"

"I know who Etta James is, Zeke. Opera isn't my only musical genre."

"Good to know."

She rolled her eyes. "Anyway . . . about my friend, Sandy . . ."

He grinned.

She realized he'd succeeded in distracting her from the heavy undertones of her grief and made the story tellable. "In the summers, we did tours all over the world."

"You and Sandy?"

"Plus a short list of company members. There was a concert series in Europe one year. That's where Anton . . ." She was aware her voice changed when she said his name.

Zeke reached for her and put his arm around her shoulders.

She sighed against him. "Anton became our principal violinist. We did this special number from *St Matthew Passion*. Lots of lovely solos. Sandy. Me. Parts for our resident tenor and bass." Tessa kept her gaze focused on the woven threads of the blanket. It was easier to tell the rest if she didn't have to look at him. She rested her cheek against the rough denim of his shirt.

He smelled like the outdoors. Clean. Fresh. Of apples. And something pleasing that was just him.

"I wish you could've met Sandy. She was the sunniest person I ever knew. Always smiling. So friendly." Tessa frowned. "Too friendly. Anton was unstable. He mistook the way she was with everyone for something else. She and our principal tenor were planning to be married."

Quickly, she told Zeke how, after the tour ended, Anton followed them to New Orleans. The violinist had stalked Sandy, and she had filed a useless restraining order.

Tessa shuddered. "When he disappeared from the city, Sandy was so relieved. We both believed he'd finally given up his obsession for her. Then one evening after a magnificent performance, the cast had planned to throw a surprise engagement party for Sandy and Dom. I'd taken off my makeup but was still in costume. The audience had gone."

He squeezed her arm.

Soaking in the light warmth of the sun on her face, she took a deep breath. The air smelled of dried grass. She steadied her pulse, finding solace in the murmur of the breeze. Taking comfort in the endless vista of billowing golden foliage undulating like the waves of the ocean. Mountain after mountain, rising one behind the other, a breathtaking progression of dusty-violet layers.

Zeke laced his fingers in hers.

At his touch, her entire body trembled.

"You're safe, Tess."

And she found the courage to continue. "It was my job to get them to the restaurant. I'd bought a special vintage of champagne. But the fire alarm went off. I grabbed the bottle—I'm not sure why, maybe because it was expensive. And I ran out of my dressing room, down the corridor—" She looked at Zeke. "It's a labyrinth below stage. The opera house is nearly as old as the city. I knocked on Dom's door and rushed in without waiting."

Tessa swallowed before telling him how she'd found Dom, face down on the floor in a puddle of blood. "His throat had been slit."

Zeke's hold tightened.

"I think I screamed. And Anton came out from the shadows. I-I hit him with the bottle." Her breath came in short, rapid bursts as if she were running the corridor again. "I ran. I-I couldn't find Sandy. The fire was so hot. I couldn't get out. Anton had barricaded the exit door."

She could still smell the smoke. Hear herself coughing, gasping for breath.

"Anton had me trapped." She looked at Zeke. "And he had his violin. He-he wanted me to . . . Anton wanted me to s-sing." She closed her eyes. She'd never told anyone that part before. Not even the police.

"He was insane, Tess. "

"Anton chased me onto the catwalk. I left her, Zeke . . ." She sobbed into his chest. "I should've fought to get past him. I shouldn't have run. But I couldn't breathe, and somehow I found the trap door to the roof."

"You can't blame yourself. You had no choice. If you hadn't, you would've died with her."

"Could I have saved her? Or was she already dead?" She choked back a sob. "Don't you see? I'll never know." Although Ouida had seemed to know . . .

He took her face between his hands. "I know that I'm glad you did whatever you had to do to stay alive." He pressed his forehead against hers. Giving her the strength she needed to tell him the rest—about the roof, the fireman, Anton's last words that wherever she went, she'd carry him with her. And about the anxiety attacks she'd battled ever since.

"Anton took everything. My friends. My career. My voice."

"He didn't take your life, Tess. And for that, I'm thankful."

"Music was my life."

He cradled her face between his work-callused hands. "You are more than the music. So much more." Swooping, his lips found hers. But almost as quickly, he drew back, giving her the freedom to break away if she wished.

Tessa didn't wish.

Instead, her hands traveled across the broad planes of his back and interlocked behind his neck. She pulled him toward her mouth.

"Tess . . ." Then his lips claimed hers again.

Something electric pulsed between them. A flame of a different sort. Kissing him, she had to remind herself to breathe.

As kisses go, it was a gentle kiss. An exploratory exercise, testing the boundaries of trust.

He held her so tenderly. As if he feared to break her. As if he held her too tightly, the moment would vanish. That she would vanish.

But she wasn't going anywhere. Despite his daredevil ways, he made her feel safe. And alive.

There was an incredible sweetness in his kiss, a carefully controlled restraint. She suspected him capable of great passion, but he allowed none of that today.

He pulled back long before she was ready. "Thank you for telling me." He got to his feet. "Dicy will be wondering what's become of us."

She figured Dicy knew exactly what had become of them. And for her own inscrutable reasons had set this afternoon into motion.

"Time to return to being a good-ole-boy waste of space." He refused to look at her, refolding the blanket. "I like you more than I should. But . . ."

Despite their true-life confessions, there was something—someone?—more than the job that stood between them.

They'd gotten sidetracked at Cane Creek. He never really explained how Brandi's sister fit into his investigation. Or about Kaci, whoever she was to him. He probably didn't realize how much emotion filled his voice when he said her name.

But he'd said as much as he was going to say today. She recognized the signs. The stoicism on his irregularly handsome features. The guarded gaze. The taciturn let's-buy-a-vowel-for-one-hundred voice.

She felt like a wrung-out dishrag of emotions. Maybe he was right. Best to pull back from the edge of no return.

They'd had fun. Shared a kiss. Maybe gone from frenemies to friends. More than enough for one afternoon's work.

Because she liked him way more than she should too.

He was a self-admitted wanderer. Wanderers, like her father, were notorious for never sticking around. Same wish-true, never-shall-be song, second verse.

Just as well. This wasn't her world. She might not know where her future path would take her, but she was pretty sure it wouldn't include an adrenaline junkie, "undercover skinhead aka cartel enforcer," chameleon like Zeke Sloane.

And yet . . . She kept her eyes trained on the hollow plane between his shoulder blades as she followed him down the side of Yonder Mountain.

She wouldn't be forgetting the kiss, nor the man, anytime soon.

Chapter Fourteen

The next day, one of Dicy's church friends offered to take her aunt to the follow-up appointment with the doctor. Tessa took the opportunity to drive to Mars Hill to update Ruth on her project. She'd just pulled in alongside the curb at The Grind when her cell buzzed.

A Tennessee number. One of the producers of Leota's album responding to Tessa's shot-in-the-dark email. Tom Connelly had been a young man starting out in the competitive music world back when Leota Byrd arrived in Nashville.

"Thank you so much for calling me back, Mr. Connelly." Tessa stayed in her car but unbuckled her seatbelt. "I can't believe I've actually found someone who remembers her. It was so long ago. Over thirty years."

He chuckled. "You're making me feel old."

After a successful career, he was now enjoying retirement, not far from where it began for him and Leota.

"No one who heard Leota Byrd sing will ever forget her voice. I'm glad you're including her in your research. She was a talent that shouldn't be forgotten."

Tessa scanned the area in front of the shop to make sure Ruth hadn't already arrived for their meeting. "I was hoping you could fill in some of the details regarding her life in Nashville, Mr. Connelly."

"I discovered her singing during open mic at a local nightclub for aspiring bluegrass musicians. It was magic. She was magic."

Tessa dug out a pen from the bottom of her purse. "When did you first hear her sing?"

"Late October 1987. It was raining cats and dogs that night in

Nashville. A smaller crowd. Their loss, my gain. She had only been in Nashville a few weeks, Leota told me."

Merritt Cozart had said Leota left school early and never returned to graduate. Tessa paged through her notebook. Bracing against the console, she added the info to the timeline she was constructing of the ballad singer's life. "What else can you tell me about the album, Mr. Connelly?"

"Stargazer Records was the pet of my college roommate and I. We were looking for fresh, young talent. Leota was that and more. She blew us away. We signed her immediately, and the recording sessions went like a dream. Because bluegrass was such a niche market, we were able to roll out the album in, pardon the pun, record time." He laughed.

"Do you know anything about her life outside the studio?"

"That spring, we kept her busy with gigs promoting the album. Radio. A bus tour. For me personally, it was a spring of boundless creativity."

"So there were plans to produce another album?"

"When she wasn't singing, she was reworking other ballads. The album was well received by fans and music critics alike. Her future was very bright. She glowed with a personal and professional happiness."

"Professionally, I get what you're saying. But personal happiness . . . What do you mean?"

He went quiet.

The window had fogged over from the condensation of her breath. "Mr. Connelly? Are you still there?" She swiped her sleeve across the glass.

"Leota promised to be back for work by midsummer. We booked the recording studio for a sequel album."

"Wait. Where did she go? And when?" But she knew the answer to that question before he even answered.

"In the fall, when I signed her, I didn't know she was pregnant. I would've signed her anyway, but at that point, I'm not sure she even realized it herself. She was barely eighteen, a child really, and yet about to become a mother."

Confirmation of what Tessa had suspected from Leota's handwritten songs. "The sequel album was going to be lullabies, wasn't it? Did she ever talk about the baby's father?"

"How did you know?" He sighed. "She took the music with her when she left Nashville in May. The closer she came to her due date, the more determined she became to return to North Carolina."

"Do you know why she came home, Mr. Connelly? There was no family waiting to welcome her back."

"She was in love. But like most musicians I've met, a passion for the music drove her toward Nashville, even if she went alone."

Tessa knew the passion firsthand.

"I think her intention in returning was to tell him about the baby. She had no doubts he'd be delighted at her news. She told me to expect three of them for the next concert tour."

"What happened, Mr. Connelly?"

He sighed. "That's just it, Miss Goforth. I put Leota on the bus that May morning. And I never heard from her or saw her again."

"Did you try to find her?"

"We eventually canceled the recording session. My partner and I hired a private investigator." Connelly sniffed. "If you're living in that back of beyond, you already know how little info he was able to acquire. The walls came down. He was an outsider."

"Do you have any theories about what became of her?"

"I spent a lot of time over the years wondering, Miss Goforth. I alternate between two scenarios. Either the baby's father convinced her to give up her music, and she became just another overworked, underappreciated mountain statistic. Or I'm left with the other far worse scenario."

"Which is?"

"I get a bad feeling the father of Leota's baby didn't receive the news with as much joy as the young woman anticipated. And that something terrible, unspeakable, happened to beautiful Leota and her much-longed-for baby. The bank account where we deposited her royalties has never been touched." He inhaled sharply. "Over the years, I've continued to check. I can't believe she or the baby's father wouldn't have wanted to access the funds to make their lives better."

She was inclined to agree with him. Some artists, for reasons of their own, chose to walk away from promising careers. None that she'd ever met walked away from money already earned.

"There is a not-so-small chunk of change that has only grown interest over the years. It's waiting to be claimed by Leota, wherever she is, or one of her descendants. If you find her . . ." Tom Connelly's voice grew hoarse. "Maybe she was too embarrassed to contact me, but would you let me know what you discover, Miss Goforth?" He cleared his throat. "I was very fond of her. And I've worried for such a long time."

"I will, Mr. Connelly. I promise, one way or the other, I'll be in touch."

She ended the call, but kept the phone propped between her neck and her ear, thinking.

May 1988. Had Leota gone from the bus to the baby's father? Or straight to Ouida's? Who else had seen Leota get off the bus in Buckthorn?

Tessa sensed answers would only be found in the songs Leota left behind. And from Ouida. But there was only one way to unlock the storehouse of Ouida's memories.

If she wanted to know more about Leota's return to Roebuck County that spring of 1988, she was going to have to return to Yonder Mountain.

And sing.

❖   ❖   ❖

Reilly had put a rush on the tests results from the rope and the mattress Zeke found in the old barn at the Cozart homeplace.

As soon as he could get away from the orchard that morning, they met at the usual out-of-the-way, deserted farm road.

"The rope fibers contained traces of human blood." Reilly grimaced at the dust coating his leather shoes. "You're sure there's nowhere else we can meet? Like maybe somewhere paved."

Zeke folded his arms, preparing for bad news. "Who did the blood belong to?"

Reilly's gaze panned over the sloping pastureland. "What happened to the millennial fixation on endless cups of coffee?"

"A match, Reilly? Did you find a match?"

"The blood was a match for Emily Murdock."

Brandi would want to know. His stomach muscles tightened, readying for the next hit. "And the mattress?"

Reilly's eyes flickered. "Semen. Blood. Exactly what you'd expect to find, based on the details Emily shared about her attack."

"Just Emily's blood?"

Reilly nodded.

"And the semen?"

"Two different samples of semen on the mattress. Can't be sure if they were deposited during the same encounter, however I'd guess they were." Reilly clenched and unclenched his hands. "Emily Murdock was gang-raped. But unless the DNA extracted from the semen is a match to other DNA already in the database, we have no way to identify the perpetrator."

"Did it?"

"Not yet. It appears the perpetrator's DNA isn't in the system from other crimes he may have committed."

"But you didn't find any trace of . . ." Zeke had a hard time saying the words out loud. "That Kaci was . . ."

"No trace of your sister at all." Reilly placed his hand on his shoulder. "Based on that evidence, whatever happened to Kaci didn't take place on the mattress."

Gibson Bascombe remained his best option—the only viable option—for finding Kaci.

Reilly studied the rolled hay bales dotting the seemingly placid rural landscape. "When I put away the cartel behind the Conquistadores street gang, I thought I'd encountered the lowest form of human life."

The case in New Mexico a few years ago had made Reilly a legend.

"Evil lurks in every corner of the globe." Reilly shuddered. "But these mountains feel more violent than any other place I've worked. Maybe because the beauty here is such a deceptive contrast."

"It's not just your imagination." Zeke broadened his shoulders. "You need to understand something about the people here. Their ancestors, my ancestors, came from the war-torn region of the Scottish borderlands to America after a detour through Ireland."

Reilly grunted. "Believe me, I get the Irish part."

"The people that settled here were born and bred to fight. Some would say it's in their blood. The wild isolation and the frontier only fed the violence."

Reilly snorted. "From where I'm standing, it still feels pretty isolated and wild."

"The Civil War was particularly uncivil in these parts."

Reilly rolled his eyes. "Must it always come back to the 'wahr' with you Southerners?"

"You know we hate it when you try to imitate our smooth, honeyed tones, right?"

Reilly grinned.

"The conflict only added fuel to the fire and became an excuse to settle old clan grievances. The bloodletting unleashed feuds that continue to this day."

Reilly straightened his tie. "The prosecutor thinks we have enough to ask for federal indictments. You don't have a lot more time to find your sister." He pushed off toward his unmarked vehicle. "I understand how personal this is for you, but watch yourself. The Cozarts bring a whole new definition to psychotic and crazy mean."

After they parted, Zeke took a circuitous route over the county line into Roebuck. He'd had the strangest feeling since leaving the orchard this morning that he was being watched, but he made sure no one followed him to his meeting with Reilly.

Yet overriding all else, he found his thoughts consumed by Tessa.

She'd left the farmhouse early. He wasn't sorry. They both needed space.

On the mountain yesterday . . . He rubbed his hand over his face. He'd meant to tell her about Kaci, but when the moment came, he'd been unable to find the words.

He turned the truck into the orchard. The last of the apples were only days from being harvested. And with the case wrapping up, there would be little to keep him in Roebuck County.

The clock was ticking. If he didn't get Gib to lead him to Kaci before arrest warrants were handed down, Zeke might never discover what happened to her. Once lawyers were brought in, Gib would have no reason to disclose further information and risk damaging his own defense.

But then there was Tessa. What was he going to do about her? What did he want to do about her?

She'd only come to help her aunt get back on her feet. Dicy was used to being self-sufficient and would never dream of tying her niece to the orchard. He had no clue as to how Tessa envisioned her future.

And where did that leave him? Them? He was an idiot. One kiss did not make a *them*.

He got out of the truck.

Dicy drove up on the little golf cart she used, even before the accident, to save steps around the farm.

He might've chickened out on telling Tessa the truth yesterday, but his moment of reckoning had come with Dicy.

As blue jays flitted from branch to branch, he sat in the golf cart with the elderly woman and told her everything. It wasn't a pretty story, but the story needed telling. About Emily. His search for Kaci. And what nearly happened to Tessa at the gas station.

Dicy's wise old face crumpled. "She never said a word to me."

"She didn't want you to worry."

"Tessa keeps too many things too close to her heart. She thinks I don't know how she continues to struggle with the past, but I do."

"On the mountain yesterday, she told me about the fire."

"I'm right tickled to hear that." Dicy smiled. "She needed to tell someone, and I'm glad it was you. There's a healing in the telling. Now if she could only find her way back to the music."

He crawled out of the cart. "She made a bad enemy with Colin Cozart."

Dicy scowled. "If somebody had taken a paddle to that boy a long time ago, he wouldn't be the vain, spoiled, little moron he is today."

His eyes darted to the empty spot under the pecan tree. "I thought Tessa would be back by now."

Dicy chewed her lip. "You reckon she decided to go to Ouida Kittrell's place? I hoped they might help each other move beyond the past into the present, but with things so unsettled . . ."

"Ouida Kittrell seems a lightning rod for conflict with the Cozarts."

Dicy held to his arm as he helped her up the ramp. "That is surely the truth."

"You're getting around better every day." He nodded encouragingly as they entered the house.

She winked. "Nothing beats the restorative powers of home."

"If you don't mind my taking off again, Miss Dicy, I'd feel better if I checked on Tessa."

"Give me some paper. I'll show you how to get there." She settled into her favorite chair in the living room. "But be careful. Ouida don't take to strangers."

He'd heard a lot of things about Ouida Kittrell. None of them good. Anjanette called her "the old witchy woman." And even Dicy appeared to harbor reservations about her cousin.

Then it hit him.

Yonder Mountain wasn't far from the part of the Trail on which Kaci had disappeared. Robertson as good as implied Kaci never came off the mountain. Ouida Kittrell might've seen something.

He was running out of hope, grasping at the wind. But the old woman might yet provide answers to his questions.

Ouida Kittrell could give him back Kaci.

❖ ❖ ❖

Nothing had changed at the Kittrell cabin since the last time Tessa had climbed the mountain and wended her way to the homestead.

Smoke curled in the bright blue sky over the clearing. A late autumn rose trailed over the porch railing, diffusing a spicy aroma. A robin sang from under a bush.

Ouida sat in the porch rocker, her gnarled hands on the armrests. The treads beat a rollicking to-and-fro cadence. Her dark eyes were fixed on the trees from where Tessa emerged.

As if she'd been waiting for Tessa to show, expecting her any moment. *Knowing* Tessa was coming.

Tessa squared her shoulders and crossed the remaining distance. "Why didn't you tell me Leota came back from Nashville pregnant?" She removed the songs from her tote bag. "These are lullabies."

Ouida looked at her. "They are indeed."

"Can't we just skip the mystery and get to what else you actually know about Leota's disappearance?"

Back and forth. Back and forth. The steady rhythm of the rocker never varied. "Are you ready to sing for me this afternoon?"

"If you're worried that I'm in cahoots with the Cozarts, I promise you nothing could be further from the truth." She adjusted the tote strap on her shoulder. "There are forces in motion that will not allow them to escape justice forever."

Ouida gripped the armrests. "Civil justice or mountain justice, one way or the other, child, we will all face a heavenly one."

"I talked this morning with Tom Connelly. I don't know if Leota ever mentioned him to you."

The old woman commenced her rocking again. "Leota trusted him. Shame she wasn't as discerning about others here."

"Connelly told me Leota left Nashville to tell the father of her child about the baby." Tessa leveled a hard stare at Ouida. "I'm guessing you were the next one to set eyes on her."

"When she arrived, she was, as the Good Book says, great with child. Didn't have to be a midwife to calculate she was breeding afore she left in October."

Tessa winced. The old-fashioned term always reminded her of farm animals. "I looked at her high school yearbook. Merritt Cozart was a classmate. Do you think he was the baby's father?"

Ouida Kittrell's mouth downturned. "I always wondered if it was Merritt. Him being a Cozart, maybe the reason she refused to tell me."

"What happened the last time you saw her?"

"First thing she done when she got to the cabin was scamper over to someplace near Cane Creek where they'd left notes for each other over the previous summer break."

"Did Leota write to him from Nashville?"

"She did, and never got no response." Ouida's eyes narrowed. "That ought to have told her something. That he didn't want no part of her nor the child."

Tessa leaned against the railing. "I'm sure that's not what she wanted to hear."

"We argued." Ouida sighed. "I regret that. But if I didn't try to make her see sense, who would? She was determined to talk to him. And she was convinced someone was trying to keep them apart."

"Over the next few days, did she work on her songs?"

"Until she got word to come meet him. Came back from Cane Creek clutching his note." Ouida scowled. "And no, I ain't got the note. She stuffed it in her skirt pocket and took it with her when she left last time."

Tessa waited for the old woman to say something else.

Ouida appeared determined to wear a groove in the porch planks. "Don't ask me where, 'cause I don't got nary an idea. But she took off like a shot . . ." She pointed her bony finger. "Through there."

For the first time, Tessa noticed the trace of a well-worn path that disappeared upward into a glade of trees. "That's the last time you ever saw Leota? When she didn't come back, weren't you concerned? Did you contact the sheriff?"

Rocking harder, Ouida glared at Tessa. "Let's imagine how that conversation would've gone." Puckering her mouth, the old woman pitched her voice. "'Mr. High Sheriff, sir, did you know your son Merritt has done got little Melungeon Leota in the family way?'" Ouida snorted. "Then maybe I'd have followed with 'I am afeared, Mr. High Sheriff, sir, your boy has done away altogether with the only thing—actually, the two millstones—that could keep him from achieving future football glory. Mayhap, you'll help me find her?'"

"Merritt Cozart's father was the sheriff before him?"

"You bet your sweet William he was."

Tessa bit her lip. "Maybe the baby's father wasn't a Cozart, but someone else. Perhaps we've been too quick to jump to conclusions."

"Where there's calamity, there's usually a Cozart." Ouida grunted. "And I never seen nothing to prove that a lie."

"Perhaps Leota continued to sing under a married name."

"Could be." Ouida's tone indicated she thought the likelihood of that about equal to winning the lottery. "Have you run across anyone in your research with a voice as pure and clear as what came forth from that child's being?"

She shook her head. That question had prompted her meeting with Dr. McClaine earlier. Ruth had become so intrigued she'd taken it upon herself to comb through the center's collection.

"Leota vanished off the face of the earth." Ouida got that strange look in her eye, as if she'd turned inward. Far, far away. "Or fell through one of the portals into another time and place."

Had the old woman lost her mind? With her living here alone all these years, no one could blame Ouida for being off-kilter. A kind way of saying crazy.

She knew she would regret asking, but she had to. "What do you mean *portals*?"

"In the old country, there were huge stone circles."

Tessa's mouth dropped. "Like Stonehenge?"

"My mam, who had both the blood of a Cherokee and a Scottish granny woman running through her veins, told me in these mountains the gateway to other worlds would only be found in three places." The old woman ticked off her fingers. "High on the balds. A deep pool in the river. Or beyond the cascade of a waterfall."

Tessa fought the urge to shiver. "There could be a thousand and one more sensible explanations for Leota's failure to return. People get busy raising a family, making a living."

Ouida steepled her hands in her aproned lap. "Only death silences that kind of gift." She gave Tessa a skewering look. "You know what I say is true. The aching need to sing is going to burn you up inside if you don't let it out, child."

A quiver of emotion spiraled inside Tessa. She'd felt the burning pressure building for days. "How can I sing when Sandy's voice has been quenched?"

"You sure about that, are you?" Ouida raised her eyebrow. "Some get short rows. But mayhap that child is making melody right now. Just somewhere else."

What do you think happens when somebody dies? She asked Zeke that just yesterday.

Did everything that made them unique die too? Or only the pain of their mortal flesh?

A leap of faith. A risk to believe. Ultimately, every choice was a risk. But the alternative was worse than unbearable.

Time to leap. To believe. To choose.

She blew out a breath. "Which of Leota's lullabies do you want me to sing first?"

Ouida had the grace not to smile, but triumph glinted in her dark eyes. "The 'Moonstone Lullaby.' For her moonstone baby. The last song Leota ever wrote."

Tessa set her bag on the step. Last night, rather than contemplate the what-might-never-be with Zeke, she'd pored over the music, memorizing each note.

After clearing her throat, she began the wistful tune.

Moonbeam beckons out the door,
And me wishing dreams
I never dreamt before.
Sleep, my moonstone baby.

Father Pine a-swaying,
Mother Moon a-shining,
Love and hope a-twining.
Silvered hills a-saying,
"Sleep, my dearest one, sleep."

Unable to continue, she fell silent.

Ouida said nothing. Just let her sort through her emotions until she could find her voice again.

"Do you think Leota ever got to sing this song to her ch-child?" Tears pricked Tessa's eyes. "Is it a wish-true lullaby? Or a never-shall-be song?"

"I don't know, Tessa. I've sung both in my time."

"What then is the point in the music, Miss Ouida? Why keep singing?"

"Because music is the crown we offer to the One we love." Her old face softened. "The music heals the hurts in our heart. We must let the music and the Giver of the gift do their perfect work. Finish it for me now, Tessa. Please."

Swallowing, she picked up the line from the final verse.

Mockingbirds a-calling,
Sound of leaves a-falling.
Sweet dreams ever more,
As older you grow.
Sleep, my moonstone baby.

Father Pine a-swaying,
Mother Moon a-shining,
Love and hope a-twining.
Silvered hills a-saying,
"Sleep, my dearest one, sleep."

A gentle hush settled over the women.

From lack of exercise, the muscle of her voice wasn't as strong as before, but sufficient. Enough. Accepted by the Giver?

"Thank you for that. I know it wasn't easy." A tear rolled unchecked down Ouida's wrinkled cheek. "But I promise you, next time won't be half as hard."

And Tessa acknowledged to herself that there would be a next time. It was who she was. How she'd been made. "Leota would've kept on singing." Tessa sighed. "You're right. Something terrible happened to her."

"Somebody, somewhere, knows the truth about my Leota." Ouida's mouth flattened. "I'm too old to be gadding about asking the right questions. But you're not."

The wind trembled through the treetops, sloughing through the branches. Leaves shivered with a brittle rustling.

"Leota left bits of the truth in that lullaby. You figure them out, and we'll find my little songbird." Abruptly, Ouida looked at the space over Tessa's shoulder. "He's come for you."

A black walnut fell, striking the porch with a *thud*.

Tessa nearly jumped out of her skin.

Chapter Fifteen

Tessa's throaty contralto stopped Zeke at the edge of the glen. His heart threatened to beat out of his chest. He couldn't have moved if he'd tried. There was a soothing quality in her voice.

She was singing a lullaby.

And an uncalled-for, vivid image floated sweet and pure through his mind. Of Tessa singing to a child in her belly. His child.

Breath hitching, he caught hold of the nearest tree and the rough bark scraped his hand. The scent of pine filled his nostrils. What was wrong with him?

"Hello, young man," the old woman called from the cabin. "Show yourself afore I fetch my gun."

As he pushed through the underbrush, Tessa spun around. The old woman had sharp eyes. Not many would've spotted him. He was sorry to have interrupted the open-air concert.

The old woman bunched her eyebrows together. "Should I be worried, Tessa?"

Cheeks pink, she shook her head. "He's nicer than he looks."

He folded his arms over his chest. "Thanks, I think."

She tucked a tendril of hair behind her ear. "You're welcome." She moistened her lips.

At the memory of those supple lips, pliant and fierce, the bottom dropped out of his stomach.

She tilted her head. "Are you following me, Ezekiel?"

"Don't hear that name every day." As she rose, the old woman's knees creaked—or was that the rocker? "Who your people be, boy?"

Her words were an invitation to come closer. Without getting buckshot. "My grandfather, Virgil Alexander, pastored in Buckthorn." He joined them on the porch. "My mother grew up here."

Tessa frowned at him. He'd surprised her by telling the old woman about his real background. He'd surprised himself.

"Don't know that I ever met your mother." Ouida Kittrell smiled, her eyes becoming dark half-moons. "But Virgil was one of the best men I ever did know. Unlike some I could name." Her eyes cut to Tessa. "He ain't one of them, is he?"

Tessa shook her head. "No, ma'am. Not at all."

Ouida Kittrell took hold of his chin.

He didn't pull away.

She tugged his face toward the light. "Blood will tell." She let go of his chin, and he wasn't sorry. "Take my hand, Ezekiel."

He looked at Tessa.

She shrugged.

He took the old woman's hand.

Lifting her face to the air, she squeezed his fingers. Hard. She stiffened, and a strange, absent look crossed her wrinkled features. Her eyes went opaque. Dicy had warned him about the spells Ouida sometimes took, but seeing it was an altogether different matter.

It was as if she left him and Tessa. Like she'd gone wandering someplace else. Some time else. Weird. And unsettling.

His gaze slid to Tessa. His eyes were probably as huge as her own.

"What is it, Miss Ouida?" Tessa rasped.

Raising chill bumps on his arms, a breeze ruffled the white hair in the old woman's bun.

"He has a gift yet unclaimed." Ouida Kittrell cocked her head, first one way and then the other, as if repositioning an antenna to a radio frequency only she could hear. "But you will find her. And later, there will be others. Many others. Yet you mustn't open the door to the darkness. 'Vengeance is Mine,' says the Lord."

Zeke went rigid.

Ouida Kittrell seemed to return to herself. She patted his hand before releasing him. "You would do well to remember an old Cherokee story my grandpappy used to tell about two wolves. It is the same terrible fight that goes on inside most people."

He tightened his jaw.

"One wolf is good, full of peace, love, hope, and faith. The other is evil, consumed by pride, greed, jealousy, and hate. Do you know which wolf wins the fight?"

He shook his head.

"The one you feed, Ezekiel. That's the one that will win."

Okay, he was officially freaked out now. How did she know about the desires churning inside him? About what he wanted to do to the Cozarts for hurting Kaci?

And she seemed so sure that he would find Kaci.

"Mercy, don't I know my belly is ready for lunch." Ouida became brisk. "I packed a basket for you two."

How had she known he was coming? He hadn't known he'd end up on Yonder Mountain today.

"It's a perfect day to climb to the bald. This weather won't last. It never does." The old woman closed her eyes and breathed deeply of the tang of autumn in the air. "It were a day like this on that bald my Foley first spoke his love to me." Her eyes opened, darting between him and Tessa. "Bring by the willow basket on your way back down the mountain."

Tessa reddened. "I'm sure Ezekiel has other things to do today."

"I 'spect he does. Yet when he gets my age, he won't remember the chores he ought to have done." She held her hands in front of her house-dress. "But he'll always regret the autumn days he let slip through his fingers."

The old woman was right. He rubbed his chin. "Would there happen to be in any pie in the basket?"

Ouida Kittrell smiled. The corners of her eyes crinkled, lifting her cheeks. "Just blueberry."

He narrowed his eyes. "Blueberry is my favorite."

A Mona Lisa smile. "I know."

Ten minutes later on the trail, Zeke hefted the weight of the basket in his hand. Clean air. Beautiful view—not the least of which included the leggy redhead striding ahead of him on the grassy incline leading to the bald.

"Why is it called a bald?"

Taking a giant stride, he caught up with her. A wind bent the tall grass, giving the swaying meadow flowers the illusion of dance.

"Because it's bald of trees, right?" She spun a slow three-sixty. "Feels like the top of the world."

Kaci would've loved Tessa's voice. He loved Tessa's voice. Was that all he loved about Tessa? He swallowed, placing the basket on a level patch of earth.

"I hate to spread Miss Ouida's quilt on the ground." She ran her palm over the stitched, bright petals. "It's so beautiful."

With effort, he removed his gaze from her mouth. "I don't mind sitting on the grass."

"She'll be offended if we don't use it. Might as well, I suppose." With a flourish, Tessa fanned the quilt over the grass.

Tomato sandwiches were the fare for the day. Probably from tomatoes plucked fresh off the old woman's vine. The last of the season.

He liked that Tessa didn't need to fill the silence. She was a comfortable person to be with. She seemed lighter today.

Perhaps because she'd been singing when he walked up on her and the old woman. Would the day ever come that she'd sing him a song?

"What did Ouida mean about you having a gift of your own yet unclaimed?" Tessa flipped onto her stomach and scissored her legs behind her into a V. "A gift of finding people?"

He didn't know what to make of the old woman's pronouncement. "You were the first. You should know."

"The rescue business." She looked at him, a question in her eyes. "Oh, like at the gas station with me." She rested her chin in her cupped hands. "I guess it does kind of fit with the whole secret agent thing."

"Special agent thing."

Tessa laughed. "That."

"Sometimes, though . . ." He didn't look up. "Sometimes it's too late for rescue. Only retrieval."

"But what's important is finding the lost person, right? Helping them find their way home."

One way or the other. And Tessa didn't even know the half of it. "Is this about helping you locate that Leota person?" He cut his eyes at Tessa. "You know I do have other things to do."

"Like the special agent thing."

He stuck his tongue in his cheek. "Like winterizing the orchard."

"And rounding up bad guys."

He touched his finger to her chin. "You are actually pretty cute."

She smiled.

"For a redhead."

She swatted at him.

Laughing, he rolled out of her reach. "You are so easy to tease, Red."

"Only 'cause I let you. Miss Ouida doesn't like strangers on her land. Good thing I was there to make sure she didn't shoot you."

"Good thing."

But in truth, getting to know Tessa had been its own gift. And no matter what the future held, he'd always be grateful.

Time to take another step of faith.

Because two weeks ago wasn't the first time he and Tessa had met.

❖   ❖   ❖

Zeke's smile faltered. "Do you remember yesterday at Cane Creek when we listened to the woodpecker and the squirrel?"

Tessa sat up and folded her legs under her. "I thought I was the only one who knew the sound game."

"What do you remember from when you were a little girl?"

"My earliest memories are sounds. There was a music to it, although in the beginning I had no idea what music even was."

"The music is your gift."

She nodded. "But after the fire, I lost the music. The gift was more of a curse. To have something like that, only to have it taken away . . ."

His eyes fastened on her face. "But now?" His voice had lowered into the raspy drawl that scraped her insides raw.

For a second, she became lost there. Glimpsing a possibility of which she'd dared not dream nor imagine. A depth and breadth of something she was still too afraid to believe in, much less reach for. Like the music, it could so easily once again be snatched away. "Now . . . here . . ." Her gaze swept over the grass softly swaying in the power of a gentle wind.

This was what shook her most about this man. Despite the rugged, gruff appearance, he was capable of such gentleness . . . at least with her.

"My voice was bigger than my little girl body. I could hear the notes in my head. When my stepmother brought me to the conservatory, the teachers said I had perfect pitch."

"How old were you?"

"Vita left me there for good when I was thirteen."

He scowled, but not at her. "Where was your father?"

"My father was emotionally distant after my mother died. He didn't know what to do with a little girl." She flashed a look at Zeke. "His military career was the excuse. A reason to always be on the move. It was my stepmother who put a name to my gift."

"When you needed him, he was never there for you."

"He looked for reasons to go." She shrugged. "Vita was desperately in love with a man who loved only his country and a dead woman. Theirs was not a happy marriage. I was better off at the conservatory. Vita let me spend summers with Dicy."

"I remember."

A white-hot awareness went through her. Gasping, she straightened. And she recalled, as if out of a dream, the slightly older, extremely quiet, blue-eyed boy who'd occasionally accompanied an old man to the orchard for a week every summer.

The younger Zeke Sloane, who first taught her the listening game, to attune to the world around her.

"It was you."

He inclined his head. "It was me."

"Why didn't you say something?"

He wouldn't meet her eyes. "If you didn't remember, it must not have mattered to you."

"After my mother died, I blocked out a lot because it was too painful. But what I do remember is almost drowning one summer and your jumping in to save me."

He twirled a blade of grass between his fingers. "A skinny, little redhead girl, who ought to have had more sense than to fall in a creek."

Baby Red. He used to tease her, calling her Baby Red. And tug at her hair.

She punched his arm. "I was nine."

"Ow." He rubbed his shoulder. "There's gratitude for you." His eyebrow quirked. "Seems like I've made a career of rescuing you."

"Seems like." She tilted her head. "But you stopped coming to the orchard."

His grin vanished. "My grandfather died." He dropped his gaze to the quilt.

She found his hand.

"Later, when I headed off to college, my mother wasn't ready for an empty nest. She said she needed someone to talk pedicures instead of football." His smile was bittersweet. "Then she hugged me to make sure I didn't feel slighted. I didn't. We made the decision as a family to foster a child."

"Your parents sound incredible."

"Kaci was sweet, cute, and funny."

Tessa stilled. Kaci was his family's foster child? That wasn't what she'd thought after what he'd let slip yesterday.

"Kaci was all mouth." He cut a glance at her. "Not unlike you."

"Hey."

"She needed a big brother. I needed . . ." He took a breath. "Someone to believe in me again."

"Why?"

"After GrandPop died, I never stopped feeling a little lost. But Kaci developed a huge case of hero worship on me."

"How old was Kaci?"

"Twelve."

She threaded her fingers through his. "Difficult years for a girl."

"I figured she'd outgrow her crush, especially when she went off to college. By that point, my parents had died in a car accident."

"Where were you?"

"After college, the urge to wander had taken me to the Army. Then the FBI."

She traced the back of his hand with her index finger. "The ultimate high for an adrenaline junkie. I'd like to meet Kaci."

"That would've been great." He extricated his hand from hers. "If she hadn't disappeared."

She listened with growing distress as he recounted the last facts he knew about Kaci's whereabouts, the real reason he'd come to Roebuck County. He also told her about Brandi's sister, what he suspected had happened to Kaci, and who he reckoned responsible.

Tessa detected the barest thread of hope in his voice that Kaci was out there somewhere. Alive. That the worst hadn't really happened to her. And Tessa heard his determination to find her.

"I'm sorry, Zeke." Inadequate words to an unimaginable horror. "I can't fathom the pain of a missing loved one." Or the desperation for answers.

Yet the more he told, the farther away from Tessa he moved, and not only physically.

She reached for him.

But shaking off her touch, he got to his feet.

She bit her lip. The emotional pulling away worried her the most. And now she understood why he'd been so overprotective every time she left the orchard. "That night at the gas station, you believe what happened to Emily would've happened to me?"

He stepped off the quilt. His nonanswer an answer in itself. He set the basket on the grass.

Tessa rose. She scooped the quilt into her arms and folded two corners together. But the wind caught the quilt, almost ripping it from her grasp.

Making a grab for it, Zeke got hold of the flapping end. He folded his half, and they met in the middle.

"You saved me, Zeke."

"But I didn't save her." A muscle ticked in his cheek.

And there it was—the crux of his issue. The guilt of not being able to save the one he loved. She'd been grappling for months with survivor guilt, for not saving Sandy from Anton.

Guilt had torn Tessa up inside. Paralyzed her voice. Trapped her in the past. Kept her from moving forward.

Just as it was doing to him.

"I should've done more for Kaci."

"What could you have done to stop her from being taken? Undeserved guilt is the cruelest taskmaster. It's irrational, and it flays its victims alive, one piece at a time."

"I should be doing more now. Instead of—" He looked away.

Instead of picnicking at the top of the world on a beautiful day with her. She tried not to feel the sting of his words. Guilt and grief were a toxic combination. He wasn't in a good place. She was just beginning to find her way out of her own nightmare.

But for him the nightmare of uncertainty hadn't yet ended.

A new fear licked at the edges of her mind. That he'd never find the answers for which he searched. "Suppose you don't find Kaci?"

"I can't accept that. I won't accept that."

She clamped her lips together. Yet another never-shall-be dream. And suddenly she was furious with him. For his stubbornness. For his determination to wreck his life.

The quilt draped over her arm, she plowed down the bald toward the grove of trees at the bottom.

He overtook her, his strides long and angry. In silence, they returned to Ouida's little house.

The old woman took the basket from him. Then the quilt from Tessa. "You two make me mad as fire. You've wasted the day by arguing."

He propped his foot on the step. "My sister disappeared off the Trail not far from here. I wonder if you saw or heard anything. Would've been April a year and a half ago."

Ouida didn't blink. "You're the one with the finding gift. Use it."

His mouth tightened. He pushed off. And not waiting for Tessa, he stalked down the path toward the road.

Tessa lifted her chin. "You said if I sang you a song, you'd let me see the rest of Leota's music."

"Can't you hear it, girl? Too much unrest in the air. The music has flown away for a better day." Ouida sniffed. "Come back tomorrow. Bring me some answers, and maybe I'll let you have a look-see at another song."

The leaves on the trees surrounding the cabin crackled in a brisk wind. The sound reminded her of dry bones rubbing together. She shivered.

So much for their bargain. But the old woman had Tessa over a barrel, and they both knew it. She wasn't sure where else to look for Leota. The trail had gone cold.

Unless she tackled Judson Cozart, who'd also attended Roebuck

High. Merritt Cozart had already warned her off. Perhaps, if she hadn't been so quick to burn the bridge with Colin, she might've gotten something useful that could've helped her trace Leota's movements.

Tears stung her eyes. After leaving the cabin, she crashed blindly through the underbrush. In light of what Zeke was going through, it seemed stupid to try to find some long-lost, obscure singer.

Suddenly, she wanted the warm comfort of Dicy.

Rushing headlong down the path, she ran smack into Zeke's solid chest.

Under the long, stabbing shadows of the pines, he'd waited for her after all. He hadn't left her.

Every inch of her burned where she'd stumbled into him. Her heart pounded. Dicy. The orchard. And yes, she wanted him too.

A fair wind riffled through the trees. A shower of scarlet leaves whirled.

She lifted her face and her arms. Twirling downward, the leaves brushed her cheek before falling to the ground.

Tessa wanted this.

Something in his features gentled. "Do you know how to tell the difference in the trees? It's easy this time of year."

She shook her head.

"That one with the red leaves is a maple." He pointed toward another. "The golden leaves are oak. Hickory is yellow."

"Where'd you learn all this?"

"My grandfather. He spent his life preaching in that little mountain church, trying to make a difference. I would've been a sad disappointment to him."

"Somehow I don't think so. Apples never fall far from the tree."

He rolled his eyes. "Spoken like a true Goforth."

She plucked an orange leaf from a bramble. "And what's this one?"

He gave her a slow, crooked smile that tumbled her insides. "See how the color almost seems to explode from that one?" He took it from her and held it to the dappled sunlight. "Elm." He twirled the leaf between his thumb and index fingers. "It matches your hair."

She scowled. "Does not."

A smile flickered at the corners of his mouth. "My favorite autumn color."

Suddenly breathless, she wasn't sure if he was talking about the leaf, her hair, or both.

"Not many that color. A rare find." He tucked the stem of the leaf behind her ear. His hand lingered on the curve of her cheek. "Like you."

"My voice used to set me apart, but I don't sing anymore."

He didn't remove his hand. "I wasn't talking about the music, Tess. I wish you could see you are so much more than your ability to perform."

When she was with him, she could almost believe . . . He made her want to believe.

Standing close, their breath mingled. If either of them moved a fraction of an inch, their lips would be touching.

Tessa desperately wanted to feel his mouth on hers. To feel the strength of his arms. To know the comfort of his embrace.

Without conscious thought, she caught his hand.

He didn't pull away. "Neither one of us are the kind who'll stay." His Adam's apple bobbed in his throat. "This isn't a good idea."

"And here I am thinking this would be a very good idea." She nuzzled her lips in his palm.

He dropped his hand.

She immediately missed the warmth of him on her skin. "I don't believe I ever properly thanked you for saving my life."

"You did. Later, in the barn."

She gave him a sideways look. "I meant when I was nine."

His mouth curved.

She took a tiny step closer, placing her hand on his shirt. She took no small satisfaction when the thump of his heart accelerated. "And by properly thanking you, I mean . . ." Fluttering her lashes, she walked her fingers down the muscles in his arm until she found his hand again.

"We shouldn't start something neither of us are able to finish." His brows drew together. "Yesterday was about satisfying our curiosity . . . Getting it out of our system."

"Oh." She let go of him. "Sorry. I'm an idiot." Face flaming, she turned sharply on her heel.

Could she have made a bigger fool of herself? She might want him. But he didn't feel the same.

Chapter Sixteen

Zeke knew he should let her walk away. But something inside him couldn't bear—wouldn't allow him—to let her go. He caught her arm. "You didn't misunderstand. I . . . I . . ." He slid his hands down her arms and back again. Cupping her elbows, he pulled her into him.

Tucked under his chin, she fit into his embrace like she'd been made for him. Perhaps she had.

"I'm the idiot, Tess. I . . ."

"Stop talking, Ezekiel." She raised her gaze. "Kiss me, plea—"

His mouth seized hers with an urgency he'd never known before. And he lost track of where she ended and he began.

The buzzing in his brain quieted.

Perspiration had curled stray tendrils of her hair around her face. Cradling her head, his hands delved into her hair. "Silk," he said against her mouth.

"W-what?" She breathed against his neck.

He brushed his thumb across the apple of her cheek.

She answered him, kiss for kiss, with a passion that stole his breath. Her hands moved across the broad planes of his shoulders. And then she was combing her fingers through the short ends of hair on the nape of his neck.

The unexpected kaleidoscope of emotion left him reeling. Long time a-coming indeed. He hadn't been truthful before.

One kiss would never satisfy. Not what was between him and Tess. He might never be able to get her out of his system.

He pulled back, keeping her within the circle of his arms. "Tess . . ."

There was so much he was feeling. Feelings he didn't know how to put into words. Things he wasn't free to express when their lives were in turmoil.

She ran the tip of her finger across his beard whiskers. "Soft, like I thought." Her husky voice sent tingles along his nerve endings.

He moistened his bottom lip. "You've been wondering about me, have you?"

At the stirring of leaves, she nestled her back against his chest, drawing his arms around her again.

Splashes of color dotted the hillsides ringing the valley below.

A ceaseless wind buffeted their clothing. He dug his heels in the soft earth and leaned the side of his face against her forehead.

"I wish-true we could stay here forever," she whispered.

So did he. But it wasn't possible. "I can't think beyond finding Kaci."

Tessa turned in his arms. "I understand bringing her justice has to be your main priority." She rested her cheek against the brushed flannel of his shirt.

Did she truly understand? Because he wasn't sure he did anymore. Justice and an obsessive need for revenge had gotten mixed up in his head.

But then there was the way he felt when he was with Tessa. He had no defenses when it came to her. A surefire way to get himself and everyone, including Tessa, killed.

He knew in a place deep inside himself that his craving for mountain justice and his craving for Tessa could not coexist. The one was bound to destroy the other. And one day—one day soon—he was going to have to choose.

There was too much unfinished business for both of them.

He wasn't free to pursue a relationship with her. Not until he'd brought closure to the other woman in his life. And after what he planned to do to the monsters who killed Kaci, he wouldn't be fit for Tessa.

What he was about to say would hurt her, but he couldn't see a way forward for them.

He thrust her away.

Startled, she parted her lips.

"We can't do this." He scrubbed his face. "I can't do this."

"Give us a chance." Her voice hitched, a half sob. "Give me a chance."

"There is no us." He scowled. "This is a mistake."

She touched her finger to her lips, still plump, slightly swollen from his kiss. "I don't believe you. You're scared of losing someone again."

"Kissing you was a mistake."

Her eyes pooled.

If she cried . . . He couldn't stand it if he made her cry. Even if what he was doing was for her own good. "You and I were each other's one that got away." He threw her the half-lidded, lazy grin country boy charm he did so well. "Let's be adults and chalk this up to the road not taken."

"Don't try to work me, Zeke. It doesn't have to be this way."

"Yes, it does. All that matters to me is Kaci," he growled. "You're a distraction I don't need."

He recognized the moment when steel entered her spine. The grit that enabled her to survive a madman. Moisture evaporating from her eyes, she lifted her chin. And once again, she became the remote, ethereal, flatlander snob.

A defensive mechanism. They were both so good at facades. If he wasn't so afraid of loving her—

Whoa. Where had that come from? Attraction, sure. A physical chemistry like none he'd ever known, yes. But he didn't do love. Love came at a price—a price he wasn't willing to pay.

She held herself rigidly erect. "Apple season is almost finished, correct?"

Zeke gave her a curt nod.

Her gaze scathed him. "Until then, I think it would be best if we kept out of each other's way. Gave each other space before I leave."

"You're planning to leave?"

"Unlike my father, I look for reasons to stay." She glared at him. "Other than Dicy, is there any reason for me to stay?"

"No," he choked.

Her lips thinned. "I didn't think so." And she walked away.

He had a sinking feeling he'd done something he'd bitterly regret.

But better that she was angry with him than the darkness inside him taint the light in her. She didn't get it, but he was saving her again. This time from himself.

❖ ❖ ❖

The next couple of days were excruciating. And maddening. Tessa wanted to scream. She wanted to yell. She wanted to throw things.

Mainly at Zeke.

It was exhausting work, avoiding someone.

Coming down the stairs at the farmhouse, she fumed. On the landing, she came to an abrupt halt. Dicy had the vacuum out.

"You shouldn't be doing that, Aunt Dicy. Please let me run the vacuum cleaner."

Ignoring her, Dicy continued to unwind the long cord of the upright.

"Why is everyone in my life so stubborn?" Tessa reached ground level. "At least let me plug it into the socket for you."

"If you don't use it . . ." Her aunt did a little two-step just to demonstrate she could. "You lose it. Miles to go afore I sleep, cinnamon bun. Miles to go."

Straightening, Tessa blew the hair out of her eyes. "Nurses make the worst patients."

"Zeke told me about Brandi's sister." Dicy's mouth quivered. "Poor girl. So sad."

She gestured at the window. "Why didn't you tell me the orchard manager you hired was Zeke Sloane?"

"I did tell you I hired Zeke, Tessie."

She threw out her hands. "But not that he was *Zeke* Zeke.

"Your Zeke."

"He's not . . ." She pressed her lips together.

She'd told her aunt what happened yesterday at Ouida's. Well, not everything. No need to go into the push-pull, non-thing happening between her and the undercover agent.

"How was I to know you wouldn't recognize each other? Oh, wait." Eyebrow raised, Dicy folded her arms. "He did recognize you."

Tessa tapped her foot on the rug. "Sarcasm doesn't become a woman of your age, Aunt Dicy."

"Sarcasm doesn't become any age, missy."

Tessa glowered.

"I thought you'd be pleased to see each other."

Pleased wasn't the predominant emotion Tessa was feeling.

"You two were thick as thieves as children. A week every summer—"

"Until he stopped coming." Her mouth twisted. "Men." She threw out her hands. "They never stay. Always looking a reason to go."

"Zeke didn't leave you. His grandfather died." Dicy's mouth pursed. "Get over it."

Her aunt didn't often take that tone with her. But when she did . . .

"I'm sorry, Aunt Dicy. I guess I might as well get over it." She tucked her hair behind her ears. "He has."

Dicy's eyes cut to the ceiling. "I'm too old for this foolishness, Lord." She shook the vacuum. "I'm about done with the two of you moping like pure-D fools over each other."

"I'm not moping."

"Don't I know I rue the day I ever sent you to Ouida." Dicy wagged her finger. "She's gotten you consumed in that sordid business with the ballad singer."

Tessa drew up. "It's research for my dissertation."

"What you call research smacks to me of deflection." Dicy made a sweeping motion toward the window overlooking the orchard. "Easier than coming to grips with what really ails you."

"That's not true."

But was it? Zeke had shut her out. His past with Kaci was a world he wouldn't let Tessa enter. Nor would he allow her to help him come to terms with his grief.

Like so much else in her life, the wish-true dream had become a never-shall-be.

So yeah, from where she was standing—*alone*—deflection sounded about right.

And Leota's fate gnawed at her.

In the cold light of day, off that haunted mountain, it seemed fantastical that a young man like Merritt would have done away with the mother of his child.

More likely, Leota had gone away with her non-Cozart lover and faded into obscurity like so many others, never quite reaching her potential.

One day, would people say the same of Tessa?

She scrolled through her phone and showed Dicy the photo she'd taken of the senior class of 1988. "Do you remember if any of these kids were Leota's friends?"

Dicy pointed to a small photo under the *b*'s. "I forgot Anjanette Bascombe was in that class." She made a face. "That was before she married the oldest Cozart brother. She and Leota were sometime friends."

"The judge's wife?"

"A real step down in the world for him. If what you say is true about Leota, Merritt wasn't the only brother to get a girl in the family way." Dicy shrugged. "At least Colin's father married Anjanette."

"I haven't met Colin's mother yet."

Dicy went back to the vacuum she'd abandoned at the foot of the stairs. "You ain't missed nothing, let me tell you. She was one of those good-for-nothing Bascombes. Enough said."

Actually, maybe Tessa had missed something.

If Merritt Cozart wouldn't answer her questions about Leota Byrd, perhaps someone else in his family would.

"Which brother married Colin's mother?"

"Ransom was four grades ahead. Went out of state to college, I think. Didn't see much of him other than during the usual holiday breaks until he graduated law school and set up practice in Buckthorn."

"And now he's the judge."

"Old Man Cozart made sure of it." Dicy pressed a lever with her foot, lowering the upright handle. "Don't go messing with that crowd." Her aunt grimaced. "Yet no matter what I say, I know you'll do what you want. I ain't the only stubborn Goforth. But mark my words, you sow the wind, you'll reap a whirlwind."

It beat agonizing over the never-shall-be, though. And running into Zeke.

But first, she made Dicy sit down, then Tessa vacuumed the house.

She couldn't remember the last time she'd used the white pages, but today Dicy's old-school phone book came in handy.

Tessa found a number listed for Cozart, Ransom. A woman with a heavy accent answered the phone. Anjanette Cozart wasn't at home, but in town for the day, the housekeeper said.

Less than an hour later, she stood outside the judge's chambers at the courthouse. The plaque on the door said Ransom W. Cozart. No one stood guard at the deserted desk in the outer office.

She rapped on the door.

"Come," barked an authoritative voice.

Twisting the gold-plated knob, she pushed into the wood-paneled inner office lined with bookshelves and heavy legal tomes.

Seated behind a huge mahogany desk, a fifty-something man in a judge's robe paged through a folder. "Just set the coffee to the side, Norma."

When Tessa didn't answer, he looked up.

His brow furrowed. His eyes were the same intense shade as the other Cozarts.

"Norma wasn't at her desk."

"So I see." He leaned back in the leather chair, lacing his hands together on his chest. "And you are?"

"Tessa Goforth. My aunt—"

"I should've recognized you. It isn't often our humble mountain burg is blessed with a singer of your caliber." He rolled a pearlescent cabochon ring around on his pinkie. "Although, as a simple man and a native son, I've always preferred traditional folk music."

The framed diplomas mounted on the wall belied his claim of being a "simple" man. Undergrad at a prestigious Virginia college, graduating in 1987. Law school at the University of North Carolina—1990.

Ransom Cozart hadn't been around Roebuck County in that last crucial year of Leota's life, but perhaps he could direct Tessa to Anjanette.

She took a step closer to the desk. "I'm sorry to interrupt. I was actually looking for your wife."

"Why?"

No one's fool, this man.

She'd need to speak carefully so as not to rouse his suspicions or make him go into protective mode over his younger brother the sheriff. Was she already doomed to failure with him because she was Kittrell kin? She wasn't sure she'd do any better at getting answers than Ouida had thirty years ago.

Tessa quickly explained her research project. He was an intellectual man, so she went into the whole shebang—the richness of the Blue Ridge ballad tradition and the folk music revival after the Bicentennial.

"And my wife would be of interest to you because . . . ?"

"Because she was friends with a talented ballad singer from Roebuck High. Her name was Leota—"

Ransom Cozart bolted upright. "Leota Byrd."

She smiled. "Her voice. Unforgettable, isn't it?"

His hand spasmed. Streaming through the tall, wide-sashed window, a sunbeam glinted off his ring. "I haven't heard that name spoken in a long, long time."

"Whose name?"

At the door, an anorexic-thin blonde glowered.

"Leota Byrd. I understand you two were friends."

Anjanette Cozart's pale lips tightened. "We *were* friends, Miss Goforth."

Buckthorn was a small place. Tessa's "fame" had preceded her. Or the Cozarts kept close watch on their enemies.

Anjanette Cozart settled her purse over her arm. "Once Leota made it big, she never looked back."

Staring into Anjanette's eyes wasn't unlike watching the slow blink in a reptile's languid gaze. A shiver oozed down Tessa's spine.

Lips twisting, Mrs. Cozart looked at her husband. "But fame and fortune takes some people that way, doesn't it, Ransom?"

Mouth working, the judge appeared to have shrunk several sizes into himself.

"Some people forget where they come from." Anjanette fluttered her hand. "Silly, vain little Leota. No better than she ought to be." The large diamond set in a platinum band had to be at least twenty carats.

Ransom Cozart's lips drew back in a snarl. "I think it is only you, Anjanette, who prefers to forget where you came from."

Unmistakable hurt flashed across the woman's features. What a not-so-happily married couple. No wonder Colin was such a piece of work.

The look Anjanette unleashed on Tessa was neither friendly nor nice. As if somehow Tessa was to blame for her husband's outburst.

Might as well go for broke.

"When Leota returned from Nashville that May of '88, did you see or speak with her, Mrs. Cozart?"

Cozart rose to his full height. "Leota came back to town?" Brow knotted, he drilled his gaze at his wife. "Did you know about this, Anjanette?" Anjanette's clawlike hand seized onto Tessa's arm. "Stuck-up little nobody." She hauled Tessa toward the door.

Tessa wasn't sure if the insult was directed at Leota or herself.

"Did you know this redheaded little tart humiliated our son Saturday night?" Anjanette hissed.

Okay, she'd meant Tessa.

She dug in her heels. "Did you know Leota was nine months pregnant?"

Cozart sucked in a breath. "Wh-what are you talking about?"

With a mighty shove, Anjanette pushed Tessa into the outer office.

"Ask Merritt about it, Judge Cozart," Tessa hollered. "He'll know."

"Get out!" Anjanette Cozart yelled. "And stay out!" She slammed the door in Tessa's face.

That hadn't gone well.

And she'd probably have bruises to show for her efforts. Perhaps she'd gotten off lucky, though. At least, Anjanette hadn't drawn blood.

In the corridor, she nearly stumbled into a mousy middle-aged woman clutching a steaming cup of coffee. Wide-eyed, Cozart's secretary stared as Tessa skirted past.

Within the hour, Buckthorn's small-town Southern grapevine would make sure Dicy knew what she'd done. Which was exactly what her aunt had warned her against.

She'd poked the bear. Stirred the hornet's nest. Sown the wind.

But it would be interesting to see what shook loose.

Midmorning, she climbed the path on Yonder Mountain.

Ouida was turning over the soil in the small garden plot beside the cabin. "You brung me answers so soon?"

"I talked to Anjanette and her husband this morning. She wasn't Leota's friend."

Ouida straightened her apron over her house dress. "I never said she was." The hemline sagged past the knotted varicose veins on the old woman's bare calves. "You been in the lion's den right early today."

Tessa was glad of the warmth of her puffy fleece vest. "Anjanette Cozart would not be the first to begrudge a talent like Leota's or her success."

"Jealousy is an ugly emotion." Ouida leaned the hoe against the chinked exterior wall of the cabin. "Walk with me, child. I could use the company and your strong back. I'm hunting sang today."

Tessa looked at her blankly.

"Ginseng. Quit standing there like you've took root and grab my poke. Just inside the door. Come on, you might learn something."

Tessa took the porch steps two at a time. Inside the house, she grabbed a burlap sack hanging from a hook. From force of habit, she shut the door behind her.

By the time they left the cabin behind, she was already panting for breath. Of course, the terrain was mostly uphill.

Dicy had been right. They should all be as agile as ninety-something Ouida Kittrell. Part mountain goat, the old woman about walked Tessa into the ground.

"Lookie, right there, why don't you?" In the filtered shade at the edge of the forest, Ouida paused beside a low, leathery plant with broad, glossy green leaves. "Late July, you find it by the small white blossoms. In fall, like now . . ." She touched the end of her stout stick to the shiny red berries. "You look for the berries. Wintergreen. Makes a good tea."

Tessa's expression must've betrayed her skepticism.

"Nature gave us her bounty to cure our ills long before there were Walmart pharmacies."

She arched her eyebrow into a question mark. "You know about Walmart?"

Ouida stuck out her black sneaker. "I'm Walden Pond, not Unabomber." She handed Tessa the bag. "Bend down and pick the leaves for me. We'll let them dry to a crisp for several days in a brown paper sack . . ."

Tessa crouched beside the plant.

"Put a handful in a pot of boiling water . . ."

Tessa plucked the leaves.

"On low heat, allow the tea leaves to steep until the water turns a dark amber ... Tuck 'em in that there bag. The aroma will fill my kitchen something wonderful."

Slinging the bag over her shoulder, Tessa rose.

"I'll brew some for you to give Dicy." Ouida moved off at a brisk pace. "You and Dicy can pour yourselves a cup, plus a dollop of honey . . ."

Something in her voluminous apron pocket clanged with each step. "The tea will put Dicy to rights in no time."

She traipsed after the old woman.

"Autumn has always been my favorite time of year. Did Dicy ever tell you about apple butter–boiling day?"

"No, ma'am."

"A popular courting activity in times long past." Ouida gave her a shrewd look. "I seen how that boy looks at you when he thinks nobody else is watching."

"That boy is a thirty-one-year-old man with more issues than you could shake that stick at." Tessa pursed her lips. "Takes more than just looking to court."

Ouida cackled, slapping her hand on her thigh. "That was the whole point of apple butter boiling, honey. It took two, in close proximity, to stir the heavy iron pot." She winked. "You children got no idea how to have fun. Not like we did."

Remembering the kiss on the mountain path, she blushed. That had been more than fun. More like earth-shattering. Until he pushed her away in no uncertain terms. He'd made his feelings plain. Zeke wasn't interested in her.

Ouida let out a shout of triumph. "Step lively."

She clambered after the old woman. "What's wrong? Are you hurt?"

"Would you look at that purty patch of yellow-gold leaves?" Ouida touched a finger to the side of her rather prominent nose. "Every sang hunter has their secret spots. Best found on a northern slope."

Tessa inspected the plant. It also contained a bunch of red berries. "You want me to pluck the leaves again?"

Ouida's head reared a fraction. "I can see your education has been sadly neglected." She jabbed the stick into the base of the plant. "Got to dig the roots on this one. That's where the money is." She whipped a small trowel out of her apron pocket.

Ah, the clanging noise.

Under the old lady's precise supervision, Tessa extracted the forked, man-shaped root from the ground.

"Give it to Dicy. She's my middleman."

Tessa tucked it into the burlap bag. "Ginseng hunting is legal, isn't it?"

"You think I'm a drug cartel matriarch?" The old woman hooted. "I have a license to hunt sang this time of year. I'm not dragging you into any illegal trafficking ring, I promise."

It was the most cheerful she'd ever seen the old woman. And Tessa was glad she'd come today. The sky was a mesmerizing azure. The mountains, a hazy blue ripple. The trees were gaudy with autumnal splendor, copper gilded and infused with a kind of magic. Or maybe it only appeared so because of the company she was keeping these days. Because of Zeke.

She was a fool. Setting herself up for heartache. Tessa shook herself. She was well shed of Ezekiel Sloane.

Ouida and her Foley. Leota and her young lover. Even hateful Anjanette and Ransom Cozart.

Tessa had only to recall the ballads to know love always seemed to end in tragedy.

Her father and Vita too. *Must love always lead to pain and betrayal? Disillusionment?* Her mother and father had been happy, Aunt Dicy said.

And yet her mother's death left Tessa's father so broken he was never the same. Left him unable to love her, the child of their love, again.

The only truly healthy, happy marriage she'd ever witnessed was her aunt and Uncle Calvin's. So where did that leave her?

Stupid to reach for more.

Tessa brushed the soil off her hands. "What was Leota wearing the last time you saw her?"

"Not those." Ouida pointed the stick at Tessa's jeans. "In warm weather, she liked flowy skirts and blouses."

"Like the album cover." After finding the photo in her phone, she held up the image of Leota at the waterfall.

"You young'uns are going to ruin your eyes with that contraption." The old woman craned her neck, studying the small screen. "Very near the same outfit as that picture. She was wearing her moon earrings. A matching ring too. The falls aren't far."

That was news. "Usually, record producers arrange photo shoots for album covers. I had no idea the waterfall was in Roebuck County."

Ouida leaned on the gnarled handle of the stick. "I've not been since I was a girl. My mam told me to stay away from that place. Mayhap, a portal."

She hoped Ouida wasn't going to start that spooky portal business again. Tessa fiddled with the zipper on her vest. "The waterfall must've had a special significance for Leota to want it on her first album."

"A secret trysting place for young lovers?" Ouida nodded. "I knew you'd figure it out."

"Maybe it means something." She shrugged. "Maybe it doesn't. I'll check it out."

The old woman shook her head. "Don't be heading off there by yourself. It's called a wilderness for a reason. Best get that young man of yours to go with you."

Only problem was Zeke wasn't her young man.

And Kaci seemed to be so much more to him than a foster sister.

It was more what he didn't say than what he did. But she had a feeling—a sad, hopeless feeling—there was a lot more between him and Kaci than he would admit. Perhaps even to himself.

When he found the answers he was seeking, would it be enough? Would she be enough? Was there any point in hanging around, hoping he'd change his mind?

Any chance for more between her and Zeke might've been doomed before it could even begin. It was that fear, replacing the terrible fire in New Orleans, that now kept her awake, tossing and turning far into the night.

Chapter Seventeen

He didn't relish the prospect of another disturbing incident with the loony Kittrell woman, so Zeke waited beside Tessa's car, which was parked by the Cozart backhoe at the base of the mountain.

Why did everything have to be so complicated?

Tessa made his life complicated. No, that wasn't entirely true. It was his feelings warring against family obligations that complicated his life.

Obligation? Is that how he really felt? Shame smote him. Kaci deserved more than obligation from him.

Despite the bright sunshine, he shivered. Whatever gift Ouida Kittrell believed he had wasn't doing him any good if he couldn't find Kaci.

But it was Tessa who occupied his thoughts. She was the last thing he thought of at night. First thing every morning. He couldn't get her out of his head.

She was right about them giving each other room. Yet here he was. Unable to go another hour without talking to her, being with her. He missed her more than he'd reckoned.

At the sound of someone coming through the underbrush, he glanced up.

Carrying a burlap bag, Tessa emerged from the shadows. She stiffened. "What are you doing here?"

He pushed off from her car. "I didn't like the way we left things the other day."

Dropping the sack, she narrowed her eyes at him. "Oh, I think you were very clear on how things stood between us." Her mouth flattened.

If he had any sense at all, he would get into his truck and leave. He certainly wouldn't have come looking for her. He wouldn't be moving toward her.

But he had. He did. He was.

He closed the gap between them. "Space is not what I'm wanting from you, Red."

She flipped her hair over her shoulder. "What is it then you're wanting from me, Zeke Sloane?"

Touching her was always a mistake. But he took her in his arms anyway. He lowered his head. "This."

And this time there was nothing tentative in his exploration of her mouth. Familiar territory that had been surveyed before, claimed now.

Melting into him, she kissed him back. Deepening his kiss. Her mouth as hungry as his own.

He felt ravenous for her. Starved for the petal softness of her lips. It seemed he'd waited his whole life for her mouth on his. For these weeks with her again.

Fire ignited a place within him he'd never thought would know warmth. His hands drifted down the length of her back, pressing into each contour of her spine.

Her eyelids fluttered, a smoldering green fire. She stifled a deep-throated groan. Her breath grazed his earlobe and his heart seized.

Zeke pulled back only for breath and returned for more. His lips brushed her cheek and burrowed into the delicate part of her neck.

She swayed against him to a melody as old as time. "Good afternoon to you too, Ezekiel."

That sultry, husky voice of hers. Sensuous as all get-out. He kissed her forehead.

He needed to stop before he couldn't.

With regret, he pulled away. "I shouldn't have said those things on the mountain path, Tess. I can't think straight right now."

"Just so we're clear, it's not space you're after but . . . ?"

"Time." He gulped. "Not being with you isn't working for me."

"Such a master of mixed signals, Ezekiel. No wonder you're so good at playing games."

"You're not a game to me, Tess. You never were."

"Time?" She folded her arms. "That's what you want?"

He nodded.

"No promises." Her mouth twisted. "Promises are words waiting to be broken. Find Kaci. And after that—" She lifted her chin. "We'll see how we feel."

He'd hurt her, and she didn't trust him. He didn't blame her. But the loss of her trust still hit him between the eyes.

Tessa tucked a tendril of hair behind her ear. "I've missed you too, Zeke."

And something, not unlike the feeling of being tossed a rope while on the edge of disaster, eased the too-rapid beating of his heart. He exhaled. "What have you and that crazy old lady been up to today?"

She hefted the burlap bag. "I've been 'sang hunting,' Ezekiel."

"What else would a singer hunt?"

She tilted her head. "Imagine my surprise to come off the mountain and find you."

"Where else would you expect to find a backwoods ninja like me?"

She clicked her key fob, popped the trunk, and stowed the bag. "I figured you might be busy with the usual mischief and mayhem."

"But no bimbos." He touched his finger to her cheek. "Seems I prefer redheads. Who knew?"

Rising on her tiptoes, she planted a quick peck on his mouth. "Redheads rule. Don't forget."

His arms went around her waist again. "I never forgot."

She scanned his features. "Is everything okay? Nothing's happened has it?"

"I'm going over to Gib's tonight. He's almost ready to spill. I feel it. I'm so close . . ."

She rested her head in the hollow of his shoulder. "I wish-true this was over for you."

He scraped his beard stubble across the red silk of her hair, and she shivered. It did funny things to his heart knowing his touch pleased her. "What were your plans for the rest of the day, Tess?"

She looked up. "What did you have in mind?"

He cocked his head.

She laughed, and play-smacked his chest. "Besides that."

"What could be better than kissing all day?"

Lips curving, she rolled her eyes. "Feel like taking a break from your cover? How about being the real Zeke for a while and go exploring with me?"

Trouble was these days he wasn't exactly sure where the cover stopped and where he started. Who was Zeke Sloane? But when he was with her, he felt more like himself. A better version of the old him.

She showed him the waterfall photo. "Ouida says it isn't far, but I shouldn't go alone."

"For once, the old lady and I agree."

Tessa tucked the phone into her pocket. "I have a feeling she's going to prove right about a lot of other things."

"Like?"

She sighed. "Ouida thinks I ought to sing again."

"I do too."

She looked at him. "Why?"

"Because I think your voice is too beautiful not to be heard." He wove his fingers in hers. "Only if you want to, though."

They smiled at each other.

"Let's drop off your car at the orchard. We can take my truck."

"Do you know where to find the falls?"

"I think I do."

An hour later, he parked in the final jumping off point into the no-man's-land of the wilderness area. They ventured past the Forest Service sign, the last remnant of civilization.

GrandPop had shown him the trail, thick with laurels, to the water-fall. Once.

It was a starkly beautiful, solitary valley enclosed within the veil of a wall of blue-green mountains. A dense forest, cloaked in oak, beech, and maple. Filled with lacy hemlocks and nestled in a brushy hollow.

He rested his shoulder against the gray lichen on the trunk of a balsam, letting her catch her breath.

Somewhere in the distance, there was a sound of water.

They followed Sassafras Creek upstream for over a mile. A brook trout flashed silver in the shallow, unpolluted creek. The perpetual, dull roaring became louder.

Suddenly, the wild beauty of the gorge rose before them and his breath hitched. He offered his hand to help her climb over a granite outcropping.

Water droplets trickled off the promontory.

"Don't look down. Find traction before you place any weight on the step."

She placed her long-fingered hand in his.

He felt a surge of warmth.

They emerged from the thicket of rhododendron into a glade that contained a wide, deep pool. Curling cinnamon ferns fringed the clearing. The current temporarily slowed before being swallowed into the churning water.

Craning skyward, they both gaped at the sheer volume of water cascading off the high rock face.

"This is the place." She pointed to a massive granite slab on the far bank. "Leota must've stood there for the photo."

Before he could call her back, she hopped her way across the path of half-submerged, tumbled rocks. Velvety and moss covered. Damp and slippery.

On the other side of the stream, she struck a pose on the slab, imitating Leota's pose in the photo.

Disquiet churned his stomach. "There's a Cherokee legend about a fish monster called the *dakwa*. It catches the unaware and drags them forever down to its lair of doom."

She laughed. "Reminds me of Ouida's deep river portal."

He held out his hand. "Come away from there, Tess. You're too close to the base of the waterfall. One slip . . ."

"You're not suggesting the fish monster ate Leota, are you?" But she must have seen something in his face. She retraced her steps and reached for his hand.

Heart stuttering, he pulled her to him. To safety. He slid his hands down her arms and just held her. "There's something about this place . . ."

She feathered his hair with her fingers. "Time out of mind, isn't it?"

"It's more dangerous than you suppose." He let go of her and pried a stick from the thick carpet of moldering leaves. He tossed it into the center of the roiling falls. As if caught in the spin cycle of a washer, the stick spiraled before disappearing from view.

"It's a hydraulic. Look at the way the water on the surface swirls. Anything gets sucked under there . . ."

Her eyes went wide. "It doesn't ever come up again."

Zeke glanced around the remote, thicketed knob. An earthy smell of leaf mold permeated the air.

"Is that what happened to Leota?" Tessa stepped closer to his side. "Do you think she came here to meet her lover and fell into the hydraulic?"

"Or was pushed. We shouldn't assume she was out here alone." He wrapped his arm around Tessa's waist. "She wouldn't be the first baby mama done away with by an entitled jerk not ready to settle down." The place gave him the willies, and he was not a man who was afraid of much. "She didn't take the picture of herself, Tess. At least one other time—if not the last—she was here with someone else."

❖   ❖   ❖

"Look at her expression." Tessa studied the photo on her phone. "Leota's smiling at the camera."

Zeke looked at Tessa. "The way a woman looks at her lover."

Without conscious thought, she opened her mouth. "Black is the color of my true love's hair, and I love the ground on which he stands . . . "

The notes rose almost as high as the cascade, floating in the air, bouncing off the granite outcropping, a lingering, resonant echo of bygone days.

Dropping her eyes, she flushed. She hadn't been able to hold in the music. Not when he looked at her that way.

Zeke touched his finger under her chin and tipped her face to look at him. "You don't have to be afraid to sing. There's nothing that comes out of your mouth that's not the most beautiful sound I've ever heard."

Her gaze misted. The longer she remained in these mountains with him, the more she felt like singing. As if she'd been given a new song, she no longer felt afraid or ashamed. And that was in no small measure owing to the man who held her heart in his hands.

For the first time, she understood what Ouida meant about "knowing." Because with devastating clarity, she knew she loved Zeke Sloane.

She loved him for his strength, his courage, his warrior spirit. His grin. Even for the pain gouging his soul. For everything that made him who he was.

But taking a page from his pay-for-every-word playbook, she bit back the words. She couldn't yet trust he was being entirely truthful with himself about his deep feelings for the young woman who'd brought him here. Perhaps he'd never feel for Tessa what he did for Kaci.

Swallowing past the emotion clogging her throat, she resisted the temptation to throw herself into his arms. "If it's all the same to you . . ." She wrapped her arms around herself. "I'd just as soon continue this conversation somewhere else."

He coiled his finger around a strand of her hair, a quizzical look in his eyes.

Shaken by the depth of her personal revelation, she removed her hair from his hand and stepped away. He turned toward the path. What would Ouida have "knowed" about this hidden glen? What undercurrents would she have gleaned here?

Hurrying after Zeke, Tessa shuddered.

Ouida would've called it a presence. Tessa preferred to think of it as an atmosphere. She cast one final glance over her shoulder at the waterfall.

It wasn't a place she'd want to venture to alone. Especially in the dark.

When they stepped out of the trees, the sun was just beginning its daily plunge behind the mountain. Late afternoon bathed the river valley in shadow. Already, the last rays of sun flecked the distant peaks a golden pink.

Zeke unlocked his vehicle, and they climbed into his truck. As he reached to turn the key, a pickup bearing the Cozart Development Corporation logo hurtled into the deserted lot.

Thirty yards distant, the truck screeched to a stop. The passenger window lowered. The cold steel barrel of a rifle appeared.

He shoved Tessa down into the seat.

"What's—?"

"Get down!"

A balaclava-clad figure squeezed off three fast shots.

Zeke threw himself over her.

The first bullet kicked dust between the vehicles. The second zinged off the driver-side mirror. The third smashed the window.

She screamed as glass exploded, showering them.

A sharp pain burned through his shirt into his back. He didn't stop to think. His training kicked in and he just reacted. He did what he had to do.

Zeke jerked the Remington from the gun rack. Crawling over her, he pushed open the passenger door.

"Don't go out there." She grabbed for him. "Stay here."

If he stayed, they'd die. He jumped to the ground. The impact jarred, and he winced at the stinging pain.

Gunshots peppered the truck.

Hands over her head, Tessa curled into a protective ball in the foot of the vehicle.

Crouching low, he snapped off the safety and levered a shell into the chamber. He was proud she wasn't one of those women who continued to shriek during a crisis.

Red was tougher than she looked. A survivor. Like he was.

Creeping forward, he used the Chevy as cover. He raised the gun to fire, fixing his gaze over the hood and onto the shooter behind the wheel of the Dodge Ram. Standing, he locked the shotgun against his shoulder.

In the same split second, the gunman sighted him and swung the barrel toward Zeke.

Zeke pulled the trigger.

The Remington blasted the side of the Dodge, and the would-be assassin drew back with a cry.

Advancing, Zeke came around the engine.

Quickly recovering, the shooter fired again, catching Zeke in the arm, winging him.

He flew backward against the truck.

Ears ringing, he chambered another shell, hard and fast. He aimed again. Fired.

The shooter shifted the Ram into gear and roared out of the clearing.

"Zeke!" She fell out of the cab. "Are you all right?"

"I think the last shot grazed him." Slumping against the hood, he flinched. "Are you hurt?"

"Your arm . . ." Her eyes widened as the dust settled. "Your sleeve is bloody."

A sudden dizziness assailed him, and he swayed.

She caught him against her side. "We need to get you to the hospital."

He shook his head. The motion nearly brought him to his knees. The earth reeled.

She hung onto him.

Good thing, or he and the ground would have become better acquainted.

"Why is everyone in my life so stubborn?" she muttered.

"Hospital . . . gives them another chance to finish the job." He panted. "Take me home."

"You need a—"

"No hospital." He grimaced as another wave of pain assaulted him. "Please . . . Tess."

She frowned. "Okay."

He let her lead him around to the passenger side. Folding into the seat, he tried to swallow the groan, but he wasn't fast enough.

She climbed behind the wheel. "Pray the truck still runs, or it's going to be a long walk to civilization."

"You pray . . ." Out of habit, he reached for the seat belt. "God will listen to you better than me anyway." At the searing pain in his shoulder, he changed his mind about safety and let the belt go.

Her mouth tightened, but she cranked the motor. When the engine started, relief flooded her face.

The truck jostled and bumped over the ruts in the old logging road.

He fell forward and grabbed for the dashboard.

She threw him an anxious glance. "Sorry."

"Don't worry about me. Get us out of here. And fast." Bracing, he leaned against the door, careful not to brush against the seat. At the moment, he hurt everywhere.

On the main highway, she accelerated.

He recalled the sensation of being watched the last time he met with Reilly. He went over and over where he could've slipped up. Who he'd ticked off most recently. What he'd said or done to expose his real identity to the Cozarts.

There could be no doubt the Cozarts had ordered the hit.

❖　❖　❖

His good arm draped across her shoulders, Tessa hauled him into the farmhouse kitchen.

Dicy took one look at them and shook her head. "What have you two gone and done now?"

She lugged him to the table. "He's been shot."

Grunting, he collapsed in the chair. "Hospital is a no go."

She wrung her hands. "You can fix him, can't you, Aunt Dicy?"

"Fix him?" Dicy snorted. "He's a man, not a broken tractor."

"She wouldn't be wrong . . ." He ground his jaw. "About the broken part . . ."

"Let me get the first aid kit." Dicy shuffled to the cabinet next to the sink. "Help him take off his shirt. Turn him and the chair around to the table."

"I don't need her help." His hand shook, fumbling the buttons. "I can do it myself."

Tessa wasn't in the mood for his pigheadedness. "Tell me something I don't know." She slapped his hand away. "You don't need anybody. You are an island. Got it."

He glared at her. "Your bedside manner needs work."

"And your attitude needs—"

"Both of you shut it." Dicy set the kit on the table with a thud. "And don't forget I used to get paid to stab people with sharp objects." She moved to the sink and disinfected her hands.

He threw Tessa a mulish look. "Have it your way."

For once, she loomed over him, undoing the buttons for him. Standing so close, she could see the vein throb at the hollow of his throat in the patch of tanned skin above his collar. She felt his heart jerk when her fingertips brushed against his skin accidentally.

Or not so accidentally.

She helped him shrug out of the ruined shirt.

Pain flashed across his face.

Her anger faded. "Zeke . . ." Dicy bustled between them, and Tessa stepped aside to let her work.

Dicy examined his upper arm. "It grazed you. Plowed a furrow on its way across, though. Let me see your back."

Leaning over, he rested both arms on the table.

"Glass." Dicy snapped on a pair of rubber gloves. "We'll have to pick it out."

His mouth curved in a mirthless smile. "And the fun just keeps coming."

"Tessa, soak the tweezers in rubbing alcohol." Dicy worked on his shoulder first, cleaning the wound. "Doesn't need stitches. Keep it free from infection, and you'll be right as rain soon enough." She tore off the packaging of a sterile gauze pad and taped it in place. "But it's gonna hurt like—"

He went rigid. "Yeah. I know."

Dicy rolled her eyes. "Can't cure stupid, but I can give you something to take the edge off the pain."

"No, thanks. Dulled reflexes would've meant we'd be dead right now."

Dicy drew up a chair to get a better look. "Tell me what happened."

"I recognized Shelton's ugly square head. He doesn't have the brains, nor the initiative, to do anything he isn't told. Somebody sent him after me."

"Hold still," Dicy muttered. "This is going to hurt you more than it hurts me."

Tessa handed her the tweezers.

He put his head in his arms to let her work. And left it to Tessa to give a blow-by-blow description of their near-fatal encounter.

She held the bowl into which Dicy dropped the fragments of glass. "Do you think Pender figured out you've been pumping Gib Bascombe for information?"

"Or Robertson decided to play both sides." He gnashed his teeth. "Against—" Heaving a breath, his torso arched as Dicy dug for a particularly stubborn shard in his flesh.

Tessa laid her hand on the dark smattering of hair on his forearm. "You're hurting him, Aunt Dicy."

Her aunt eyed the splinter of glass she held between the tweezers. "More proof of why the good Lord sent me to nursing school and you to music school." She dropped the glass with a clink into the bowl and resumed her probing.

The muscles in his arm convulsed beneath Tessa's palm.

"Maybe one of the Cozart brothers decided I'm a loose end that needs tying."

"I think I've got it all." Her aunt sat back. "Course my eyes ain't what they used to be."

He straightened. "That doesn't make me feel better, Dicy."

"Be still. I ain't a-through with you yet." She dabbed ointment on his back.

He yelped. "That stings!"

"Means it's working, killing the germs." She screwed the cap onto the antiseptic tube again. "Your shirt's too far gone, even for the rag pile. You best cover yourself with another. Tessie, you clean off the table. And I'll commence to putting supper on it."

"None for me, but thanks for the doctoring." He rose, sending the chair scudding. "If the Cozarts are onto me, this could be my last chance to get Gib to talk."

Tessa tried getting between him and the door. "If the Cozarts are onto you, they could be waiting for you to step off the farm so they can finish what they started."

Both hands on either side of her shoulders, he gently but firmly moved her aside. "I'll be prepared next time."

"Call Reilly. You shouldn't go out there without support."

"This is what I do," he snapped. "Go back to obsessing over your dead singer and let me do my job."

"You want to talk about obsessing over dead women? Do you really want to go there with me?" She got in his face. "Are you so *obsessed* with finding Kaci you're willing to die to see her again?"

"Get out of my way, Tessa. This is my fight." His mouth set in a hard line. "Not yours."

Tessa balled his shirt and threw it at his bare chest. "Since you're so determined to spill more of your own blood, why waste another perfectly good shirt?"

Zeke snatched the shirt off the kitchen floor and stomped out the door.

Her chest heaved.

Dicy shook her head. "And here I thought you children were starting to get along so much better."

A disconcerting thought struck Tessa. She slumped. "You don't suppose . . ."

"What?" Dicy's eyes sparked.

She shook her head, but she couldn't shake her sudden misgivings. "Zeke was the intended target." She put her hand to her throat. "Wasn't he?"

Chapter Eighteen

After getting shot at and cut up in the process, Zeke wasn't in the most patient or understanding of moods.

He wasn't sure how much more he could take of Gibson's pathetic, self-pitying whining. How much longer was he going to have to pretend to be best friends with this dirtbag before Gib spilled his guts and told the truth?

Although Gib probably wouldn't recognize truth if it hit him square in the gut.

He glanced at the slathering excuse for a man stuffing his face with the burger Zeke bought him.

Gib started to choke.

For a second, Zeke considered letting him. But it wouldn't do Kaci any good if he died before pointing Zeke in the right direction. "Slow down, Gib . . ." He pounded Gib's back. "Take a breath. Not so fast."

Gib coughed.

Zeke handed him a bottle of water. "Drink something."

Gib shook his greasy head. "Need something stronger. Can't seem to settle my stomach these days."

No surprise considering Gib had death-spiraled into a regimen of booze, cigarettes, and weed.

"Where's the liquor you promised me? I need a drink."

Need. Need. Need. He'd worked hard to make sure what Gib needed he was the one to supply. But enough was enough.

What he wanted to promise Gib was a trip out to the woodshed. With a long, sharp knife, cutting off his fingers one by one until Gib told him where they'd taken—

Sickened with himself, he ran his hand over his face. At some point he'd become less concerned about justice and more interested in closure at any cost.

But that's how angry he was. How infuriated a piece of trash like Bascombe could get to go on living while Kaci rotted somewhere.

He was so close. Zeke could feel it. And still, Bascombe wouldn't give him what *he* needed.

Perhaps it was time to up the ante. Interject some "tough love." Maybe Pender knew best when it came to a loser like Gib. Bascombe seemed to respond to bullying.

Rising, Zeke shoved his chair back with his heel.

Gib's red-rimmed eyes flew open as the chair scraped across the dirty, linoleum floor.

"I'm sick of you making demands, Gib. I'm the only one standing between you and the law, man." He got in Gib's face, too angry to flinch at the nauseating smell of his unwashed breath. "Don't think if the Cozarts get pinched they won't squeal your name."

"They won't be giving me up, or they'd be giving up themselves." Gib's piggy eyes narrowed. "Besides, no law in this state will ever touch them."

"Stop lying to me, Gib. Stop lying to yourself. I know you did something to that woman hiker. You know what you did and where she is." He yanked Gib to his feet by the scruff of his collar. "You're a drunk. And an addict. You run your mouth too much. You're a loose end to the Cozarts. One day they're going to decide it'd be in their best interests to shut you up for good."

Gib shook his head, whiplashing Zeke with strands of oily hair. "No."

"Maybe they'll do to you what you did to her."

Gib wrenched free, eyes wild. "It wasn't my idea, I swear."

"It doesn't matter whose idea it was. You participated, didn't you? You as good as killed her." He slammed Gib against the drywall. "I'm the only hope you've got of saving yourself. The only one on your side. The only one who can keep you safe when the Cozarts come looking." He raised his fist. "Tell me, Bascombe. What did you do to her?"

"The girl wasn't supposed to die," Gib bleated. "The others didn't."

Zeke let go of his shirt. Although he'd known in his heart Kaci had to be dead, Bascombe's confirmation fell like a boulder into the pit of his stomach. "What others?"

His back against the wall, Gib quivered. "Three or four, I forget."

"Three or four?" Rage engulfed him. "Which is it? Who were they?"

"I-I'm not sure. I was drunk and high those times. Pender and Shelton . . ." Bascombe looked away.

"Tell me everything. From the beginning."

"It started when Pender's girlfriend dumped him and left the county."

Only way she could probably get away from him.

"That first time, Shelton was raving about his no-good ex-wife who'd taken his children and yet expected him to still pay for their support while she was shacking up with another guy. Pen and Shel got to cursing uppity women who needed to be taught a lesson." Gib swallowed. "It was late. We was holed up drinking in Pender's truck, raising hell at the bridge over the branch outside town."

An isolated spot on the highway that stretched over the mountain to Tennessee.

"She just come along off the mountain. Pender recognized the car as belonging to the high school guidance counselor. She wasn't from around here."

And without local ties or the support of a local family, vulnerable. Easy prey to someone like Pender Cozart. The only guidance counselor Zeke had run across was a Cozart cousin. Which meant the previous woman had been the one they assaulted. A woman who'd abruptly tendered her resignation and left the county.

"Pender pulled the truck across the bridge so she couldn't cross. When she had to stop, Shelton was waiting. He had her door open—it wasn't locked—and yanked her out before she knew what was what."

"What were you doing?"

"Pen told me to drive her car. I followed his truck to the old Cozart homeplace on Yonder. And then he told me to stay with the vehicles until they were finished."

"And when they 'finished,'" Zeke sneered. "What happened then?"

"They kept her there all night. Let her go when daylight come." Gib shook his shaggy head. "Later, Pender said he'd let her go too soon." His voice dropped. "Wouldn't make that mistake again."

Once Reilly dispatched the forensic team to the barn, no doubt traces of the other victims' DNA would show up as well. "Why did Pender target these women?"

Head in his hands, Gib recounted their "strategy." The counselor had been a crime of opportunity on the dark, deserted road—wrong place, wrong time. Late May, two years ago.

Next time, the night of Labor Day, Pender had been primed for another victim. A similar situation—an outsider with no more connections or protection than the counselor.

She was one of the out-of-state college girls working the summer rafting season. Since Labor Day marked the end of summer, everyone was headed home to begin fall classes. No one wondered at the girl's sudden departure.

"Pender says she was asking for it. Parading herself around like they do in those tight clothes. Drinking. Smoking weed by the river. Teasing men."

"What was her name?"

He didn't meet Zeke's eyes. "The river hussy, Pender called her."

Zeke could find her name on the white-water rafting company records and obtain the counselor's name from the school. He'd locate the women. Get Reilly to persuade them to testify.

No matter how it sickened him, he had to keep Gibson talking. Get him to tell the rest of the sordid tale.

"And what happened when you took her?" he growled.

"Pender kept her a whole day and night. He sent me to make sure I did his job at the garage so his father didn't find out he never showed for work. Boss didn't care as long as them motors got fixed." Gib pushed back his scrawny shoulders. "I'm better at repairs than Pender anyway."

"The third time was Emily Murdock, wasn't it?" She'd been attacked in late November. "Why her?"

Emily was the only one who didn't fit the pattern. Born local, although her family had never been on good terms with the Cozarts.

"Bad blood between the families. A Civil War thing."

Zeke stared at him. "What are you talking about?"

"Bascombes and Cozarts was Confederate. Murdocks were Union, Pen said."

That was crazy. An age-old clan feud couldn't have been the reason Emily was chosen as their next victim, could it? But perhaps no crazier than the war he'd once been a part of.

Maybe bushwhacking, rape, and murder were things passed through the Cozart bloodline. Knowing what he did of the Cozarts, not beyond the realm of possibility.

"I reckon you know what they did to Emily." Gib poked out his lip. "Brandi's done told you, I'll bet. You're not going to make me say all that again, are you?"

"You were the one who held Emily down."

Gib shuffled his feet. "Just the first time. After that, they kept her tied in the barn. I had to do both Shel and Pen's jobs so they didn't get into trouble. And bring them food until they got tired of messing with her."

"Emily was nothing but a child, Gib."

"I know," he whispered. "My little sister was same grade as her."

The rapes had taken place with growing frequency. Yet between the attack on Emily and Kaci's disappearance had been a long gap. He asked Gib about it.

"Emily's suicide scared Shelton. He'd had enough. Said we was going to get caught. That we ought to stop."

"But Pender didn't want to stop . . ."

Gib's gaze lifted. "By that time, Pen couldn't stop."

It might have been the most honest, truest thing Bascombe had ever said.

Zeke had known soldiers like Pender. Men who'd gotten a taste for violence, for blood sport. Suddenly weary, he sank onto the kitchen chair. "How did Pender target Kaci?"

Gib gave him a blank look.

"The woman hiker."

"Pen has a drinking buddy who is a park ranger. One night, he spouted off to Pen about having to deal with stupid through-hikers. About how the flatlanders from away get themselves into such crazy fixes, miles from help."

Which would've set Pender scheming.

"There was this girl the ranger had met that day. Alone on the Trail. Pretty, he mentioned."

Anger licked at Zeke's innards toward the ranger who'd run his mouth to the wrong person and painted a target on Kaci's back.

Zeke had begged Kaci not to do the Trail alone. To at least take her dog. But she'd been so determined to prove something to herself.

He'd done the same. Anything to shake the restlessness he'd felt since he was a boy. Wasn't he still doing it?

"When was this, Gib?"

"April."

That fit the timeline he'd established for her disappearance. Most through-hikers started in Georgia. By April, the natural attrition rate would've thinned the crowds, leaving greater and greater distances between the hikers. Isolating Kaci. Exposing her to a danger she had no way of imagining.

"Take me through it exactly as it happened."

"Pen parked on an old logging trail. I stayed with the truck while he and Shelton went looking. They found her in her sleeping bag."

Where Kaci would've been taken completely by surprise. At their mercy.

"They drug her to the truck. She was kicking and screaming and fighting them."

She wouldn't have gone quietly.

"They kept hold of her while I drove to the barn. And this time, Pen said I . . ." Gib gulped.

Zeke clenched and unclenched his hands. "What did you do? Say it."

Pressed against the wall, Gib slid onto his haunches. "He said it was time for me to be a man. This time I'd get first taste. I didn't want to. I told him." He buried his head in his arms. "But he called me names. So I—"

"So you raped her. And then the other two raped her."

Gib's shoulders shook.

Zeke closed his eyes against the horror of the images the men had perpetrated upon Kaci. Imagining her fear. Her pain. Her anguish. The helplessness.

"It never got that far with her."

Zeke opened his eyes.

"She wouldn't stop fighting. She was like a wildcat. She wouldn't lie still and just let me . . ."

"What happened? What did you do that killed her?"

"Pen told me to tie her up till she calmed down."

"To the post in the barn?"

"No, not there."

Explaining why only Emily's DNA had been found on the rope.

"What did you tie her with then?"

"An old rope Pen had in the truck." Gib's chin jutted. "It was supposed to only be for a while. Till he finished smoking and was ready to start on her. But—"

He yanked Gib to his feet.

Bascombe yelped.

"Show me how you tied her."

Gib placed his wrists together behind his back. "Then I wrapped the rope around her ankles." He clicked his shoes together. "I didn't tie her neck. She could lift her head off the barn floor. I had to pee, so I went outside for just a minute, but when I came back, she wasn't breathing."

A searing hatred exploded before Zeke's eyes. His fist went through the drywall next to Gib's head.

Bascombe flinched, moaning.

Knuckles bloody, he drew back to strike Gib.

"It was an accident," Gib whined. "We didn't mean for her to die. Pen was going to keep her the usual few days, and after he'd had his fun, return her to the Trail. No one would've missed her. She could've gone on her way. But something went wrong."

What went wrong was that they'd hog-tied her. And placed her prone, her weight pressing on her chest. Kaci—sweet, tough, little Kaci—had died from positional asphyxia.

It hurt him to think of her gasping for breath. Unable to fill her compressed lungs. Dying like an animal—tied like an animal—on that filthy, wooden floor.

"Pen said it was my fault. That I was too dumb to tie her right. We was all scared. Shelton was swearing. Pen made a call . . ."

The high sheriff had known from the beginning. That's what he'd meant at the Cozart ranch when he'd said he was tired of cleaning up Pender's messes. Accessory after the fact. He'd enjoy pinning Merritt's hide to the wall.

"Cozart told Pen he didn't want to know anything about it. Pen sent me to get rid of her."

He seized Gib by the throat and jacked him against the wall. "Show me where you put her."

"I'll take you there," he squeaked.

Zeke shoved him toward the door. "Now."

In the deepening twilight, the dashboard in Zeke's truck bathed their faces in an eerie, green glow. Gib slouched on the edge of the seat. His sullen instructions led them into the Pisgah.

Zeke parked on a side road used by park personnel. He grabbed the short-handled spade out of the toolbox in the truck, and they walked to the end of the trailhead.

Gib pointed his stubby finger. "Underneath the trees on the bank."

Below the bank, the creek gurgled. Curled brown leaves drifted in slow motion from the overhanging canopy of tall, leafy trees. Rotting leaves littered the ground.

In daylight, he imagined this to be a peaceful spot. Innocuously innocent. Like Kaci. As much as she loved the outdoors, she would've loved it here.

But this should never have been her final resting place. There were people who missed her. Who desperately needed a grave to visit. Friends. Coworkers. People who loved her.

He had loved her.

Gritting his teeth, he thrust the spade at Gib. "Find her."

Bascombe shrank from him. "But . . . But—"

Zeke growled low in his throat.

Using the spade, Gib scraped away the leaves and then plunged the tip into the soft, loamy soil. A sharp thud resounded against the steel plate.

Zeke wrenched the tool from him. Crouching, he brushed more of the topsoil away with his hand. In the half light, he spotted the pale, white sphere of a human skull. "This is her? You're sure it's her?"

Gib shook like a birch in winter. "Course it's her. Who else would it be? I don't go around killing people. I'm not like Pen and Shelton."

Zeke fisted his hands in the dirt.

Gibson Bascombe was exactly like Pender Cozart and Shelton Allen.

Trash. Scum of the earth who'd snuffed out the beautiful light that was Kaci.

Clawing the soil, his hand encountered something more flexible than human bone. He dug deeper.

Something crinkled inside the rotting threads of what had been Kaci's jacket pocket. Unearthing a small, leather book wrapped in weather-proof plastic, he caught his breath.

Removing it from its protective shield, he stared at the scratched, cracked spine of the little blue New Testament.

The book fell open. The pages fluttered in the soft breeze.

Kaci . . .

Lazy to the end, Bascombe had buried her in a shallow grave. Zeke hoped the animals hadn't gotten to the rest of her bones, but he wouldn't excavate any further. He didn't want to run the risk of destroying any physical evidence for the crime scene investigators.

He'd found Kaci at last. The search was over. But would he ever live long enough to stop missing her?

The wind sighed through the barren trees around them, a lament of mourning and death.

"I don't like it here." Gib whimpered. "There's haints in this place."

Zeke stuffed the New Testament into his cargo pants. "Don't be a fool." The book wasn't anybody's concern, but his. "Nobody's here but you and me."

The sky was a dark-blue velvet. Wherever Kaci was now, she was well. She wasn't here.

What do you think happens when you die? Tessa had asked him that day on the mountain.

It was a choice to believe. A risk to hope. A leap of faith, she'd said.

She was right. There had to be more beyond this. Beauty, love, the bright essence of Kaci—they couldn't simply end. Somewhere they must go on.

If hell existed, so must heaven. But the things he'd done . . . the darkness he felt inside . . .

He knew to which one he was destined. The distance between him and Kaci felt untraversable, her loss, irretrievable.

Knees creaking, he rose. He was getting too old for this kind of thing.

Peace and happiness held an increasingly irresistible appeal. Not that he had much chance of finding either.

"Whatcha going to do with her now, Zeke?"

"The Pisgah is federal land, which means you and I are going to take a ride to Park Headquarters."

"I can't do that." Gib backed away. "The Cozarts will kill me."

"Cozarts don't have any power over federal law enforcement, Bascombe. Your best bet is to come clean with them."

"Why can't you call them? An anonymous tip. Why does it have to be me?"

He took a steadying breath. "They'll keep you safe in protective custody."

"I can't." Gib stumbled. "They'll find me . . ."

"The Cozarts are not God," he shouted. "For once in your life, stop being such a sniveling coward. Be a man."

Gib's face paled in the moonlight. "You said you'd help me."

"This is me helping you, Bascombe. You can't go on pretending this never happened. You can't drink your way out of forgetting. The only way is to step forward and own what you did."

"You said you were my friend. You've been lying to me. To get me to spill on the boys. To turn on my kin." The look in his eyes was not unlike a bewildered child. A child who had somehow managed to crawl into a hole way over his head. And found no one to lift him out.

"Bascombe, trust me—"

Gib shook his head so hard, Zeke was surprised his brains didn't rattle. "I did trust you. Like I trusted Pen to look out for me. You're-you're just like Pender."

Remorse knotted his gut. The gray murky area of undercover work. It never used to bother him. Did the end ever justify the means? "Bascombe, listen—"

Gib took off into the underbrush. Zeke gave chase, but he wasn't as familiar with the land as Gib. Zeke soon lost him among the trees. He searched for a while, but eventually gave it up as futile.

It was time to call Reilly. Come morning, he'd track down Bascombe. Gib wasn't that bright. He'd surface sooner or later. Hopefully Gibson had enough sense of self-preservation to realize he'd find no refuge by running to the Cozarts for protection.

But even if he did, all that mattered now was getting Kaci out of here. Reilly and the CSI team arrived within the hour. The temperature plunged as soon as the last rays of light went behind the range. He didn't feel the chill. How could he when his heart had already frozen solid?

His voice clipped and hard, he retold Gib's version of events. And also about Shelton's earlier attack that afternoon.

"I'm sorry, Sloane." Reilly stood with him as the team set up floodlights, taped off the surrounding area, and got to work recovering Kaci's remains. "This is not the result I hoped for you."

"Maybe not, but it's the answer we both expected."

"Still . . ." The older man blew out a breath, fogging the cold night. "She was your sister."

Zeke stayed through the exhumation. Every stage in the process photographed by men and women who knew him. They knew what this victim meant to him personally.

Victim. Kaci. The world tilting, he squatted and placed his palm on the dirt. It was as close as he could get to touching her now. As close as he'd ever get to her again.

With a respect he appreciated, the team transferred the last of her bones from the soil into the body bag. His heart nearly ripped in two as they zipped the plastic over her body.

"There's nothing else you can do here tonight, son." Reilly pulled him to his feet. "Go home."

Where was that exactly?

It started to rain.

Later, he was never sure how he made it to the orchard in one piece without plunging over a guardrail. He welcomed the numbness. Anything was better than the agonizing pain he knew would come.

A kitchen light was on when he pulled into the orchard. Giving in to an impulse, he stopped at the farmhouse and got out.

Tessa must've been listening for him. She waited for him at the top of the ramp, then pulled him inside the kitchen and scanned his face.

He didn't know what she saw when she looked at him. He felt like stone. Impenetrable as granite.

"Zeke . . . What is it? Shelton? Did you . . . ?"

He shook his head. "Gib confessed. I found K-Kaci . . ." He shuddered.

Tessa's arms went around him. "Oh, Zeke. I'm so, so sorry."

For a second, he allowed himself the comfort of her embrace. Closing his eyes, he inhaled the clean, lavender fragrance of her hair. Tried desperately to block out the images he feared he'd forever see. Kaci's bones, white in the moonlight . . . the empty eye sockets.

"It's over." Crushing him to her, she stroked his back, making small circles with her hand. "It's finally over."

"How can it be over?" He pushed her away. "Pender and Shelton better pray the law gets to them before I do. Because I'm going to hunt them down."

"If they don't kill you first." Her nostrils flared. "When will it finally be over? After you kill one of theirs, the Cozarts will never let you live."

He scowled. "It's an eye for an eye."

"This vendetta only makes you like them." She tugged at his coat. "You're upset right now. Not thinking clearly. Don't do this. Please. If we ever hope to have a future—"

"I have no future." His eyes blazed. "Not without Kaci. Why can't you understand that?"

She reared as if he'd struck her. "Why can't you mourn Kaci and leave the vengeance to God?"

"I can't mourn Kaci. Not yet." He jerked free. "I won't grieve for her until everyone who did this is as dead as she is."

Her mouth trembled. "You mean dead like you?"

"That's exactly what I mean." He looked at her as if she was a stranger. "Dead like me."

Chapter Nineteen

Searching for Pender, Zeke drove around in the rain for hours. Unsuccessful, he returned to the orchard before dawn, dropping exhausted into bed. He'd sleep a few hours and start the hunt again.

But he came awake to the insistent rumble of his cell on the nightstand. Groaning, he scrambled for his phone. He clicked On.

"This is a fine mess of—"

He winced at Reilly's expletive. "What are you talking about?"

"I'm talking about a dead body. Your informant."

He jackknifed upright. "What's happened to Brandi?"

"Don't think it's a her." A harsh bark of laughter. "Though there's not much left to tell one way or the other."

If not Brandi, who? A sick feeling welled inside his chest. Bascombe.

"Girl Scouts ran across the remains early this morning. Troop leader called 911. Since it's on national forestland and after one look at the corpse, the park rangers called the FBI field office. And lucky me, here I am."

"Where's here?"

"In the middle of the wilderness. I'll send you the coordinates." There was a stumbling sound on the other end of the phone. Reilly cursed, loud and long. "I hate the woods. I hate nature. Why can't people get murdered in nice, easily accessible, paved—"

"You think it was murder?"

"The rangers are tracking the bear as we speak."

Zeke scrubbed his face. "A bear murdered Bascombe?"

"Son," Reilly sputtered. "I am not in the mood to repeat myself. I'm dealing here with a buttload of hysterical people—and I'm not talking about the scouts. I've got veteran investigators hurling inside my vehicle."

Reilly groaned. "Of all the places in these United States of America, why did I ever come here? You Southern people are unhinged. I hate, hate, hate sweet tea. And barbecue. And the smell of magnol—"

"Reilly. You're sure Bascombe was murdered?"

"Gee whiz, Mountain Man. I think I'm still competent enough to know the bear that mauled Bascombe to death didn't first tie him to the tree," he growled. "But what do I know? I'm old-fashioned that way!"

Flinching, Zeke pulled the cell away from his ear.

"Get down here ASAP. Or it's going to be your—"

"I'm coming," he shouted, trying to be heard over the cussing.

Reilly hung up on him.

The sky was a pewter color, and it was raining again. Today, the mountains felt oppressive, making Zeke vaguely uneasy.

He parked next to a bevy of law enforcement vehicles and a white Mecklenburg County Girl Scouts van. A handful of preteens hovered around an older woman seated on the bumper. Her face was ashen.

Zeke tromped through the bracken, keeping to the path established outside the crime scene tape.

Around the bend, looking miserable and cold in his khaki green parka, a park ranger waited for him. "You Sloane?" Rain dribbled off the brim of his hat.

Nodding, he reached for his pocket before realizing he had no identification—not the official kind anyway. Keeping that sort of thing on him while undercover was a good way to get killed.

The ranger gave him the once-over. "You look like Reilly said you'd look."

He would've loved hearing the description.

"The agent's waiting for you." The wiry officer rested his hand on his gun belt and shook his head. "He sure doesn't like to be kept waiting."

"No." Zeke exhaled, his breath fogging. "He doesn't."

The ranger motioned him on. "Better you than me."

Pushing through a dense patch of rhododendron, he registered the stench of carnage before his brain processed the sight that met his eyes. When it did, he rocked to a standstill.

Gibson Bascombe—what was left of Gibson Bascombe—had been

tied spread-eagle to the trunk of a giant oak. Claw marks sharpened the bark around the ravages of his battered skull. Flesh clung precariously to his shattered cheekbones. His scalp was gone.

If not for the ropes, his left arm would no longer have remained attached to his torso. As it was, his right leg dangled from the hip socket by only a tendon of flesh.

Zeke threw his hand over his mouth.

Breaking off from a conversation with several figures in hooded crime scene overalls, Reilly stalked over to him. "Not so much to look at now, is he?"

Gib had never been much to look at. But this? Zeke's stomach heaved. Only with great difficulty did he keep the contents of his stomach where it belonged. He was glad Reilly pulled him away before he'd eaten breakfast. Or else, combat veteran though he was, his breakfast would've been all over the forest floor and Reilly's crime scene.

"They bloodied him first. Knife marks on his upper body. We've lifted fingerprints from where they smeared the blood across his clothing. We also found donut crumbs scattered around the area."

"Blood lure and bear bait." Zeke swallowed. "Did you get more than one set of prints?"

Reilly nodded, his lantern jaw tight. "Oh, yeah."

Zeke tore his gaze from Gib's mutilated form.

"Real nasty fellows to do that to someone." Water droplets quivered on the blunt edges of Reilly's buzz cut. "You've been made for sure. No telling how quickly he sang once they started on him. In his situation, I'd sing on my own mother. Little good it did him, though."

He didn't want to think about the terror Gib must've experienced in those last horrible seconds. The bear charging toward him. Unable to move, unable to get away.

Just like what he did to Kaci . . . A voice in Zeke's head shrilled. *What Gib Bascombe deserved.* But the pain? Unimaginable pain. The terrible sounds of searing retribution. *Vengeance is Mine . . .* This time it was the old woman's quavery tone that played in his mind.

The crack of a gun split the air.

He jolted.

Reilly grimaced. "Rangers have bagged the bear."

"I should've made more of an effort to find him when he ran off. He knew, once we unearthed Kaci, they'd know it was him who told. He knew they'd come after him."

"You live by the sword, you don't die well." Reilly shrugged. "It's the black bear I feel sorry for. But until you put 'em down, no one is safe. Once an animal has gotten a taste of blood . . ."

A taste for blood. That's what Gib had said about Pender.

"Don't bother returning to the orchard to pack your stuff. You're done, Sloane."

He was far from done. "I'm not going anywhere. I have to see this through."

"You got a death wish? The Cozarts aren't stupid. They'll realize Brandi Murdock had to be in on it too." Reilly jutted his thumb at the ruined corpse, sagging against the tree. "They're just as likely to take their revenge out on your friend."

"Exactly why I can't leave. Not until the Cozarts are in custody. I have to warn Brandi."

Reilly muttered something under his breath.

Zeke figured it wasn't complimentary.

"I've put in a request for agents as far afield as Raleigh, but there are a lot of Cozarts to round up. They're as slippery as eels."

"All the more reason I can't evaporate yet."

Reilly's granite-gray eyes narrowed. "Is that the reason you're not ready to do your usual vanishing act? This reluctance wouldn't have anything to do with that redheaded gal you're sweet on?"

"I'm not—" What was the point in lying anymore? He was lying to himself most of all. "You do your job, Special Agent Reilly. And let me do mine."

"And if it means your life?"

He pursed his lips. "Then so be it."

Reilly glared. "After what they did to your sister, are you sure you haven't moved to what the cartels call *venganza*?"

"What if I have?" He fisted his hands. "Somebody has to pay for what happened to Kaci."

Reilly gripped his shoulder. "Somebody already has."

He shook him off. "Until Pender Cozart is put down, no one in Roe-buck County is safe."

Reilly wagged his finger. "These people are the filth of the earth. But hear me, Sloane, you make sure they're the only ones who've developed a taste for blood."

❖ ❖ ❖

She had fallen asleep watching for Zeke to return to the orchard. During the long, lonely night, it started to rain. And didn't let up. Tessa awoke to the squelching rumble of tires over the bridge.

Thankful he was safe, she had fallen asleep once more. When she awoke several hours later, however, his truck was gone from the meadow. She hadn't heard him leave the second time.

She was losing her mind from worry. If he succeeded in carrying out his terrible vengeance, what would the revenge do to him?

The sweet, shy, quiet boy who loved the woods . . . She feared he'd disappear forever. Consumed by the bloodletting.

Maybe she could talk sense into Ouida, if not Ezekiel Sloane. Time was running out for the old woman ensconced in her mountain fortress. Tessa feared time had already run out for any chance of something more with Zeke.

There were only seven days left until Ouida's eviction. Tessa dressed quickly, belting a tan raincoat over her jeans and sweater. She left a note for her aunt.

Outside, the rain had slackened to an annoying light drizzle. Seeking a distraction, she turned on the car radio, but the forecast proved as dire as the day itself.

A powerful storm front was predicted to sweep through western North Carolina. The same system had spawned tornados in Oklahoma and hail in the Mississippi River valley. Additional bands of heavy rain and gusty winds would strip the final color from the trees. Much colder air was forecast to move in behind the severe storms.

With the ground already saturated, flash flooding was a real possibility. Ouida needed to see sense. It was time to leave Yonder Mountain.

After parking beside the backhoe, Tessa quickly climbed through the brush. The path was slippery with rain-slicked leaves.

The trail had become nearly as familiar to her as the orchard. Hard to believe, a week ago she hadn't known Ouida Kittrell. Truth to tell, she was beginning to wish she'd never known Leota Byrd ever existed.

But a week ago she hadn't remembered Zeke existed either.

Yet in some undefinable way she'd known him forever. Like a deep place inside herself had been marking time. Until she found her way back to the orchard. To Dicy. And him.

Reaching the edge of the grove, she helloed the house.

Ouida shuffled onto the porch, moving as slowly as Tessa had ever seen her, for once showing every one of her ninety years.

Perhaps the rain bothered her bones. There was an air of fragility about her today. And sadness.

Ouida waved her forward. "Didn't think you'd come in this weather."

Tessa pushed off the hood. Dark storm clouds hovered over the mountains toward Tennessee, obliterating any sense of where mountain ended and sky began. She must somehow persuade the old woman to begin packing. "Even in the rain, it's pretty up here."

Ouida's face lightened. "Right pretty, it is. Any time, any day." Her gaze wandered over to the trees at the edge of the clearing.

Water plinked off the leaves.

"There's a storm coming, Ouida."

"I know." Ouida held her arm stiff against her side. "The dampness has been talking to my bones." Her dark eyes returned to the color-daubed treetops. "I won't see another display like this."

"What's wrong?"

Ouida shrugged her stooped shoulders. "Something else I feel in my bones. Storm clouds are gathering. We're entering a season of dying today." She heaved a sigh. "I'd as soon get on through my dying, so I can start living again."

She bit her lip. "Don't talk that way, Ouida."

"If you've got what I've got to look forward to, you wouldn't wish-true me to stay."

Since coming here, Tessa had made her choice. To believe there was yet something beyond the darkness, beyond the end.

Not just wish-true hopes or never-shall-be dreams, but the faith-becomes-sight happily-ever-after that God had made them for from the beginning.

As for the other risk she'd taken—loving Zeke—that hadn't worked out as she'd hoped.

Ouida took her arm. "I want to go to the ridge."

"But it's raining. We should stay inside on a day like this. Especially if you're not feeling well."

Ouida shook her head. "It's a crossroads kind of day." She lumbered toward the laurel.

Pulling her hood up, Tessa sloshed after the old woman.

Amidst the oaks and sycamores, Ouida seemed to become stronger with every step she climbed. A wind sprang up.

Leaves of saffron yellow and crimson red danced on the breeze before floating gently downward to carpet the path.

Smiling, Ouida plucked a curled, orange leaf off the shoulder of her jacket. "It's done finished the dance and reached its time to rest. Like me."

Unease stirred in Tessa's chest.

Ouida twirled the stem in her hand. "Come spring, I want you to promise me you'll climb the mountain again. That's what spring teaches us. Hope reborn."

After she turned in her dissertation, she had no idea where she'd be come spring.

Or where spring would find Zeke. Restless, wandering Zeke. He'd probably once more be embedded somewhere far away with another set of dangerous criminals.

She touched Ouida's sleeve. "Dicy wants you to come to the orchard. In the first flush of spring, you can see the apple trees for yourself. And in summer, smell the sweet scent of white apple blossoms."

"A beautiful path for sure. But not my path." Ouida tucked the leaf behind Tessa's ear. "Don't you look a sight. Autumn's your season."

"The hair." She grimaced. "Yes, I know."

"Your hair is your beauty."

She'd believed Zeke thought so. But now . . .

"Listen to the story the leaves tell, Tessa. There's a beauty to each season. I've had my time—spring, summer, autumn. But winter's not the end. You don't need to be afraid. The sound of falling leaves is a thing of beauty. I promise."

Tessa's eyes blurred.

Ouida patted the rough bark of the tree. "Just you watch. For folks who choose faith, new life begins anew. Just someplace else."

They walked around the clusters of evergreen spruce and rhododendron till they came to the bottom of the grassy bald. Ouida held out her arm, and Tessa helped her to the top.

Like parting a curtain, a wind blew the mist off the mountain. In the distance, the silver ribbon of the ancient river glistened.

"A final gift. Thank You, Lord." With a sigh, the old woman rested against the granite outcropping. "I came out onto the porch at first light to greet the day. A white dove flew right out from underneath the steps." Closing her eyes, Ouida lifted her face to the brisk wind that plastered her housedress against her legs. "I knowed what that means."

Tessa wrapped her arms around herself. She hated it when Ouida "knew" things she couldn't possibly know. The old woman was in a strange, introspective mood today.

"It won't be much longer. And it came to me plain as you and I are sitting here that Leota would be waiting for me. How I loved that child. But she's long dead. I know it now."

After her attempts to find a single trace of the missing singer, Tessa feared the same. Leota and her baby had not survived the summer of 1988.

"In the water-soaked light, I saw him. Short time here, a long time gone," the old woman whispered. "Too long."

The hair prickled on Tessa's neck. "Who?"

Like lines on a map, the wrinkles fanned out from her apple rose cheeks. "Foley, my own true love. Smilingest, happiest man I ever knew." Her chicory-brown eyes lit. "Stood at the edge of the glade. He'd come from up here. The selfsame path you and I just trod."

Tessa leaned against the boulder. The wind caught the leaf in her hair and sent it fluttering over the edge of the drop. "Please, Ouida. Let me take you to Dicy."

"Bless you, child, for your concern. But I don't aim to set one foot off this mountain. Won't need to. I've done heard from my Foley. I'm headed home. Not yet, but soon."

"A trick of the light, Ouida . . ."

"I know what I saw, child." Her work-worn palm cupped Tessa's cheek. "The time for sorrow has past. Joy cometh in the morning. You wouldn't deny me that, would you? You and Dicy must let me go. I'm ready." Her gaze roamed over the ridge. "Ready for home."

Chapter Twenty

Leaving Reilly at the crime scene in the forest, Zeke headed toward Brandi's house. If he'd been thinking straight last night, he would've warned her then. But after finding Kaci, he'd unraveled, his thoughts full of grief mixed with a bloodlust for revenge.

And there was another thing he should've done yesterday.

From the truck, he called Tonio. When he explained the situation, Tonio didn't sound overly surprised. Maybe Zeke wasn't as good at undercover work as he'd believed.

"Not so, *mi amigo*." Tonio blew out a breath. "It is just we have of necessity developed a sixth sense about who are the good guys and who are the bad. You are one of the good."

He wasn't so sure anymore. And once he got his hands on Pender, it definitely wouldn't be true.

The rain started up again.

He flicked on the windshield wipers. "The Cozarts may come to the orchard, Tonio. They might retaliate against Miss Dicy and Tessa." He had to make sure the people he cared about were safe.

"*Doña* Dicy is a good woman. Luis and our cousins, we will keep watch. No one who does not belong will set foot near the apples."

Zeke exhaled. "Thank you, Tonio."

His next call was to Luther. "If you care about Brandi, meet me at her house in ten minutes. I'll explain when I get there. The Cozarts are going to come after her. I've got to get her out of the county."

Zeke clicked Off before Luther could launch into heated slurs regarding his character. As in, lack thereof.

Next, he speed-dialed Brandi. "Pack a bag," he barked into the phone.

"Hello to you too," she rasped.

"Everything's about to hit the fan, Brandi. You need to disappear until the Cozarts are behind bars. I'm headed your way now."

"Does this mean . . . ?" She gasped. "You found Kaci?"

He swallowed hard. "Yeah."

The wipers swiped left, then right, in a steady beat.

"It's really going to be over?"

"Be ready to go, Brandi. Don't answer the phone. Don't come to the door unless it's me."

"Oh, Zeke . . ." She started crying. "Emily . . ."

"Focus," he growled. "We're not out of the woods yet."

Brandi gulped. "I'll be ready."

Skirting downtown Buckthorn, five minutes later, he pulled into the Murdock driveway. He threw himself out of the truck.

A quicksilver, jacked-up Chevy screeched in behind him. Luther got out, brandishing a gun in his direction.

"Whoa, Luther." He backed a step, hands raised. "We're on the same side here."

The veins in his massive neck engorged, Luther's free hand went for Zeke's throat. And he rammed Zeke into his own truck.

Feeling the cuts from yesterday's attack, Zeke flinched when his shoulder made contact with the unforgiving steel. Had he made a mistake in calling Luther? Had Luther been in the Cozarts' pocket all along?

Cocking the pistol, he pressed the barrel to Zeke's temple. "What have you done, Sloane? What have you dragged Brandi into?"

Movement erupted from the house, and Brandi threw herself between the two men. "Stop, Luther. You've got it wrong."

Unable to breathe, Zeke tugged at the meaty fist clenched around his throat.

"Zeke's an undercover agent with the FBI. We've been working together to bring those monsters who hurt Emily to justice." She strained at Luther's arm.

His grip on the gun didn't slacken.

Best case scenario, Luther's steel would leave a small, round circle imprinted on his temple. Worst case, his brains would be scattered over the hood of the truck. If he didn't suffocate first.

"Listen to me." She laid her hand over Luther's fist, coiled around the gun. "They killed his sister too."

The bartender's eyes flicked to her. "What are you talking about?"

She touched Luther's face. "The hiker who went missing on the Trail last year."

His unibrow furrowed. "The one they never found?"

"I found her," Zeke choked. "Gibson Bascombe showed me before he died."

Brandi sucked in a breath.

Stepping back, Luther released his hold on Zeke.

Coughing, Zeke bent double. Chest heaving, he gasped for air.

She took hold of him.

"I'm sorry." Luther's bald head glistened under another heavy downpour. "I didn't know."

Zeke rubbed his throat. "You don't have to apologize for protecting the woman you love."

Brandi let go of him. "Luther, what does he mean?"

Still clutching the gun, the bartender folded his arms across his leather jacket. "I'll keep 'em busy long enough for you two to get across the county line."

Her lips parted. "No . . ."

Zeke frowned. "That's not why I called you, man." His wet jeans clung to his skin. Would it ever stop raining? "It's you who should take her away from here."

Luther shook his head. "It's not me she's wanting."

"Tell her how you feel."

"I know what I've seen. How it is with you two." He fished his keys out of his jacket. "They'll nail you for sure if you take your vehicle. Take mine."

She stepped away from Zeke. "It was part of the cover. Zeke and I—it wasn't real."

"Looked real to me." He extended the keys toward Zeke. "Let's exchange vehicles. It will buy you valuable time."

She took Luther's hand. "I can't leave you here. To fight them alone."

He trembled, but his gaze darted over her head to Zeke. "You make her go. Keep her safe."

"I'm not going with Zeke. Not without you." She hung onto Luther. "I won't leave you here."

He looked away. "I want more than anything for you to be happy. To get the life you deserve."

One by one, she unfolded the fingers of his clenched hand.

He didn't fight her.

"Please tell me how you feel." She removed the keys from his grasp. "Do you feel something for me?"

"I love you, Brandi. I've always loved you." The big man gave a helpless, hopeless shrug. "But ever since high school . . . after I got out of prison . . ."

"You've been such a good friend." She lifted her face to the rain. "I wasn't sure what you felt for me."

"I didn't want to risk losing our friendship." He tried to pull his hand free, but she didn't let go. "Or make it so awkward I couldn't see you every day."

Raindrops sparkled like dew on the edges of her lashes. "I was scared too. After what happened to Emily . . ." Her voice broke. "But you were there for me." And she moved his palm to her cheek. "I'm not scared anymore, Luther."

Something transformed his features. Hope. An aching vulnerability. Love.

Brandi didn't wait for the gentle giant to make the first move. She rose on her tiptoes and brushed her lips against his with a kiss as gentle as falling rain.

Zeke turned away. For a moment, he missed Tessa with an intensity that robbed him of breath.

But she was safer at the orchard. Anywhere away from him was safer.

He cleared his throat. "I'd love to stand here in the rain all day and watch you two kids declare your undying love for each other, but you need to go and so do I."

She settled onto her heels. "You're not coming with us?"

"Unfinished business." He glanced at the sky. "Before I'm through, the rain won't be the only thing pouring today."

❖ ❖ ❖

Failure dogged Tessa as she wended her way from Ouida's cabin. There was nothing left to do but return to the farmhouse. And wait for a phone call, maybe a knock at the door.

She wasn't sure how the FBI would deliver the bleak news, or when. That either Zeke was dead or he'd been arrested for murder.

Halfway down the mountain, she stumbled and started to slide off the trail toward the ravine. Crying out, she flung herself at a tree, scratching her face against the bark. She only just caught hold, stopping her momentum from plunging her into the chasm below.

A close call. Her chest heaved and her temples throbbed. She touched her hand to her burning, welted cheek.

Suddenly, Colin Cozart stepped from behind an old-growth tree. At the malevolent look in his eyes, she bolted.

Her hood fell away, and her hair streamed behind her. Scrambling toward the laurel, she raced into the hell. Branches whipped back, smacking her. Wet leaves batted at her face, sticking.

But Colin was quick on his feet. Quicker than she. He got a fistful of her hair and jerked her backward.

Fire ignited the nerve endings on her neck. Screaming, she groped, hands flailing, clawing at his hand, anything to reduce the pressure on her scalp.

"Shut your mouth!" Colin yanked her hard against his chest, ripping her gaze to the glowering sky.

Tessa found his hand, tried to break his hold. But he wasn't alone.

Black trench coat flapping, Anjanette Cozart stepped onto the path. Cradling a shotgun in her arms, she caressed the stock like an old friend. "Bring her."

Colin dragged Tessa out of the hell.

Her black rain boots crunching the leaves on the forest floor, Anjanette headed downhill.

Colin wrenched Tessa along, moving too fast for her to keep pace. Snatching her upright when she stumbled.

He threw her into the clearing, and she fell against the backhoe. A green Range Rover sat parked beside her BMW.

She calculated the distance from where she sat on the ground to the tree cover, but Colin hovered too close. She'd never make it. He'd be on her in a second.

Anjanette opened the trunk of the Rover and deposited the shotgun inside the cargo hold. "We're going to take a little ride. You won't be needing your car, though."

Colin dragged Tessa upright.

She fought him all the way to the Rover. Biting and kicking. Holding onto the frame.

He slapped her, hard.

Stunned, she fell onto the back seat.

Colin wiped his hand along his cheek and stared incredulous at the thin red line of blood. "Look what that hellcat did to me, Mother."

"Buckle up, darlin'." Anjanette crawled behind the wheel. "We have several situations to deal with before we can rendezvous with your father."

"What about her?"

Anjanette click-locked the four doors. From the rearview mirror, her gaze bored into Tessa. "You want to find Leota so bad? Let me take you to her." Her eyes cut to her son in the front passenger seat. "If she tries anything, shoot her."

Colin pulled a gun from the glove box and pointed the weapon at Tessa's head.

It took a while for Anjanette to drive around the perimeter of Yonder. Huddled against the door, Tessa did her best to memorize the route. Once she escaped, she'd need to be able to find her way to civilization. She wasn't going down without a fight.

After skirting the wilderness area, Anjanette finally came to a stop at the end of an old logging road. "We're here. Get her out." She popped the lock on the doors.

Colin hopped out and flung open Tessa's door. "If I have to come in there after you, I'll break your arm." He ran his hand over the cut on his cheek and sucked the blood from his finger.

At the look in his eyes, she got out of the car. "Where is 'here'?"

He took hold of her arm and shoved her forward. "Move."

"A quicker route than using the Cane Creek trail." Anjanette led the way through the dense underbrush. "Not many still alive to remember, but Cozarts never forget."

Tessa didn't hurry, playing for time. Dicy would eventually send someone to look for her. But who? Probably not High Sheriff Merritt Cozart, who'd murdered a pregnant teenager thirty years ago.

Zeke.

She fell over a branch.

Zeke would find her. He had a gift. He'd found Kaci.

She grimaced. Only after she was dead, though.

But would he come looking? If he did, only after he'd exhausted his thirst for revenge. Too late for her too?

"Stop dawdling." Colin pushed her, sending her sprawling.

Tessa landed facedown on a bed of pine needles. She had only a moment to inhale the sharp, pine-scented fragrance before he hauled her up by the scruff of her jacket.

He jabbed the gun in the small of her back. "Walk!"

She lurched forward, but she was tired of being the victim. She hadn't survived Anton to die in this primeval forest alone. If she could somehow gain possession of the gun . . .

Following the bank of the creek, they walked a long way. No longer placid or gentle, the water ran high. After the heavy rains, the brook had become a bubbling cauldron at full spate. The stream, a tributary of the ancient river, drowned other sounds.

Alert to any opportunity of escape, she scanned the terrain as she marched along.

But Colin stuck close, and he'd shoot her before she had time to dash to the nearest tree cover.

Her gaze cut to the embankment. Perhaps she could drag him into the raging torrent with her. She imagined the water carrying them along. Best case scenario, Colin would lose the gun and the current would separate them, taking her farther downstream. Maybe to town.

In the stream, half-submerged logs bobbed like corks. If she could latch onto one of the logs . . . But the log could also roll over on her, and the branches could snag her clothing. Her feet could get tangled by debris, trapping her underwater until she drowned.

Before she could decide if she was a strong enough swimmer to take the risk, Anjanette decided for her. "Through there." The woman motioned toward the rhododendron.

Colin shoved her forward.

Breaking through the vegetation, she found herself at the base of the waterfall. The roaring she'd heard hadn't only been from the frothing creek.

Colin crowded in behind her.

The bank had all but disappeared. The three of them stood on the opposite side of the pool from where she and Zeke talked only a few days ago, though it seemed an eternity.

Her heart pounded. Her eyes darted to the foaming water at the bottom of the falls and riveted on the hydraulic.

Was this where Leota had lain for decades? Not lain. Fomented, swirled, agitated like a washer set on a spin cycle. An illusion of movement, of life. A forever dance of death.

And if the Cozarts had their way, she would join Leota.

She dug in her heels. "No . . ."

"Not there." Anjanette's mouth hardened. "A few more yards." She walked into the watery veil descending from the cliff face and disappeared.

One minute she was there, but the next . . .

Tessa shrank back. "The waterfalls are portals," Ouida had said.

Colin nudged her with the gun. "Go."

Beneath her feet, the slab thundered from the vibration of the cascade. She drew her raincoat around her, scant protection against the spray. Taking a breath, she stepped through the watery onslaught. And into a world she couldn't have begun to imagine.

A place time forgot.

The cavern behind the waterfall was large, soaring above her head. A fraction of a second later, Colin passed through behind her. Water dripped from her clothes and hair, forming a puddle in the dust of the hidden cave.

Waiting for them, Anjanette clutched a lighted lantern. Which provided a feeble glow, a vain attempt to push back the darkness. But it lent enough light to see the markings etched onto the stone walls. Drawings in a place visited by the ancients.

How long since the last human had ventured here? Had Ouida known about this place? Tessa didn't think so, but Leota must have.

"I don't like this place. It's creepy, Mother. It would've been easier to bury her in the woods." Colin scowled. "Or push her in the creek and let the water do our work for us."

The lighting of the lantern cast an eerie jack-o'-lantern glow onto Anjanette's face. "Far more fitting that the two songbirds lie together, silenced for eternity."

His brow knotted. "Two?"

When Anjanette stepped aside, Tessa spotted the hole gaping in the cavern floor. And the slatted wooden rope ladder at Anjanette's feet.

A trembling began at the base of Tessa's spine and traveled the length of her body. "You put Leota . . . there?"

"I visit her from time to time." Anjanette smiled. "When I'm feeling blue, I come here to sit and remember." She tilted her head. "Sometimes, I think I can hear her singing the old ballads from her underworld prison. And I laugh."

Her blood ran cold. "Was it you or Merritt who left her to die?"

"I was younger then." Anjanette ran a critical eye over Tessa. "That's why, this time, I brought Colin with me."

"Why are you doing this, Anjanette?"

"Old Mr. Cozart hated you nasty Melungeons. He was only too happy to help me intercept your letters to his grandson."

She blinked. *Her* letters?

"His grandson was beginning to love me. But you just had to come back to spoil everything. The way you spoiled everything for me. I followed you over the summer." Anjanette's eyes glittered. "I discovered the secret places where you left notes for each other."

You. Your. Had Tessa become Leota in Anjanette's deranged mind?

"What's going on, Mother?"

Anjanette's mouth trembled. "I saw him kiss you at the falls."

She lifted her chin. "You spied on them."

Anjanette's lips drew back into a snarl. "You were never good enough for a Cozart, Leota."

"That's rich coming from a Bascombe like you," Tessa spat.

Colin brought the gun down across her back.

With a cry, she fell to her knees.

"No one speaks to my mother like that."

Anjanette gave her son a fond, approving look. "We'll have to go away for a while, darlin', but things will calm eventually. We'll return to claim what's rightfully yours."

Fighting off the pain, Tessa gritted her teeth. "Federal agents are rounding up your family as we speak. You'll never run this county again."

Anjanette squatted in front of her, eye to eye. "Never is a long time, my dear." She set the lantern between them. "I'll be back to hear your ghost songs." She reached for the gun in Colin's hand. "You fooled me, changing your hair to red." Anjanette hefted the gun in her palm as if testing its weight. "I couldn't find your baby last time."

Colin frowned. "What baby?"

"But I know where to find him now. I overheard Merritt talking to Ransom." Anjanette's brow furrowed. "He shouldn't have told him. But it won't matter much longer. I'm going to kill your baby, once and for all."

"What baby, Mother?"

"Anjanette thinks I'm Leota Byrd. Your mother's unhinged."

"Shut up." He backhanded her across the face.

Tessa tasted the metallic tang of her blood on her lip.

"Who's Leota Byrd, Mother? What's she talking about?"

Anjanette rose, towering over her. "Mother will take care of everything, darlin'. Like I did before, I won't let Leota's misbegotten spawn take your place." Gripping the pistol, Anjanette threw back her arm. Her eyes wide and burning, like an avenging Valkyrie from the Wagnerian opera, she brought the gun down in a swooping arc.

Tessa didn't have time to cry out. There was a cracking, blinding pain.

Darkness engulfed her.

Chapter Twenty-One

With Brandi and Luther safely speeding away to destinations unknown, Zeke turned his truck onto Main. At the intersection, a dozen flashing blue lights zoomed in the opposite direction, sirens blaring.

State troopers. State Bureau of Investigation. And the unmarked SUV contained federal agents also involved in the Cozart takedown. Reilly was as good as his word.

Zeke had the vague notion of confronting Merritt first. Of somehow luring him away from the police station and his deputies. But the high sheriff's car wasn't parked in the lot across the street.

Half of the law enforcement vehicles screeched to a stop on the sidewalk in front of the courthouse. Troopers spilled out, then took the granite steps two at a time. Probably looking for Ransom.

Others ran next door to the law enforcement center. Merritt's deputies wouldn't be Zeke's problem once he located Merritt.

Down the block, the SBI vehicles braked in front of Cozart Development Corporation. The Yukon was there. They'd soon have Judson in custody.

The SUV continued the length of Main, leaving the town limits behind. On their way to the Cozart enclave for Colin and Anjanette, where they'd run into Pup and Runt too. He wished them luck.

Which meant Pender and Shelton were his.

His cell rang.

Zeke grabbed the phone off the seat. "Sloane."

"It is Luis . . ."

His gut tightened. "What's wrong?"

"The *señorita*, she is not here, *mi amigo*."

A roaring that had nothing to do with the sirens filled his head with noise. "What do you mean she's not at the orchard?" She'd been there when he left this morning.

"Doña Dicy say to call you. She is very afraid. Her niece went to bring the old woman off the mountain."

He closed his eyes.

Neither Tessa nor Dicy could've possibly envisioned how the events of the day would spiral out of control. Or imagine the danger in setting foot off the orchard. He should've called them after he talked to Tonio and warned Tessa not to leave. He'd meant to but had imagined Brandi to be in more immediate danger.

"Thanks, Luis," he grunted, and clicked Off.

Likely as not, though, she'd have gone warning or no. But if Pender caught Tessa on her way to Yonder Mountain . . .

Wrenching the wheel, he sped after the SUVs. He shot past the courthouse, past the Cozart building. The truck rattled over the bridge spanning the river. He blew by the chapel on the promontory overlooking town. At the fork, he slung the curve.

Foot to the floor, he speed-dialed her cell. Pressing the phone to his ear, his panic mounted. "Pick up. Pick up. Where are you?" Dread gnawed at his belly. His inability to reach her wasn't good. Couldn't be good.

The call rolled to voice mail.

Frustrated, he clicked Off and threw the phone into the console tray. He needed to think.

He swiped his hand over his face.

From the moment she got out of her car that first day, hadn't somewhere inside him known it would come to this?

Known . . . He sounded like Ouida. And Tessa's persistence in sticking her nose where it didn't belong hadn't helped.

But instinct or the highly honed gut that kept him alive in the white separatist stronghold—whatever he wanted to call it—his senses were at full alert now. Screaming that something had happened to her and that the something wore the face of a Cozart.

The phone buzzed.

He groped for the cell.

A text message. From Tessa?

Then he glanced at the screen, and fear knifed his gut. No, not from Tessa.

"At the barn. Having fun. But it's you we want."

The barn . . . Pender and Shelton. What had they done to Tessa? Had they hurt her?

Horrific images of what had happened to the other women raced through his mind, robbing him of rational thought. Making it hard to breathe.

A blinding, killing fury consumed him. His blood roiled in his veins, begging for release. For vengeance to be satisfied.

If they touched her, he'd kill them.

No . . . too quick. He'd flay every inch of—

Rain pelted the windshield. Dark woods rose on either side of the road. Storm clouds unfurled on the wind.

The swirling darkness inside himself cleared for a moment. They'd threatened to hurt her. That's why they were taunting him. But hurt wasn't dead.

Gib said what happened to Kaci was an accident, an anomaly.

There was still time, if he could reach her. Trade himself for her life. It was his treachery they wanted to punish.

Lightning severed the sky. The tops of the trees writhed. A thunderous boom shook the ground.

He was aware he was walking into an ambush. The odds were in their favor, not his. But he didn't care. He wouldn't allow what befell Kaci to happen to Tessa.

Zeke took the twists and turns much too fast, setting the brown leaves carpeting the shoulder of the road aflutter.

They'd be looking for him to come down the logging road. But he had a better idea. Something to even the odds. The element of surprise.

Robertson's farm. He'd hide the truck at Robertson's, then hike through the woods to the old Cozart homestead.

Suddenly, a Dodge Ram came out of nowhere and T-boned his truck, running him off the road and spinning him onto the shoulder.

Fighting for control, he barreled into the woods.

Saplings beat at the hood. A giant tree loomed ahead.

Headed on a collision course, he jerked the wheel and stomped on the brakes.

The rear fishtailed.

Inches from impact, he brought the truck to a rocking halt. Quaking with the aftereffects of adrenaline, his chest rose and fell.

Pender and Shelton jumped out of their vehicle. Small, oozing cuts from the earlier shoot-out pockmarked Shelton's face.

Zeke was reaching for the Remington when the men flung open both truck doors.

Pender snatched the shotgun out of his grasp. Shelton dragged him from the truck and threw a punch.

Zeke deflected it.

Off balance, Shelton teetered on the steel toes of his boots.

Zeke followed with an uppercut, nailing his jaw.

Shelton fell to the leaf-covered ground.

Zeke went for the Glock he'd stashed in the waistband of his jeans.

But Pender was on him in an instant, wrestling for control of the gun.

Zeke threw back his arm. His fisted hand connected with Pender's jeering face.

Pender dropped like a rock.

Still lying on his back, Shelton swiped Zeke's legs out from under him. They rolled on the ground as Pender scrambled to his feet.

A booted kick whooshed the air from Zeke's lungs, and it sounded as if a couple of ribs cracked. His grip on the Glock broke. The gun clattered across the ground, out of reach.

Pender pounced, pressing his knee into his back, mashing his face into the earth.

Zeke thrashed. "Where is she?"

Shelton seized a fistful of his shirt and then yanked him upright. "Shut up."

He turned his face from the blast of expletives and Shelton's sour breath.

"Look at me when I'm talking to you, rat face!" Shelton shook him.

No small feat, considering Zeke topped the Aryan Nations reject by three or four inches. But what he lacked in stature—or in brains—Shelton made up for in mouth and brawn.

A flurry of punches followed to Zeke's midsection. Blood gushed onto his lip from his nose.

Striking out, he pummeled Shelton's solar plexus. The skinhead grunted.

Then the butt of Zeke's own rifle nailed him in the temple.

Stars exploded. Excruciating pain shredded his brain, momentarily blinding him. He twisted to catch himself and went down on one knee.

Pender swung the stock again, but Zeke ducked, saving his life, receiving a glancing blow rather than a death blow. Still, it caught him broadside and set off a reverberation in his skull, rattling his teeth. He pitched forward, unable to stop himself this time.

Over the high-pitched noise in his head, he heard the sound of tires on the road.

Another car. Doors slammed. Crunching gravel.

Through the sweat and mud stinging his eyes, he beheld a pair of black leather rain boots and a pair of Italian loafers. Sometime during the melee, it had stopped raining.

"You better not have killed him." Colin of the Italian loafers.

Pender placed his boot on Zeke's shoulder blades, pushing him down. "Why not?"

Shelton kicked him.

He muffled a groan.

Colin's feet circled. "Because he may be our ticket out of the country."

"I'm federal." Zeke clawed the dirt unable to rise. "Let Tessa go. Take me. We can make a deal."

The rain boots approached. "You are not in a position to make deals."

His stomach knotted at the voice.

Anjanette snapped her fingers. "Take him to the barn."

Each taking an arm, Pender and Shelton hauled him vertical.

The barn was where he wanted to go anyway. To where they were holding Tessa. He didn't have a plan. But he'd figure something out.

He had to.

❖   ❖   ❖

Zeke blinked as sudden light poured into his eyes. After being stuffed into the Dodge Ram, he must've blacked out. But for how long?

The overcast day had turned into a gloomy afternoon.

Shelton tore him from the vehicle. Shoved forward, Zeke staggered.

They were in the clearing at the old Cozart homestead.

His head throbbed.

Pender strode out of the old barn. "It's done like you said, Aunt Angie."

"Let's lynch him like the old days." Shelton kicked Zeke again, as if he was a sack of potatoes. "You dirty—" Expletives dropped from his mouth like pine cones onto a roof in a hurricane.

Cradling the double-barrel, Anjanette's face flickered with annoyance. "Such language, Shelton Allen, is not appropriate in the presence of a lady."

Some lady. But there was no sign of the Cozart brotherhood. Reilly must've managed to corral them at least.

Colin stood off to the side, paging through his phone. "We need to go, Mother. We've already taken far too long. Dad risked capture to warn us."

She flicked a skeletal hand. "I acted too quickly last time, and the past grew up to bite me." She threw Zeke a venomous look. "I won't make that mistake again."

Colin leaned against the open door of the Range Rover, looking petulant and bored. "Dad says to put him in the car and go."

Shelton shook his fist. "Not till I've done had my fun with this federal piece of—"

The shotgun came up and pumping the trigger, Anjanette unloaded a barrel into Shelton.

He flew backward, landing on his back. Parts of his midsection scattered into the muddy earth.

Colin fell into the Rover.

Zeke hit the ground and stayed there.

Pender's eyes went as wide as silver dollars. "Aunt Angie?"

With a glacial glare, she swung the smoking barrel in his direction.

Palms raised, Pender backed away, terror in his eyes.

"I warned him about his language. He didn't listen."

Colin retched into the ground near the tire. "Mother, what are you doing?"

"You're going to have to be strong, darlin'. Hard times are ahead until we get across the border. Hard things are going to have to be done."

Zeke's best recourse was to remain quiet. In the insanity, maybe they'd forget about him. Or he might take to playing dead.

Anjanette lowered the shotgun. "Drag Shelton's body into the barn, Pender."

Pender moved with an alacrity Zeke hadn't known he possessed. "Yes, ma'am." After taking hold under Shelton's armpits, he towed the dead man into the barn.

"Get the fire going, Colin. Loose ends need to burn along with the evidence those fools left in the barn."

Zeke jerked. "Tessa—"

Anjanette trained the shotgun on him. "She ain't there. That's just what I told Pender to say to bring you running."

His gaze cut to Pender and Colin, who were setting fires around the perimeter of the old barn.

It didn't take much for the flames to take hold. Pender must've been spreading accelerant while Zeke was in the Rover.

The evidence of what had happened to the three rape victims and to Kaci would go up in smoke.

Anjanette jabbed the barrel into his chest. "Don't even think about it."

He froze.

But as long as Tessa wasn't in there, what did it matter if they torched the place? Good riddance to that hellhole of misery.

The building deserved to be wiped off the face of the earth. Extinguished. Gutted. Obliterated.

A more immediate problem involved his own well-being. His life and Tessa's weren't worth a plugged nickel in the hands of the murderous Cozarts, and the cavalry didn't know where he was.

He was going to have to save himself. And stall long enough to find out where they'd stashed Tessa.

Returning, Colin raised his hands to his face and wrinkled his nose. He reeked of gasoline.

"Make sure you get the fire going good inside the barn too, Pender," Anjanette called.

Nodding, Pender disappeared into the barn.

Anjanette nudged the gun toward the barn. "Bar the door, darlin'."

Colin blinked. "While Pender is still inside?" His mouth opened and closed like a fish on a line. "But he's family."

"You remember what I used to tell you about the baby birds of prey?"

Colin's face went ashen. "Only one nestling is allowed to live."

She nodded. "Go. Hurry."

He ran to do his mother's bidding.

Zeke set his jaw. "What have you done with Tessa?"

Anjanette fixed her eyes on him. "It's your fault she had to die."

"She can't be dead." He shook his head against the darkness spiraling before his vision. "I don't believe you." It couldn't be true. It mustn't be true.

"That white girl was never meant for the likes of a mongrel like you. Even if she hadn't spurned my boy, I'd have sooner seen her dead than mix her pure blood with yours."

What crazy was she talking now?

Coughing, Colin ran back to them.

Smoke curled above the structure. Flames shot skyward from the corners of the barn.

From inside, Pender pounded on the barred double doors. And as the dry wood tinder of the barn became engulfed with tongues of fire, he took to yelling to be let out.

Orange smoke billowed into the gray sky as the shouting became pleas. Flames crackled along the eaves. The roof buckled and Pender begged for release.

Even from a distance, the stifling heat sucked the oxygen out of Zeke's lungs.

Colin threw his arm over his face as Pender's voice morphed into nightmarish screams.

Zeke placed his hands over his ears. Anything to stop from hearing the unearthly, inhuman howl or the licking, gloating hiss of the fire monster devouring his prey.

Anjanette's eyes glittered but she didn't turn her face from the inferno. Not once.

Fiery vengeance was a terrible thing to behold. A divine ferocity. Worse than he could've possibly imagined, much less exacted. Part of him relished Pender getting what he deserved.

Another part—the good wolf on his shoulder?—shrank from a reckoning so horrible. So complete. Without mercy.

Exactly what Pender deserved, said the bad wolf on his other shoulder. Yet for some of the things Zeke had done in the name of justice, didn't he deserve the same?

Then came a searing silence.

Colin jabbed his smoke-blackened thumb at Zeke. "Why not him too?"

Anjanette had the stone-cold face of a killer. No remorse. No regret. "His turn will come. Very, very soon."

Zeke doubted Shelton or Pender had been her first kills. A taste of blood only whetted an appetite like hers for more.

Turning to her son, she softened her steely gaze. "I'm going to have to ask you to do another brave, brave thing." She handed Colin the shotgun. "I've done everything else, but this kill must be yours."

Colin cringed from the outstretched gun in her hand. "What are you talking about?"

"This is where you prove yourself a Cozart. Where you become a man and take your rightful place in your father's eyes."

Even if the feds in town spotted the smoke, they'd never get here—much less find this place—in time. A heaviness settled over Zeke. So this was how it would end. On a deserted mountain in a wilderness. Alone. Unable to save himself or more importantly, Tessa.

But if this was it, he wouldn't go a coward. He wouldn't let them put him down like a dog.

Trembling, Colin took the gun.

"I need to find your daddy." Anjanette patted his arm. "He's not like you and me. He doesn't always see what needs to be done." She gave her son a baleful smile. "I've had to save him from Leota twice."

Zeke didn't have many cards left to play, but he'd just as soon go out fighting and take both of them with him.

Enrage. Distract. Disarm. Destroy.

It wasn't much of a chance, but it was the only option he could come up with. Last ditch. Suicidal.

"Yeah, sugar boy . . ." Zeke drawled. He made a grotesque innuendo regarding Colin's relationship with his mother.

Colin went rigid.

Anjanette's face contorted. "Your mother was a Melungeon harlot.

Dead in the hole I put her in all those years ago." For a second, her pale eyes clouded with confusion. She waved her hand in front of her face as if brushing away cobwebs. "I mean, today."

"I don't know what you're—"

"Go ahead." She nudged Colin. "Only one harpy eagle can rule the roost. This has to be your kill, son."

"She still wipe your drawers for you too, sugar boy?"

Colin white-knuckled the stock. "I-I . . ."

"Shoot him," screamed his mother. "Everything I've done was for you."

"A hostage, Mother. Dad said to bring him."

"He may be your father's eldest, but I'll never let Ransom put Leota's mongrel in your place."

Zeke and Colin both gaped at Anjanette.

The Leota Tessa had been looking for? She wasn't his mother. That was ridiculous.

Anjanette was a raving lunatic.

Yet . . .

Over the years there had been things said between his parents but quickly hushed when he walked into the room.

Missing pieces suddenly fell into place. The secrets he'd always sensed that left him feeling an outsider. Of not belonging. Of being lost. The hints, the whispers that now made a terrible sense.

The horrifying revelation made his head spin. The world as he'd known it, who he'd always believed himself to be, vanished into a dark mist.

Anjanette took her phone from her jacket pocket, glanced at it, and tucked it away. "Devil's Circle as we planned. Take Pender's truck. Like always, I'm sure he's left the keys in the ignition. Daddy and I will wait for you." She blew him a kiss.

Colin made a face at her back.

After squelching away in her squeaky rubber boots, she hopped inside the Rover and took off.

Moments ticked by. Still Colin hesitated.

There was the sound of a vehicle. Just as the high sheriff's cruiser rolled into the clearing, with a final tremor, the framework of the barn collapsed.

Having nothing to lose, Zeke grabbed the business end of the shotgun, but he slipped in the mud.

Colin took advantage of his fumble to move out of reach.

Propping open the door, Merritt got out of the patrol car. He leaned his elbows on the roof. "What's going on here, Colin?"

A malignant jealousy had taken hold of Colin's pretty boy features and transformed him into something hideous. Into his mother.

"Did you know, Uncle Merritt?"

"Know what, Colin?"

"About him being Daddy's firstborn." Colin pointed the barrel dead center to Zeke's chest. "After all these years, is that why you crawled out of the slime? To take my place, Sloane? To take my father?"

Merritt lifted his gaze to the sky. "I'm so sick of this. The lying. The cheating. The killing. So tired of carrying the brutal weight of the Cozarts on my shoulders. This poisonous legacy that runs through our blood ends now." His eyes cut between Colin and Zeke. "But this time, I'm the one doing the choosing." Merritt dropped his hand to his side arm. In a blur of motion, he withdrew his weapon and fired.

Flinching at the deafening retort of the Glock, Zeke tensed, preparing for sudden pain. For the bullet to tear into his flesh. For the descent of darkness.

Yet as the sound reverberated, echoing over the hollow, he was still standing. No blinding pain. No onset of eternal twilight.

The force of the blast knocked Colin onto his knees and the shotgun mingled with the mud. Eyes bulging, he stared at his uncle as choking sounds emanated from his throat. He fell on his back, his gaze locking on the circle of sky above the trees. The bright-blue intensity dulled from his Cozart eyes.

"Muscle memory." Merritt lowered his arm and the gun. "The training never leaves you."

Chapter Twenty-Two

As Colin's body cooled on the ground, Zeke braced for the next bullet to find him.

Death by Colin. Death by Merritt. Either way, death.

"You were in the Marines, right?" Zeke jutted his jaw. "Somalia. The Gulf War. Liberia. Close quarter battle."

"You've done your homework on me. But I wouldn't expect anything less from a former Army grunt like you."

Zeke inclined his head. "You've done a background check on me too, I see. Now kill me, or tell me where I can find Tessa."

"Son, if I'd wanted to kill you, you'd have been dead thirty-one years ago."

Nothing was making sense. He clenched his fists. "Where's Tessa?"

"We'll get to that. But first, there are things you need to know about your family."

He gnashed his teeth. "The Cozarts aren't my family."

"I've saved you from yourself." Merritt holstered the Glock. "I've done your killing for you. Your need for vengeance ends with Colin."

"How's that?"

"Pender called Colin that night from the barn in a panic to dispose of the girl's body. Later, Colin couldn't help but brag how he was a real Cozart now. How the boys were his to run, not mine."

Zeke's stomach knotted. "Kaci."

He'd always assumed Merritt was in it up to his thick neck. He'd never even considered a squeamish weakling like Colin might be involved.

"I didn't know what they'd been doing to those women. I wouldn't have allowed, much less covered up, that kind of thing." Merritt propped his boot on the bumper of his SUV. "And after what happened to your sister, it was like Leota all over again. That's when I realized I couldn't do it anymore. But I had to stay in the game long enough to stop them."

"You are Reilly's inside informant?" Zeke stared at him. "You're turning state's evidence on the family?"

"I'd already figured out who you were." Merritt gave him a faint smile. "The Cozart eyes. And I've been keeping overwatch on your well-being ever since."

So he hadn't imagined those times he'd felt eyes on his back.

Zeke stabbed his finger at Colin's body. "You think once I knew about his involvement I would've killed him?"

Merritt pushed the brim of his hat off his forehead. "Was I wrong?"

He swallowed.

"Leota would've wanted me to save you from the Cozart bloodlust."

Had Merritt saved Zeke from the worst in himself? Knowing the truth, he wasn't sure what he would've done if Colin had fallen into his hands. Staggering, he put out his arm and braced himself against the cruiser.

Something crinkled in the pocket of his cargo pants. The New Testament he'd forgotten he'd stashed there.

A whisper floated across his mind. Kaci's voice. His grandfather's too. Merritt's solution wouldn't have been the way of escape—the choice—that God promised in the little blue book.

Merritt opened the passenger door. "You should sit down, son. You've looked better."

Zeke sank onto the seat, keeping his feet firmly on the ground.

"Leota once told me my hands were a gift. We were the same grade through school. Muscle memory . . . football or gun. Some gift, huh?"

Would Zeke have given into the dark, burning drive for revenge? With the men responsible for ending Kaci's life already dead, he'd never know for sure.

The sheriff stuck his hands in his trouser pockets. "After what happened to your mother, I turned my back on football. Ran away to the Marines."

Zeke scrubbed his face. "My mother really was Leota Byrd?"

Merritt motioned toward the smoldering ashes. "You were born on the floor of the barn." A shadow of a smile curved his lips. "She sang a song about the moon to you."

Zeke recalled the unexplainable sensation he'd felt that day in the barn. Goosebumps prickled his arms. The memory shook him.

"Leota was on the run when the birth pains hit her. Hiding from my grandfather who was trying to keep her from contacting Ransom. Alone in the world, she called me."

"Why didn't she go to Ouida? That's what Ouida did. Deliver babies."

"They'd quarreled. I don't think Leota trusted her to birth the princeling of the Kittrell's arch enemy. Maybe she was afraid it'd be a life for a life."

"What do you mean?"

Merritt shifted. "My grandfather lynched Foley Reaves."

"But why then did she trust you, a Cozart?"

Merritt drew a deep breath. "We'd been friends since we were children. A part of me hoped in saving Leota's baby I might save myself. And it did, for a long time.

"Why did you ever come back here, Merritt?"

He closed his eyes. "It was home. Same reason as Leota. Eventually, I just wanted to come home."

Zeke ran his hand over his head, trying to wrap his mind and heart around an identity he'd never suspected. Not in his wildest nightmares. "You were here when I was born?"

"She begged me to save her baby. I wanted to save *her*. I didn't know Anjanette was in league with my grandfather. I didn't know when she left the barn, Leota was walking into a trap."

"Where did Ransom fit into this?"

"Until I told him the other night, he didn't know Leota came back for him. Nor about the baby. She'd run away to sing in Nashville. When he wrote and didn't hear from her, he went into a despair . . ." Merritt rubbed his chin. "My grandfather made sure any correspondence was intercepted and destroyed."

"Playing into Anjanette's schemes."

Merritt blew out a breath. "During spring break the year Ransom was to graduate, Anjanette caught my brother at his weakest. He proposed out of guilt. He was to start law school at Carolina in the fall. You ever been to Deep Holler?"

Zeke nodded.

"I'm the last person to defend Anjanette. But she'd been abused by her father since she was a girl. Determined never to go back there, she wasn't going to allow anyone to usurp her or her child."

"Ransom wasn't the only one who loved Leota, was he, Merritt?"

The stoic lawman's face turned bleak. "We all loved her. In a weird way, I think Anjanette did too. But the hate in Anjanette was stronger than the love."

Zeke sighed. "The hate had been fed more."

"At the barn, I explained about Ransom's engagement. Near about broke Leota's heart when I told her." Merritt's eyes glistened. "I was desperate to get her to see sense. But she wouldn't leave with me. Not without Ransom. There'd been a foolish lover's quarrel when she left town in October."

The high sheriff gave him a crooked smile. "Charming Ransom. She kept talking about the goodness in him. Couldn't see him for what he was. What he would become." Merritt grimaced. "What we would all become. I waited with you at the barn a long time. When she didn't come back, I took you straight to the best man I knew—"

"Virgil Alexander." Zeke owed Merritt Cozart his life.

"I can't go to prison like Judson." The sheriff's gaze lifted to the rosy streaks painting the evening sky. "I wouldn't survive without the trees. And the mountains."

"Merritt . . ."

"I don't want you to think we didn't know better." Merritt's eyes returned to the blue jon over the hills. "There is this something deep inside each person that knows Someone is out there. A higher judge."

"You made a deal with Reilly." Zeke inched forward. "It doesn't have to be this way."

Merritt heaved a sigh. "Oh, but I think it does. Probably foreordained from the moment of our Cozart birth."

"Life is what we make it." Zeke shook his head hard. "A choice. And yours doesn't have to be over. Reilly will make sure—"

"You need to stop worrying 'bout me, son, and save your woman."

His gut clenched. "Where is she? What have they done with her?"

"Once I delivered you to the preacher, I searched for Leota. But she was gone." He glanced at Colin's lifeless body. "You'll find what you need to save her in the cruiser."

Zeke was tired of ancient, bloody feuds. "Where is Tessa, Merritt? Where did Anjanette take her?"

"The wilderness is nothing but a bunch of laurel hells. There's tales of men getting lost in there and not finding their way out for weeks, if ever. But in the middle of one of those labyrinths is a waterfall, a place Leota and my brother loved."

His heart skipped a beat. "The hydraulic?"

Merritt nodded. "Colin texted me when they left your gal there this afternoon. He didn't understand the strange things Anjanette said to the Goforth girl. But that's when I understood what she'd done to Leota. Behind the cascade, there's a cave. And within the cave, a dark hole. An abyss."

Love is as strong as death . . . Jealousy as cruel as the grave . . .

"Save your woman. Don't let Anjanette win again. God, forgive me . . . I wasn't able to save your mother."

Even as Zeke rose off the seat, it was too late.

The sheriff's hand fell to his gun belt.

Muscle memory—

He raised the gun to his temple and pulled the trigger. There was a sharp retort. Like a puppet with its strings severed, the high sheriff fell face forward to lie forever still.

Zeke set his jaw.

It was time to use the gift he'd been given. To save the woman he'd loved most of his life. Loved more than life itself.

And to pray for God's mercy—that he wasn't already too late.

❖ ❖ ❖

When Tessa awoke, it was dark. Not just dark. The blackness was as complete and as deep as hell.

Tessa's heart pounded and she moved her hand to her face. She couldn't see her hand. She couldn't see anything. Total light deprivation.

Had she gone blind?

The darkness bore down upon her. Not merely an absence of light, but a heavy, suffocating shroud blanketing her limbs. A weighted pressure upon her chest, filling her nasal passages, clogging her ears.

Or—was she dead?

Listen, listen. What do you hear?

An involuntary scream ripped from her throat. She screamed again—anything to relieve the unremitting silence. She felt the warmth of her breath on her face. Her hand touched her lips, tracing their outline.

Dead people didn't breathe. And though her skin was cooler than usual, her breath reassured Tessa she was still alive. Dead people were cold, not warm.

What had happened to her? Why was she here? Where was she?

She lay on her back, arms and legs laid straight. Pressing up on her elbows, she tried sitting up.

Her forehead banged into something solid.

With a startled cry, she fell onto her back again. Her hands shook as they explored the space above her face.

The cold stone was no more than five inches from her nose.

Her temples pounded. The last thing she remembered . . . Colin. Anjanette. She bit back a sob.

Refusing to give into the terror building in her mind, she dropped her hands to her sides. Methodically, she examined the perimeters of her prison. Her shoulders brushed the confines of the walls. There was no room to turn.

The pocket of rock would've been too tiny for a man like Zeke.

She moaned. Tessa ached for him so badly it was a palpable thing, and, in a way far beyond the physical. *Mustn't think of him. Not now.* The longing for him demoralized her.

Tessa squeezed her eyes shut. At least, she believed she did. In the all-consuming blackness, she wasn't sure if her eyes were open or shut. She could only lie inert, listening to the sound of her own ragged breathing.

Had they entombed her in some sort of stone vault?

Deprived of the most vital of senses, her other senses kicked in. The smell of earth, dust, and something she could only think of as ancient rock filled her nostrils.

Not a sepulchre as she'd first believed. She was underground. Blind panic robbed her of coherent thought. Claustrophobia descended like a smothering curtain. She was buried alive.

She screamed and she screamed again. Until her naturally husky voice grew hoarse. *Wait* . . . She had to stop before she used up the oxygen—

Oh, God. Help me.

In a frenzy of terror, she clawed at the enclosing rock coffin.

Warm liquid touched her cheeks. She tasted the salt of her tears on her tongue, and also something metallic. Blood. In her flailing, she'd mangled her own flesh.

Stop. Think. Listen.

No one knew where she was. *She* didn't know where she was.

Like the night at the opera house, no one was coming to save her. No one had been there to rescue her from Anton. She hadn't been able to find Sandy, but Anton had found Tessa. He'd chased her down the corridor. Pursued her onto the stage. Scrambled after her.

Gasping for breath that night, she thought only of getting higher to escape the noxious fumes. A primal instinct for survival drove her away from the blaze. Desperate for air, she'd clambered onto the scaffolding of the catwalk.

But his hand reached, grasping for her. He seized upon the hem of her costume.

She'd torn free, probing for the latch on the ceiling. Finding the handle, she'd put her shoulder into it and shoved the door open.

Then she'd been free.

Scrambling out, she'd run across the roof as far as she could go and clung to the balustrade.

In the Quarter, the nineteenth-century Italianate edifice overlooked the streets of Royal and Bourbon. Behind her, the fire raged, a scorching heat. Even in the open air, the black smoke boiled, curling around her, choking her lungs.

Tessa had heard the distant wail of sirens. Then the hiss and spray of the water hoses. Far below, firefighters clutched their axes. They battered the windows and doors of the grand old lady. Braver than her, they fought to get into the inferno she'd run away from. They'd arrive too late for Sandy.

Anton had crawled onto the roof, calling Tessa's name. Cajoling her to come away from the edge, to come to him. To sing—for him.

Without letting go of her death grip on the railing, over her bruised, bleeding shoulder, she'd stared at him.

Anton stood outside the open trapdoor, wreathed in black smoke. His blond hair was coated with ash. His classically handsome features, grimy with soot.

Her choice. To jump or to burn with a madman.

God, help—

The wind had whipped the folds of her garment around her bare legs. She closed her eyes.

When she opened them, a man in a helmet was reaching for her.

"I'll never let you go," Anton screamed at her in the final moment as the flames engulfed him. "Wherever you go, you'll carry me with you."

The rescuer on the extension ladder never gave any indication he heard Anton.

Perhaps Anton's parting words only resonated in her head.

The man in the turnout gear pulled at her none too gently.

With a wild cry, she scrabbled over the balustrade and into his waiting arms. They'd barely touched the ground when the entire structure collapsed in a heap of fiery sparks and groaning beams.

A death throe of twisting steel girders. Popping, percussive, explosive bursts. Yet despite the unbearable heat, she'd felt a faint breeze on her bare arms. A wind off the river . . .

She jerked back to reality.

The air current wasn't in her imagination. She could feel a dank, stale breeze on her face. Where there was air flow, there had to be a way out. Escape.

She thrust her hand behind her head and discovered a nothingness.

The draft of air accelerated into a gust. The gust became a gale. And the blast had a voice. Like that of a wailing, writhing banshee. Or an oxygen-stealing, limb-flattening cyclone that threatened to suck the air from her lips.

She had to get out of here. But which way was out? Down or up? The deafening bellow crescendoed, drowning other sounds. Including her galloping heartbeat and frantic breath.

Wiggling her hips, she reached her arms above her head. She inched and contorted, fighting to be free of the stone cocoon. Lacerating her skin in the process. And then her hands felt the edges of the rocky chute.

Tessa squirmed out. She dangled, only to find herself dropping into the blackness. No boundaries. No walls. No sense of up or down. Free falling, she struggled to right herself midair.

She landed on her belly with a whoosh. A sharp, jagged rock poked through her raincoat into her abdomen. Momentarily, knocking the air from her body.

Fearing she might fall farther into a bottomless crevasse, she remained motionless. It took some time to gather her courage to move her feet. Stretching, sliding, praying for something solid not far beneath her, a floor she could not see.

One shoe—thank God she'd worn her running shoes—found purchase. Then the other. Whimpering, she crawled her hands and body to join her feet.

Breathing heavily, she remembered her phone. Had they searched her before dumping her here to die? But patting her pocket, she felt the bulge of her cell.

"Please, God . . ." Prying it out of her jeans, her hand fumbled. "Don't drop it. Don't . . ." She touched her finger to the screen.

Light blinded her eyes.

Her eyes soon adjusted to the glare. No cell reception. But she quickly located the flashlight app in the settings and shone the light around, illuminating the cavern. She exhaled with audible relief.

The room itself was as large as a football field. Once on her feet, she turned slowly around, letting the light splay over the darkened chamber. Pushing back the blackness.

Halfway up the rock wall was the cylindrical fissure from whence she'd slithered.

The wind and the moaning had stopped. The ceiling was so high as to be indeterminate.

One of the cast at the opera house had been a devoted, hobbyist caver in the hill country of Texas, so Tessa recognized the groaning for what it was. Not an ancient, demonic phantasm. There was a rational, scientific explanation.

Caves had their own air pressure systems. The sound she'd heard was the cave breathing. The cave's way of trying to maintain equal pressure with the air pressure on the surface.

It had sounded like science fiction when Jules described it to her once. Now that she'd experienced the phenomenon firsthand? She took a steadying breath, because he hadn't described the half of it.

She came off the rock ledge onto a level patch of terrain. The underworld contained no color. Only browns and grays. As for life? It appeared she had the cave to herself.

While that was terrifying in itself, she was grateful there were no other creatures like insects, bats, or spiders. But more frightening creatures called from the dark recesses of her fear, and she regretted every horror movie she'd ever watched. She closed her mind to cinematic conjurings of bone-chilling specters. If she gave in to the fear, she'd be lost.

Think about something else. Where there was air pressure, there was a way out. Hold on to that.

She glanced at her cell. It contained only about five-percent battery life. When the light went out, she'd be delivered once more into the unfathomable darkness. And once her cell died, how long before she died too?

Don't think that way.

She needed to inspect the environ for an escape hatch before she lost the light.

But help would arrive. Zeke would look for her.

She lifted her chin. *God, as You sent the firefighter, please send Zeke to me.*

Like a director blocking the stage during a rehearsal, she made mental notes of the layout of the cave and the positions of the immense, jagged boulders scattered across the space.

The tomblike capsule was upstage. Across the circumference of the cavern, downstage. Upward, in the center, the flow of air ascended.

Stage left, she blundered into a jumble of stones. She beamed the light at her feet.

Not rocks. A skull.

She reeled.

With two curved, dagger-length incisors, the skull was monstrous.

But curiosity overcame her fear. Her besetting sin, which had landed her in this hellhole in the first place. She hobbled forward for a closer look.

The skull and pile of bones didn't belong to a monster, but to a prehistoric creature that once roamed the ancient mountains.

How long had the saber-toothed tiger lain in the darkness, undisturbed until now? And how had it found itself below the surface of the world?

Perhaps while chasing prey, it had fallen into the chasm. Or created a den here, and for whatever reason—illness or injury—been unable to climb free.

Tessa backed away. Its misery had ended long ago. Hers, however . . .

Someone had carried her unconscious into this hole. And very deliberately placed her feetfirst into that wormhole sarcophagus. Someone had left her to die in the most horrible place imaginable. Bereaved of light, sound, life. Alone. Someone hated her very much.

For a brief irrational second, she considered that somehow Anton had survived the maelstrom of death. But no, he couldn't have done it. His charred body had been positively identified in the smoking wreckage of the opera house.

Yet could there have been a mistake? She shivered. Had his boast proven all too real? That despite death, he'd follow her wherever—

Tessa swung around. The light from the cell bounced off stage right.

Anton was dead. *Stop freaking out.* The dead couldn't hurt her. With every fiber of her being, she believed Anton still continued to exist, but in a place far worse than this tunnel under the earth. A place of forever doom.

Her current situation was the evil work of the very-much-alive Anjanette and Colin. Her head ached. She remembered the lacy curtain of falling water. The cave behind the falls. A quick, stunning whack.

She winced, fingers finding the goose egg at the base of her hairline. She had a thick skull and a heavy cushion of hair to thank for her injuries being no worse. She rotated her neck, trying to work out the knots of tension. And her gaze latched onto a splash of color.

To the left of a broken boulder, there lay something yellow.

She blinked to be sure and squinted. Something blue too.

Tessa moved closer.

In the perfect humidity of the chamber, black strands of wavy hair still clung to the human skull. The slender bag of bones wore a faded blue broomstick skirt and a sunshine-yellow peasant blouse, similar to the one on the album cover. And scuffed red Keds of a now-vintage origin.

This had to be the mortal remains of Leota Byrd. Arms flung wide, the ballad singer's empty eye sockets stared into the black netherworld above her head.

"Oh, Leota," she whispered to the darkness. "What did you do to Anjanette to earn you this?"

But she knew.

Tessa crouched beside the woman whose voice had been so effervescent, whose life had been so short. All these decades, she'd lain here. Alone.

A gift like Leota's—like what Tessa once possessed—drove those around them in one of two ways. Into an admiration of beauty, an appreciation for a taste of Eden lost and a whisper of paradise to come. Or, like Anjanette, into a jealous rage. Attempting to destroy what they themselves could not possess. An ancient, murderous envy. As old as the mountains and the river itself, a malice straight from the gates of hell.

Metal glinted on the bony knuckle of Leota's thumb.

A man's ring. The cut stone, a pearly opalescence. She'd seen its smaller, female twin. And at last, she knew the identity of Leota's long-ago erstwhile lover.

Ouida had said Leota left wearing moon earrings and a matching ring. Tessa had envisioned half-moons in sterling silver. But Ouida meant moonstone, like the lullaby.

As if on some spiteful cue, the light from the cell flickered and died, leaving Tessa stuck in this graveyard devoid of life. Devoid of sound. Devoid of everything.

Shivering, quavering, she began to sob.

Like the dead woman, she'd been betrayed and abandoned by every man she ever loved. But not by God . . . She'd been too bitter to see the truth before. On the roof of the opera house, He'd been there. Always faithful.

Despite the darkness, she beheld everything clearly now.

A portion of a sacred music cantata from her conservatory days came back to her. Based on a psalm . . . She could see the title and the words in her mind's eye.

Where can I go to flee from Your presence . . . The darkness and the light are both alike to Thee.

A gentle whisper drifted across her consciousness.

Sing.

Tessa stiffened.

Sing, came the insistent command.

Tessa railed at the darkness, a seething, visceral entity pulsing against her sanity. Anton had wanted her to sing that night too, as a perverse mockery of everything good.

Not like that. Sing to Me.

She opened her mouth, unsure of what notes her dry, tightly closed throat could produce. But what emerged was the aria, the high point of Bach's *St Matthew Passion*, "Erbarme dich."

Lord, have mercy on me.

Chapter Twenty-Three

It was the longest drive of Zeke's life. Inside the cruiser, the police scanner broadcast reports of the river at flood stage. Emergency personnel were up to their eyeballs in mudslides and swift water rescues.

The cruiser had been equipped with climbing ropes, an LED camp lantern, a flashlight, gloves, and a machete. Merritt, his uncle, had provided everything.

His uncle? *No.* He couldn't think about that now. He wasn't sure he ever wanted to think about the blood-soaked family into which he now found himself an unwilling member.

Zeke drove as far as the road allowed. After grabbing the gear, he stuck his head through the coil of rope and let it hang around his torso. He stuffed the tactical light into his cargo pants and slid the handle of the lantern over his arm. Gripping the machete, he took the incline at a run. He charged past the lavender shadow ruins of the once vibrant Cane Creek community.

Only ghosts lived here now.

He jogged around the broken, tumbledown headstones of people whose time had come and gone. The light was failing. Night would drop like a blackout curtain.

But he didn't utilize the flashlight or lantern. Not yet. He didn't want to put a drain on the batteries until he had no other choice.

Cozart blood ran through his veins. The same blood as Merritt. Judson. Colin. Pender . . . *Dearest God,* the evil his clan had done.

The drugs. The murders. The brutality.

Something twisted inside him. *Stop thinking about that. Focus.* If he didn't get through the laurel hell and on the other side before the darkness descended . . .

Tessa. He kept her image before him as he hacked his way through. He could barely see the path. If he lost the trail, if he lost her . . . like he'd lost Kaci?

His breath became ragged. *Blood will out. Ouida was right. Blood always prevails.*

Kin to the Cozarts, his previous life choices took on an altogether different meaning. No matter how innocuous, every event suddenly took on a new, sinister interpretation.

Everything he'd ever touched, believed true about himself. Everyone he'd ever loved. Tainted by the blood ties he bore. Polluted. Contaminated. Fouled.

How could he ever have a future with Tessa? How could she ever love someone like him? How could God?

Zeke burst out of the rhododendron at full bore, nearly toppling into the rising creek. He teetered on the sandbank, throwing himself back just in the nick of time.

The fast-flowing stream had become a raging torrent.

A well of despair opened in his chest. His own internal dakwa threatened to drag him down and swallow him whole. He had to keep fighting. He wouldn't, couldn't, give in.

Not until Tessa was safe. After that . . . Maybe Merritt was right. Perhaps the wicked heritage of the Cozarts could die with Zeke.

Taking a shuddering breath, he gauged the distance, stone to stone, from the bank to the granite slab. Soon the path to the falls would be completely obscured.

Stepping onto the first rock, he wobbled. It was slick with moss on a good day, and this was anything but a good day. Nearly afraid to breathe, he stretched for the next one. And the next one.

Midway across, he lost his footing and flailed.

The cold shock of the water almost stopped his heart. The flash flood had loosened debris from the muddy bottom. He couldn't get his feet under him. He struggled to right himself, frantic to avoid the looming falls. But in the thrall of a power mightier than himself, he became caught in the current's riptide. Sweeping him ever closer in an inexorable trajectory to the hydraulic.

Something solid slammed into him and a churning log crashed over him. Holding him down. Rolling, tumbling over him.

He couldn't breathe . . . Desperate to stop his momentum, he reached but couldn't find anything to grasp on to. Splashing the water around him, he stretched out his hands.

Rock scraped his knuckles.

He seized hold and popped up on the other side of the cascade.

The log spun into the mud-red cycle of the hydraulic and vanished.

He clung to the granite ledge. Not the easiest way to get inside the falls, but he'd made it. That was what counted.

Zeke heaved himself out of the mind-numbing cold of the pool. Lumbering to his feet, he took stock of his gear. The lantern and machete were gone, wrested from him.

But the rope was still strung around his body. And the flashlight, if it worked, was still tucked in the side pocket of his pants.

He stepped farther inside the cave, out of the spray. "Here goes n-nothing . . ." His teeth chattered.

Zeke flicked a lever, and light streamed out of the florescent, water-proof flashlight. Shining the beam, he quickly ascertained the lair lay empty. His heart sank. Where was she? *Tessa* . . .

The interior of the cave contained pictographs of ancient warriors scraped time out of mind on the walls. A people with hugely drawn eyes, big as moons, long vanished. Pushed out, vanquished by the later Cherokee.

White settlers would later expel the Cherokee. And Roosevelt's park-way would dislocate the settlers' descendants. But here, stylized render-ings of near mythical creatures were preserved pristine. Mastodons. Saber-toothed tigers. A bird he didn't recognize.

Hearing something, his ears pricked. The sound was not quite intel-ligible, not English.

Zeke played the light over the walls. Across the floor. To an opening.

A cleft too small for the bulk of his shoulders to fit through. But a wirier build like Anjanette or Colin would fit . . . and a slim woman like Tessa.

Dropping to his knees, he didn't understand the words at first.

Then apparently, she switched to English, singing, "Have mercy, My God, for the sake of my tears. Look here, my heart and eyes weep before you bitterly."

It was the most beautiful sound he ever heard in his life. "Tessa!" he yelled.

A sudden gust of air blew out of the pit.

Dust flew into his eyes, blinding him, and he was blown back by the force of the wind.

Music ceasing, the chamber filled with an unholy yowling, raising atavistic hackles along his spine.

Fighting the velocity, he stuck his head over the gap. "Tessa!"

Like the flicking off of an electric light, the wind ceased as suddenly as it began.

"Tessa, are you there?" His heart pounded. "Are you all right?"

Just when he believed he would lose his mind from the silence, she called to him. "Zeke?" She sounded on the verge of hysteria. "I can't see you. It's so dark down here."

"I'm here, baby." He shone the light in the direction of her voice, but he couldn't see her either. "I can't get through to you. I'm going to throw down a rope."

Yet how would she find the line in the dark?

"I can see your light. It's very high." Her voice darkened. "The wind . . . Sometimes it changes direction. Sucks things inside. We won't have much time before it starts again."

Zeke jumped to his feet and unwound the climbing rope. "I'm attaching the flashlight. Don't let it hit you," he shouted. "When it drops, tie the end around your waist."

How far did the drop-off extend? Would the rope be long enough to reach her?

God, please let it be enough. He anchored one end of the rope to an immoveable boulder. After putting on the climbing gloves, he positioned himself on the floor, bracing his feet against the shelf of the opening. He needed traction to bring her out. The last thing he did was to secure the flashlight to the other end of the line.

Once the light went through the rift, he would be operating in darkness.

Zeke cupped his hands around his mouth. "I'm sending it now, Tess. Watch yourself." He tossed the rope into the shaft.

Silence . . .

"Tess!" His mouth went dry. "Red?"

"I've got it."

His chin sank onto his chest. *Thank You, God.* The line went taut between his hands.

"I'm ready, Zeke." She gave the rope a gentle tug. "Get me out of here, please. I want to go h-home."

Home. The most beautiful word in the universe from the lips of the most beautiful woman he'd ever known. He'd need her emotional strength to get them both through this terrible night.

"I'm going to pull you up."

"O-kay." A querulous tremor in her voice.

"Sing to me, Tess, while I haul you up."

Below him in the crater, a laugh. "'Cause it isn't over till the fat lady sings?"

"Figured you'd appreciate a little opera humor," he bellowed.

She required something to take her mind off the ascent. He needed a tune to take his mind off what would happen if the rope slipped.

He grimaced. He wouldn't lose his grip. He wouldn't let her fall. "Here we go." He yanked on the cord. "Hold on tight. And sing, Tess."

"Black is the color . . ." The notes floated upward. "His face so soft and wondrous fair. The purest eyes and the strongest hands—"

"Nice touch," he called down.

"I thought you'd appreciate that part," she yelled.

He would appreciate her standing next to him more. "Keep singing," he shouted.

"Oh, I love my lov-er and well he knows."

Hand over hand, he pulled. Straining. Panting for breath. Digging his heels into the ground. Grappling deep for reserves of strength.

"Yes, I love the ground on where he goes." There was a subtle change in her voice. "And still I hope that the time will come. Still I pray that the time will come."

Closer and closer. Higher and higher. Her voice louder. Nearer. The muscles in his arms were on fire. Almost . . . Almost . . .

"When he and I will be as one—" Her head breached the top of the gap. Holding the flashlight, she gasped at the sight of him.

"Your arms," he croaked, stretched full length, his feet counterbalancing her weight. "Get your arms over the ledge."

She shimmied her shoulders through the slit. She propped herself on her elbows, and scuttled free.

Only then did he let go of his death grip on the rope. He reached for Tessa, grabbed under her arms, and jerked her farther from the jaws of the gaping orifice. Losing his balance, he landed on the dirt of the cave floor.

She fell on top of him.

They lay there. Stunned and exhausted, perhaps neither quite yet believing they'd made it.

One hand fisted on his shirt, but her other hand hadn't let go of the flashlight.

"And he and I will be as one," she whispered. Then she buried her face in his chest. "You came."

He flung off the gloves, sat up, and ran his hands over her hair, her face. Desperate to make sure she wasn't hurt, that she was okay.

She laid the flashlight between them and snagged hold of his hand. "I'm fine." She brushed her mouth across his palm. "Scared within an inch of my life, but . . ."

He pressed his lips to her hair and closed his eyes, inhaling the scent of her, imprinting it into his memory. "That was too close."

"I'm mountain tough like Dicy. And you."

Not like him. He told her everything that had happened while she was in the depths of the earth. The flooding. Reilly arresting Judson. Anjanette gunning down Shelton. The barn burning with Pender inside. The showdown with Colin. And the sheriff's bitter, personal revelation of how he hid Leota's baby from Anjanette's wrath.

"I found Leota." Tessa tugged at his shirt. "She's down there. Anjanette was saying crazy things. She thought I was Leota. She wanted to know where I'd hidden the baby." Tessa told him all she'd uncovered in her research about Leota. About the record label in Nashville, Tom Connelly's memories of the young singer, and what Ouida had revealed.

Something pinched inside his chest. His mother, the mother he never knew. He scoured his hand over his face. "I was the baby, Tess."

If only he could erase the nightmare his existence had become. He was cursed now. Because he was a Cozart.

❖ ❖ ❖

Tessa had a desperate need to be close to him. Refusing to let Zeke venture far, she wrapped around him, hugging his arm. "I had plenty of time to think in the dark. I suspected it might be you. Looking back on the things she said to you, I think Ouida must've suspected as well."

"GrandPop knew." Zeke extricated himself from her hold. "The only one who didn't suspect was me." He made a face. "And the Cozarts. Because if they had, I'd already be dead by now. I wish I—"

"Don't say that. I know what it feels like to have everything you've ever believed to be true of yourself ripped away. To feel betrayed. To doubt yourself."

He shook his head. "It makes me sick to my stomach that I share anything with the Cozarts. Makes me feel rotten to the core. Just like them."

"You're nothing like them, Zeke."

"Only difference is I had a badge. And a license to justify the lies I told. I know the feelings I carried inside." He thumped his chest. "The corrosive hatred when I saw what they'd done to Kaci. It's my fault what happened to Gib. I could've done something. I should've done something."

"You couldn't have known."

"I knew what they'd do if they caught him. Deep down, I didn't care." He jutted his jaw. "Somewhere inside me hoped maybe they'd catch him. Do my dirty work for me," he spat. "But for the grace of God . . . What a cosmic joke. On me."

She placed her hands on either side of his face. "I don't believe it was an accident or a coincidence that Merritt carried you to a godly man like Virgil Alexander. Nor a fluke that his daughter and son-in-law, the Sloanes, raised you far away from Roebuck. The fingerprint of God has been on your life from the beginning. Don't you see? His hand is on you still."

He jerked free. "How do you figure God's grace to Kaci?"

A tear rolled down Tessa's cheek. "He gave the Sloanes to Kaci too. And you as a foster brother."

"Some brother I proved to be. I let her go off alone to be killed."

"That wasn't on you." She raised her hands. "In this twisted, fallen world, there are Antons and Anjanettes everywhere. They get a choice too. But there's grace at the top of a burning building." She let her hands drop. "There's grace, even in a pit."

"I wish—" He bit off a moan.

She captured his hand. "Grace allowed you to find Kaci. Grace brought you to my rescue. Grace . . ." She bit her trembling lip. "Grace is waiting for you to allow Him to save you. From yourself."

He stared at her, brow furrowed. "You don't understand. I'm under a blood curse."

She blew out an angry breath. "What I understand is that God is the only chance you've got to be free of the stain."

Abruptly, he rose.

"I need to get you off this mountain." He glanced toward the hole. "Excavating her will have to wait." Closing off his emotions, he'd reverted to type.

He absolutely infuriated Tessa. She clenched her teeth so tight her molars ached. "By her, you mean your mother, Ezekiel?"

"My mother died in a car crash." The look he flicked her way was less than friendly. "It won't be easy getting out of these mountains."

"Not to mention that Anjanette and Ransom are also on the loose."

"Not for long." He snorted. "Not when I'm done with them."

"You can't kill your own father, Zeke."

It was hard to recollect how only a few moments ago he'd hung onto her. Kissed her hair. Breathed in her very essence. Almost allowed himself to love her.

The expression in his eyes sent shivers down her arms. "The judge is no father to me."

For the first time she saw the Cozart in him. And it terrified her.

Chapter Twenty-Four

When they cleared the waterfall, Zeke realized how cold he truly was. He'd fallen into the frigid water, but a deeper, down-to-the-bone chill had frozen him to the core. In the place his heart, hopes, and dreams used to reside.

A pale moon chased scudding clouds.

Carriage stiff, Tessa snatched her arm free when he tried to guide her over the perilous, unsteady rocks. "I've got it," she grunted.

Just as well. When he got through with the woman who'd wrought such misery, he wouldn't be fit nor free to be a part of Tessa's future. And when he got his hands on the man—his father—who'd failed to stop what happened to Leota . . .

Like he'd failed to stop what happened to Kaci?

With the cessation of the rain, the creek had crept back into its usual boundaries, but he kept a watchful eye, only a hand's reach away, as Tessa traversed the creek.

He wasn't sure what he ought to do to Ransom Cozart when he caught him. Zeke wasn't sure what ought to be done to himself for not protecting his foster sister.

Once Tessa was safely ashore, he put his head down and concentrated on bridging the last slick rock. He leaped across the final gap and landed on the rain-saturated soil of the bank. His boots sank into the mud.

"Zeke." Something in her voice . . .

His head snapped up. And he found himself on the wrong end of Anjanette's Smith & Wesson.

"You came for your mother." There was a crazed look in Anjanette's eyes. "I suppose even brute animals possess some feeling for the vixen that bore them."

He pushed Tessa behind him.

Anjanette's glacial-blue gaze flitted to the top of the falls. "The helicopter will be here soon."

"What helicopter? Where do you think you're going?" he growled.

Her mouth hardened. "Our business associates have airstrips and landing pads from here to Mexico. Did you think we wouldn't have a contingency for everything?"

Tessa spoke over his shoulder. "I think, Mrs. Cozart, you are a very intelligent woman." She took a step around him.

He grabbed for her, but she eluded his grasp.

"You've been the real power behind the Cozart throne almost from the beginning."

What was she doing? Using herself as a shield, putting her body between the gun and him.

He took hold of her shoulders.

"No . . ." She dug in her heels, refusing to budge.

"Where is my son?" Anjanette hissed.

Standing her ground, Tessa gritted her teeth. "Colin's waiting for you to join him."

Zeke wrapped his arms around her torso and shoved her aside. They jockeyed for position.

"Stop it," Anjanette yelled. "Or I'll blow both of you into the creek."

They froze.

"We're going to Devil's Circle." She jabbed the gun toward the moonlight-silvered path. "Move."

The gun prodding his back, he took hold of Tessa to help her climb. Her hand was so cold.

Shivering, she squeezed his fingers.

He wished he could stop and warm her hands between his. The crisp chill of the night air meant, come morning, they'd see frost on the apple trees.

If he and Tessa lived to see it.

A creamy orb, the hunter's moon glowed through the bare branches of a sycamore. A wind set the branches astir. Like skeletal arms, the tree limbs reached for the sky.

The trail wound over the rocky bluff from which the waterfall spilled. Tilted outcroppings loomed on either side. At the top, a series of enormous natural boulders lay haphazardly tumbled like semi-upright matchsticks. As if a race of giants had simply left the bizarre game of dominos where they'd fallen.

Anjanette drove them into the circle and beyond, forcing them to the cliff's edge.

In the gorge below, the ancient, angry river roared.

Tessa's breath hitched. "Zeke . . ."

"Don't look down," he whispered. "Hang on to me."

Rescue wasn't coming.

But then a figure emerged from behind a crag.

"This has gone as far as it's going to go, Janette." The judge's silvery hair shone in the moonlight. "It's time to stop. Judson's been arrested. Colin is . . ." His voice hitched.

Ransom must have come upon Colin's body at the burned-out barn.

Anjanette's face twisted. "It's not over until she's dead. I thought I killed her once . . ." The gun wobbled in her hands. "But she won't die. She just won't die!"

Clutching the back of his shirt, Tessa trembled. She tottered on the brink.

Rock scree skidded down the cliff at their backs, sliding and rolling before striking stone at the bottom.

Zeke grabbed her and held her fast against himself.

"I won't let you hurt him, Janette. I won't let you kill Leota's son too." He angled toward Zeke. "I never knew she was pregnant, I swear. Not until Merritt told me yesterday. I never heard from her after she left. I thought she'd found someone else. Someone from the world of her music."

"You were meant for me." Anjanette writhed. Her eyes had gone feral. "You were never meant for that crossbred strumpet who enticed you with her sloe eyes and honeyed tongue."

"I want you to understand, Zeke." Ransom turned his back on Anjanette. "The summer before my senior year, Merritt brought Leota to sing at a party. I heard her, really saw her that night, and . . ." His voice broke.

"Why did she always get everything?" Anjanette screamed. "You brought *me* to that party. After all those years, you'd finally noticed me.

Why did I always end up with nothing? She had everything. The voice
. . . the songs . . . the applause . . . your firstborn son," she shouted into
the wind. "It wasn't fair. She never loved you. She left you for the music."

"That summer was the happiest of my life. We spent it everywhere
together. The falls. The barn that Judson's son desecrated." Ransom
lifted his face, tears rolling down his cheeks. "I didn't know what Pender
had done there until Merritt told me."

"You want me to feel sorry for you?" Rage overtook Zeke. "You bent
the law to line your pockets."

"Zeke . . ." Tessa mouthed into his shoulder.

But he wasn't about to let Ransom Cozart off the hook so easily.
"You looked the other way while your family ran roughshod over this
county for decades."

"Law school was my grandfather's idea. I never wanted anyone or
anything the way I wanted her."

"Don't say that," Anjanette wailed. "The helicopter is coming. We
can start over. See me this time. Look at me . . . Look at *me!*"

"The helicopter isn't coming," Ransom snarled. "I never called them.
I'm sick to death of everything."

"Where's Colin?" she hollered. "What have you done with our son?"

"Leota and I exchanged rings." Ransom took the pinkie ring off his
finger. "Moonstones. Leota had a thing for the moon. Some old superstition about true lovers."

Anjanette shook her head. "You've worn *her* ring all these years when
I could never get you to wear a wedding band?"

"Leota and I said our own version of vows late that summer at the
falls."

"The album cover . . ." Tessa whispered. "A wedding photo."

Zeke didn't want to hear this. Any of this. "Didn't take you long to
find comfort elsewhere did it, old man?"

Ransom shook his head. "When I came home for fall break, Leota
told me she couldn't wait any longer to go to Nashville. We quarreled.
At school, I was beside myself when I didn't hear from her. Wallowing
in self-pity, I was drinking too much. And one night, Anjanette . . ."

"You betrayed the girl you supposedly loved," Zeke roared. "You got
exactly the life you deserved."

"Leota was the most beautiful thing I ever saw or heard." Ransom's eyes were tortured. "Anjanette stole my life as much as she stole Leota's life from her." He opened his hands. "I would've loved you, my own true son, the way I've never loved anyone besides your mother."

"He's not your true son!" screeched Anjanette, coming closer. "Colin is—"

Twisting her wrist, Ransom wrenched the gun from her hands. "You murdered her."

"Because I love you," Anjanette sobbed.

He yanked Anjanette close, trapping the gun between them. "But I . . . I always loved her." Pressing her against his chest, Ransom pumped the trigger.

Anjanette's spectral-thin body jerked in his arms.

Tessa screamed.

Anjanette's pale eyes went wide in disbelief at the final, horrific betrayal. "R-Ran-sommm . . ."

He threw the gun to the ground. "Love is as strong as death . . ." His gaze flicked toward Zeke.

If he lived to be a hundred, Zeke would never forget the look in the judge's overly bright blue eyes. Eyes so much like Zeke's own. But there was also in Ransom's gaze an expression of consuming grief, remorse, and something just for him, his firstborn son.

Then, the moment passed.

Ransom grabbed both sides of Anjanette's face. "For my sins." The life slowly draining out of his wife, their gazes locked.

"Love . . ." he shouted. "As cruel as the grave." He lunged, pushing Anjanette backward, leaping into nothingness.

Anjanette shrieked as they disappeared over the precipice.

"No!" Zeke cried.

There was a thud on the jagged boulders below.

He would've rushed after them—for what purpose, he wasn't quite sure unless it was his dark blood calling—but Tessa caught hold of him.

As if by sheer willpower, she restrained him from going over the edge. "Let them go." She wept. "Let the misery be done with them. I'm *your* reason to stay, Zeke. I'm your reason."

His shirttail ripped in her hand.

Chest heaving, he looked at her.

"I love you." She sank to her knees. "Love me more than vengeance. Let me love you."

And it was her love that held him in place, rooting him, grounding him. He cast one quick glimpse over the drop. It was too dark to see the shattered body of his mother's killer or the wasted form of his mother's lover.

No one could survive that kind of fall. They were gone. Dust to dust. Ashes to ashes. As if they'd never been.

But that wasn't true. He was still here. And because he was alive, something of Leota would go on too.

Listen, listen. What do you hear?

Zeke cocked his ear to the sky. He could almost swear he heard a low, soft singing coming from somewhere far distant yet as near as the ever present blue jon lying on the horizon. He gulped. "Do you hear that, Tess?"

The wind whipping her hair, she shook her head. But her eyes were huge. "A moonstone lullaby . . ." She quivered.

He shook himself. This was crazy, his imagination playing tricks on him.

But whatever he'd—they'd—heard, the sound faded gently away.

Zeke turned his back on the mountain and the stones. He held out his hand. "Let's go home."

Chapter Twenty-Five

It wasn't easy getting off the mountain. By the time they made it to Park Headquarters and civilization, it was dawn. The news of his parentage had left Zeke reeling.

Working nonstop after the flood, crews cleared the roads made impassable by downed trees. Tessa fretted and worried, but it wasn't possible to check on Ouida right away. The orchard required as much cleaning up after the storm as the rest of the county.

Early the next day, Reilly arrived at the farmhouse. "I've got a team of forensic accountants poring over the documents and laptops we seized at the Cozart compound. Figured you'd want in on it."

Zeke tossed another load of branches into the barrel for burning. "Track the money, and you'll find the rest of the Cozart cronies."

"The tentacles of Cozart corruption reach to the state capital." Reilly folded his arms over his chest. "I'm headed to Raleigh to continue working the corruption side of the case. You interested in coming too?"

Propping his hands on his hips, Zeke took a long look over the rows of apple trees. "You might've been right about my career. I think I'm done with the Bureau."

Reilly shook his head. "You don't have to be done." He frowned. "I managed to keep your nose looking clean in the official report. What went down in your personal life doesn't have to impact your professional life."

"I've lost the taste for undercover work."

"There are other things you could do in the Bureau besides work undercover."

He sighed. "I think it's time for me to move on to something else."

The case supervisor cut his eyes to the farmhouse on the knoll above the orchard. "Someone else, maybe?"

Zeke swallowed. "I'm not sure that's going to work out." He wasn't sure about anything.

"I'm sorry to hear that." Reilly's lips pursed. "But I promise you there will be more arrests to come."

Zeke offered his hand. "Thanks for everything you did, Reilly. Happy hunting."

His grip was firm. "Takes a long time for dead trees to fall. But one stiff wind, down they come."

Zeke grinned. "And you, my friend, are a typhoon."

Reilly laughed all the way to his car.

That night, Dicy drove her golf cart over to his cabin across the meadow. He heard her coming when the cart rattled over the little bridge.

He opened the door and helped the elderly woman hobble inside.

"I think you've stewed in your own juices long enough, dear heart."

"Any idea why my grandfather saddled me with the name Ezekiel?"

"No clue."

He scowled. "Then I've really got nothing to say, Miss Dicy."

"That's just fine." She eased into an armchair. "'Cause I've got plenty to say for the both of us."

Perhaps it was best that she'd come. Dicy might be the only one alive who could answer some of his questions. He sank down onto the couch.

"Tessa and I are worried about you. It's not good, you keeping your feelings bottled inside." The old woman's face gentled. "How are you doing?"

He blew out a breath. "Guess I owe my year-round tan to Leota Byrd, eh?"

"I hope you won't allow the events of the last forty-eight hours to make you bitter. It was a bitter seed of prejudice that yielded a crop of hatred that spawned three generations of evil." Her gaze dropped to Kaci's Testament on the burled wood table between them. "What's this?"

He scraped his hand over his face. "I've been looking through Kaci's New Testament."

"That's the best place to start when you've got questions." Dicy picked it up and flipped through the pages. "Looks like she highlighted some favorite verses."

He leaned forward on the edge of the seat. "I have so many questions, Miss Dicy, I don't know where to start."

She looked at him. "There are things in this life we will never know, and we have to accept that." Dicy ran her finger across one of the pages. "Kaci's life might've ended in the Yonder Wilderness, but these verses she marked tell me she knew the way Home. I'm here to make sure you know how to find your way too."

He shook his head. "I'm not sure that's possible for someone like me."

"Your mother—"

"My mother is Jean Sloane," he growled.

Dicy nodded. "That's who I meant. Jean Alexander Sloane was a woman with a lot of love to give. I did not know Leota Byrd was your birth mother."

He rubbed his forehead. "I wondered . . ." It made him feel less alone somehow, knowing Dicy hadn't been lying to him this entire time.

Dicy gave him a pensive look. "Looking back, though, I suspect your grandfather told my husband. Calvin told me it would be better, having once left, if Virgil stayed as far away from the county as he could get. At the time, I didn't understand why he would say such a thing about his best friend."

"Why did he bring me here every summer, Miss Dicy?"

"These mountains grow into your heart. Your grandfather couldn't resist the hankering to breathe sky-country air." She laid the cane across her lap. "Perhaps he knew you'd have to return someday to the land which gave you birth, and he wanted to give you a foundation. Roots. A place to begin."

Like an unbroken chain, it seemed the people of this place always came back to the mountains, those ancient mountains. True for Leota. His grandfather also.

And one day he, too, would be gone, but the land . . . The land continued.

He exhaled. "We visited the orchard, but never went to town or even the chapel where he'd spent his adult life. And we never visited any of his parishioners except for you."

Dicy smoothed her housedress. "He must've been afraid someone would see you and connect you to the Cozarts. You and Colin were the same age. Someone might've seen the resemblance. He couldn't take the chance."

"No wonder he swore our trips to secrecy. My parents would've been livid."

"And terrified. Old Mr. Cozart was a vengeful sort. If he or Anjanette had got hold of you, he would've had you exterminated from the earth as surely as King Herod killed the Bethlehem babies."

Zeke leaned his elbows on his knees. "So when Merritt brought me to Virgil Alexander . . ."

"Your grandfather would've known he had to get you as far away from the Cozarts as possible. It was the only chance to save your life. And in saving your life, he gave you the chance for a new life. A different kind of future."

"It cost him a lot, didn't it? Giving up his home, his pastorate. Why?"

Dicy smiled. "He told me one time he took one look at you and saw the fine, young man you'd become one day. He moved you as far away as he could from the evil, corrupting influence of the Cozart clan. He did it because he loved you."

Over the last few days, Zeke had felt as if everything he'd shared for thirteen years with his grandfather had been a lie. Dicy's words gave him no small measure of comfort.

"The Lord works in ways often beyond our understanding." She tilted her gray head. "Leota's sacrifice filled another woman's empty arms. Don't lose sight of the legacy of the two women who loved you. That's more than some folk ever get. Virgil took you to a place where you'd be cherished and protected. Their silence was never meant to hurt you, but to keep you safe. The Sloanes poured themselves into you. They loved you until their last breath."

Jean and Will Sloane had loved him. He would not forget what they'd meant to each other as a family. Perhaps one day when he was older, they would've told him the truth about his origins. "I'm not sure how I feel about my birth mother, Miss Dicy."

"You should feel however you want or need to feel. I expect, like a lot of things in life, your feelings for her will take time to settle. I pray, though, one day you will think of her with great compassion. Like the rest of us mortals, Leota made mistakes."

He knotted his hands. "She loved unwisely. A mistake that cost her her life."

"Yet it was Leota's love that saved your life."

He threw out his hands. "But what do I do with the irrefutable fact that my blood remains Cozart?"

"In the end, the only blood that will matter is the blood of Christ. It is that blood God sees when He looks at those who belong to Him. Not the blood that runs through our veins, but the blood that washes our heart." Dicy held Kaci's blue Testament out to him. "There are two things I know, Zeke. God is a good, good Father. And He loves you devotedly."

He took the book from her.

"There is an old hymn, one of your grandfather's favorites." Dicy's wrinkled mouth curved. "Don't worry. I won't sing it to you. Tessa's the singer in this family. But it goes like this—" She cleared her throat and spoke the words. "What can wash away our sin? Nothing but the blood of Jesus. What can make us whole again?"

"Nothing but the blood of Jesus," he whispered.

She smiled. "I never did think putting a child's backside on a pew every Sunday a mistake. The Sloanes taught you well." She thumped the cane on the floor.

He set aside the Testament and moved to help her to her feet.

"You can't choose your beginning. But oh, my dearest heart, each of us do get to choose our destination." She touched his arm. "That's what the blood of Jesus does—it gives us a choice. The love of God is a gift. The love Tessa has for you is also a gift. I hope you won't waste either one." Leaning heavily on the cane, Dicy shuffled out to the golf cart.

He watched from the porch, making sure she made it safely across the creek and to the farmhouse.

Tessa came out onto the ramp and gently assisted the old lady into the kitchen.

Back inside the cabin, he stared at the blue New Testament. Sitting down in the armchair Dicy had vacated, once more he opened the book.

A verse leaped out at him.

"You were redeemed from the empty way of life handed down to you from your ancestors . . . with the precious blood of Christ."

Tears stung his eyelids. He thumbed through the other verses Kaci had believed important enough to mark.

"No condemnation for those in Christ Jesus . . ."

His heart pounded.

"If anyone is in Christ, the new creation has come: The old has gone, the new is here!"

The words reverberated in the deep places of his soul. This was the way home. The way to peace, to his mom and dad, to his beloved grandfather.

He choked off a sob. And to Kaci.

This was the answer for what happens when a person died, the only answer he ever needed to know. And somehow, at that moment, everything came together for him. At last.

He longed to be a new, better man than the man he was. Maybe whose child he was born to was less important than whose child he became, his family of origin less important than his family for eternity.

The words of the Scripture, the words of Kaci's heart, became the words of his heart's desire too.

He squeezed his eyes shut. *Forgive me, Lord. Wash me in Your precious blood. Please make me clean. I want to belong to You.*

Zeke opened his eyes. Nothing appeared changed inside the cabin. And yet everything inside him felt different. Lighter. Free. Clean. New. *Where do I go from here, Lord?*

Or perhaps this time, going was not what God required from him. Was there something else that God wanted him to do? Some purpose higher than serving himself?

In light of salvation, any gift Zeke possessed was incomparably small. But maybe there was something with which he could gift the Savior who'd given him His life-atoning blood?

His grandfather had risked much to give him roots to this place. It was time to stop wandering. And with his spiritual heritage also came responsibility to give back to others. What did God want the rest of his life to look like?

Gradually, an idea took shape, a path that might still be inclusive of all the characteristics that made him who he was. Utilizing his curiosity, the same adrenaline drive, only now redeemed. Like Zeke himself.

He'd spoken with Tom Connelly and knew the extent of the money kept in his mother's royalties account. Money that now belonged to him. There'd been a God-driven purpose for it all along.

But what did the amazing transformation inside him mean for him and Tessa? Could his new purpose, new life, include her? She'd said she was leaving. Was there a place for him in the future she envisioned for herself?

Zeke's heart thumped in his chest.

At cross-purposes with her for so long, he'd hurt her. Too badly for her to forgive him? She'd probably given up on him. She couldn't possibly love him anymore.

He wasn't good with words. He wasn't even good at admitting his feelings to himself. What did he have to offer someone like Tessa Goforth?

Zeke was back to more questions than answers, but now he knew where he must seek the answers. He spent the rest of the long night reading through the little blue book. Praying for God's strength and wisdom to do what was best for Tessa.

Even if God's best for her might not include him.

Chapter Twenty-Six

In the forty-eight hours since the reckoning, there had remained between her and Zeke a world of hurt. Despite what they'd been through on Yonder, there were a host of things left unsaid and unsettled.

Zeke had gone somewhere inside himself, shutting her out. Likely wrestling over his blood. Wrangling with God and tormenting himself over a past that couldn't be changed.

Then on the second night after the flood, Dicy went over to the cabin to "talk sense into the boy."

She wished her aunt good luck with that.

But whatever Dicy had said, the next morning, Zeke actually emerged from his self-imposed isolation and ate breakfast with them in the farmhouse. And he shared the momentous step of faith he'd taken.

Dicy hugged his neck while Tessa cried.

In characteristically Zeke-like fashion, however, he didn't say anything else about it. Although Tessa *did* notice he carried a blue New Testament in his back pocket. And something inside him no longer seemed as tightly coiled.

That afternoon, she came up on him reading through the little book in the barn. "Sorry." She fluttered her hand and turned to go. "I didn't mean to interrupt."

"Wait, Tess." He pushed up from the workbench and stuffed the Bible in his pocket. "If you're not too busy, I wondered if you would help me."

Zeke Sloane wanted to spend time with her? She fought a valiant fight to keep sheer elation off her features. "I'm not too busy. What do you need?"

"Uh . . ." He scrubbed his chin. "I was wondering if you'd help me work on the tractor."

She blinked at him. "The tractor?"

He motioned to the John Deere. "Maybe you could hand me the tools?" He dropped his gaze to his boots. "What do you think?"

When she told him she'd help, she was proud of how even she kept her tone.

He went over the names of the tools he needed.

"Got it." She nodded. "I won't let you down."

He almost smiled. Almost. Before he caught himself.

She felt ten times lighter. With hope. For them.

They worked for a long time together. When he brought the old John Deere roaring to life, she applauded, and he grinned down at her.

She told herself not to get her hopes up too much too soon. Men were notoriously unreliable in her experience. Wish-true dreams were too often never-shall-be realities.

But things were easier between them. And for that, she was grateful.

That day, the news broke on every front and the outside world descended on Roebuck County.

It took a team of trained professionals the better part of another day to bring Leota Byrd's remains out of the pit. Once they widened the opening, Zeke insisted on climbing into the hole with them.

He needed to be there, he said. Just once. With her. The mother he never knew.

It was an unimaginable horror to contemplate that the teenage girl might have lain there in the pitch-blackness for hours or days. Waiting for death to come while knowing her baby had been ripped away, her lover lost to her, and her heart broken.

Had she called for help with that lovely voice of hers, until she was hoarse? How long did it take for the average person to die of starvation? Weeks.

Tessa didn't imagine that scenario likely.

How long before a person died of thirst? A handful of days. No more than a week. Suffering the effects of afterbirth, how long before exposure to the cold extinguished all sparks of life?

But the medical examiner discovered a deep fracture on the back of

Leota's skull. His preliminary findings indicated that she'd hit her head when she fell. After Anjanette pushed her into the abyss.

There was a good chance she either died instantly or within minutes succumbed to internal bleeding inside her brain.

No one would ever know for certain. As with most things, there existed a choice in which to believe. Tessa knew which she would choose. She prayed that in the years to come, whenever Zeke thought about his poor mother, he would choose the same.

Leota would receive a proper burial soon, not far from Emily Murdock's grave. The spot Zeke had picked out at the old church cemetery offered a glorious view, befitting the Songbird of the Blue Ridge.

Following the removal of Leota's remains, a motley assortment of specialists from the university and the state natural history museum took over the cave. Geologists. Anthropologists. Lots of -*gists*. The pictographs of the mysterious moon-eyed people and the saber-toothed tiger made the evening news.

Tessa could hardly wait to tell Ouida. The hills themselves would save the old woman's mountain. State officials had brought an unequivocal halt to development plans, and the governor declared the entire wilderness area a region of "historic and cultural significance."

Scientists would be studying the cave and searching for other clues to the region's prehistoric and pre-Columbian past for decades. There was even a revival of interest among the historians in recreating the Cane Creek community as a testament to Appalachian life before the Park and to highlight the hamlet's tragic demise in the scattering.

It was a story that had long since needed to be told. Tessa hoped Ouida would agree to be a part of it. It wasn't only the mountain's natural resources that should be preserved. The old woman's knowledge of the music and people that once inhabited the land must be captured in the oral tradition before it vanished as completely as the morning mist over a mountain ridge.

Tessa had spent the last few days thinking about what she wanted to do next. And with whom. Maybe if she didn't push, didn't make demands . . . If she controlled her expectations, didn't ask God for too much . . .

Maybe one day, Zeke would learn to love her. The way he loved Kaci?

She took a deep breath. Okay, perhaps he'd never love anyone the way he loved Kaci. But if he loved Tessa at all, even the tiniest bit, it would be more than she'd ever had before. A little love from Zeke was better than a whole lot of anything from someone else.

Or so she told herself in the wee hours of the night. Yet another worry niggled at the edges of her mind. How long would she have with him before he left her for something else?

Be thankful. Take what you can get. It will be enough.

Wouldn't it?

That morning, she awoke with a strange sense of urgency. "I'm going to check on Ouida today."

Zeke scowled over his cup of morning coffee.

He wasn't the only one who could scowl. "You can go with me, or I'll go by myself."

Their gazes locked.

"Fine." He pushed back his chair. "I'll get my jacket. Or I'll never hear the end of it."

"I've made a decision," Dicy announced as they turned to go. "I've decided to reinstate the annual apple butter boiling to celebrate the end of harvest. Got me a taste for some apple butter." She winked at them. "Wouldn't mind seeing some good old-fashioned courtin'. Think you two could help with that?"

He grinned. "I think something could be arranged." He rapped his palm on the doorframe. "What do you think, Red? Up for some apple butter courtin'? Wouldn't want to bore a sophisticated, uptown girl like yourself."

She made sure he saw her roll her eyes. "This uptown girl has had enough excitement to last a lifetime."

Back on familiar footing. This bantering thing they did, they did well.

And just because she could, she tilted her head, looking at him slantways from beneath her lashes. "I hear that country life—and country boys—possess a charm all their own."

He ran his hand over his mouth, but not before she saw his lips twitch. "I can be charming."

"I expect you can." She stuck her tongue in her cheek. "But talk is cheap."

With a blinding flash of even, strong white teeth, he brushed his lips against the tendril of hair hanging over her ear. "Allow me to demonstrate."

Her toes curled in a delicious shiver.

Dicy cleared her throat.

Nearly twined together on the threshold of the screen porch, they sprang apart.

"Like I said, time for some good *old-fashioned* courtin'."

Tessa blushed.

"Yes, ma'am." Zeke's laughing eyes were anything but repentant. "Later," he whispered, and brushed his mouth against her earlobe when Dicy thumped over to the counter with the cane. His voice scraped deliciously low.

Her heart beat faster.

"Tell Ouida I expect to see her there." Dicy rummaged through her recipe box. "And if she's got any wintergreen tea left, I'd love some."

"We'll be back." Tessa started to grab the wicker basket, but Zeke got to it first. Country boys were good about things like that. She smiled at him and he smiled back.

"Now where did I put Granny's apple butter recipe?" Dicy muttered as the screen door banged behind them.

In the truck, he gave Tessa a quizzical look from behind the wheel. "You know the heater in this old pickup doesn't always work as well as it should."

"And you're telling me this why?"

He shrugged. "Suit yourself. Just thought it might be warmer if you sat over here."

She arched her brow. "You mean closer to you?"

"Just a thought."

Resisting the urge to smile, she scooted as far as she could in the seat, her shoulder brushing his.

One-handing the wheel as he drove, he interlaced his fingers with hers.

Her heart leaped. "I was thinking . . ."

"Uh-oh."

She elbowed him. "Hush."

Zeke's lips quirked.

"As I was saying before I was so rudely interrupted . . ." She paused, arching her eyebrow.

He squeezed her hand, but kept his gaze fixed on the road.

"I'd like to sing again. Professionally."

His hand tensed in hers, and his face resumed that maddeningly impassive mask. "Another opera company." His voice was flat. "Another tour. Away."

Why could he never tell her what he was feeling? Why did he leave her guessing how he felt? She'd told him she loved him at Devil's Circle.

Yet not once had he uttered those words to her. She turned her face to the window as the rolling meadowland slid past. He cared for her, she knew he did. He'd proven above and beyond as much.

Were the words no longer in him? Had those kinds of feelings died with Kaci? Did his vision of the future even include Tessa?

She shook her head. "Not the opera. My heart has gone elsewhere these days."

Her heart now resided with the man beside her. But despite the flirting and banter, she wasn't sure, though, if he wanted hers.

"The songs of the mountains are calling me." She half turned in the seat, letting go of his hand. "I'd like to record the rest of the music Leota wrote. An album in her memory." It seemed only fitting she ask Leota's son for his permission.

Perhaps together, they could tackle Ouida. Convince her to share the rest of Leota's portfolio.

"Unless you'd rather I didn't. If not me, then someone else—maybe a lyric soprano like Leota." She spoke in a rush, as she did sometimes when she was nervous. "You might find it painful for anyone to sing those songs she never got to sing, but I hate to think of her work forever languishing unsung. Unheard—"

"I-I think Leota would be honored. Thank you."

She released the breath she'd been holding.

"Your voice would be perfect. I think she would have loved you."

But do you? She swallowed against what he'd left unsaid.

His gaze seemed glued to the road. "So where will you go to make the recording?"

"Dr. McClaine has a top-notch studio contact." She shrugged. "Tom Connelly loved your mother too, so he's vowed to come out of retirement to finance the project."

"Nashville?" Zeke looked at her then. "That's not far."

She looked back at him. "No, it isn't."

"Oh" was all he said.

She fought a nearly overwhelming urge to physically throttle him. She lifted her eyes to the roof, sending out a plea for patience. "Also, maybe I'll record a collection of church music." She twirled a strand of hair around her finger. "The old hymns, especially, are such a rich storehouse."

"I like old hymns."

"And I'm also thinking about opening a coffeehouse in Buckthorn."

He cut his eyes to her. "For real?"

"For real."

He blinked. "In Buckthorn."

"In Buckthorn."

He smiled. "Café du Roebuck?"

Seriously, that smile ought to be licensed. Tessa sniffed. "I'll take your suggestion under advisement."

He scratched his head. "So why are you sitting so far away again?" He reached for her.

She looked up to find his gaze fixed on her hair, a sweet hunger in his eyes. She slid over.

At the end of the Yonder Wilderness service road, he parked the truck. The construction equipment was gone, put to better use somewhere else.

Burning with energy, announcements, and impatience, she left Zeke to handle the basket. She clambered up the wooded slope through the trees, quickly outpacing him. She sped through the overgrown deer trail that had become somehow more familiar to her than the street on which she'd lived in New Orleans, then burst out of the forest into the cabin clearing.

Tessa pounded up the porch steps. It was only as she stepped across the open threshold that she noticed the unnatural quiet. "Miss Ouida?" she called into the darkened interior. Suddenly hesitant, she lingered on the porch.

Zeke lumbered up behind her. "What's wrong?"

Tessa cocked her head. "I don't know. I just feel something isn't the same. Listen."

He frowned. "I don't hear anything."

"Exactly." She pushed inside. A search of the two rooms quickly revealed the cabin was deserted. "Where could she be? It's so early."

He set the basket on the scarred butcher-block counter. "Some of us work for a living. And get up with the chickens. You should try it sometime."

She made a face at him.

The bed was neatly made, but there was a depression in the coverlet. As if Ouida had only grabbed a quick nap there, not slept through the night under the covers.

"You need to see this, Tess."

At the strange sound to his voice, she hurried back into the great room. Standing beside the farm table, he gestured to the items on the table. After lifting the drawstring bag to his nose, he sniffed. "Wintergreen tea leaves."

Underneath the bag, stained and the ink faded, there was a recipe card. For apple butter.

Prickles broke out along her arms.

A beautiful pastel wedding ring quilt made from floral pieces of feed-sack cloth was draped over the back of a chair. And siting on the woven rush seat, a tattered old folder.

Leota's songs.

Tessa's breath caught.

Widening his stance, Zeke planted his hands on his hips. "Where can she have gone?"

Her gaze returned to the wedding ring quilt and to the note pinned on top. Written in Ouida's shaky, spidery script was "True love is as strong as death."

"He came for her." Tessa's voice hitched. "The by-and-by." She turned on her heel and ran out the door.

"Tess . . ." he called after her.

She dashed down the steps. "I know where Ouida is."

"Wait." He raced after her. "Let me go first. Tess . . ."

But she couldn't wait. The truth was a boulder on her chest. She could scarcely breathe for its weight, for the sorrow pressing down upon her.

She darted into the forest once again, and Zeke wasn't far behind. She bounded up the incline through the winter-dying, tall grass. Tears pouring down her cheeks, she pushed forward not stopping until her lungs were bursting for oxygen. A stitch in her side threatened to bend her double.

No . . . This couldn't be right. For Ouida to die so alone. As alone as she'd lived.

He caught up with her at the approach to the bald. "Tess . . ." There was a helpless quality in his voice. He tried to put his arm around her, to comfort her.

Sobbing, she shook him off. "Ouida died as she'd lived on this mountain. Totally alone."

He furrowed his brow. "Which is exactly what she wanted."

They found the old woman in a Sunday go-to-meeting dress. Her back against the boulder, she sat in the grass. Her white hair—longer than Tessa would've imagined—hung loose down to the small of her back. Her eyes were closed, but her face was upturned to the golden glow of the ascending sun. There was something in her features of the young woman she'd once been.

Zeke touched Ouida's hand, which was cupped in her lap. "She's still warm to the touch. It hasn't been long since—"

"Since she flew to heaven's beckoning call," Tessa whispered. "She and her great love are at last together again." Gazing into the beyond, she did what she always did. She allowed the music to express what was in her too deep for words, and sang, "Fare thee well my own true love and farewell for a while. . ." She took a steadying breath. "I'm going away, but I'll be back if I go ten thousand miles."

There was a silence between them as the echo of her voice softly receded across the mountains.

He pulled her around to the other side of the boulder. "You haven't asked what I plan to do now that harvest is over."

She hadn't asked because she feared what he'd say. And she hadn't wanted to hear it. Not yet. She'd just wanted to enjoy being with him a little while longer. Tessa let the air trickle slowly from between her lips.

His need to wander wouldn't allow him to be still for very long. She should've known he would broach the subject, sooner or later.

"Where's Reilly sending you now? A new domestic terrorism case in Wyoming? A drug cartel in Arizona?"

"I resigned from the Bureau, Tess."

She reared a fraction. Not what she'd expected. "Where will you go?"

"Is it inevitable that I go?" His brow furrowed. "Do you want me to?"

"No, I don't want you to go, but I thought you said . . . The restlessness . . . What are you thinking?"

"I do have a gift for finding people. There are so many who don't ever make the milk cartons. I'd like to get my private investigator license."

She stared at him.

"I can help the lost ones come home, one way or the other." His gaze dropped to the ground. "But only in between orchard responsibilities. If Dicy doesn't kick me out."

She laughed and he glanced up. "Aunt Dicy adores you. You've got a home for life. If you want it."

His eyes locked onto hers. "I want it."

A sibilant breeze blew a strand of hair across her cheek. She moved to brush it away, but he beat her to it.

He rubbed the tendril between his thumb and forefinger. "Red silk. I want you, Tess. I want you in my life."

Both of them were so wounded and so broken. Maybe she was wrong to expect more. Yet did the past always have to determine the future? "I want that too."

He searched her face. "I want to make sure you understand where I'm coming from."

In other words, don't hold too tight.

He might never say the words to her. Could she live with that? Could she become her stepmother and be content with what Zeke was willing to give of himself? Doubt ate away at her stomach. She bit her lip. "We should call someone about Ouida." Head bent, she retraced her route down to the base of the bald.

"Tess . . . ," he called after her.

She'd reached the shelter of the trees before he caught up to her and tugged her to a standstill.

"Wait." Frustration laced his voice. "I'm choosing to believe that to give oneself totally to another risks great loss, but—"

"You don't have say anything else." She suddenly became frantic not to have this conversation with him. Was the tenuous happiness she felt between them already slipping from her grasp? "I understand about Kaci."

He frowned. "What is it you think you understand?"

"Don't make me say it, Zeke."

"Say what?"

Tessa glared at him. "Say that I understand you'll never love anyone the way you loved Kaci. Admit that I'm willing to accept whatever crumbs of love you have left to offer." She threw out her hands. "Because I do. I am."

"Is that what you think?" His eyes widened. "Why would you think so little of me? Of yourself?"

"Must we talk about it? I get it." Hot tears prickled her eyelids. "Don't worry about me. It's a lesson I learned early from my father."

"I'm not your father." He ground his teeth. "I'm not going to leave you. Don't you know I can hardly breathe at the thought of you not being in my life?"

She tossed her hair over her shoulder. "How could I possibly know what you're feeling or *if* you're feeling anything when you don't tell me, Ezekiel?"

He reached for her. "What I feel for you is so much bigger." He swallowed. "Bigger than anything else I've ever felt for anyone. There was a lot of guilt bound up in my feelings for Kaci. She was my sister. But you are my world."

"Zeke . . ." Her throat felt raw from unshed tears.

"You told me once you looked for reasons to stay. You asked me if there was a reason for you to stay. I lied to you and told you there wasn't, because I was afraid of losing you."

The longing in his eyes humbled her.

He touched her chin with the tip of his finger and lifted her gaze to his. "But I'm promising you right now I won't ever lie to you again. I want to become the kind of man you can love. A man who looks for reasons to stay, not reasons to go." His voice hitched. "You are my reason to stay."

And it was as if the dam of words stored inside him had been suddenly released.

"I want you to lie next to me every night. I want your face to be the first face I see . . . I want you to love me and bear my children."

Tessa's heart squeezed.

His eyes, those wonderful eyes of his, welled. "I want you to sing to me. A song just for me."

She feathered her fingers through his hair. "Would every day work for you?"

He wrapped his arms around her. "Every day would be perfect. Like those long-ago summer days. You were always singing little songs to me then." His hand made a slow trek to the small of her back.

She drank in his words.

His thumb brushed across her chin and swept over the apple of her cheek. "And I think a secret place inside of me has loved you ever since. That I was waiting for us to find each other again."

"Zeke, I love you so much."

"I love you, Red."

Cupping the back of her head, his hand sank into her hair. "And I will love you until the last breath leaves my body." He sifted his fingers through her curls.

Her mouth trembled.

"I know the answer now to what happens when we die." He cradled her face between the warmth of his palms. "I know the answer."

Her breath hitched.

Zeke pressed his forehead to hers. "Because when death takes me home, I will be there, Tess, loving you still." His mouth found hers.

In that moment, time stopped. Nothing existed but Zeke and her.

Nothing but the gentle sound of falling leaves.

Discussion Questions

1. One of the themes of *The Sound of Falling Leaves* is finding home. "You had to first have a home before you could go back to it," Tessa claims. Do you think this statement is true? Where have you found "home"?

2. Who was your favorite character? Why? Which character resonated most with you? Why?

3. What was your favorite scene? Why?

4. Throughout *The Sound of Falling Leaves*, the past plays an important role in shaping the present. What were some examples of this in the story? How has this been true in your own life?

5. "An irretrievable tipping point. When life irrevocably changed for good or bad. No going back. No do-overs. Eternity in a moment." Tessa experiences this feeling before a highly charged scene in chapter four. Have you ever experienced a moment like that? What was it? Did your life change for good or bad?

6. What were some of the metaphors used in *The Sound of Falling Leaves* to illustrate a deeper truth? For instance, what deeper meaning did you see behind Zeke's obsession with the tractor?

7. What was something you learned in reading this story? What surprised you?

8. Ouida told Tessa that God has given good gifts to us all, and our gifts—including Tessa's gift of music—are the crown "we offer to the One we love." What is your gift to Him? Or as Dicy admonishes Tessa, have you neglected "the gift that is in thee?"

9. Had you heard of the scattering during the Great Depression before reading *The Sound of Falling Leaves*? Great Smoky

Mountains National Park is one of the most visited parks in the nation. Preserving the natural landscape for generations to enjoy, however, came at an enormous cost for some families. What are your thoughts on individual rights versus the common good? Eminent domain and progress versus property rights and the environment?

10. How do you feel about Dicy's statement, "You get about as much justice as you can pay for"? Is this true? Why or why not?

11. What was your take on Ouida's gift? Was it a blessing or a curse? From the Lord or not? What did Ouida believe about the source of her gift? Have you ever known someone like her who seemed to know unexplainable things?

12. Do you agree with Dicy's belief that "God is a whole lot bigger than the box most folks try to keep Him inside"? Why do you think that?

13. Which do you believe is greater: nurture or nature?

14. Does the end ever justify the means? Why or why not?

15. Both Tessa and Zeke wrestle with guilt. What effect did their guilt have on each of them? Deserved or undeserved, have you ever struggled with guilt? How did you handle it?

16. Ouida reminds Tessa that not many go through life unscathed by sorrow, and some people get more than their fair share. Have you been touched by sorrow? How so?

17. After undergoing a horrific ordeal in a fire, Tessa thinks she's lost her faith. Part of Ouida's attachment to her mountain may have been a misplaced belief that her strength came from the mountains. Ouida even quotes "I will lift up mine eyes unto the hills" (Psalm 121:1), but the rest of the Bible verse clearly states that our help comes from the Lord, the maker of heaven and earth. Have you ever misplaced your faith by trusting in something or someone other than God? What does Ouida say to Tessa to reassure her about mislaid faith?

18. The bronze plaque on the churchyard gate reads, "Remember me as you pass by. As you are now, so once was I. As I am now, so you must be. Prepare for death and follow me." What do you think happens when you die? How have you prepared for that

eventuality? Ouida states that she is ready "for home." Will you be ready? How do you know?

19. After listening to the singing at Aunt Dicy's church, Tessa reflects, "For those with eyes to see, ears to hear, the music was but a shadow of what was to come. For those with hearts to sing, the music was a dim reflection of the eternal Glory." Where or how have you experienced this dim reflection of the eternal Glory to come?

20. "Blood will tell," Ouida says to Zeke. Must "blood" always prevail? How important is our blood to what we become? What do you believe about generational curses?

21. In this twisted, fallen world, the blood of Adam runs through all our veins. And yet, as Tessa says to Zeke, there is grace at the top of a burning building. Grace in a pit. Grace waiting to rescue us from ourselves. Where have you found grace?

22. What does Tessa tell Zeke is the only way to be free of the stain of his blood? And ultimately whose is the only blood that matters? What choice does that blood give us? Whose blood does God see when He looks at you?

23. Dicy tells Zeke that there are things in this life we will never fully understand and we have to accept that. What are some of those things in your life? What two things did Dicy want Zeke to know about God?

24. One of the greatest truths of the gospel is that while we don't get to choose our beginning, we can choose our destination. What have you chosen? I pray you have chosen wisely, because that choice is your way home.

25. What story do the leaves tell? What does the sound of falling leaves represent? And at the end of the novel, what is Tessa's conclusion about the sound?

KEEP READING WITH AN EXCERPT *from* ANOTHER EXCITING LISA CARTER TITLE

978-1-68370-094-4

Caden Wallis lost friends, his girlfriend, and even his leg to the ravages of war. He arrives on the Outer Banks broken and still reeling, struggling to make peace with his new life.

McKenna Dockery has been stuck in limbo since her fiancé died three years ago. Now, when the handsome yet heartbroken Caden arrives at her doorstep, she starts to wonder if there may be hope for her heart after all . . .

But no sooner do they meet than a man is found murdered on McKenna's property—and Caden is the prime suspect. The two must learn to trust each other, or no one will be safe in the tangled web of conspiracy, greed, and deceit lurking in the tidal marshlands of the Outer Banks.

Prologue

Sergeant First Class Caden Wallis grinned as his CO whistled—perhaps the fifteenth time today—that same tune again. On the floor of the Humvee, the six-year-old Belgian Malinois' ears perked. And Caden's canine friend, K9 Sergeant First Class Friday, barked.

Caden laughed. "Even Friday's sick of that song."

His team leader, Master Sergeant Joe Nelson, was the closest he'd ever come to a best friend, and to the younger guys Joe was a father figure. They'd all—Caden and Friday included—follow him without hesitation into a death trap if so ordered.

From the front passenger seat, Joe angled. His eyebrows arched, vanishing underneath his combat helmet. "Not just any tune. A hymn, but also a love song. 'Here is love,'" he warbled in his terrible off-key baritone. "'Vast—'"

The vehicle rattled over the bomb-pitted road, jostling them. Bracing, Caden grabbed hold of the side to keep from lurching forward.

Sanchez, team medic, cut his eyes at Caden and nudged Pulaski at the wheel. They took up where Joe left off, but in a shrill falsetto.

"'Vast as an ocean, loving kindness as the flood . . .'"

Joe rolled his eyes as they hammed it up.

"'Who his love will not remember? Who can cease to sing His praise?'"

Biting the inside of his cheek, Joe tolerated the impromptu concert. Anything to lessen pre-mission tension.

"'Through the floodgates of God's mercy flowed a vast and gracious tide . . .'"

Friday howled.

Sanchez and Pulaski broke into laughter, as did Joe.

Caden smiled. Joe was the best man he'd ever known. A godly man, the real deal. Caden wasn't into religion, but he'd come to believe that Joe's faith had somehow buffered them, protected them by proxy, throughout their long deployment thus far.

The only thing on Caden's radar was getting home to his girlfriend in one piece. Thinking of Nikki, his stomach cramped. She hadn't answered his calls in over a month. Sensing her handler's disquiet, Friday insinuated her head underneath her hand and licked his fingers.

Had Nikki, as threatened, grown tired of waiting for him?

The armored personnel vehicle jerked to a standstill. And the dust—always the dust—swirled through the open windows. In terms of mileage, the village wasn't far from base camp, but lately anywhere outside the wire had become a killing zone. Out of the other Humvees in the convoy, the rest of their team emptied onto the deserted street. Including the Afghan military officer.

Caden had taken a dislike to him during their extensive pre-mission planning. Maybe he was hyperparanoid, or maybe on his third tour he didn't trust any of the locals. The officer was a necessary evil in his opinion, considered essential in brokering the agreement between coalition forces and the tribal leader.

"Keep your head on a swivel for unfriendlies." Joe made eye contact with each member of their twelve-man Alpha team. "We're on foot from here."

Yazz—Navajo Hosteen Yazzie, their communications specialist—grunted. Caden seconded the feeling.

The dirt street disappeared into a maze of mud-brick dwellings three stories high. Row after row of potential sweet spots for a sniper. Or an entire terrorist faction. Silence reigned as the men assumed a defensive posture, clutching their M-4 rifles.

Joe adjusted the black-checkered shemagh around his neck. "I don't need to tell you how kinetic this area has been. The headman's support will pave the way to peace in this province."

Weapons Specialist Tavon Miller's dark face tightened. "So where is everyone?"

Scruggs—the newest and youngest team member—snickered. "Maybe the spooks didn't hand out enough chocolate when they set up this meet and greet."

Pulaski's mouth thinned. "Or we're walking into an ambush."

"What they pay us the big bucks for," Scruggs smirked.

Yazz sighed. "Not."

One look from Joe silenced the chatter. Their nerves were frayed. Too many back-to-back encounters of a deadly kind. But the quiet was unnerving. Caden grasped a tighter hold on Friday's leash.

"Glad you go first, Sergeant Friday," joked Pulaski, breaking the eerie hush.

The men had grown to love and depend on Friday. Her bomb-sniffing capabilities had saved their lives on more than one occasion.

Joe cut his eyes at the narrow street ahead. "And we've got your six."

Venturing deeper into the village, Caden and Friday did their job. The team and the Afghan officer followed Friday's lead. Only the sound of the men's boots on the hard-packed road broke the stillness. As Friday pulled forward on the leash, Caden's arms prickled. He felt the unseen force of a hundred eyes behind the mud-brick walls.

Suddenly, from somewhere behind Caden, the Afghan officer's shrill cry shattered the calm. "Allah Akbar!"

Caden's gaze swung over his shoulder just as the Afghan fired point blank at Joe. Tavon opened fire on the Afghan, pink mist spraying. Caden took a step intending to pivot, but Friday pulled down on the leash, sniffing his foot.

"What're you doing, girl? Hold—"

Something beneath his boot clicked. He half turned. Friday rammed her body against him. And at that moment he realized a second too late that he'd missed her signal.

The blast lifted him into the air amidst a searing pain. A percussive roar drowned out further sound. Darkness engulfed him.

When he regained consciousness, he found himself flat on his back. Blackened debris lay scattered in every direction. He blinked, waiting for the swirling dust and smoke to settle.

Gunfire erupted from the shadows, followed by the retort of the

M-4s. Savage yells reverberated off the walls. Responding with curses, the men hunkered behind whatever cover they could find.

Fear gripped his chest. "Friday? Where are you, girl?"

He struggled to rise, but his legs wouldn't cooperate. And despite the broiling noonday sun, a glacial coldness crept from his toes to his torso.

Where was his rifle? If he could find it . . . leverage himself upright . . .

But it had either been scattered out of reach or demolished beyond repair.

Someone slid to a stop beside Caden. Two others crouched as a defensive shield, protecting them and responding to small-arms fire from their unseen enemy.

"Helo inbound," Yazz shouted from a doorway.

Sanchez ripped open Caden's medical kit, the one-pounder every soldier carried in his gear.

"The sergeant first," Caden rasped.

Sanchez ignored him. Velcro ripped.

"A tourniquet?" His heart accelerated. "Where's—"

"I've got three or four minutes before you bleed out." Sanchez's lips flattened. "With all due respect, Wallis, shut up." He secured the tourniquet onto Caden's leg, positioned the Velcro strap, and tightened the attached rod.

Flinching, he bit back the scream of pain threatening to explode from his lungs.

Sanchez swallowed. "I'm sorry . . ."

It felt as if flames licked at his legs. "I'm on fire," he groaned.

The *rata-tat-tat* of gunfire continued. Amid the searing pain in his lower extremities, he heard the distant whir of the bird's rotors.

"Rick," he whispered.

Something in the New Mexican's face flickered before Sanchez clamped down his emotions again.

Caden fought against an onslaught of pain, so terrible it threatened to suck the oxygen out of his lungs. "I need you to put out the—"

Sanchez forced a fentanyl lollipop between Caden's clenched teeth.

Caden's hand inched toward his leg. Toward the wrenching,

mind-numbing pain. Instead of flesh, solid muscle or bone, a gushing warmth spurted between his fingers. A flowing fountain . . .

Echoes of Joe's favorite song filtered through his mind. He raised his hand and stared. A stream of crimson flowed between his fingers.

A vast and gracious tide . . .

His breath hitched as an unknown, helpless horror skyrocketed from the marrow of his bones. The white-faced figure of Sanchez blurred. The last sound he heard was Sanchez yanking open his own medical kit.

And Velcro ripping on another tourniquet.

Chapter One

The explosive cawing of seagulls jolted her heart into overdrive. At the edge of the beach, she spun around on the deck of her boat. A gaggle of birds darted upward, their cries echoing on the wind, warning of danger.

Of predators.

McKenna Dockery clutched her camera, pressing it against her chest. She went still to identify the source of the misplaced noise that had almost sounded like gunfire. The island was narrow at this end, but on the other side of the dunes all was quiet, except for the relentless, pounding waves of the Atlantic rolling onto the shore.

Over the weekend, a tropical storm had battered the Outer Banks. Now the desolate yet wildly beautiful Yaupon was a treasure trove of sea glass. But no one except her ever ventured to Yaupon Island anymore, and it'd been a while since she visited.

She climbed out of the boat and reached for her plastic bucket. Ankle deep in the channel waters, she dug her toes into the sand, resisting the pull of the outgoing tide. Though late September, it was warmer than usual.

Curiosity overpowered her fear—and often her good sense, her father complained. Yet leaving her boat anchored in the sheltered cove, she traversed the beach and climbed the sandy trail winding over the dune. At the top, a stiff ocean breeze whipped tendrils of her hair into her eyes, obscuring her vision. She raked the strands out of her face and, lifting the camera hanging around her neck, peered through the telescopic lens. Her finger clicked the shutter button, the camera making faint whirring sounds as she scanned the deserted shoreline. Nothing she saw accounted for the *boom* she'd heard moments before.

Probably her imagination working overtime. Her dad had been ill last night. She'd awakened every time he struggled to make his way to the hall bathroom.

She tilted her head, listening, but heard only the soothing sound of churning waves and the skritching of the sand crabs on the beach below. Had she imagined the sound? Silence thrummed, underscoring the wind-swept abandonment of the isolated island off the coast of North Carolina.

Neither her dad nor Bryce liked her going off alone in the boat. She'd grown up on the Banks and knew how to handle herself on the water, but today . . .

Her skin prickled.

Gripping the camera, she gazed across the turbulent inlet that separated the small barrier island from the larger island of Hatteras. The air hung thick with trepidation. An early-morning fog snaked above the dark waters of the wetlands.

Suddenly the ever-present wind that buffeted year-round residents died. And quiet descended like a smothering blanket. No bird calls. As if they, too, waited. But for what?

An eerie stillness reigned, broken only by the tide lapping against the seashore. She fingered the cell phone tucked into the pocket of her denim shorts. No signal this far from Hatteras. A village had thrived here once beside a life-saving station, until repeated storms forced the villagers to relocate to Hatteras. Now only wild creatures remained.

She shook herself. This was ridiculous. Probably high school kids playing hooky. Though there had been a recent rash of more violent crime farther north on the Banks. Her dad, Tuckahoe's police chief, blamed it on a new player in the drug market. Connected to a Central American cartel, an unknown dealer was peddling an even more powerful and deadly drug. And where there was money to be made, so also came ruthless criminals to the otherwise peaceful Outer Banks.

As the police chief's daughter, she should've known better than to come here. Her hand shook as she replaced the cap over the lens. From Blackbeard to the gin runners of Prohibition, the barrier islands had proven a haven for unsavory elements.

Feeling eyes on the back of her head, a shiver of uneasiness traveled the length of her spine. She backpedaled the way she'd come. Underneath her windbreaker, tentacles of cold fear crawled up and down her arms. On the back side of Yaupon again, she sloshed through the knee-deep water of the cove. But she never took her eyes off the rotting stumps of the dock, the long-abandoned husks of boats. She groped behind her for the familiar fiberglass bow of her boat and heaved it off the sand, putting her back into it. Only then did she clamber onto the deck. Breathing heavily, she padded over to the controls. Turning the ignition, she brought the engine to life. And above the humming of the motor . . .

On a distant sandy rise behind the stark outline of stone foundations, a babble of voices. The words indistinguishable. Angry, loud voices.

Throwing open the throttle, she gunned the engine and headed for the safety of home.

❖   ❖   ❖

TUCKAHOE, HATTERAS ISLAND, NC

Caden startled awake, not quite sure where he was. But at the rolling crash of the waves, he remembered. And immediately wished to return to the oblivion from which he'd awoken.

As impossible as returning to his life before. He'd come to the end of the world. The end of the road. Soon the end of everything.

He rubbed the sandy grit from his eyes. Leaning heavily upon the piling underneath the pier, he strong-armed his way to his feet. Or rather, what remained of his feet.

Caden grimaced, stiff from his overnight sojourn on the sand. The last island ferry had dropped him off at Hatteras Village at midnight. The long journey to North Carolina had depleted his small cash reserve. First the train, then a bus. A fellow vet offered him a ride to the ferry landing in Swan Quarter. Once on Ocracoke, he'd caught another ferry—the free ferry—to Hatteras Village. Then he'd walked north on Highway 12 until he could go no further.

But this was as far as he needed to go. To fulfill one last desire. To complete one final mission.

Joe . . . Friday . . . Red-hot memories sizzled his brain. His chest tightened. He fought the panic. The urge to run. Not that running was an option anymore.

A pinkish glow bathed the shoreline in striations of golden light, shining through the breaks in the dunes. Caden ran a shaky hand over the stubble on his face.

He'd dreamed last night of running the long, grassy field at his old high school, a football tucked underneath his arm, his feet pounding the turf, darting and dodging the defensive line.

Nine months ago he'd awoken at Reed to the sensation of a blow-torch on his feet. And the pain hadn't lessened. How could anything no longer there still hurt so much? The bomb—a pressure-sensitive homemade device—had shattered his leg. Shredded his tissue into shards of flesh. Severed his left leg below the knee.

He owed his life to Sanchez. But Sanchez had done him no favors.

"Keep breathing. Stay awake. Don't you rack out on me." Sanchez had refused to abandon him until the C-17 deposited him at the combat support hospital in Kandahar, where they stabilized him.

There had then been a blessedly unconscious flight to Bagram Air Base outside Kabul. From there to Germany, where they'd removed the breathing tube in the Level One trauma center at Landstuhl. And ultimately to Walter Reed.

Seven days. Seven thousand miles. From Afghanistan to DC. From vibrant life to a living death. From wholeness to utter brokenness.

He'd endured multiple surgeries during his stay on Ward 57 to remove scraps of metal from his wounds. But as his calls and texts to Nikki went unanswered, the festering, gnawing fear inside him quadrupled.

"Take one day at a time," the doctor advised.

Many soldiers were wounded far worse than he had been, yet they'd overcome their disabilities. So he worked hard, harder than he'd ever worked in his life, to take back his life. To return to Nikki. To create a home with Nikki. To be the man Nikki deserved.

"You watch," he'd told the physical therapist in the amputee wing. "I'm going to climb those nine flights of stairs in record time. One month tops."

Caden glanced out from underneath the pier. Guys like him were trained to never quit. If one solution didn't work, they devised another plan. And if victory proved impossible, they died still trying. But this . . . He didn't know how to move forward from what had happened.

Nikki's last words had slashed his insides sharper than shrapnel, confirming everything he'd ever suspected about himself. And when she walked out of Reed . . . for the first time he heard oblivion call to him.

Stomach clenching, Caden scanned the blue-gray waters of the Atlantic. He'd always yearned to see the ocean—a desire fueled when the nurse deposited a brown parcel on his hospital bed. Inside the package he'd found ocean waves in the folds of fabric. A quilt. But it was the label on the reverse side he couldn't forget.

Always come home.

Foster homes didn't qualify as home—part of why he'd joined the army. And he'd found there for a time a family of sorts.

He pushed away thoughts of Joe and the brothers he'd left behind. There was no going back. Only forward.

"Your only limitations—" He could hear the prosthetist in his head."—are the ones you make for yourself."

The quilt had gotten him through bad bouts of pain after intense PT. Wrapping around him like the arms of the mother he never had. The quilt kept him fighting.

Could he rebuild his life? Or was his life over? Eight months ago Nikki had answered that question for him.

He'd lost more than his leg in Afghanistan. He'd lost his pride, his chance for a life. And worst of all, hope.

That's when he made his decision. He had to end this—before the pain wore away at his resolve. No matter what, he'd not give into the temptation to numb the pain. He wouldn't—he'd rather die than become his parents.

A quick internet search revealed everything he needed to know to see the ocean for the first and last time. Everything he needed to find the quilter—*M. Dockery, Tuckahoe, NC*—named on the label.

Caden nudged the duffel in the sand beside him with his boot. Soon as he returned the blue-and-white quilt to its rightful owner, he'd return here. Stick to the plan. Go in deep until he could no longer see the beach. Waves would roll over him. He'd lose his footing. Saltwater would fill his lungs. Choking, gasping, he wouldn't be able to breathe. And then he—

He took a deep breath, the sea breeze bringing a briny aroma to his nostrils. Propping his hip against the wooden piling, he carefully—every movement minutely planned these days—hoisted the bag, ducked his head, and slung the strap over his shoulder. He fought to maintain his balance on the shifting sand. His knuckles whitened on the strap. He was hanging on by only a thread, and not just to his ruck.

Caden practiced the breathing techniques. Didn't help much, but the stabbing intensity of the pain abated somewhat.

He straightened. Refocused on his mission. He was tethered to this world by only the threads of a quilt. At least until eventide.

McKenna's heart continued to thump long after the island disappeared behind the boat's wake. She steered across the channel toward the sheltered bay. Slowing the boat, she pulled back on the throttle and chugged into the Tuckahoe marina, maneuvering past a recreational boater headed out, a man with stringy gray-blond hair and brawny arms at the wheel. His short-sleeved tropical shirt with a riotous display of flora belied the beer gut above his cargo shorts. One of those aging hippies on a never-ending quest for the magic elixir of eternal youth. A stereotype of island escapism.

Before she got a close look at his face, however, the boater slipped Maui Jim sunglasses over his eyes. But she'd seen him before at Skipjacks. Odd he was still hanging around. Unless he was one of those weird writer types renting a house for the winter to pen his version of the Great American Novel.

Still, it was within a Banker's best interests to be friendly. Tourists were their bread and butter. She raised her hand to wave, but as the adrenaline escaped down her arm and through her fingertips, her hand shook.

His teeth flashed, a contrast against his peeling, sunburned skin, and then their boats were past each other.

Once inside the Tuckahoe harbor, she eased the boat into the rented berth and cut the engine. In one leap, she bridged the gap between the boat and the dock. The silver-weathered planks felt solid beneath her. She reached for her bucket—

"Top of the mornin' to you."

She whirled.

Beside his charter boat, a grizzled waterman lifted his hand in greeting. Laddie Ferguson, longtime family friend.

She willed her heartbeat to subside. It wasn't like her to get spooked. But after her unsettling experience on Yaupon, her nerves were frayed.

"Out early, aren't you now?" Beneath the brim of a stained ball cap, Laddie's bushy gray brows lowered. "Where you been?"

"Hunting sea glass." She secured a mooring line to a cleat on the pier. "You're heading out late, aren't you, Laddie?"

"Business to take care of this morning." Coming alongside, Laddie tied off another line for her. "I'll be out and about soon enough."

She glanced at her watch. "Thanks for your help." Still time before her shift, if she hurried. "Next time you're in the diner, I'll owe you a danish."

Behind the bristly beard, the waterman's lips curved, and creases from a lifetime of gauging sea horizons fanned out from his faded blue eyes. "Tell that grandmother of yours I said hello."

After leaving the bucket of sea glass in the bed of her truck, she crossed the marina parking lot to the public access path. At the bottom of the dune, she took the wooden steps two at a time. Topping the incline, she took a cautious, exploratory breath. Her pulse quieted. The sound of the waves always made her better, and she cast aside the strange foreboding she'd experienced on Yaupon.

She plodded through the sand until she stood at the water's edge. But despite the healing power of the wind and the waves, the old ache she'd come to consider a part of herself resurfaced. Grief had proven as slippery as an eel. Just when she believed she had a solid grip on it, a tsunami of breath-stealing anguish rolled in, taking her completely by surprise.

"Will it always be like this, God?" she whispered toward the leftover streaks of pink in the morning sky.

Silence, except for the sighing of the waves.

Three years since Shawn had died. She'd almost begun to believe there'd never be an answer. The tide frothed at her feet, flowing in and ebbing out. Kind of like her hope.

Every day, she lost more of Shawn. And one day—soon?—she feared she'd lose the memory of his laugh completely. Already, she no longer recalled the exact shade of his eyes. Blue-green? Or more green than blue?

Was this it for her? And if so, why did something within her yearn to find herself again—find her heart again—in someone else's arms? Why couldn't the life she had now be enough? A life with her dad and her grandmother, Lovey. Keeping the business afloat was a full-time job. So many had so much less. Was she ungrateful?

God, forgive me if I am.

Her eyes flicked upward toward the gulls wheeling in acrobatic figure eights in the sky. Something—Someone—whispered for her to wait. To be patient. To not lose faith.

To hold on to her hope.

But she'd become mired in a kind of emotional paralysis. Stuck between her life *Before* and an *After* she was afraid to embrace. Not if the future meant letting go of Shawn. She couldn't betray him like that.

Her heart ached at a sudden, quick memory of how Shawn used to smile when he watched her dance on stage.

Kicking off her flip-flops, she lifted her face to the morning sun. Soaking in the blessing. Claiming the promise. Lulled by the waves. The gentle sea breeze fluttered across her skin, imparting peace and strength. She staked her life and her heart on the fulfillment of that which she had yet to see. Choosing, despite the empty void, to trust while her dreams remained unfulfilled. When the pain and loneliness were at their height.

When, perhaps, faith meant the most.

❖ ❖ ❖

Rounding the curve of the shoreline, a flicker of movement at the water's edge caught Caden's attention. He noticed her legs first, homing in upon that which he no longer possessed. Encased in denim shorts, her legs went on forever.

She was a tall woman in a seen-better-days navy windbreaker. The unfurling of the sun highlighted the straight blonde hair skimming her shoulders. Eyes closed, arms outstretched, she arched one foot over the water and made a circling motion with her pointed toe, balancing on her other leg. She raised her arms above her head, her fingers artfully posed. Leaning sideways, she kicked upward. Her feet scissored above the surface of the water. He held his breath, transfixed. Yet she landed nimble, soft and sure footed as a butterfly lighting upon a leaf. Her knees flexed and straightened.

Poetry in motion.

Caden scowled at his useless leg and bit his lip until he tasted the coppery, metallic taste of blood. "Why do you hate me so much, God?"

As his sibilant whisper floated across the sand, the woman reeled midmotion. Her arms lowered from their duet with the sky. And she rotated, as graceful as the opening of a door, toward him.

For a long moment, they stared at each other. An eternity as they weighed the measure of the other. Until her eyes—blue like the Carolina morning—sharpened.

Something in those fathomless depths rocked him. Jarred him. A frightening intensity tugged at him. Read him down to his soul.

The soul he used to have.

His heart skipped a beat. He had to get away from here, from her, before she distracted him from his purpose. Before—

She stretched out her hand. Absurdly panicked, he pivoted without thinking.

And fell flat on his face.

Chapter Two

IN THREE STRIDES, MCKENNA REACHED THE MAN LYING ON THE sand. His pant leg had ridden up to his shin, revealing not actual flesh but a prosthesis.

Judging from his tactical pants, maybe a veteran. Dark hair feathered over the collar of an army-green T-shirt. Around his neck a metal chain glinted. Dog tags?

Something warned her not to help him. To save his pride and allow him to stand on his own.

"I got it," he grunted and rolled onto his side. "I don't need your help."

By sheer force of will—and locking her arms behind her back—she stopped herself from rushing to his rescue. "I wasn't offering."

At her tone, he stiffened. Using the duffel as a prop, he counterbalanced and crawled to a kneeling position.

She'd seen death in his face. His unvoiced intentions hit her like a blow. She'd seen a coming grave in those large, dark eyes of his. Sad, weary-of-life eyes. And a seething anger at an all-too-familiar enemy surged within her heart.

The man, perhaps a few years older, was gaunt. Late twenties. But he'd once been powerfully built with broad, muscled shoulders. His bent, emaciated frame was probably just under six foot. And behind the scraggly beard that framed his mouth, she imagined he'd also once been almost handsome. High cheekbones. A rugged jawline. Before pain wracked his features and flattened his lips into a thin, straight line.

Gasping, the man righted himself into a standing position. He tossed her a triumphant look. "I told you I could do it."

She shrugged. "Never doubted it."

The man glared at her. She glared back until his eyes darted over her shoulder to the waves. "What's that?"

Her breath hitched at the sight of the black-green object floating on the tide. She sped toward the water as the sea turtle flopped onto the shore. Sinking to her knees, she performed a cursory examination. A front flipper remained entangled in a fishing line. One of the back flippers had been severed, perhaps by the blades of a boat's propeller.

Belatedly, she remembered the other wounded creature by the dunes. But he was exactly where she'd left him. Still scowling.

She scrambled to her feet. "I could use some help here."

He jolted, nearly unsettling his carefully contrived balance. "You want me?"

She planted her hands on her hips. "I want you."

He blinked. And she blushed.

Averting her gaze, she brushed away the sand encrusting her knees. "I mean I need you. Really need—" She cleared her throat. "I need your help."

Pity demoralized. Responsibility inspired.

She studied him as indecision fought with something akin to dignity. Finally, he moved forward as self-respect gained the upper hand. His gait was jerky, uneven. She'd be willing to bet he'd ditched physical therapy too soon, before the benefits outweighed the pain.

He flushed when he caught her staring.

McKenna turned away, giving him the chance to approach without scrutiny. Reaching her side, he leaned closer. She prepared to be overwhelmed by the homeless stench of him, or alcohol. But he only smelled of the salty sea air, like everyone in Tuckahoe. Like her.

So maybe he wasn't homeless. Or homeless long. As a police chief's daughter, she knew enough to recognize a drug-induced haze in a person's eyes. This man's eyes were clear . . . except for the crushing weight of fear and a heart-wrenching childlike disbelief in the face of desperate pain.

McKenna pushed away a helpless feeling. This was why she hadn't gone into nursing. Her natural empathy unraveled her, rendering her useful to no one.

"I thought sea turtles lived in the ocean."

He had a strong, deep voice.

McKenna tilted her head. "When sea turtles get hurt, sometimes they get lost."

She resisted the temptation to point out the similarities between the turtle's injuries and his own. Despite the pain, intelligence also shone out of his dark eyes.

The man wasn't stupid. Suicidal, yes. Stupid, no.

His mouth twisted. "Where I come from, they'd shoot a horse in this condition."

A cowboy? Maybe the bow-legged gait wasn't solely a war wound.

She frowned. "We don't shoot turtles here."

His mouth hardened. "Maybe you should." A thread of anger flitted across the broad planes of his face.

She preferred anger to the other thing she'd seen in his eyes.

"Here's what we'll do." She outlined how she'd retrieve her truck, drive as close as she could get on the beach, and fill the baby swimming pool she kept in the truck bed for emergencies like this.

"We'll lift Cecil into the tub, then take him to the sea turtle rescue hospital."

"Cecil?" A laugh barked from between his lips. A rusty laugh, but a laugh all the same. "You know this turtle?"

Her lips curved. "Dr. Thompson lets me name the wounded ones I bring him."

The man raked a hand across the top of his dark hair. "A veterinarian?"

"Marine animal specialist. We share him with the aquarium over the bridge." She dusted off her hands. "We'd better hurry before Dr. Thompson heads to Manteo."

"You work at the animal hospital?"

She shook her head. "The turtle rehab is staffed by volunteers like me. We provide a temporary home for the wounded until we can equip them to survive on their own."

The man gave her the strangest look. "A labor of love."

Crinkling her eyes, she smiled. "Exactly."

Her smile dazzled him. Like a string of diamonds glinting across the water. A glittering trail of hope-encrusted bread crumbs. A commodity Caden had no use for. Not anymore.

She trudged toward the dunes. Sea oats waving in the wind, the woman disappeared from view. For a second he wondered if he'd imagined her.

But the creature—Cecil?—hunkered in the sand. So he wasn't going crazy. Or at least any crazier than he'd been when he arrived.

The injured turtle was real, so she must be real. The turtle-rescuing, beach-dancing woman. Tall, willowy, and blonde. Totally unlike Nikki. Her winsome smile had caught him by surprise. As did his unbidden response to the embodiment of hope she brought with her.

He stuffed the good feeling down. He'd help her with the turtle. Maybe she'd give him a ride to the diner.

Caden paced around the animal, his footprints sinking in the wet sand. He'd known the instant she noticed his leg. He could always tell by the slight hesitation, the hitch of breath. He'd steeled himself for the usual pity. But instead of pity—or disgust, in Nikki's case—there'd been something unexpected in the woman's face. A ferocity he recognized from fellow warriors in the height of battle. Though what Beach Girl believed she battled he hadn't a clue.

His gaze lifted as a blue Chevy truck rumbled onto the beach. Jumping out, she hurried around to open the tailgate. She handed him a plastic jug. "Fill 'er up."

Caden wasn't sure he could trust his footing in the foaming surf. What if he fell on his face and made a fool out of himself again? But she moved away, not giving him the chance to refuse.

Unscrewing the cap, he waded ankle deep into the water. So far so good. The water felt cool against his real foot, and sloshing, gurgling liquid filled the jug.

Heading up the incline with a confident stride he could only envy, she dumped the contents of her own container into the baby pool. "Just enough to make the ride to the clinic comfortable for him."

Sand was tricky, slippery. He moved cautiously up the slope and emptied his jug into the pool, pleased he hadn't disgraced himself. He retraced his steps to where she knelt beside Cecil.

"Loggerheads aren't as heavy as leatherbacks. And Cecil isn't full grown. Probably an adolescent, lucky for us."

Caden scowled. "Lucky for us."

Her eyes flicked at the bitterness in his voice. His knee protested as he lowered himself on the other side of Cecil.

"The hardest part," she warned, "will be lifting so you don't lose your balance."

He squared his jaw. Everything was hard. "Let's do it already."

"Okay. One . . . two . . . three." She hoisted her side free of the cloying sand.

Caden heaved and bit back a groan. But he toughed it out and took the brunt of the turtle's weight. Which was the way it should be. Soaking wet, Beach Girl probably wouldn't weigh much over a hundred pounds.

Together they lowered Cecil into the tub. The turtle fluttered what remained of his flippers. The woman clambered into the bed, gently splashing water over Cecil's pitted shell.

Breathing in short spurts, Caden was ashamed how such a small effort took so much out of him these days.

She gestured toward the crew cab. "Would you mind riding to the clinic to help me settle Cecil in case we don't catch the doc?"

"As long as you'll drop me off in town."

Jumping down, she slammed the tailgate shut. "Deal."

He yanked open the passenger door and tossed in his ruck. After inserting his torso into the cab like the therapist had shown him, he swung his legs inside.

Sliding behind the wheel, she inspected the dashboard clock and grimaced. "I'm supposed to be at work in fifteen minutes." She turned the key in the ignition. The engine sputtered before catching.

"Is the clinic far?"

Both hands on the wheel, she maneuvered off the treacherous sand. "Nothing in Tuckahoe is far."

He gripped the armrest, trying to cushion his joints against the jolt. "H-had the shocks checked r-recently?" He gritted his rattling teeth.

"Too expensive right now." She flung a sideways look at him. "You offering?"

"No . . . I'm not . . ." He made a motion toward his leg. "In case you forgot . . ." His lips clamped together.

"I didn't forget." She faced forward. "But maybe you should."

She had some nerve. Clenching his fists, he angled toward the passing scenery. Three minutes of blessed silence ticked by.

"Visiting someone on the Banks?"

This woman talked too much. He drummed his fingers on the armrest.

"Well?" She wasn't going to let this go.

"No." He cranked down the window, letting the wind buffet him.

They passed a post office and a grocery store. Two minutes passed. He knew because he fixed his gaze on the clock, waiting. And sure enough—

"Just passing through?" Her lips twitched. "Tuckahoe isn't exactly on the beaten path."

These never-met-a-stranger southerners didn't understand how to mind their own business.

He folded his arms across his chest. "I'm returning something to its rightful owner. I've got no use for it anymore."

"Nice of you. And then you're off to someplace else?"

"To nowhere else," he muttered under his breath.

"Only two ways on or off Hatteras Island—the ferry at Hatteras Village south or north on Highway 12 across the Bonner Bridge. How'd you get here?"

He glared. "Ferry."

She motioned toward the notch between the dunes lining the highway that revealed a tantalizing glimpse of blue ocean. "It's a nice place we call home. Tuckahoe has everything you'll ever need."

He snorted. "Like?"

"Like good people, ocean breezes, gorgeous sunrises or sunsets—take your pick." She smiled.

And something—it wasn't pain this time—banged against his rib cage.

She pointed to a clump of twisted, stunted trees where a white steeple pierced the azure sky.

"God and I aren't on a speaking basis."

She threw him a look. "Suit yourself."

He surveyed the terrain. "Not many people around."

"Summertime we get about forty thousand visitors. Bankers—that's what we year-rounders on the Outer Banks call ourselves—we work two or three jobs during tourist season to earn most of what we make the whole year." She quirked her eyebrow. "Like squirrels storing nuts for winter. But past Labor Day, we get the Banks to ourselves again."

"With no room for an outsider like me."

She turned off Highway 12 into the parking lot of a low-slung concrete building. *Tuckahoe Turtle Rescue Center*, the sign over the entrance read.

"There's always room." She glanced in the rearview mirror. "What's *he* doing here?"

A Town of Tuckahoe police cruiser pulled in behind them, and a thirty-something man in a short-sleeved, gray police uniform got out.

"Hey, Bryce." She left the door dinging as she hurried around the truck. "I'm glad you're here. I could use the muscle."

The athletic man with frat-boy good looks caught her around the waist. "I went to the marina. You took the boat out again, didn't you?" He shook his head. "You shouldn't take off with no one knowing where you are."

She lifted her chin. "As you can see, I'm fine."

Ice-blue eyes narrowing, the policeman tightened his arms around her in a proprietary way. "Aren't you supposed to be at work?"

Beach Girl and the man obviously had some sort of relationship. Caden's brow furrowed. None of his business.

Ever-fluid motion, she glided out of the man's hold. "I'm going to be late if you don't help me." She tugged him toward the pickup. "I ran into a situation this morning—"

Spotting Caden, the policeman's chiseled features underwent a transformation. "What have you done?" Lip curling, he jerked her to a standstill.

Caden's nostrils flared. He didn't like the guy manhandling her. Inside the cab, he unfolded his arms, his fingers flexing.

"Let go of me, Bryce." She pulled free. "He isn't the situation I'm talking about. I found an injured loggerhead on the beach."

Bryce's patrician nose wrinkled. "You don't even know his name, do you? A bum. A drug-crazed addict you picked up on the beach."

She slapped his hand away as he reached for her again. "Stop it, Bryce. He'll hear you. And he's not—"

"He's another stray," the policeman hissed.

"My ears aren't missing. Just my leg." He leaned out the window. "And the name's Caden Wallis."

She flashed him another one of those killer smiles. His gut quivered. The look Bryce threw his way was far from nice.

Her silver dolphin earrings jangled as she sidestepped the policeman. "But if you're on a call, I'm sure Caden—" She emphasized his name. "—can handle relocating Cecil to the tank inside the center."

The police officer's face darkened. "I came looking for you because Dispatch radioed me," he snapped. "Your dad was a no-show for roll call this morning."

She bit her lip. "He had a rough night. I realize he's been MIA a lot lately, but I'm sure he's on his way to the station."

An older man in surgical scrubs stepped out of the building, and she let out a breath.

"I thought I heard voices." The doctor peered into the truck bed. "A new patient?"

Caden fumbled for the door handle, but the officer leaned against the door, keeping it shut. "Wouldn't want a man in your condition to hurt yourself."

While Caden fumed in the truck, the three of them wrestled the kiddy pool with Cecil into the facility. Minutes later, she emerged with the policeman on her heels. He strolled toward Caden's open window.

"Somewhere I can drop you?" Not so much a question as a command.

Beach Girl yanked open the driver-side door. "I got this, Bryce. Stop being such a worrywart."

"You are so hardheaded," he growled, raking his hand over his close-cropped blond hair. "When will you learn not everyone is a good guy? Not everyone deserves to be rescued."

Anger flashed across her features. "I'm not the naive fool you think I am, Bryce."

His face fell. "I didn't mean . . . I just . . ."

She pulled the door shut. "Don't you have a drug dealer to catch, Officer Hinson?"

His eyes flitted to Caden. "How long are you staying in Tuckahoe?"

"Not long." Caden jutted his jaw. "No worries."

Bryce Hinson's brows lowered. "I'm not worried. But I consider the chief's family to be my family. And we take care of our own here on the Banks."

She revved the engine. "Goodbye, Bryce."

With a final death glare at Caden, he stepped away as she put the truck in motion.

On the highway again, her forehead scrunched as she glanced at the clock. "Where to now, Caden?" She favored him with another smile. His heart skipped a beat. Irritation shot through him at the pleasure he felt in its sunshine. There was this little dimple in her chin. An extremely friendly southern person, she probably smiled at everyone, turtles and dogs too.

"Drop me off at Skipjacks, please. If it's not out of your way." The ferry captain had told him the Dockerys owned Skipjacks. He'd go there, return the quilt, then leave. For good.

"I'm headed there too." Her cheeks lifted. "Although my grandmother is going to skin me alive for not being there when the doors opened."

"Good." He coughed. "I mean, not good that you're going to be skinned alive, but good that I'm not taking you out of your way. We're both headed in the same direction." He scrubbed the back of his neck. "Your dad's the police chief?"

Her face clouded. "With everything that's been happening, there's talk about him being forced to resign."

"What's been happening?"

Her fingers tensed on the wheel. "We serve a great breakfast at Skipjacks."

Okay, her dad's work was off limits. Not like he'd ever see her again once he got out of the truck.

She steered into the crushed oyster shell parking lot of a cedar-shingled restaurant on stilts. "Thanks for helping me rescue Cecil. How about the Fisherman's Breakfast Catch? On the house."

He bristled. "I don't need your charity."

She eased into the space nearest the ramp. "I park around back, but I'll let you off here." The engine idled in the handicapped spot—designed for a cripple like him.

Teeth on edge, he threw open the door and swung his legs over the side. He inched his way down and flinched when his leg made contact with the ground. The jarring motion set off a new round of aches in his stump. He bent to retrieve his ruck, hiding his pain.

He looked across the seat at her. "Thanks for the lift. For . . ." For one last chance to be useful.

She glanced at him through her lashes. "Maybe we'll run into each other again."

"Run?" He tightened his hold on the bag. "No chance of that."

Chapter Three

As the truck disappeared around the corner of the restaurant, he realized she'd never told him her name. And he'd not asked.

Caden reached for the glass-fronted door, and a bell jangled overhead. Inside, he hesitated, grateful for the cool current of air from the whirring ceiling fan. A placard read *Make Yourself at Home*.

He was here to make sure the quilt did just that.

The dining area boasted a smattering of blue-checkered tables with chairs. Booths lined the outer walls. Floor-to-ceiling windows provided a lofty view of the waterfront and the tidal marsh meandering to the Pamlico Sound. A larger-than-life menu was mounted on the back wall. A pass-through cutout revealed a commercial kitchen.

An auburn-haired seventyish woman perched on a stool behind an antique brass register. In a lavender shirt and charcoal-gray trousers, she chatted with a handful of men in ball caps and Wellingtons. Just the kind of woman he'd always imagined his own grandmother might resemble.

If either of his grandmothers had ever bothered to retrieve him from Child Protective Services.

Caden hobbled toward an empty booth. The lady at the register—his quilt lady?—looked busy. He'd order coffee and wait until she was free.

He thrust his ruck into the booth, then wedged himself on the opposite side. The enticing aroma of hash browns and scrambled eggs made his stomach growl. He hadn't felt like eating for a long time. But there was no need to fill his belly. He'd be nothing but shark food by sunset.

Balancing a tray of pancakes and orange juice, a fifty-something waitress in tight-fitting black jeans and red stiletto heels emerged from the swinging door of the kitchen. "Be right with you, hon. Soon as I deliver Pastor's order."

She rushed past, the aroma of breakfast meat and cloying perfume trailing in her wake. He barely had time to identify the scent—Shalimar—before she returned.

"What can I do you for, hon?" She plucked a pencil out of her upswept, golden blonde hair and tabbed through her notepad until she found a blank page. According to the name tag pinned to her fluttery red blouse, her name was Earlene.

Although his wounds weren't visible, out of habit he tucked his feet under the blue Formica table, keeping his leg hidden. "Coffee."

She made a note and paused, pencil poised.

"That's all."

Her red-tinted lips quirked. "Hon, if you don't mind me saying so, you need some meat on your handsome bones."

Caden shook his head. "Just coffee."

Her heavily mascara-rimmed eyes narrowed. "Cream and sugar?"

"Black."

"How did I know you'd say that?" She poked the pencil into her bun again. "Coffee coming right up, shoog." She ambled toward the pickup window.

Shoog. Southern for "sugar." An endearment Virginia-born Joe Nelson had used for his wife.

Earlene returned with his coffee just as a tall, lanky man in jeans and boots stormed inside the restaurant.

"Walt, honey, slow down," Earlene called out. Caden winced at the raw vulnerability in her eyes.

About Earlene's age, the man combed his fingers through the short ends of his gray-blond hair. "Didn't hear Baby Girl leave. I got a call about her."

The man appeared frazzled, his movements jerky, an all too familiar expression on his weary, once handsome face. There was a hint of pain in his blue eyes, and barely masked exhaustion. Which over time had apparently carved deep lines upon his face.

Caden swallowed past the boulder in his throat. Not going to happen to him. Not once the sun descended below the horizon.

"Where have you been, Walt?"

"S-somewhere I had to be." Walt tugged at the cuffs of his green plaid shirt. "But my girl—"

"Walt, it's fine. She's in the kitchen."

If Earlene could have curled herself into the man's angular frame, Caden reckoned she would have. As it was, she still held his coffee. Should he reach for it?

"Pour yourself a cup and go talk to her." Earlene flitted a hand toward the far wall.

Caden's gaze followed her gesture, and for the first time he noticed the trophy case on the other side of the counter. Not filled with the usual trophies, the case contained lots of ribbons—mostly blue—and a photo of the old lady cashier standing beside a large quilt.

So she *was* his quilt lady.

"Relax, Walt." Earlene patted his arm. "Take a breath."

Walt's thin mouth creased into a vague smile as he shoved off toward the kitchen.

She peered after him for the duration of a heartbeat, her eyes consumed with an unrequited longing. Caden fiddled with a sugar packet. After Nikki's betrayal, he knew that feeling.

Earlene's breath caught in a small half sob as she swung around and plunked the mug in front of him. Hot black liquid sloshed over the rim of the cup. She grabbed a handful of napkins. "I'm—I'm so sorry, shoog." Her hand shook, dabbing at the tabletop.

He should've ordered the cream—anything to take the pinched, hopeless look out of her eyes.

"I might take some cream after all, Miss Earlene." Using a napkin, he caught a rivulet of caffeine flowing toward the edge. "If it wouldn't be too much trouble, ma'am."

A pool of moisture welled in her ocean-blue eyes. Maybe all the islanders—Bankers, Beach Girl had called them—sported blue eyes.

Earlene gave him a tremulous smile. "Wouldn't be any trouble at all, shoog. What else can I get you?"

He almost smiled back. Almost.

"I'm looking for M. Dockery." His gaze drifted toward the old woman. "I'd like to speak with her when she gets a chance."

Earlene pushed the soggy napkins to the far side of the table. "Will do. And I'll be back with a cloth to clean up this mess."

Wending around the throng of tables, she nudged one old codger with her hip before heading behind the counter. "McKenna," Earlene yelled. "A man wants to talk to you."

Caden jerked, the cup halfway to his lips. The old woman at the register stilled. Like someone had flicked a switch, the chatter instantly died. Every head turned in his direction.

He reminded himself yet again that his wounds didn't show.

"Soon as I flip this omelet," someone hollered from the kitchen.

His eyes darted to the cash register. The old lady hadn't budged.

Remembering the need to map out his moves, he carefully got to his feet and unzipped the bag. Extracting the quilt, he angled as Beach Girl ambled out of the kitchen, a white apron wrapped around her lithe form.

She swiveled to Earlene. "Who'd you say was looking for me?"

Earlene gaped at him, a dishcloth limp in one hand. "Sweet tea and hush my mouth . . ."

When Beach Girl caught sight of him, genuine warmth lit her face. "Caden, I'm so glad you decided—"

Her gaze latched onto the quilt. She froze. Color drained from her face as her knees buckled.

And with reflexes he hadn't used since Kandahar, he caught *M. Dockery* in his arms as she fell.

❖   ❖   ❖

Her first coherent thought? Somebody ought to shut up the squawking hen.

Actually, not true. Tucked beneath someone's chin, encircled in strong, masculine arms, McKenna's initial sensation had been one of extreme comfort.

A hand, callused but gentle, brushed a lock of hair out of her eyes. "McKenna?"

His beard scraped against her earlobe. She nestled deeper.

"McKenna?"

Her name sounded different coming from him. She liked the low scrape of his voice.

"Somebody call 9-1-1!" Earlene screamed. Ah, the squawking hen.

McKenna's eyes popped open.

Caden Wallis let out a breath, the warmth fanning her cheek. Mortification mounted. She—who'd never fainted in her life—had collapsed into a stranger's arms.

Her weight had unbalanced him. Both of them were sprawled across the booth. She'd knocked over a wounded vet. A man who struggled to stand upright.

"I'm so sorry. Did I hurt you? Let me . . ." She struggled, trying to get off him. Would the embarrassment never end? "For the love of sweet tea," she whispered.

Caden's chest rumbled beneath her.

Her eyes darted to his face in time to see him crack a smile. *Crack* being the operative word. He quickly clamped down as if his face might break from the unaccustomed strain.

She scrambled free. "This isn't funny."

His eyes held amusement as he righted himself. "This is the most fun I've had in a year."

"McKenna!" screeched Earlene.

Other voices shouted for her dad, and the cacophony rose. "Who is he, hon?" "What's going on here?" "What's he doing with Shawn's—"

Placing two fingers in her mouth, McKenna unleashed the ear-splitting whistle Dad had taught her at the tender age of eight. Earlene winced. Lovey, a funny smile plastered on her wrinkled face, didn't budge from her stool behind the register.

"Everybody calm down. I'm okay."

"I'm not." Caden fell against the upholstery, hands to his ears. "Warn a guy next time."

Her father stepped forward with one hand on his gun belt.

She stood and gestured to the booth. "Everyone, I'd like you to meet Caden Wallis."

Her father scowled. "Bryce said there was a man . . ."

Fresh irritation with Bryce flared inside McKenna.

The quilt in his arms again, Caden pushed to his feet. "I'm looking for the quilter who made this."

And once again McKenna felt herself going cold. How did he— Where did he—

Dad wheeled toward the cash register. "Do you know this man, Mother?"

McKenna held up her palm. "I've got this, Daddy."

"Leave the boy alone." Lovey fluttered her hand. "She said she's got him."

Chuckles rang out as diners returned to their tables.

"That's not what I said, Lovey."

"Mother? Earlene?" Dad barked. "What's going on here?"

Earlene retreated to the drink dispenser. Lovey didn't look up from counting change. "Go on about your business, son. No harm will come to McKenna."

McKenna stared pointedly at her father. "Yes, *Chief.* Don't you have places to be?"

"I'll be at the station." Dad scowled at Caden. "Across the street." He stalked out, the bell jangling.

She sank back into the booth, Caden on the other side. She fingered the quilt lying on the table between them. "This is what you were returning to its rightful owner?"

Caden's dark eyes softened. "Did you make this quilt?"

"Where did you get this?"

"At Walter Reed. After . . ." He swallowed.

"I sent it to a group who takes quilts to wounded veterans." Her voice went husky. "I couldn't bear for it to never be used."

"The quilt blocks capture the movement of water . . . like the way you danced—" He bit his lip.

Her cheeks reddened. She hadn't danced in front of anyone since she left the troupe. Since Shawn.

"The quilt spoke to me. Made me feel better. Comforted." His eyes, as dark fringed as a raven's wings, dropped away. "I'd never seen the ocean. It gave me a good excuse to come."

She straightened. "Never?"

"I'm from Oklahoma."

"A cowboy."

His lips twitched. "Sort of."

She smiled. "Thought so."

His eyes fastened on the region of her mouth. A curious, melted-butter feeling warmed her.

"I spent my high school years on a ranch for foster kids who didn't adopt out. We were expected to work."

Unexpected pain jabbed her heart. She reached across the table for his hand. "I'm sor—"

A frisson of electricity sizzled between them. Stung, she drew back. He stared at the place where her fingers had touched his skin.

"Quilt static. Sorry."

A pulse jumped in his cheek. "Those people were good to me." He sighed. "Long as I helped the football team win championships." He scrubbed his forehead. "I aged out. We haven't kept in touch."

Something inside her ached at what he'd said. And hadn't said. He'd worked for approval, and something told her Caden Wallis had continued to perform.

Until he couldn't anymore.

But there was something else going on beyond his injury. Something worse?

Soldiers with strong support networks recovered faster from the wounds of war. Those without that kind of support . . . didn't.

Turning back a corner of the quilt, she traced the words on the label with her finger.

He leaned forward. "*Always come home.*"

She found herself unable to look away from his eyes. "So you did."

His mouth opened. He closed it with a snap. "I brought the quilt home." He laced his hands together on top of the table. "To you."

Strong, capable hands. Capable of expertly palming a football, she imagined. And yet also capable of a gentleness she'd experienced firsthand. Her heart thudded. "You said the quilt was something you had no use for anymore."

He gripped the tabletop and pushed to his feet. "Correct."

Inexplicable panic streaked through her. "Wait." She placed a restraining hand on his arm. Another crackle of electricity. He froze. The skin on her arm goose pimpled.

"Before you take off somewhere—" She allowed the unspoken "nowhere" to hang between them for the space of a breath.

He sank into the booth again.

"I wondered if maybe you'd help us out at Skipjacks today." The words tumbled out of her mouth. "Our cook, Alonso, didn't show again. Since Lovey's hip surgery, she doesn't do well standing for long. Earlene's alone on the floor and Dad . . ." She blew out a breath. "Dad doesn't seem to be having a good day."

His face remained a stoic, maddening mask.

She started to squeeze his hand, but thinking better of it, she placed her palm flat on the table. "I've stepped in to cook, but the dishwasher's not working. If you could wash the dishes so we don't get behind on the orders . . ." She couldn't seem to stop jabbering. "I'd pay you a fair wage. You'd be doing me—us—a tremendous favor if you'd stick around." She inhaled. "For a while."

"I don't have a while to spare." The coldness of his words hit her like a punch to the face.

"Till sundown, then." What could she say to make him stay? Why did she care if he did or not? "Sunsets on the island are not to be missed."

A flame of interest—in the sunset?—flickered in his dark brown eyes. She resisted the urge to drown in those pools of liquid chocolate.

"Just today. Till you kick me out." His lips twisted. "You won't be the first."